SUNIL GANGOPADHYAY was one of India's most prolific and well-known writers, writing in Bengali. He wrote novels, short stories, poems, children's adventure stories and started the journal *Krittibas*. The translations of his novels *Sei Samay* (*Those Days*), *Pratham Alo* (*First Light*) and *Moner Manush* (*The Fakir*) have all been best-sellers. He has won many awards, among them the Sahitya Akademi Award for *Sei Samay* and the Saraswati Samman for *Pratham Alo*.

ARUNA CHAKRAVARTI is a well-known writer and translator. Prominent among her eleven published books are five translated works: *Songs of Tagore, Srikanta, Those Days, First Light* and *The Way Home*. Her creative writing includes a book of short stories, *Secret Spaces*, and two critically acclaimed novels: *The Inheritors*, which was short-listed for the Commonwealth Writers Prize 2004, and the recent best-selling *Jorasanko*. She has received several awards, including the Sahitya Akademi Award and the Sarat Puraskar.

PRIMAL WOMAN

Stories

SUNIL GANGOPADHYAY

Compiled and translated from the Bengali by
ARUNA CHAKRAVARTI

HARPER ● PERENNIAL

NEW YORK • LONDON • TORONTO • SYDNEY • NEW DELHI

HARPER PERENNIAL

First published in India in 2014 by Harper Perennial
An imprint of HarperCollins *Publishers* India

Copyright for the original text in Bengali © Swati and Shouvik Gangopadhyay
English translation copyright © Aruna Chakravarti 2014

P-ISBN: 978-93-5136-498-6
E-ISBN: 978-93-5136-499-3

2 4 6 8 10 9 7 5 3 1

HarperCollins *Publishers*
A-75, Sector 57, Noida 201301, India
77-85 Fulham Palace Road, London W6 8JB, United Kingdom
Hazelton Lanes, 55 Avenue Road, Suite 2900, Toronto, Ontario M5R 3L2
and 1995 Markham Road, Scarborough, Ontario M1B 5M8, Canada
25 Ryde Road, Pymble, Sydney, NSW 2073, Australia
10 East 53rd Street, New York NY 10022, USA

Typeset in 10/14 IowanOldSt BT at
SÜRYA

Printed and bound at
Thomson Press (India) Ltd.

For Bhulu-da,
the best brother-in-law in the world…

CONTENTS

PRIMAL WOMAN

THE WOMAN ENTERED the garden at dawn. It was also the dawn of creation...

Not a sound anywhere. Sheets of green dappled with trees, palms, vines and shrubs stretched before her. Some were covered with rainbow-hued flowers, others bent to the ground, heavy with clusters of ripening fruit. They were nameless and their pristine fragrance had not a whiff of the bittersweet pungency of natural flora. Rivulets of limpid water danced and pranced between the trees, the pebbles in their beds sparkling like pieces of crystal. A light breeze blew, soft and sweet.

The only other thing that moved in the primeval garden was the mist, a diaphanous veil dripping slowly from the clouds, longing to touch the earth. But its hopes were shattered. A virile young sun, aggressive and impetuous, was devouring it by degrees. For the mist is the sun's breakfast.

The woman walked slowly, her footsteps muffled. Her body was bare, bereft of clothing or adornment. Her only cover was the sheet of hair that fell down her back to full rounded hips, smooth as silk. The fuzz that nestled in her armpits and between her thighs was warm and soft as down. She had a high, arched nose with finely cut nostrils and eyebrows like birds' wings. Her lashes were long and curved. Her breasts with their deep cleft, seemingly carved out of marble by a master sculptor, were buoyant waves on whose crests floated twin buds about to open and yield their scent. Below them rested a navel that rippled and shimmered like a half moon.

The woman's movements were languid, her eyes unseeing.

She was ageless. Of infancy, childhood, prime and decay she had no knowledge. They did not touch her. She lived and breathed the essence of youth. She had seen only a few seasons so far—spring, summer, rain and autumn. Now she felt a nip in the air as she walked. A delicate chill passed over her limbs. A taste of the approaching winter.

She had been banished from the garden on a night of pouring rain and taken refuge in a cave set deep in the mountains. She had been forbidden re-entry but the longing for the place of her birth was so intense at times that she felt a whirlwind seize her. It tossed and turned her in motions so fierce, she felt herself flaming to the tips of her fingers and the lobes of her ears. She was consumed by a thirst so deep that all the water of the land could not quench it. Night after night she lay awake staring into the dark. Like the last one...

Leaving the cave, she had bathed in a stream and started walking in the opposite direction. But how and when her steps turned towards the garden she did not know. Humans, when driven to despair by loss and loneliness, turn unconsciously, involuntarily, to the place of their origin.

The garden had no tracks or pathways. The woman moved slowly, skirting bushes and parting boughs as she went. Sometimes she had to cross stretches of water, sometimes she stopped to untangle her feet from creepers.

Suddenly, a shower of rain came pelting down and she took refuge under the spreading shade of a tree. There was another creature there, a cow with a coat that shone like gold and udders swollen with milk. Its eyes were moist with unshed tears. The woman stretched out her hand and caressed the velvety dewlap. The cow moaned in ecstasy and a spurt of milk ran down its legs. It knew the hand and had recognized its owner. The woman turned her eyes this way and that. The trees waved their branches at her and the fruits and flowers nodded their heads. They knew her. All, all of them knew her. Bittersweet sensations pricked her veins.

'How are you all?' she asked, smiling. 'Are you happy that I've come back to you?' The smile was visible but the words were unuttered, for language had not yet been born. The woman knew how to laugh and weep. A few sounds emanated from her throat but they held no meaning. She knew no words. There were no words on her lips, only expression in her eyes. And with her eyes she spoke to everything around her and they answered, for they too knew only the language of silence. 'You've come after a long time,' they said to her. 'You've grown even more beautiful.' From the branch above her head a ripe fruit, full and round, dropped at her feet. It was the tree's way of welcoming her.

The woman had wept all night but now she felt a load lift from her chest. Picking up the fruit, she sat on a boulder at the edge of a stream. The rain had stopped and a magnificent rainbow lit up the sky. She looked at it and spoke, as to a friend, 'How are you?' From the cave that was now her dwelling she could see no rainbows.

Turning her eyes away from the sky, she looked into the

water. Her own face looked back at her. It was the only human face she had seen in a long time. It was the only human she could speak to.

Suddenly, she saw a creature gliding towards her from the opposite bank. It was a serpent with a vast, undulating body. It stared at her through bulging eyes. Resolute, unblinking. She felt no fear. She knew the creature and had seen it often. It never came too close. It always stopped a few yards away and gaped at her as it was doing now. As if … as if it wanted to say something to her. But the waves of the creature's mind were out of sync with hers. She looked at it with blank eyes. 'Go away,' she said. But the serpent did not move. It continued to stare at her, its coiled body half concealed by moss and pebbles. The woman rose and began to walk towards the cusp where another stream met this one. A man stood in the water which rose to his thighs. Long, waving locks of hair fell to his shoulders and a dark, velvety stubble covered his cheeks and chin. His chest was as broad and massive as a stone wall. His magnificent physique was stark naked.

At the sight of him the woman trembled. From the lashes of her eyes to the tips of her toes. Then the shivering left her limbs and turned into a raging passion of desire. Her heart burned as though a flaming tornado was passing over it. She wanted to fly on its wings to where he stood and fling her body, tender as a flower, on his stony chest. To merge every particle of her being with his. But she controlled the urge. The garden was forbidden territory. In entering it she had broken the rules. He might reject her, might cruelly thrust her aside. Three of the Maker's sentinels guarded the garden day and night. What if he alerted them?

'Beloved,' her heart spoke within her. 'You are left companionless just as I am. We have quarrelled, it is true. Yet ... yet I cannot bear our separation. Doesn't your heart ache for me as mine does for you? Why, oh why did you not come looking for me? Is your anger greater than all your other feelings?' Her body stood poised for flight but her mind held it back with a firm hand. She swayed where she stood. The hues of the rainbow still filled the sky. The trees, flowers and fruits were as bright and beautiful as ever, the breeze as honeyed. But the woman's eyes saw nothing. Only the man before her...

After a while he stepped out of the water and was lost in the shadows of the forest.

'Titriv!' a bird circling above her head called sharply. 'Titriv!' Or it may have been 'Lilith'. The woman came out of her trance and looked up at the sky. She had heard this particular cry often but never seen the bird. She narrowed her eyes and scanned the greenery around her. She knew it was nestling in the branches of one of the trees. But which tree? 'Dear bird,' she implored, 'come out of your hiding and call me again. Call louder. If my man hears you, he might remember me.'

It was from the call of this bird that the woman had been given her name. It was Lilith.

The first human form wrought by the Creator out of earth, air and water was the male. After breathing life into it, he had looked at his handiwork in admiration and said, 'I give you the name Adam. This garden is yours. Enjoy its delights.' But Adam, though he was surrounded by objects of sensuous pleasure, was often downcast and unhappy. He did not know why, but his Maker, who watched over him from afar, did. Like all other living creatures, Adam needed to procreate and live through successive generations. And for that purpose he needed a mate.

The Maker realized that he was guilty of a grave error. He had moulded the man in his own image, given him the genitals of a male. What cast would He use for the female? He himself was not a woman, not even in the smallest part. And He didn't need to procreate. He was the One and Only. He was Elohim.

Once again He set himself to the task of creation. Choosing the best and finest, strain by strain, from all his earlier work, He fashioned the female—a creature of unsurpassed beauty and grace. Strength and power were the male's attributes, an exquisite delicacy and sensibility were the female's.

As the breath of life entered her form, the woman rose and stood face to face with her mate. The two looked long and deep into each other's eyes. It was at that moment that the bird flew over their heads calling, 'Titriv! Lilith!' The Maker heaved a sigh of relief. The task of creation was complete. 'Adam and Lilith,' he said, 'the earth is yours to live in and rule. Complement one another and find fulfilment. The gift of speech will be yours when you are ready for it. Until then, converse in the language of silence. Sense one another's needs with your eyes, hearts and the flow of your blood.'

Adam turned to the woman. 'You have dust on your body,' he said. 'Come, let us wash ourselves in a stream.'

The days passed, each one brighter and more beautiful as the pair wandered through the garden like deer and doe. They bathed, ate and slept together and even in their dreams saw only each other. But one morning, when Lilith raised her arm to pluck a ripe fruit, Adam stopped her. 'Not that one,' he said.

'Why not?' Lilith asked curiously.

'I'll teach you to distinguish the good from the indifferent. I'll pick the best and give it to you.'

'I'll take them from your hands with pleasure.' Lilith smiled.

Another day, just as Lilith was stepping into the cool green waters of a lagoon to wash her sun-warmed limbs, Adam grasped her arm. 'Not here,' he said.

This time something flickered in Lilith's eyes. 'Why not?' she asked sharply.

'I haven't seen this waterbody before. Besides, there are flowers floating on its surface. I'll take you to another one. Its water is purer and clearer.'

That afternoon the sky was angry. The sun disappeared behind black clouds, stone-hard and menacing. They clashed against each other with a terrible sound. Flashes of light, more brilliant than the sun's, dazzled the sky—as though in defiance of their Maker, threatening to destroy His creation. Lilith's heart trembled but Adam knew no fear. The Creator had told him that these were periodic bursts of rebellion and easily quelled. Taking Lilith's hand, Adam led her to a dried-up riverbed partially screened by a wall of hills. They sat side by side, waiting for the storm to subside. Presently, the cloud cover melted away and turned into a gigantic lake from which sheets of water came splashing down on their bodies.

Lilith shivered.

'Your limbs are cold and wet,' Adam said. 'Lie down. I'll cover them with mine.'

Adam lay on Lilith, protecting her from the elements with infinite love and care. Breast to breast they lay; mouth to mouth. Thigh resting against thigh. Lilith stopped shivering. A balmy warmth spread through her limbs, entered her bloodstream and touched her heart. Her body melted into his.

'Adam.' She took his name for the first time. There was wonder in her voice.

'Lilith,' he whispered.

Adam entered Lilith. He reached deep within her. Could any sensation be sweeter? Then, deeply fulfilled, they clung together and slept, a blessed, dreamless sleep.

From that day on Nature took over. They loved and mated at all times of the day—morning, noon and night. Beneath the boughs of flowering trees, in the waters of streams and rivulets and under the open sky. And now their eyes beheld what had been hidden from them so far. They saw the same game being played around them. Birds and beasts, worms and insects, even trees and creepers came together from time to time in ecstatic union.

One evening, as they sat by a river, Adam took Lilith by the hand. 'Come,' he said.

Lilith recognized the mating call but instead of obeying, she pressed her face against Adam's chest and said, 'We've come together so often, and each time it has been your body above mine. Why don't we try another way? You below and I...?'

'I below you!' Adam was stunned. 'But why?'

'To see what it feels like.'

'That's impossible.'

'Why impossible? We could try it once.'

'No. It goes against the law of Nature.'

'What is Nature?'

'Nature is one of the manifestations of the Maker.'

'And what does it say?'

'That man commands and woman obeys.'

'But the Maker told us to complement one another.'

'And that is what we do. I give you protection and you delight me with your sweetness.'

'But can we not complement each other more equally? Just as we do in other things. One day I dive into the water first and you follow. On another day I am led by you. Can't our love-making admit an element of change?'

'It is not the same thing.' Adam's voice was grave. 'Come, lie down. I am ready.'

Lilith obeyed but a shadow fell over her heart. And their union, for the first time, lost its perfection. The heat and passion of the male failed to evoke an answering warmth in the female. Rising, she walked into the river and stood neck deep in it. She stood in the water for a long time.

The same scene was played out the next day. Lilith begged Adam to try out her way but he was steadfast in his refusal. He reasoned with her, coaxed, cajoled and commanded but Lilith pleaded plaintively, 'Once. Just once.'

Adam was appalled. He hadn't dreamed that a woman, fragile and tender as a flower, could have such an inflexible will. They sat in silence for a while. And then Lilith said the strangest thing. 'We are alike in every way. We have the same needs, enjoy the same pleasures. Yet, every time, it is you who determines what I must do. You tell me what I can and cannot eat, where I must bathe and sleep. And it is you who always gives the mating call. Why is it so? Are my brains and senses duller than yours?'

Adam was silent for a moment. Then he said, 'Cast such

thoughts aside. I am your protector. I am responsible for your well-being. Obey me in all things and no harm shall come to you.'

Lilith was not convinced. 'The same elements have gone into the making of our bodies,' she said, 'and our hearts and senses. Why, then, can we not be equal? I don't understand...'

'You don't need to understand anything. Wear these flowers in your hair. You will look even more beautiful.'

'I don't wish to look more beautiful. I want us to share our lives in equal measure.'

'Man and woman can never be equal. What you are saying goes against the Maker's command. Can we disobey Him?'

'Why does the Maker speak only to you and never to me?'

Adam ignored the question. 'Look around you,' he said instead. 'Observe all other forms of life. They follow the same law. The male above, the female below.'

'You speak of the animal world. But we are not animals. We rank supreme in the order of the Maker's creation.'

'Don't say *we*,' Adam said testily. 'Aren't our bodies different? Is yours not smaller and weaker?'

'That's true,' Lilith murmured thoughtfully. 'Quite true. But ... but is my heart smaller than yours? Are my brains and senses inferior?'

'These questions are not for you to ask.'

Silence. Lilith placed her head on Adam's chest and said gently, 'Let us not quarrel, dear one. Let us make love in a different way. For once?' Her eyes were soft with pleading. 'It might be more pleasurable for both of us.'

'Have you felt a lack of pleasure all these days? Have you not reached the summit each time, and felt fulfilled?'

Lilith did not reply. She rose and walked away.

A few days later, on a dark, shadowy afternoon, when a sweet breeze blew and birds and beasts, trees and shrubs were calling out to their mates, Adam took Lilith in his arms. 'Come,' he said. Lilith rose and, pressing her soft breasts to his chest, whispered, 'Can't you indulge me once? Just once?'

At this, Adam's patience reached its end and his brow grew dark with anger. Lifting her in his powerful arms, he flung her to the ground and pinned her body beneath his. 'You dare belittle me, woman!' he shouted, thunder rumbling in his voice. 'Why should I indulge you? I am your master. Obeying me is your duty and your supreme fulfillment as a woman.'

Lilith strained and struggled, then slipped away from him and ran into the woods, as nimble as a doe. Adam followed her, roaring like a lion. But Lilith wouldn't let him catch her. Laughing, she darted this way and that, hiding behind bushes and circling tree trunks. She expected him to join in her mirth but heard no responding laughter. Adam gnashed his teeth and his eyes turned into balls of fire. His voice grew louder and more menacing—so menacing that everything in the garden trembled in awe and fear.

At the sound, three creatures flew down from the sky and dropped to the ground. Their bodies were shaped like Adam's but they had wings like birds. They were angels, the Creator's sentinels. Their names were Senoy, Sansenoy and Semangelof.

They caught Lilith in a few seconds and asked, 'Why all this commotion? What is going on?'

The question had been put to Lilith but it was Adam

who answered. 'This woman the Maker has given me is disobedient,' he said, his chest heaving with indignation. 'She questions my right to do with her as I desire. I would rather not have a mate than have one like her.'

Lilith's lips trembled. She tried to speak, to defend herself. But the angels wouldn't let her.

'Have you gone mad, woman?' one admonished her sternly. 'Don't you know your happiness lies in that of your man? Disobedience will bring you nothing but trouble and sorrow.'

'Listen to me,' Lilith pleaded. 'I...'

'There's nothing more to be said or heard,' the second angel cut her short. 'Do your duty. Follow your man.'

'Minor quarrels might occur now and then,' the third one said. There was a hint of amusement in his voice. 'That is because the Maker has given you reason, something he has withheld from the rest of His creation. Bickering a little and then making up enhances the love game. Go, resolve your differences and enjoy yourselves.'

Lilith's face hardened at these words. Her winged brows came together. 'Listen to me,' she said firmly. 'You *must* listen. The man just said he doesn't want a mate who is disobedient. Can I not say the same? Can't I reject one who does not respect my will?'

'You can't be serious!' The third angel smiled at her. But the first one was not so indulgent.

'You do not have the right to accept or reject,' he said harshly. 'You were created to satisfy the needs of the male. Never forget that.'

Adam came forward and, grasping her arm, pulled her roughly towards him. The angels pushed her from behind. 'No!' Lilith cried out, trembling and panting like a wounded doe. 'You shan't have me against my will. Never.' Adam let go. He knew he had the power to subdue her body and enter her by force. But the sweetness of surrender and the ecstasy of a shared union would not be his.

The three angels looked at one another. 'Adam,' they asked grimly, 'do you take or spurn this woman?'

'I spurn her,' Adam answered. 'I do not wish to see her face again.'

The angels turned to Lilith. 'We banish you from this garden!' they pronounced in a terrible voice. 'You are impious! Unholy! You have no place here.' The four of them dragged her to the edge of a precipice. A sharp shove and her tender body went tumbling down the jagged crags. Reaching the bottom, she fell into a river in a dead faint. She floated on the water for days. Then, on gaining consciousness, she rose and walked into the cave that was now her home.

She spent her days wandering in the mountains, weeping incessantly. There was vegetation here, not as rich and refulgent as in the garden, but there were briars and bushes that bore wild nuts and berries. On these she sustained herself. And all the while she wondered, 'What did I do to be punished thus? I wanted us to share our lives in equal measure. I asked for nothing more.'

How deep lies the source of human tears? Why do they know no end? But tears, though given by the Maker only to the highest of his creation, do not answer questions. At times, when the pain and humiliation of Adam's rejection became too grievous to bear, she thought of embracing death. Of flinging herself from the top of a cliff or drowning in a mountain lake. But in the end she couldn't. Life pulled her back with invisible strings.

Time went on. The days were long and weary and the
nights were worse. Desolation sat on her chest, heavy as
stone. She lay awake for hours, staring into the darkness,
waiting for dawn. Gradually she started to weaken. This
life is no life, she thought. Better to live as Adam's slave
than away from all that I love. She decided to go back and
seek his forgiveness. To tell him that, henceforth, she
would live under his obedience. If such was a woman's
destiny, so be it.

Yet something pulled her back each time...

One day, the three angels appeared before her.

'We banished you from the garden,' Senoy said coldly,
'but we are prepared to take you back. On one condition.'

Lilith looked up eagerly.

'You must not think of yourself as equal to Adam ever
again.' Sansenoy's voice was stern, inexorable. 'You must
submit your will to his in all things.'

Semangelof smiled at her. 'Great happiness lies ahead
of you, Lilith,' he said gently. 'Everything you wish for will
be yours in the time to come. Only, don't ask for it. Are you
willing?'

'Quite willing,' Lilith murmured. Joy leapt up in her
veins at the thought of returning. Yet a nagging fear pricked
at her heart. 'I have a question,' she said meekly, eyes
downcast, voice quivering. 'Is Adam prepared to take me
back?'

'We will persuade him to do so,' Senoy answered. 'He
will agree when he hears that you are carrying his child in
your womb.'

A child! What was that? And what was a womb? Lilith

looked up, bewildered. She had noticed some changes in her body of late. Her belly had swelled and she felt something move inside it from time to time. A child! A wave of injured pride and self-pity washed over her. Adam would take her back not because he missed her but because she was carrying his child. Sansenoy saw the disappointment in her eyes and said gravely, 'You see yourself solely as a companion to Adam. But that was not the Maker's intention in creating you. Another man would have served that purpose. Like all living things, Adam needs to procreate and he can do so only through a woman. You will receive his seed, nurture it within your body and yield it to him when the allotted span is over. Again and again, for all time to come. Thus shall man multiply and fill the earth. As for you, yours will be the glory of the primal womb.'

A tiny flame flickered in Lilith's eyes at these words but she doused it in an instant. 'Very well,' she said quietly, 'I shall receive Adam's seed and nurture his child in my womb. But the season and clime shall be of my choosing. It is my body and only I will know when it is ready.'

'Your body!' Senoy exclaimed. 'It is only a receptacle! Besides, the privilege of choice has not been bestowed upon you.'

Suddenly a current of white-hot rage darted through Lilith's veins. Her eyes blazed in defiance. 'I scorn such a union!' she cried. 'One in which my needs and desires are so totally negated! Go and tell Adam that I shall return to the garden only if he comes and pleads with me. If not, this cave is good enough shelter.'

The angels stared at her, speechless with shock. Then, collecting themselves, they tried to make her change her mind. They reasoned and hectored, coaxed and threatened

by turns. But Lilith was adamant. She wouldn't go back
with them. Adam must come to her. He must tell her that
he still desired her.

Sansenoy wagged a menacing finger and hurled
imprecations at her. 'May your womb turn to dust,' he
thundered, 'and the child in it shrivel and die. Lustful,
licentious woman! You are cursed with sterility from this
day forth.'

Lilith swooned and fell to the ground.

When she regained consciousness, the angels had left.
Her limbs burned and shuddered with excruciating pain.
Her battered womb felt as empty as air. Yet, so great was
her life force, Lilith did not die.

Strength and beauty returned slowly. And now she
made a resolution. She wouldn't think of Adam any more.
She didn't need a mate. She would live in the midst of
nature and all the flora and fauna would be her friends. The
sky would be her closest companion. Gazing on its changing
face, hour after hour, she would conquer her desolation.
But as water flows spontaneously towards water, so Lilith's
mind and body craved Adam's. So vast, so all-consuming
was her yearning that she knew no peace. Her nights were
long and sleepless, her days arid and barren. And then, one
night, she couldn't bear her isolation any longer. She rose
at dawn and entered the forbidden garden.

She wanted to see Adam once. Only once. To ask him the
question that had haunted her ever since her banishment.
'Do you love me, Adam? Put your hand on your heart and
tell me the truth. Does the sweetness and beauty of the
time we spent together mean nothing to you? If that is so, I
shall bid you farewell. You shall never see my face again.'

She saw him from afar but, lacking the courage to face him, she followed closely, stealthily, like a shadow. If she heard him pronounce her name or saw him pause even momentarily at their favourite mating places, she would know that his yearning for their time together was no less than hers. But Adam passed the riverbed where their bodies had first awakened and known the ecstasy of union hurriedly, absently. As though his mind was somewhere else. And now she noticed changes in him. There was a sound coming from his throat. A strange, unprecedented sound to which his lips were moving in unison. It was a word and he was repeating it over and over again. Presently he stopped and picked an armful of flowers. Squatting under a clump of palms, he began to weave them into a garland. He had never picked flowers before, only fruits. And he had never woven a garland. Lilith smiled. Who was it for? Himself? Or could it be for her?

Stringing the last flower, Adam got up and ran into the woods, Lilith following him on silent feet. He was calling out louder now, the same word. What was it? A name?

Suddenly, she stopped and slipped behind a tree. Her mouth turned dry and all the breath went out of her lungs. Another woman stood before Adam. She was a replica of Lilith, just as well-formed, just as beautiful. But her nose was smaller and softer, her eyes dim and dreamy. The woman smiled and, taking Adam by the hand, led him to a patch of moss under a tree. Some large leaves piled with fruits, berries and nuts were spread on it. Lilith noticed that she had peeled and segmented the fruits and shelled the nuts. Adam dropped down on his haunches and placed the garland around her neck. The woman looked pleased. She stroked the flowers and kissed them. Picking up the fruits one by one, she fed Adam with her own hands. Lilith was surprised. She had never thought of doing that. They had eaten together from the same leaf. At times they had even bitten into the same fruit turn by turn.

The stranger ate what remained after Adam had had his fill. Then he turned his back to her and she moved towards him. Curious to see what they were doing, Lilith inched closer. The woman was stroking the man's broad, perspiring back and gently easing out the ooze from some pistules that had formed on it like beads. He uttered soft moans of pleasure, then lay spread-eagled on the velvety moss. The woman kneeled at his feet and began to press and knead the powerful muscles in his legs and thighs. Adam's body heaved luxuriously. His breathing became regular and his eyes grew heavy with sleep. The woman moved away. She lay down at the edge of the patch of moss, curled up her body and went to sleep.

Lilith looked on in wonder. She had no such skills. She hadn't even known they existed. Her eyes burned with pain and humiliation at Adam's betrayal. Walking away, she sat down by a small spring. Tears rolled down her cheeks and fell into the water. Her destiny lay before her, crystal clear. Adam didn't want her any more. He didn't need her. She knew now that the word he was muttering over and over again was the woman's name. It was *Eve*.

Lilith wept by the stream for hours. Then, exhausted in mind and body, she drifted into an uneasy, fitful sleep. When she awoke, the daylight was gone. The sun had set and a radiant moon shone from a cloudless sky. Its beams shimmered over the leaves of trees and turned the water bodies into sheets of silver. The scent of night flowers entered her nostrils. She raised her head to a sky sprinkled all over with stars. 'Beautiful!' she whispered, as though to a friend. 'Beautiful! But it is not for me. I must go.'

She must go, she knew that. But her feet were rooted to the ground and she could not move. 'I've lost everything,' she said to herself. 'I am a destitute. Even hope has abandoned me.' Even as she thought this, the old Lilith asserted herself. Her nostrils flared, her breath grew hot and heavy, angry sparks flashed in her eyes. 'Why should I leave everything I love?' she muttered rebelliously. 'Why should I submit to such gross injustice? The Maker formed us both from the same elements but he treats us differently. He is partial to Adam and unfair to me.'

The Maker had created Lilith but the complexity of his own creation had eluded him. He thought he had given her beauty and sweetness, sensitivity and subservience. A modicum of self-pity perhaps, and a touch, a mild touch of self-respect. But he was totally unaware that another element had gone into her making. Something called *jealousy*.

This primal passion swept over Lilith in waves, swamping her body, heart and mind. Every organ, every vein, sinew and nerve rose in revolt. She walked swiftly to the spot where the two lay sleeping. Adam was sprawled on the carpet of soft moss, Eve was lying at the edge at an awkward angle, as though fearful of constricting his space. She looked around. This was *hers*, this clearing surrounded by waving palms and sweet-scented flower bushes. This bed of emerald moss. This vast night sky. This glittering moon. They were hers, all hers. How dare Adam replace her with another woman? The night was cold but Lilith's limbs burned as though with fever and beads of sweat appeared on her brow. She would take what was hers. No one would be allowed to intimidate her. Not Adam, not the angels. No … not even Elohim. The angels had called her lustful and licentious. She would be just that. She would take what she desired by force.

She sprang on Adam's sleeping form and spread her limbs over his. 'Mine. Only mine,' she muttered. Adam's eyes sprang open. From the feel of her body he knew it wasn't his present consort. It was Lilith. 'You!' he cried out in shock and revulsion. 'How dare you come here again?' He tried to throw her off—this woman as frail and tender as a flower—but couldn't. He tried again and again. Then he panicked and let out a fearful shriek.

Eve heard him and woke up. She stared at the scene, eyes wide with horror. Who or what was this apparition? Another like herself? Or a fiend in the guise of a woman? And indeed Lilith felt herself imbued with the strength and power of a dozen demons. Adam thrashed and struggled; Eve strained every muscle as she tried to pull Lilith away, but their combined strength was nothing before hers.

Suddenly, the three angels dropped from the sky. Seizing Lilith by the hair, they plucked her off Adam's body as lightly as a leaf. Not content with showering slander and abuse, they started beating her into submission. So harsh, so cruel was their assault that Lilith's body was bruised and battered in seconds. By the time they were done, it was a mass of broken bones and bloodied flesh. Picking her up with two fingers as he would a loathsome worm, Sansenoy flung her out of the garden. 'You go back with your life for the last time,' the three spoke in a single voice. 'Death will be your due if you dare violate these holy premises again.'

But their threats failed to frighten or subdue Lilith. Her blood boiled and seethed. Her eyes blazed with fury. Licking her wounds like an angry tigress, she took a vow. Come what may, she would avenge her humiliation.

She saw something slither down the trunk of a tree. It moved rapidly towards her, coiling and uncoiling its giant form a few yards from where she sat. The creature had changed since she had seen it last. Its body was as obese and ugly as ever and covered with scales. But it had a human face now and two curved horns had sprung out of its head. 'You don't know me, Lilith,' the serpent spoke for the first time. 'My name is Samael. I am no less powerful than the Creator. We have both suffered at His hands and we both seek revenge. Be my consort. Let us fight and overthrow Him together.'

Lilith had been Adam's mate, the power and beauty of whose physique was no less than the Maker's. The thought of embracing this bizarre creature disgusted her. 'Get out of my sight,' she screamed. She would take revenge, but she would take it alone.

The events of the night had shocked and frightened Eve so much that she couldn't stop weeping and shivering. Adam spent hours consoling and soothing her. Eve had been created after Lilith's banishment to serve as Adam's companion. But this time the Maker had taken a precaution. He had formed her out of a rib taken from Adam's own body. She was only a part of Adam, a tiny part. And as such she would be completely subservient. Her life would be subsumed in his. 'Do not be fearful, dear one,' Adam said, wiping away her tears. 'That hateful creature will never come into this garden again.'

But Lilith came...

One night, when Adam lay sleeping on his mossy bed, he felt a soft body drifting down on his. He knew it was Lilith. He tried to thresh his arms and push her away but they seemed weighed down with lead and lay powerless by his side. He wanted to scream but her burning mouth was crushing his and he couldn't utter a sound. He tried to heave himself up but her soft breasts and silky thighs were pressing down on him with phenomenal strength. And now he felt her taking him in, draining him to the last drop, consuming him. He could neither move nor breathe, for she was above him and he below. Yet an ecstatic joy, a rapture sweeter than any sensation he had ever known, suffused his blood and ran through his veins, warming every cell in his body. A delicious lassitude descended on his limbs as they melted into hers.

Adam sat up with a start. Where was Lilith? A faint scent of her hair, dimly remembered, clung to the air. But there was no sign of her. No sound, either. Adam strained his ears to hear her footsteps on the grass and fallen leaves but the night was silent. Not a breath of wind stirred in the trees. The Maker's creation was wrapped in slumber. And now, something, someone, willed Adam to look down at the proud flag of his arrogant manhood which hung like a limp rag between his loins. The moss was splattered with semen.

Seasons came and went. The years stretched into aeons. Adam fathered many children and Eve's was the glory of the primal womb. Then, replete with the joy and triumph of proliferating and filling the earth with their own kind, they embraced death.

But Lilith did not die...

Spurned and humbled, baulked of all her desires, deprived of love, thirsting for fulfilment and burning for revenge, Lilith lives on. Her carnal body turned to dust in due time and vanished from the face of the earth. But she comes, as she came to Adam, in the adolescent dreams of youth.

THE GREAT WORLD

WITH NO EXPECTATIONS from life, Subal had little sense of his misery. In fact, these days he looked almost happy. And this when his business had hit rock-bottom, when his two nets were gathering dust in a corner of his kitchen. And why not? All the big fish seemed to have disappeared from the vicinity. The best he could do was to buy shrimps and small fish from wholesalers and sell them in the local bazaars. Making three or four rupees at the end of the day was such an effort that his bones were turning to dust. Soon he would find grass growing on them. Yet a secret happiness bubbled in his breast. Four-thousand-five-hundred rupees! And all he had to do to get it was smear his right thumb with ink and press it on a piece of paper. He stole loving glances at the precious organ, his heart swelling with the pride of possession. Four-thousand-five-hundred! Had anyone in his fourteen generations of ancestors even seen such a sum?

There were about two-hundred-and-fifty grams of bele fish left in Subal's basket, their translucent white flesh turning opaque yellow with the passing hours. Huge blue flies buzzed angrily above them. Subal had brought the price down by degrees to two rupees a kilo but still there were no takers. Only one old man hovered around, eyeing them greedily. Subal knew he was waiting for the moment when he would get them at the price he had offered—one-rupee-fifty paisa. But Subal would be damned if he sold his goods at a loss. Far better to take it home and eat it himself.

Turning to his friend Nitai, who had sold his own stock and was waiting patiently for him, he said, 'Let's go. My back and shoulders are stiff from all this sitting around. Do you have a bidi?'

'No, dada,' Nitai answered. 'I'll buy some on the way out. And a kilo of rice.'

'What's the price of rice in this bazaar?'

'Two rupees thirty paisa. That too for broken rice.'

'We'll buy it from Baguihati. It's bound to be cheaper there. At least fifteen paisa less.'

Nitai was a bit of a dandy. He wore a shirt and kept his money in a plastic purse. Subal didn't care for show. A coarse dhuti that came down to his knees was good enough for him. He could tuck his cloth pouch securely at the waist, which was the main thing. Wearing shirts and vests was a nuisance. Besides, washing them involved expense. All you needed to do with a bare torso was take a few dips in the pond and you were clean.

Reaching Baguihati, Nitai bought some rice and red chillies. Subal, who had drawn his rations only yesterday, bought half a kilo of salt. He was about to buy some bidis when better sense prevailed. If he had his own he wouldn't be able to freeload on Nitai. He would wait till Nitai took the turning to Keshtopur and then buy a pack. The two men walked along at a leisurely pace until they reached the main road.

Nitai lit a bidi and looked around. 'How this place has changed!' he marvelled. 'It used to be a desolate swamp full of water bodies. And look at it now! Houses sprouting like mushrooms everywhere.'

Subal thought of his thumb and his voice shook with elation as he said philosophically, 'Change is a part of life. I remember a time when giant sharks floated past exactly where we are standing now. Their mouths were like caverns.'

'Sharks?'

'Yes, yes, sharks. As for fish, the place was teeming with chital and boal. Each a yard-and-a-half long. Now there are buses running where water used to stretch as far as the eye could see.'

'Are you thinking of selling your land, Subal-da? I'm told the price has risen to three thousand.'

'Three thousand! Pooh!' Subal dismissed Nitai's question with the contempt it deserved. 'Just wait and watch, it will be ten thousand in a year or two. Then we'll see. I'm not letting go of my land in a hurry. I'm not such a fool.'

Nitai's house was a mile-and-a-half away from the turn for Keshtopur. Subal's was a few minutes' walk. He could see his house from where they stood. There was a palmyra growing behind it, studded with huge balls of heavy black fruit. A pair of vultures sat on it day and night. Shaala! Subal cursed under his breath. He would chop that palm tree down one of these days. Where would the buggers go then? He looked around. Two canals ran parallel on either side of the road. The one on the left was old, a natural strip of water. The other canal was new and man-made. In order to raise the road to its present level, the earth had been dug in a straight line down the right side. The long pit was flooded now. In fact, the whole area was flooded with the rain that had been pelting down, unceasingly, for the last two months. Tiger prawn flourished in fresh rainwater.

Subal pulled up his dhuti, tucked it around his middle, and stepped off the road. He pushed his way across waves of water that rose to his knees, even to his waist in places. Reaching home, he discovered that the yard had turned into a swirling pond. Shaala! This fucking rain was killing all his plants. His pumpkin vine was hanging from the thatch like a length of rotten string. His chillies were completely submerged. Even they would die. God! Had anyone ever seen rain like this before?

Subal muttered curses but his heart sang a little tune. His yard had disappeared, his plants were dead, his house was swaying like a sinking boat and water had entered the kitchen. But who cared? With all this rain, the fields, meadows, streams, canals and ponds had become one. A great sheet of water. The rich were just as badly affected as the poor. The car in the Senguptas' garage was lying idle, useless, sunk to the neck in dirty water. The babus were walking to office, dhutis up to their thighs, feet slipping in mud and slush. How Subal laughed when he saw them. Even their maid, arrogant whore, had to pull her sari right up to her buttocks on her way to and fro. And best of all, shoals of big fish had come swimming from other ponds into his. This was because he had done something very clever. He had lowered a sack of cow dung into the middle of his pond. Fish loved the smell of cow dung. He would wait till the water went down a little and then bring out his nets. But the tulsi! He felt a pang of anxiety. His tulsi plant stood on a pedestal in the yard. It was safe for now, but...

It was all because of the tulsi. The entire region had once been wild and marshy. All one could see for miles were stretches of water and waving reeds, dotted here and there with primitive fishing dams known as bheris. A couple of them had once belonged to his family. Subal had faint memories of his childhood. They had been quite well-off then. His grandfather had supplied fish to the royal household in Paikpara every day. Then, who knows what got into him, he decided to buy another bheri in Mahesh Bathaan. That turned out to be a disaster. Not only did he lose his money and his bheris, he had to sell most of his land. And what was the price of land then in these parts? Seventy, or at the most seventy-five rupees a bigha? That too with highly erratic and arbitrary measuring. As a result, the man became a pauper.

Soon afterwards, such is the irony of fate, the government entered the scene. The villagers woke up one morning to find tents being hoisted and water being sucked out of the bog. And then earth from the Ganga was brought in huge iron pipes and the low land was raised and levelled. On one side, an impressive strip of asphalt called VIP Road came up and on the other, a network of smaller roads. The area was given a new, fancy name: Salt Lake. The price of land rose overnight. The few fishermen and betel-growers who still had land were delighted to sell it off at a thousand or fifteen-hundred per bigha and move to Bhatiara or Koikhali. Subal's six brothers did the same with the small patches they had inherited. But Subal was stuck. Being the eldest son, the old house with the tulsi plant had fallen in his share. His mother, Bagala, screamed and cursed at the very mention of a sale. Sobbing bitterly, she flung herself on the earth next to the tulsi. 'Have I borne sons in my womb, Ma?' she demanded of the plant. 'Or a bunch of thorny scrubs? Doesn't everyone know that selling a family house is followed by the death of the eldest son? That the hand that uproots a tulsi plant rots with leprosy? Money! Is

money all that matters to you?' She turned angry, red eyes
on Subal. 'Choke me to death first, scum of my womb, then
do as you please...'

Subal, of course, paid no attention to her threats and
entreaties. What weight did an old woman's irrational
fears have against the sum of four-thousand-five-hundred
rupees? But the matter got somewhat complicated when
his wife joined ranks with her mother-in-law. Even then,
Subal would have ignored them both for the foolish, ignorant
women they were. But Bagala threw herself at his feet and
knocked her head against them. 'O baba Subol!' she wept.
'Don't put me through the agony of watching you die. Wait
till I'm gone. After that...' Subal drew back hastily. The
sight of his mother grovelling at his feet unnerved him.

While Bagala was throwing tantrums, the government
was acquiring large stretches of land swiftly and arbitrarily.
Luckily for her, Subal's house stood opposite the road
where all the activity was going on. If it were not for that,
her raving and ranting would have come to nothing. Like
poor Haridas Sapui's. He hadn't wanted to sell to the
government. The Marwaris were offering him a better price.
But what power could the poor man wield against the
forces of officialdom? He resisted as long as he could but
had to admit defeat in the end.

The government wasn't interested in Subal's property
but others were. A cycle company had approached him, so
had the Senguptas. His tiny plot of one kota and nine
chhataks adjoined theirs and they wanted to sell it off in
one lot. He was being offered four-thousand-five-hundred
rupees. But Subal refused to sell. He had to wait till his
mother died, he told them. But these days, it didn't bother
him too much. He smiled often, in anticipation of the

happy event. Then all he would need to do was smear his right thumb with ink ... meanwhile the price would go on rising.

At forty-one, Subal had fathered nine children of whom seven were still alive and kicking. His wife was the sort of woman who believed in entering the birthing shed once a year at the very least. She had given him a break for the last two years but who knew how long that would last? The eldest boy was the only other earning member but he had cut himself off from his family. He sold vegetables in Hathibagan Market and lived there with his wife. They didn't get a paisa out of him.

Subal entered the yard to find the other six frisking and gambolling in the dirty water like a shoal of fish. Blood rushed to his head in fury and, as always, he took it out on his daughter, Kushi. She was nearly sixteen, a woman, but she behaved like a tomboy. Instead of being a mother to her siblings and keeping them out of harm's way, she was the ringleader in all their games. The bitch was the bane of Subal's life. As greedy as an alley cat, she thought nothing of stealing whatever she could find in the kitchen and stuffing her maw. Mischief lurked in every bone of her body. A moment's inattention and one of her hapless brothers would find his share of food snatched away from his hands and crammed into her mouth.

'Kushi!' Subal lowered his basket on the dalaan and called out sternly. 'Come here.' Kushi's torn rag of a sari was tucked so high around her waist that Subal could see her thighs and flashes of her swelling breasts. The girl quailed at the sound of her father's voice. Hastily rearranging her sari, she walked up to him timidly. 'Haramjadi!' Subal grabbed her hair with one hand and slapped her hard on

the cheek with the other. 'What were you doing in the
water?'

'A ... a ... a catfish!' Kushi's head hung on one side
under the pressure of her father's hand and her voice came
out high and tinny. 'I saw a catfish near the t-tulsi.'

'A catfish!' Subal snarled. His free hand came down,
again and again, leaving red marks across the downy cheek.
'I'll stuff it alive into your mouth, spawn of a whore! Good
for nothing but eating and rolling around naked in the mud
and slush! Dragging the others in too! Even the little one
with his fever...'

Now Subal's wife entered the scene and took over from
her husband. Raining a shower of blows on the girl's back,
she shrieked, 'The shit-eating bitch doesn't listen to a word
I say. Didn't I tell you to grind the chillies half an hour
ago?'

Of all their children, Kushi was the only one with some
flesh on her bones. Consequently, Subal and his wife got a
lot of pleasure out of beating her and they did so with or
without reason. She never cried or protested and she didn't
do so now. Her face turned sulky and she walked slowly
towards the kitchen to do her mother's bidding.

Every morning, Subal rises before dawn and walks to the
warehouse in Datta Bagan. Buying whatever fish he can
afford, he goes to Naager Bazaar to sell it. The sun is close
to the zenith by the time his work is done and he has
walked the long miles home. He is tired and hungry but he
has to perform his parental duties first. The pernicious
vermin his wife spawns year after year are god's curse on
him! It is for them that he has to toil in the hot sun. A few

blows, some threats and abuses have to be administered before he can think of his own comfort. The job well done, he slaps a palmful of mustard oil on his burning pate and takes a few dips in the pond. After this, he sits down to his meal. Subal has made a rule and insists that it is meticulously followed. He eats first, as much as his stomach can hold. Then whatever is left is shared among the others. His health and well-being are essential, for isn't he the one who feeds them all? If, god forbid, something were to happen to him, if he fell ill or died, would anyone come forward with even a grain of burned rice in his hand?

Subal's wife comes out of the kitchen with an enamel thaala heaped with rice. Subal makes a well in the centre of the mound and pours a bowlful of dal in it. Mixing it together, he stuffs large fistfuls into his mouth with slurps of relish. The thaala is refilled twice or thrice with more rice, dal and whatever else has been cooked—pumpkin-vine chochchori or shrimps in fiery mustard sauce. By the time Subal has finished, the thaala shines as though it has been polished. Subal rises with a giant belch of satisfaction and, after washing his hands and rinsing out his mouth, stretches out on the floor of the dalaan and goes to sleep.

It is late evening by the time he awakes. After another round of beating and intimidating the children, he does odd jobs about the house. Some days he climbs up the thatch to inspect his gourds and pumpkins. He counts them and checks them for insect bites. He tends to them lovingly, turning them over and applying lime on their wounds. Other days he repairs the fence or stuffs straw in the holes of the roof. But he works only till sunset. They have no lantern.

When the lights on VIP Road are lit and their beams

play on the waters of the canal, he makes his way to Keshtopur, where his friends are waiting. He spends five or six annas on toddy and discusses the possibility of starting a fishing business in partnership with Nitai. He comes home high and merry and eats a large stack of rutis with a bowl of treacle. Then he pours half a pot of water down his gullet, and lies down and waits for his wife. They have only one bedroom in which husband, wife and children sleep together. A tiny square of the dalaan has been cordoned off for Bagala. Subal lies down by the door and smokes one bidi after another. A familiar heat rises in his loins. But the worthless woman takes her own time washing her pots and pans and wiping down the kitchen floor. His restlessness increases by the minute. How many pots do they have that she takes so long? She is nothing but a shiftless, lazy bitch with no care for her husband's needs.

He grabs her as soon as she appears and flings her down beside him. Without caring if the children are awake and watching, he kneads and squeezes her emaciated body and mounts her. The poor woman's bones creak under his weight and she gasps and wheezes like a pair of bellows.

'Another...' she whimpers, 'another imp of Satan is growing in my belly, draining me to the dregs. Will you never give my bones rest?' Subal cackles with laughter as though it is a good joke. And thus life goes on for them, day after day and night after night...

When Subal is away, the children play and roam about freely. Sometimes they stand on one side of VIP Road and watch the cars go by. They stare in wonder at the fair, handsome gentlemen and the beautiful ladies in pretty saris and jewels who sit within. The boys pick up whatever they can find—pieces of coloured paper, cigarette butts and bottle corks and stoppers. Sometimes they even find crusts of bread. None of them go to school except twelve-year-old Haran.

Subal's wife can't manage her children and doesn't even attempt to. The only one she tries to keep an eye on is Kushi. 'Eyi Kushi!' she hollers from time to time. 'Where are you, haramjadi? Come here at once.' If Kushi fails to make an appearance, she coaxes one of her sons to look for her. 'O re, find out what that slut is up to. Tell her I want her.' At the slightest sign of hesitation, she snaps, 'What are you waiting for, mukhpora? Go!'

At this point Kushi comes running in, panting and breathless, her hair wild and her clothes in disarray. 'Why are you screaming your head off?' She glares at her mother. Her mother glares back.

'What else can I do but scream? Sing kirtan? Such a great big hulk of a girl and not a bit of work is to be got out of her! Where were you?'

'I was just outside the door, looking at the cars on Bhaipi Road.'

'Looking at the cars! A-ha-ha-ha!' Kushi's mother grimaces and flings out her arms threateningly. 'Haven't I told you not to stand by the road?' Her eyes fall on her daughter's form, and her face blazes with fury. 'Is this how you tie a sari? Tits and all showing! Just wait till your father comes home. I'll make him give you the thrashing of your life.'

'I keep telling you to buy me a blouse,' Kushi mutters ruefully, tugging the end of her short four-yard sari, trying unsuccessfully to cover her burgeoning breasts. 'Everyone wears a blouse.'

'A blouse! I'll give you seven licks with a broomstick. No rice in the house and she wants a blouse. I should keep you locked in the house, naked. Worthless slut! Good for nothing but eating and sleeping...'

Subal was standing at the door when two cars came down VIP Road and stopped outside his house. Four gentlemen got out and struck up a conversation with him. Bagala watched the scene from the dalaan, her eyes as sharp as a hawk's. Again! Again the city rascals were trying to tempt her boy! 'Subal!' she cried in a high, cracked voice. 'Don't talk to them, son. Come away.' Subal ignored her. The men continued talking, pointing this way and that. Then, climbing down the side of the canal, they looked in the direction of the house. Kushi, who stood with her grandmother, saw one of the men staring at her. His eyes raked her form, taking in the swelling contours, the smooth skin, moist and dark as moss. Bagala saw it too. Pushing the girl behind her, she screamed, 'O Subal! Don't you dare play tricks with me. This is my father-in-law's house, the house I was brought to as a bride. You'll sell it over my dead body. I'll...'

'Chup!' Subal turned around and gnashed his teeth at his mother. 'Stop your caterwauling, you old crone, before I choke your breath.' Turning back to the gentlemen, he listened patiently to what they were saying, nodding his head in approval from time to time. He came inside a little later, his face beaming, thirty-two teeth bared in a grin. He held a wad of notes in his hand. Bagala's face crumpled like a dried mango. Her toothless mouth quivered as she clawed at her son's chest and sobbed. 'What have you done, you scum of my womb? You've given your thumb print and sold the property!'

'Hoonh.' Subal smiled snidely and looked at his mother out of the corners of his eyes. 'That's just what I have done.'

'A-a-a-a-h!' Bagala let out a long moan and sank to the floor in a heap. Her eyes went blank as she mumbled, 'You couldn't wait till I died? You couldn't...?'

'O ki! O ki!' Subal pulled his mother up. 'Women are all the same. They don't have the patience to listen to anything. Always jumping to conclusions! Arre baba, haven't I promised I won't sell in your lifetime? Not that you'll go in a hurry. Women never do. They live on and on, especially in poor families...'

'Don't talk in riddles. Who were those men and why did they give you money?'

'Not for the house re, Ma. I didn't sell the house. All they want to do is hang a picture outside. They'll give me fifteen rupees a month for that. They've given me an advance of thirty rupees.'

'Money for hanging a picture!' Bagala's jaw fell open. 'What picture?'

'It's called an advertise. I can't believe my luck. I wonder whose face I saw when I woke up this morning! The money just flew in and fell into my lap. I'll go tell Nitai...'

'Fifteen rupees! Every month?'

'That's what I'm telling you!' In his excitement, Subal became generous and promised his mother a blanket and Haran an exercise book and pencil.

'O go!' Subal's wife put in her bit. 'You must buy a blouse for Kushi. A four-yard sari doesn't cover her properly. She's grown so big—people stare at her.'

It seemed to the whole family that the extra fifteen rupees would take care of all their needs, solve all their problems.

A few days later a truck arrived with quantities of material. Three or four smartly dressed boys jumped down and got to work. Iron poles were planted on either side of Subal's house. On top of them they erected a huge tin sheet painted in the richest, most glowing colours. The scene was charming. On the right hand was a silver airplane in flight. At the other end was a city with towers so tall they seemed to be nestling among the clouds that floated in a vivid blue sky. Below the plane, a young couple ran hand in hand, laughing and gazing at each other. The girl had green eyes and auburn hair and a full bosom with a deep cleft. Her skirt had risen to her waist in the strong breeze, revealing a pair of plump pink thighs. The caption 'FLY QUANTAS TO THE WORLD' appeared in the centre of the hoarding in large black letters. It took about three hours to put up. Their work done, the boys leapt into the truck and drove off.

The children—why just the children, even Subal—gazed at it, eyes struck with wonder. They had never, in all their lives, seen anything so beautiful. And it was theirs, their very own. The tiny, dilapidated house in which they had lived for as long as they could remember was transformed. It had been touched by a magic wand! Everyone on VIP Road stared at it.

More than the beauty of form and colour, Subal and his children were mesmerized by the dynamism of the picture. It seemed to them that the plane was actually flying, the boy and girl actually running. Slowly at first, then faster and faster. They could almost feel the wind, that was lifting the girl's skirts, on their limbs. The sun, which was turning the clouds into masses of spun silver, on their faces. As for the houses, who lived in houses like these? Had the skies parted somehow and shown them a glimpse of heaven?

Subal checked the iron poles to see if they were firm. Then he stroked the picture lovingly with a rough, work-worn hand. He let out a sigh of satisfaction. Thanks to the hoarding, the palm tree behind the house was hidden from view. Only its tip could be seen. But the vultures, damn them, were still there, huddled precariously on the highest frond. He thought of cutting down the tree, then changed his mind quickly. Deprived of their nesting place, they might come and perch on the poles, and that would be a disaster.

For the children, the day was one of great excitement. It was almost like Durga Puja. Kushi was so affected she kept stealing out of the house to gaze at the picture with wondering eyes. More than anything—the blue sky, the silver plane and the beautiful houses with their domes and towers—her eyes were drawn to the young couple who ran hand in hand. It wasn't as if she hadn't seen sahebs and mems before. Many drove down VIP Road on their way to the airport. But when was the last time her eyes beheld such beauty? The boy's shoulders were so broad, so manly. The girl's lips, it seemed to her, would start trickling sweet juice at any moment. They were like ripe fruit, full and red. And her legs! Smooth and plump with a colour like milk mixed with alta. As for her dress, who knew how much it cost? A hundred rupees at the very least! She gazed and gazed and her heart pounded with the strangest sensations. She longed to share her thoughts with someone. But who?

The only one in the family who knew a smattering of

English was Haran. It was to him that everyone turned for enlightenment. Haran read out the words painstakingly, letter by letter, explaining them as he went along. 'F-L-Y... fly,' he read. 'Fly means *maachhi*.'

'Maachhi!' the others exclaimed. 'You mean the insect?'

'Hoonh.'

'Nonsense. There isn't a single maachhi in the picture.'

Haran's face was solemn as he said ponderously, 'I'm only reading what's written. Is it my fault there's no maachhi in the picture?'

The youngest boy, Nobu, was a snide brat, far more knowing than his five years warranted. 'See! See!' He winked and giggled. 'The mem is showing her bums. They're so round and fair!'

For some reason this remark infuriated Kushi. She sprang forward and slapped her brother smartly on the cheek. He set up a wail and his mother came running to his rescue. 'How dare you raise your hand to the boy?' She dragged Kushi away by her hair. 'That too at dusk. Wait till I find a strip of bamboo to break on your back.'

Kushi had thought that the day was special, a day of rejoicing. She had hoped that her mother would cook rice for the evening meal but she did nothing of the sort. As soon as Subal left to celebrate with toddy and friends, Kushi's mother set her to knead a pat of dough. Kushi's heart sank. The children got two rutis each which only added fuel to the fire that raged, day and night, in her stomach. She felt hungry all the time. A handful of rice, just one handful, quenched it—at least for sometime.

Dusk crept slowly into the yard as Kushi sat on the dalaan kneading the dough. The air began to fill with sounds: the chirping of crickets, toads croaking in harsh voices. One of them sounded like a long wail. It is being gulped down by a snake, Kushi thought. The area was infested with snakes. They stayed hidden in their holes all summer and wriggled out as soon as the rains hit the earth. Kushi craned her neck but she couldn't see the hoarding. It had been swallowed up by the dark. From the top of the palm behind the house she heard the flapping of wings. The vultures were getting ready for the night.

Suddenly a whistle, like the shrill cry of a squirrel, came to Kushi's ears. She looked up sharply. 'Thak-ma!' she called out to her grandmother. 'I've kneaded the dough. Start rolling out the rutis. I'll be back in a few minutes.'

'Why?' her mother's voice came from the kitchen. Wary, suspicious. 'Where are you going?'

'I'll be back in a minute.'

'From where?' her mother snapped. 'Where do you need to go at this unearthly hour?'

But Kushi had also learned the art of snapping. 'Baba re baba!' She thrust her face through the kitchen door menacingly. 'Can't I even go to the shithole?'

Stealing out from the back, Kushi walked to VIP Road. Dodging the cars, she ran across it, climbed down the side of the canal, and waited by an ash-sheoda bush that grew next to the water. Within seconds a young man's powerful arms were around her waist. Pulling her deeper into the shadows, he thrust a greasy paper bag in her hands. 'Look,' he said, 'I've brought you some potato chops. I know you like them.' At home all Kushi got were beatings and abuse. And the food her mother gave her didn't fill even a corner of her stomach. Hunger pangs assaulted her day and night. There was only one person who cared for her and brought her good things to eat. His name was Tabu and he worked as a fitter in a cycle shop.

Kushi fell on the chops and devoured them in large, greedy bites. While she was thus occupied, Tabu slid his hands under her sari and started squeezing and pinching her soft breasts. 'Eyi! Eyi!' Kushi giggled and squirmed. 'You're tickling me. Hee hee hee!'

'Chup,' the young man whispered. 'People will hear you.'

'Don't touch me there. It makes me laugh.'

'Okay, I won't. But you must be quiet. Don't make a sound.'

Tabu's hands stole up her thighs. They lingered over her buttocks and then pushed her down gently. The two lay side by side on the grassy bank. Above them were the lights and sounds of VIP Road.

'You know something?' Kushi whispered. 'Some people have put up a picture outside our house.'

'What picture?'

'Haven't you seen it? Oh my goodness! It's so beautiful … so beautiful. You won't believe your eyes.'

'Where?' Tabu raised his head.

'You won't be able to see it in the dark. Come by tomorrow morning.'

Suddenly, the headlights of a passing car fell on the hoarding. The fluorescent colours sprang into life. Kushi sat up, startled. 'Did you see it?' She clutched the boy's shoulder. Her voice shook with excitement. 'Did you see it?' she asked again and again. 'Did you? Did you?'

'See what?' The boy looked this way and that, then put his hand over her mouth. 'Why don't you lower your voice? Who knows who is lurking in the bushes, waiting to pounce on us?'

'That … that…' Another car passed and again the picture came to life. She pointed a finger. 'Outside our house.'

'Oh, that!' Tabu lay down again. 'It's only an advertise.'

'What does that mean?'

Tabu didn't bother to enlighten her. 'Who hung it there?' he asked carelessly. 'It's quite pretty.'

'Isn't it? Did you see the boy and girl? Aren't they … aren't they beautiful?'

Car after car drove down the road, flashing their lights on the hoarding. And now Tabu's hands were groping her all over, his fingers touching the most secret spaces of her body. But she didn't stop him. Her face was aglow, her limbs quivered in delight. His mouth was crushing hers, his teeth cutting into her lips. She could taste blood. But all she said was, 'Why are they running, Tabu-da? Where are they going?'

'Mmn … mmn … mm.'

'Will they catch the plane, do you think? Do they live in one of those houses? What place is that?'

'London maybe … who knows?'

'Why did they hang the picture outside our house?'

'Why don't you keep your mouth shut? Someone will hear you. Mmn … mmn … I love you, my little pagli, my golden girl … I'll bring you some cutlets tomorrow.'

'Their faces are so beautiful. So very beautiful!'

Kushi craned her neck to look at the hoarding each time a car passed. And wave after wave of ecstasy, a sensation she had never known before, passed over her.

LONTTON SAHEB'S BUNGALOW

JERKED AWAKE IN the middle of a powerful snore, Hamilton saheb raised his shaggy white head. 'Ke da!' he croaked. 'Ke ohane?' The words 'Who is it! Who's there?' were spoken in the rustic dialect of Kumarkhali, the accent and intonation perfected from decades of living in rural Bengal.

No answer.

The veranda where he sat was long and wide, with a tiled roof and a lantern hanging from one of the beams. The flame had gone out from lack of oil or perhaps it hadn't been lit at all. Flowing beneath the bungalow, the Gorai was in spate, a stretch of dark water flecked with flickering lights. The lights came from the lamps on the fishermen's boats which still floated on its surface. On moonlit nights the river was transformed into a wrinkled sheet of silver.

Two lounging chairs, one of them with Hamilton saheb in it, stood side by side with a three-legged stool between them. The decanter of port that he had been drinking from all day was placed on the stool along with a glass and a jug of water. His hand groped about in the dark. The glass was empty and so was the decanter. As empty as air. Not even the dregs remained. Hamilton lost his temper. 'Ke da!' he roared. 'Why don't you answer me, you rogue?'

Still no response. It must be the wind, he thought.

When it blew hard, the wooden bungalow creaked and swayed like a ship. There was hardly any wind tonight yet there was that noise again, and then again. It was clear now that some living creature was lurking in the dark. Hamilton saheb picked up the gun that lay next to his chair and rose to his feet. The officials of the Company had threatened to oust him from the bungalow, so he had to be prepared all the time. Stumbling and tottering from drinking all day, he made his way to the door. 'Haala!' he cursed roundly. 'Son of a whore! Motherfucker! You've come to kill me, have you? Just you wait. One bullet and your wife will be widowed—'

Hamilton was so drunk he didn't stop to think that his killer could have shot him while he was asleep. Why would he hide and make indistinct noises?

Pushing the curtain aside, the first thing he saw was a pair of eyes glowing in the dark. They were too small and too close to the floor to belong to a large animal. Ah, it was a cat. As his eyes grew accustomed to the dark, he realized that it was holding a mouse between its teeth. The mouse was struggling to free itself and the cat was banging it on the floor. It saw the saheb but didn't run away in fright. It wasn't about to let go of its dinner.

Hamilton saheb hated cats. Creepy, cunning creatures. Besides, what right did they have to hunt mice in his bungalow? They were *his* mice, weren't they? He saw them scurrying about all day. Sometimes they slithered down the arms of his chair and scampered across his feet. He didn't mind in the least. But this devil of a tomcat came in and out of his bungalow as if it belonged to him. 'Haat! Shoo! Get lost!' He waved his gun at the glittering eyes but the stubborn creature refused to budge. Shooting a cat for trespassing would be rather excessive, he thought. But this whoreson was staring at him in defiance. He had to be taught a lesson. Raising his gun, he fired a shot out of the open window. The cat dropped the mouse and leapt out of the room, tail high in the air.

Hamilton grinned from ear to ear. He loved the sound of gunshots and made it a point to fire at least one each day whether he needed to or not. It was his way of exercising control over the people around him—servants, villagers. The only other gun in these parts belonged to the indigo planter, Mr Frazier.

Kasem, the orderly, heard the sound and bounded up the stairs. 'Who is it? What happened?' he cried out, bursting into the room. 'What is the matter, saheb? Whom did you shoot?' His eyes were round with anxiety.

'Come closer,' the saheb ordered.

The moment Kasem was within reach, Hamilton saheb gripped his ear and wrenched it hard. 'Haramzada! Sheikh-er po!' he snarled. 'You eat of my salt. Heaps and heaps of rice! But when it comes to work, you disappear. How dare that tomcat enter my house? Why didn't you drive it away?'

Kasem's face was contorted with pain but he burst out laughing. 'Ha ha! Let go of my ear, saheb. It hurts … The cat came in through the kitchen window. It's Phaitka's job to keep a lookout there…'

'Chup!' the saheb thundered. 'Phaitka's job is to cook, not to do chowkidari. That's your job, along with all the other work in the house. Why didn't you light the lantern? And who's going to fill the decanter? Haala! Whoreson!'

'There's a bottle in your room, saheb.'

'How dare you talk back! Want a thwacking kick on your behind? It's your duty to see that the decanter is full, morning, noon and night, not to tell me that bottles may be found in my room or in the shops.'

'Sorry, saheb. I'll—I'll fill it. Forgive me.'

Returning to his chair, Hamilton put down the gun and stared out at river and sky. Kasem brought the bottle, poured out a large peg and handed it to his master. 'Phaitka wanted to know,' he said easily, 'what you would like to eat tonight.'

'I'd like to eat your head!' Hamilton snapped but there was a twinkle in his eye. 'What can you give me?'

'Whatever you wish.'

'Whatever I wish! Can you give me Yorkshire pudding?'

Kasem shrugged and stuck out his lower lip. 'I've never heard of it but I'll tell Phaitka.'

'Phaitka!' The saheb let out a roar of laughter. 'You think he has even seen Yorkshire pud in his life? Is there milk in the house? Raisins? Tell Phaitka to make some payesh. It won't be Yorkshire pudding but who cares? I'll have Kumarkhali pudding. Ha ha ha!'

Sobering down, he crinkled his brow and continued, 'Hyaan re, Kasem, how's your youngest son? Has the fever gone?'

'No, saheb.'

'Does he feel cold? Is he shivering?'

'No, saheb, he's as hot as hot can be. To touch him is to scorch your hand.'

'Hmm, not good. Not good at all. Take him to the hospital in Jessore tomorrow. He needs a good doctor. Don't worry about the expense, I'll pay for everything.'

'You're very generous, saheb.'

'Would you like a sip from my glass, Kasem?' Hamilton's yellow teeth flashed in a malicious grin. 'Just to see what it tastes like?'

'Tobah, tobah!' Kasem touched his ears and bit his tongue. 'Liquor is haraam according to our faith. Even such a thought is sin.'

'What if I pour the stuff down your throat some day? Can you stop me?'

'I'll hold my breath. I'll die before I let a drop go down. Phaitka takes a swig from your bottle now and then. I've seen him ... the thief.'

'Chup!' Hamilton saheb thundered. 'Complaints, complaints, complaints! I'm sick of the two of you. Phaitka tells me you steal my sona-moog and send it home. What about that?'

'A lie, saheb!'Kasem jerked his head and hands agitatedly. 'A shameless lie! You eat no other lentils, only sona-moog. Don't I know that? If I did such a thing, wouldn't I go straight to hell? Phaitka is a liar and a selfish rascal. He keeps the fish head for himself every day. Not once has he shared it with me.'

'And what about you? Don't you stare at his wife with eyes as big as rosogollas?'

'Chhi chhi chhi!' Kasem shrieked in outrage. 'Is that what he says, the lying bastard? Lakshmi is like my daughter. She and my Fatima are the same age. I'll tear his tongue out of his throat.'

Hamilton roared with laughter and dismissed Kasem with a wave of his hand. Taking a leisurely sip, he smirked into his glass. He had deliberately employed a Hindu cook, Phatik Das, and a Muslim orderly, Kasem Sheikh. They bickered and quarrelled all day but he didn't mind. In fact, he enjoyed it. Sometimes he even added fuel to the fire. But he noticed one thing and it pleased him. For all their spats, they had something between them, a bond of empathy and co-dependence that rose to the surface whenever one of them was threatened.

Hamilton gulped down two stiff pegs in quick succession. Then, turning his head, he saw her. She was sitting in the other chair—a woman in a mulberry-pink gown and a white lace scarf pinned to her breast with a cameo brooch—his wife, Jenny. His dim, befuddled eyes gazed fondly at her. 'Darling,' he murmured, 'look at the sky. Clouds are gathering. Still one can see the moonlight flickering over the river. By the way, do you remember the three lemon trees you planted? They've started bearing fruit. I had the first one today.'

An hour later, Phatik came up the stairs to ask his master if he was ready for dinner. But Hamilton saheb was fast asleep, his head tucked into his neck. Phatik called out a couple of times but he knew his saheb would not wake up. He was far too drunk, dead to the world. And if, god forbid, he or Kasem tried to shake him awake, there would be hell to pay. He would mouth the most obscene curses and cuff and kick the offender with unimaginable violence. It was best to leave him alone. Phatik shrugged his shoulders and decided to go back to the kitchen. Before leaving, he picked up the half-empty glass and poured the remains down his throat.

The pargana or administrative division in which the village of Kumarkhali was located had once belonged to the East India Company. The Company was defunct now and the region, indeed the whole of British India, had come under the rule of Queen Victoria. Consequently, the Board of Directors in England was in the process of selling off its properties in the country to wealthy natives. It was far easier than collecting rents from individual tenants.

The pargana of Ibrahimpur had been bought by a Bengali zamindar residing in Kolkata. It was but natural that he would prefer a native manager to Mr Charles Hamilton, who had ruled the estate with an iron hand all these years. The zamindar had acquired the land but was up against a stupendous hurdle where the bungalow was concerned, for Hamilton refused to budge. The East India Company was in a quandary. The terms of the contract were crystal clear: the Company would transfer all its properties in Ibrahimpur, including the bungalow, in return for a sizeable sum of money. At first, Hamilton was asked to vacate with polite requests and gentle prodding. Notices and warnings followed. Finally, the Company had no option left but to dislodge him. The new zamindar had threatened to move the courts if full possession was not given within the stipulated time.

Hamilton's refusal to vacate was totally without rationale. If the Company no longer existed, how could it employ a manager? And if there was no manager, on what grounds was an Englishman occupying the manager's bungalow? But Hamilton wouldn't see reason. The Company offered him a house in Kolkata but he refused. And he wouldn't go back to England either.

Charles Hamilton, a native of Yorkshire, had come out to India at the age of seventeen as a clerk with the East India Company. After training in the Civil Services, he moved from district to district before settling down in the village of Kumarkhali in the Ibrahimpur pargana. He had lived here for the last thirty-five years, first as assistant manager and then as manager. His present residence, overlooking the river, had been built under his supervision and its furnishings and décor chosen by his wife. The surrounding greenery still bore a touch of her presence. Jenny had loved her garden and lavished all her care on it. She had roamed the villages of Ibrahimpur, collecting roots and cuttings of different trees and shrubs, and planted them here. And, in accordance with her dying wish, she lay buried in a corner of this very garden, under the gnarled star apple tree.

Hamilton had no desire to return to England. He didn't consider it his country any more. On the few occasions that he had visited his birthplace, he felt restless and unhappy and yearned for India. It was on his return from one of these trips that he met Jenny. It was a shipboard romance and they got married as soon as they landed. The lovely young girl with her passion for trees had never gone back to her native land. She had fallen in love with rural Bengal, embraced it and made it her own.

Hamilton had spent more than two-thirds of his life in India. England held no charm for him. Besides, all the old ties were gone. His parents had died and his relatives barely knew him. He had no friends either. A lot of Englishmen went back home with huge fortunes amassed from their years in India. They lived lavish lives, spending money like water. Yet they were looked at askance and accorded scant respect. Lord Clive had to commit suicide. Charles Hamilton would be a non-entity in his native land. Here he was somebody. He was *Lontton saheb*. The locals respected and feared him. But they also loved him because he knew their language and customs and involved himself intimately in their lives. Besides, his Jenny was here...

After Jenny's death, Hamilton's drinking had increased

steadily and now, with nothing else to do, he drank every day, deep into the night. He loved getting drunk, for it was only in a completely sodden state that he found himself reunited with Jenny. Sitting by her side and sharing his thoughts with her, he felt his loneliness receding...

Occasionally, very occasionally, Hamilton saheb became his old self. On those mornings, he woke up in a crisp, carefree mood and went for a walk through the village. Pulling on a pair of baggy trousers and a threadbare black coat over a striped shirt, he laced his long boots, slung his gun across one shoulder and set off, splashing through puddles and stumbling over potholes. He was a strange sight with his giant frame and shock of white hair atop a face as red as a rupi monkey's bottom. Calling out to everyone he met, he exchanged news and made enquiries. Had Haradhan replaced the thatch that was blown away in last week's storm? Any news of Motalef's daughter, the one who had disappeared while bathing in the river? Had she really been dragged away by a crocodile like everyone was saying? He remembered everything about everyone in Kumarkhali and involved himself actively in their lives, sometimes with curses and abuses, sometimes with words of comfort and promises of help.

The children of the village were scared of white folk as a rule and ran away whenever they saw any. But not one of them was afraid of Charles Hamilton. 'Lontton saheb! Lontton saheb!' they clamoured around him, tugging at his coat and eyeing his gun curiously. Hamilton stroked a girl's cheek, ruffled another's hair, even pinched a little boy's bottom quite hard. Then he searched his pockets for the bits of candy he always carried.

And it wasn't just the children. Adults too came running

when he approached and stood before him with folded hands. But if anyone attempted to touch his feet, he took three leaps backwards and cried out, 'Arre, na na! I'm a mlecchha, a non-Hindu. Do you want to lose your caste, you numbskulls?'

The villagers knew about the saheb's refusal to vacate the bungalow and were glad of it. But it worried them too. How long could one man, even if he had a gun, hold out against an army of lance- and stick-wielding paiks and lathyals? Hamilton's strength lay not in his weapon but in the love and dependence of the people of Ibrahimpur. They didn't want him to leave. The moment they saw a stranger in the village or any other suspicious activity, they ran to the bungalow to inform him. Unable to pronounce his name correctly, the villagers called him 'Lontton saheb'. Some even referred to him as 'Pagla saheb'. Hamilton was aware of this, but instead of annoying him, it made him laugh. He hadn't the slightest objection to being called 'the crazy Englishman'.

When Hamilton first came to Kumarkhali it was an obscure hamlet with no amenities whatsoever. People had to walk to the weekly haat in Mansabganj, several miles away, to buy even their basic provisions. It was worse during the rainy season when the roads were flooded. There was no option then but to go by boat. Moved by the plight of the villagers, Hamilton set up two shops on the river front from where they could obtain their daily requirements at reasonable prices. That was seventeen years ago. Now there was a regular bazaar here, with thirteen or fourteen shops. And this was entirely owing to his efforts. The Company had nothing to do with it. As a result, the villagers named it Charles' Bazaar which, with constant repetition, got corrupted and became Chalia Bazaar. Chalia Bazaar was now a landmark on the map of Ibrahimpur and its importance had increased substantially with the entry of steam ships up the Ganga.

Hamilton saheb's income came from the rents of this bazaar, which the shopkeepers gave him voluntarily. He didn't require much money and rarely bothered to collect his dues. In fact, much of what he received he gave away to the poor. He was a whimsical character, unlike other white folk, and highly approachable. But if a man came to him for help with a daughter's dowry or a mother's funeral rites, he was sent packing with a flea in his ear. On the other hand, if he heard of someone's illness or a father's inability to educate his son due to lack of funds, he would empty his pockets to the last paisa.

Hamilton walked to the new sweet shop that had been set up a few months ago and sat on the bamboo bench outside. 'Koi re!' he called in a booming voice. 'Bring me what you have. Jilipi! Halwa!' A middle-aged man with a sacred thread across his chest came out of the shop and stood before him with folded hands. He knew the saheb had a sweet tooth and didn't care for savouries like kochuri and nimki.

'Pronam, saheb,' he said humbly. 'There's no halwa left. Only jilipi.'

'So be it,' Hamilton endorsed heartily. 'Bring jilipi.'

The man went inside and returned with four jilipis on a piece of banana leaf.

'Only four!' the saheb glared at him. 'This is just a pinch of snuff for a corner of my nostril. My stomach is an empty cave. How many do you have in your basket? Bring them all, bring them all.' The shopkeeper rushed inside and came back with a huge basket brimming over with crisp, curled golden rings shining with oil and syrup.

Hamilton saheb cackled in delight and crammed a whole jilipi into his mouth. Then, noticing a couple of half-naked infants staring at him with round eyes and thumbs thrust deep into their mouths, he cried out, 'Why do you suck your thumbs like ninnies? Do they have honey on them? Aaye, aaye! Eat jilipi. See how sweet they are. Eat as many as you want.'

The children ran to him with shouts of glee. Almost on cue, a host of others came running from different directions and fell on the basket till it was buzzing like a hive of honey bees. 'Eat!' Hamilton saheb shouted in encouragement. 'Eat all you want but no pushing or shoving!'

Sitting back, he watched the jilipi festival, his face crinkled in mirth. Suddenly his eyes fell on a little girl. There were tears streaming down her cheek but they didn't look like tears of joy. Besides, they only fell from one eye. 'Eyi, chheri!' He fondled the girl's chin. 'Why are you crying?'

The girl looked up in surprise. 'I'm not crying,' she said and licked up the syrup running down her hand.

Hamilton saheb realized she was suffering from an eye ailment. He had seen it in several other children in the village. He made a mental note to send for a doctor from the city to test the eyes of all the children. Left untreated, a disease like this could lead to blindness...

There were evenings when Hamilton saheb's inebriation failed to take full possession of him and he couldn't find Jenny.

Restless and unhappy, he murmured her name over and over again. 'Come, Jenny,' he whispered. 'Please come. Where are you, my darling?' He waited for a response but all he could hear was the soughing of the wind in the trees. Rising, he leaned over the rails and, fixing his eyes on Jenny's grave, called out to her at the top of his voice, 'Jenny! Jenny! Why don't you come to me?' The agonized cry floated on the breeze like a weary night bird's call, its echoes dying in the waters of the river. Above, a velvet sky glimmered with stars and snatches of song wafted up from the fishermen's boats. The saheb shrieked until his voice cracked but Jenny did not come.

On such nights, Hamilton fell asleep with the dawn and didn't rise till noon. The servants didn't disturb him. But one day they were forced to do so.

A stranger, obviously a man of some distinction, stood at the front door, demanding to see Mr Charles Hamilton. With him were three guards holding spears in their hands. A terrified Kasem informed him with folded hands that the saheb was asleep and could not be disturbed but the gentleman refused to believe him. It was early afternoon. How could anyone be asleep at this hour?

Unable to convince him, Kasem went up to his master's bedroom and called out his name.

Hamilton sat up with a howl of protest. 'How dare you wake me up, you son of a pig?' he roared.

Kasem stood trembling at the foot of his bed and, in a shaking voice, told him why. Hamilton rose instantly and pulled on a shirt. Picking up his gun, he marched down the stairs, the boards creaking under his heavy tread. His face was unwashed, his eyes bloodshot.

As he reached the front door, he saw his guest standing

outside. He was an imposing personage in a gold-embroidered tunic and a round turban. The arrogance and self-esteem that proceeded from generations of wealth and exalted lineage were etched on his face. But Hamilton saheb wasn't impressed.

'Who are you?' he asked gruffly in Bengali. 'What do you want?'

The stranger didn't answer the question. 'May I speak with you for a while?' he asked instead in flawless English.

'Who sent you? I don't need to talk to anyone.'

'I will take only a few minutes of your time.'

'You're Bengali,' the Englishman barked at his guest, 'why don't you speak in Bangla? Who are you? Have you been sent by the zamindar's nayeb?'

A smile flickered across the stranger's lips. 'Na, Hamilton saheb,' he answered in the tone and diction of a Kolkata aristocrat. 'The zamindar's nayeb didn't send me. I have come on my own. My name is Srijukta Dwarkanath Thakur.'

'He's the zamindar,' one of the guards said.

Saheb frowned. 'Thakur! So you're the new zamindar! Why are you here? Have you come to evict me from your property? Let me tell you straightaway that I shan't vacate this kuthi. You'll get it only over my dead body.'

'No.' Dwarkanath smiled. 'I haven't come to evict you. If that was my intention I wouldn't have come in person.'

'Why? What ... then?' Hamilton stammered and looked blank.

'You are my guest,' Dwarkanath answered. 'Protecting you and your interest is my duty. I have come to know that your late wife lies buried here. The bungalow is replete with her memories. I have no wish to disturb them. Mr Hamilton, please feel free to stay on. For the rest of your life, if you so wish. It will be my honour and privilege. The estate will bear the cost of all repairs and renovations as and when you think they are due.'

Hamilton stared at him. He had heard that the new breed of native zamindars was exceedingly greedy and grasping. They extorted heavy rents and spent the money in lives of luxury in Kolkata. They hardly ever visited their estates or took an interest in the welfare of their tenants. But what he was hearing now was the opposite.

'I'm very sorry to have kept you standing outside, Thakur babu,' he muttered in a shamed voice. 'You are my zamindar and I your subject. I should have shown you more respect. Please come in and sit down.'

Dwarkanath bent down to slip off his nagras.

'E ki!' Hamilton exclaimed. 'Why do you take off your shoes?'

'This bungalow is a temple to your wife's memory. In our culture we are taught to enter such places barefoot.'

'Arre, na na. We Europeans don't believe in all that.' Pointing to a corner of the garden, Hamilton said, 'Do you see that star apple tree? My wife's grave lies beneath it. Bury me beside her when I die. Do that for me and it will be enough.' He looked around the dusty, uncared-for room in which they now stood and continued, 'Please sit. I'm afraid I don't have a chair worthy of a guest of your stature. Things have deteriorated since my wife...'

'Do not agitate yourself. This house is yours and I shall leave shortly. I just want to say that you needn't lug that gun around any more. My lathyals will protect the village from now on, and you too.'

'Now I would like to say something,' Hamilton replied. 'I'm British. We take what is not ours with the power of arms. We are not used to accepting gifts. You have very generously given me leave to occupy your house until my death. Now you must allow me to give you something in return.'

'Forgive me.' Dwarkanath folded his hands. 'I didn't come here in the hope of any return.'

'Thakur babu,' Hamilton went on as though he hadn't heard what his guest had said, 'there is a bazaar by the river which belongs to me—not to the Company. It is small but the location is strategic. As more and more steam ships come up the river it will boom with business and rents will go up. I wish to make it over to you.' Dwarkanath tried to say something but Hamilton stopped him with a raised hand. 'Don't look upon it as a gift. It is a grave responsibility that I am thrusting on you. A lot of work needs to be done. Roads must be laid and sanitation taken care of. I am too old and tired to undertake all that. You are young and dynamic. Please take charge. Another thing, the villagers are poor and deprived. Their children suffer from malnutrition and various diseases. There is an eye ailment common in these parts that strikes many blind before they attain puberty. If you could do something for them...'

'Your word is my command,' Dwarkanath said, his voice quivering with reverence and wonder. 'I shall do all I can.' He rose to his feet. The two shook hands.

Dwarkanath's generosity to the eccentric Englishman pleased the villagers of Kumarkhali and made him the most popular zamindar in the district. The members of the ruling class too were struck by his magnanimity. Not only were they relieved at the solution to their problem, they were beholden to him for his kindness to one of their own. His fame as an able yet compassionate administrator spread throughout Bengal.

And Charles Hamilton was free of tension and anxiety. He no longer required his gun. It stood against a wall in his bedroom, gathering dust. But the peace and tranquillity that followed weren't exactly palatable. He liked challenges, he liked to confront his fears. They kept him vibrant and angrily alive. But now there was no challenge and nothing to fear. Something went out of him slowly but surely. His life force began to ebb and he became drowsy and dull. He rarely found Jenny in the armchair beside him these days. He increased his drinking but still she eluded him.

One night, just as the moon was rising slowly over the river, Phatik and Kasem heard their master shouting at the top of his voice: 'Jenny! Jenny!' It didn't worry them at first; of late, he had often been seen leaning over the railing, calling out to his dead wife. But tonight his cries were louder and more hysterical. They tore through the sleeping village like the howls of a soul in hell. The two looked at one another with round eyes but dared not go to their master. They could not go to sleep either.

Once he entered his bedroom, Hamilton did not leave it before daylight. But that night he came lumbering down the dark stairs and ran across the garden to Jenny's grave. 'Jenny! Jenny!' he burst into loud jerking sobs. 'Don't leave me behind, my darling. Take me with you.' Phatik and Kasem heard him and froze. This time there was no question of ignoring what was happening. Rushing out of the house, they came and stood by their master. Hamilton lay sprawled, face downward, on his wife's grave. They turned him over and found no sign of life.

Hamilton was buried, as he had wished, under the star apple tree. A few days later the Nayeb of Khurshiadpur took possession of the bungalow. Dwarkanath was in

England at the time. The sahebs and memsahebs looked with stars in their eyes at his fabulous wealth, munificence and exceedingly lavish lifestyle. Aristocrats fawned on him and even the queen gave him a private audience.

Dwarkanath had left his country for good soon after his meeting with Charles Hamilton, so there wasn't much he could do for the blind children of Kumarkhali. Besides, even if he had, how many people would have come to know? The wealthy philanthropist redeemed his promise in another way. He sent the staggering sum of ten thousand pounds to a charitable organization raising funds for the blind. The nobility of his gesture was talked about through the length and breadth of England and earned the native zamindar the title of 'prince'. Henceforth, he was known as Prince Dwarkanath Tagore.

A Piece of History

IF YOU TURN the pages of a Kolkata street guide, your eyes will fall on a name: Duel Avenue. The place seems to exist only on paper. What do we envisage when we hear the word 'avenue'? Doesn't the image of a wide street shaded by trees on either side float before our eyes? But there is no such place in the area demarcated. There is Belvedere at one end, then the zoo, and at the other, on the road to Diamond Harbour, is a vast square. The meteorological office is located here alongside blocks of government flats. And somewhere in between is a thin strip of lane named 'Duel Avenue'. The trees have long disappeared. Even of the giant banyan, once known as 'Horror Oak', there is no trace. No one can show you the way barring the peon at the post office, who delivers letters addressed to 'The Regional Meteorological Office, 4 Duel Avenue'. 'That's Duel Avenue,' he will tell you, pointing with his forefinger. But once you reach the place, a thrill of excitement will pass over you, more so if you know the history of the period.

17 August 1780. 5.30 a.m. Sir Phillip Francis was pacing up and down agitatedly, glancing at his watch every two minutes. His limbs were trembling with fury. Why was

Hastings taking so long? Was he shying away from his appointment? Was he afraid of keeping it?

His worries were unfounded. He had no notion of the kind of man he was dealing with. There were many sides to Warren Hastings and they were often seen as conflicting. He was a chauvinistic Englishman but he believed in good governance for the colonies. An idealist at one level, he was an astute politician at another. And if there was one thing he wasn't, it was a coward.

Several scandals had sullied his fair name—Nandakumar's hanging, the swindling of the Begums of Oudh. But he was a strong supporter of the indigenous language Sanskrit, and facilitated its promotion. He admired the arts of India. A good writer, he wrote letters to his wife in a beautiful, flowing hand. But above all these qualities was his admirable strength of mind. He fought his opponents single-handedly in the battle to protect his reputation.

The directors of the East India Company had set up a council of four members and sent them out to India. Their job was to oversee the actions of the governor general and act as regulators. Warren Hastings understood, quite clearly, that this had been done with a view to curtail his powers. He found himself having to bow down to the pressures of the council time and again, and felt outraged and humiliated. One of the members was Sir Phillip Francis, an arrogant egotist who thought everyone beneath him, even the governor general, and was contemptuous of his position. A notorious gambler and womanizer, his affair with Madame Grande was the talk of the upper echelons of Kolkata society. Everyone knew how, after being caught red-handed, he had to pay the irate husband a sum of forty thousand rupees. There were many who believed that the duel between Francis and Hastings was over a woman. But in this they were wrong. Theirs was a clash of two strong personalities, a battle of powerful wills.

It all started in 1774 when Sir Phillip Francis stepped off the boat that had brought him from England and first set foot in the city of Kolkata. The cannon boomed seventeen times to announce his arrival. Sir Phillip frowned in annoyance. He was an English aristocrat of the first rung, a scion from one of the finest families of the land. He should have been welcomed with twenty-one rounds of gunfire— why were there only seventeen? Thus began his lifelong animosity with Warren Hastings. A series of minor clashes followed. Fortunately for him, he enjoyed a position of power. He could confront the governor general, needle him, create hurdles for him in whatever he wished to do. And Hastings had no means of hitting back.

Matters came to a head just before a meeting of the council. Francis was unwell at the time, and Hastings and his wife were enjoying a cruise along the Ganga, on their way to Chinsura for a short holiday. The latest dispatch from London was expected any day now. A dispatch that would in all probability strip Hastings of his position and recall him to England.

On 15 August, Warren Hastings read his historic 'Note', a long impassioned speech in which he vilified Sir Phillip Francis in the words: 'I judge of his public conduct by my experience of his private which I have found to be void of truth and honour.' He claimed that he had substantial evidence in his possession and regretted the fact that he had to submit to the counsel of one such as he.

Sir Phillip looked furious but he didn't say a word.

When the meeting was over, he summoned Warren Hastings to his private chamber and said without preamble, 'I wish to make a befitting reply to your speech. But words will not suffice, a physical blow is necessary.' In those days the English valued reticence and civility above all other qualities. No voices were raised, no harsh words exchanged. Hastings accepted the challenge calmly. The date, place and time of the duel were set. 17 August, 5.30 a.m., in the open ground next to Alipore Bridge. Pistols would be used instead of swords.

'It's six o'clock,' Sir Phillip Francis said coldly the moment Hastings arrived. His second, Colonel Waters, then chief engineer of Bengal, nodded. Hastings glanced at his own second, who drew out his watch. 'No,' the latter said gravely. 'It is five-thirty. Their watch is fast.'

They took some time to decide on the exact location. Sir Phillip was finicky and objected to several suggestions. Hastings, on the other hand, calmly declared that that he wouldn't mind even if the combat took place in the open street. The party moved slowly towards Sir Elijah Impey's mansion. And on the way, they found the perfect spot: a stretch of level ground under a giant banyan tree that found favour from all. Duels had to have witnesses and there were several on both sides.

A famous duel had been fought between Fox and Adams in England several years ago, a historic one that had set the rules for all duels that followed. Francis and Hastings agreed to abide by these. A line was drawn in the centre, from which each combatant had to take fourteen steps backward. Hastings demurred a little over the distance. He feared that the bullet might fail to reach its mark. But Francis was ready. He checked his pistol and changed it.

Then, both fired. Hastings's bullet lodged itself in Sir Phillip's leg and the latter sank to his knees.

'I'm a dead man,' he declared.

'Good,' Hastings answered gravely and then added with a smile, 'I hope not.'

Everyone ran to the wounded man.

Warren Hastings walked over slowly. 'I didn't expect this, sir.' He shook his head regretfully. 'I hope your injury is a minor one. If it isn't, and you die from the wound, I shall surrender to the chief sheriff.'

Then Sir Phillip made a confession that left everyone gaping. He said he had never fired a pistol in his life. This was his first time. Hastings furrowed his brow in astonishment. Using pistols had been his opponent's suggestion. What sort of man was he?

Though Sir Phillip Francis recovered from the wound, his ego had taken a tremendous knock. He went back to England but his hostility remained. After Hastings was recalled, some members of the Company proposed that he be given an earldom. Francis stood firmly against it. He even lobbied with brilliant orators like Burke and Sheridan and brought them over to his side. Then came the famous case of the *Impeachment of Warren Hastings*. Everyone has read about it in history books. But a tiny lane in Kolkata, buried in oblivion, still stands, a mute witness to the events that led to it...

Towards the end of the sixties I found myself in the grip of a powerful infatuation. No, not for a woman. For the history of Kolkata. The idea of writing a novel set in colonial Bengal was forming slowly in my mind. I had the seed but I needed to find a fit soil to plant it in where it could take root and grow into a vast tree with spreading branches. Though I meant to set *Sei Samai* (*Those Days*) between 1840 and 1870, well after the period in which the historic duel took place, it was important for me to get a complete picture of British rule in India. I started researching the entire period—from the advent of the East India Company. The dry facts, culled from old, yellowing pages at the Archives weren't enough for me so I took to walking about the streets trying to pick up bits of living history. And every time I found something I felt a ripple of excitement run through my spine. It was on one such afternoon that I stumbled upon Duel Avenue. Many scholars and historians know about the duel that was fought between Francis and Hastings but I doubt that any of them has seen the location. 'Is there really such a place?' Binoy Ghosh asked me once and was surprised when I told him I had actually stood there.

Sir Francis had been a colourful personality, a fascinating character. Immensely wealthy and fired with the pride of lineage, he believed in unlimited opulence and magnificence in his style of living. The splendid mansion in which he lived alone was run by a staff of one-hundred-and-seventeen servants. And he was unashamedly wedded to the pleasures of the flesh. His affair with the notorious Madame Grande resulted in a scandal the proportions of which were unheard of in the elitist circles of Kolkata. But he treated it as a feather in his cap. Aristocrats, he believed, were meant to have liaisons with beautiful women. Not one—many. Only men with petty middle-class mentalities were satisfied with one woman. Warren Hastings had tried to prick a hole in this armour of arrogance and pomposity. And he paid dearly for it.

It took me a long time and a great deal of walking about in the hot sun to find the place. Finally a postman directed me. There was nothing to see there, yet a tremor of excitement passed over my sweating, fatigued body. The very fact that I had found the spot was enough for me.

I stood there for a moment, eyes closed, trying to evoke the ambience of a faraway time. Then, sighing, I turned to leave. And that was when I saw them, a white couple in their early thirties, their backs bent under heavy rucksacks. Their clothes were threadbare and filthy, their hair unkempt. At the time I speak of, a lot of young white men and women were coming to Kolkata from America. Popularly known as hippies, they were draft dodgers who had left their shores to escape being sent to Vietnam. I thought the couple belonged to that category. The young man had a week-old stubble on his chin and a map in his hand. The girl was so scantily clad I felt embarrassed to look at her. I watched them for a while. They were enquiring something from passers-by but were obviously not getting any answers. Perhaps their accent was the problem. Presently they came up to me and said, 'Could you help us find a place? We're looking for Duel Avenue.'

I was startled. Why were they looking for Duel Avenue? I showed them the spot. The man took out his camera and clicked several times.

As we were walking back, we got talking. The young man was British, not American, and his companion was French. He was a freelance journalist who picked up a little money from time to time by writing articles in newspapers. They had spent the last two years hitchhiking all over the world and were now in India. But why were they looking for Duel Avenue? When I asked him this, the young man said he wanted to write a piece on the duel that took place in 1780 between Warren Hastings and Phillip Francis. This made me curious.

'There are far more interesting stories scattered about in the streets of Kolkata,' I told him. 'What made you choose this one?'

He smiled. 'It is easier for me to write this story,' he said. 'I have the background material. My name is Chris Francis.'

'Does that mean … you are … are you…' I stammered, 'related to…'

'Sir Phillip Francis was my great, great, great, great, great-grandfather.'

I stared at the young man, at his filthy shorts and grimy t-shirt, the blond stubble on his long, white chin. Sir Phillip Francis lived in a mansion and was waited upon by one-hundred-and-seventeen servants. And this boy, bearing his name and blood, was walking all over the world in tattered clothes and frayed shoes. The thought staggered me.

HOT RICE—OR JUST A GHOST STORY?

THEY COME EVERY night of the new moon. At an hour when the darkness of the sky is impenetrable. When there is no sign of life anywhere and the world seems dead and faded. All you hear are sounds. A grating noise—k-r-r-r ... k-r-r-r—from the tips of the bamboo fronds as they rub against each other. Bats swoop down to the branches of the lychee tree with a rustle of papery wings and a pair of owls screech in pained voices. A takshak glides slowly up the trunk of the ancient peepul that stands at the crossing called Panchlar Modh. *Takshak!* It hisses seven times. Exactly seven. *Takshak! Takshak! Takshak!* The snake is said to be three-hundred-and-fifty years old.

They come at that hour. The flames of their lanterns quiver with their quivering shadows and the anklets on their feet ring *jhum jhum jhum.*

Khokh khokh khokh! A man coughs. An old man for whom his cough has been a companion for a lifetime. A couple of children cry out shrilly in their sleep. It is evident that life flows like an undercurrent beneath the dark, silent vault of the moonless sky.

Now some windows open and shadowy figures cluster in the verandas. Flickering lights and tinkling sounds approach, and stop under the peepul of Panchlar Modh.

There are eleven young men with two lanterns between them. Four of them have anklets on their feet and two carry spears in their hands. The night is cold. Putting down their spears and lanterns, they rub their hands vigorously and slap their thighs, shoulders, even their cheeks, to ward off the mosquitoes that have descended upon them in droves. Raising their voices, they shout: *Re re re re re re re/ Wake up, oh, villagers awake!* The summons is repeated, four times from four directions: east, west, north and south. Then they stand in a ring. The dancers take their positions in the centre and begin stamping their feet. Their anklets jingle and jangle. The others clap to the rhythm and sing in horribly tuneless voices.

> We've come to buy a ghost, o go!
> We need to buy a ghost.
> Someone told us in a dream—
> ghost bones and fat when ground and melted
> in Bipin Khuro's new contraption...
> with gangajal and tulsi leaves
> make a syrup sweet and luscious.
> We drank that great concoction
> and now we want some more.
> We've come to buy a ghost, o go!
> We need to buy a ghost.

A bunch of crows nesting peacefully in the branches of the peepul tree are rudely awakened by the song and fly off, squawking in fright. A couple of jackals slink away. From the courtyard of a nearby house, the pop and crackle of a flaring hookah comes floating in the wind. The men resume their singing:

A ghost, a ghost … any one will do.
Sons or daughters, distant kin,
young or old, white, black or brown.
Be it Brahmin or Musalman,
the price placed on the spirit's head…
Not one, not two, but takas ten.
Buy sweets and savouries, bags of rice.
Just show us one and claim your ten.
Ghost fat and bones when mixed and melted
make a nectar fit for kings.
Give us one and take your ten
still fresh and warm from the mint.

The dancers continue stamping their feet and clanking their anklets long after the song has ended. Nitai, the midget, is the most energetic of them. He loves dancing and can never get enough of it. It is only when Surendra holds out a bidi that he stops.

Surendra's chest is like an iron door and his head like a bush of black flames. He holds a great spear in one hand. He has composed the song himself and is pleased with the way it has turned out. His face wears the contentment of an artist satisfied with his creation.

The second spear is carried by Binod. He holds it high above his head and waves it about like a flag. Stuck to the blade is a small creature that wriggles and whines. It is a hedgehog.

'Shaala!' Binod curses under his breath. 'Still alive and kicking!' He thrashes the spear on the ground and the hedgehog lets out a pitiful squeak.

The eleven drop down on their haunches and light bidis. They will rest here awhile and then go to Malo Para and resume their singing.

'O, Paban thakurda!' Surendra hollers in the direction of the crackling hookah. 'Are you awake?'

'Hyaan re,' an ancient voice quakes and quavers. 'I'm wide awake.'

No one knows Paban's age, not even he himself. It could be eighty, it could be a hundred. His back is bent in a neat bow and the bones sticking out from the skin on his chest can be counted even in the dark. He has fathered five sons, two of whom are dead. Two of his grandsons have passed on too but Paban refuses to die. He remains doggedly, stubbornly, determinedly alive.

The group gathers in the tiny yard adjoining Paban's shack and, putting down their lanterns, enquire casually, 'Where's the water pot, Paban thakurda?' Their throats are parched and their bodies gleam with sweat in the cold, misty night.

Paban's son, Nibaran, enters the yard, rubbing the sleep out of his eyes. He is carrying an earthen pot of water. Tilting it above his mouth, he pours the water in a steady stream between his tongue and palate. The pot is half empty when he puts it down. Nibaran's children cower at the door, their eyes curious.

As soon as Paban puts down his hookah, Nitai grabs it and takes a deep pull. 'Thoo! Thoo!' He spits forcefully on the ground, his face twisted with disgust. 'Ram, Ram! What have you put in the chillum, thakurda? This isn't tobacco.'

'Hee hee hee!' the old man cackles, baring his toothless gums. His eyes crinkle in mirth.

'Give it to me!' Ghanai snatches the hookah from Nitai's hand and takes a pull. His insides somersault in shock and he retches.

'Not for you! Not for you!' Paban wags his white head. 'You youngsters don't have stomachs like us older folk.'

'But what is it? It's not tobacco.'

'Do I have the money to buy tobacco? Does this worthless son of mine give me a paisa?'

'Then what have you put in the chillum?'

'Dried mango leaves and cow dung crushed and mixed together. I've been smoking all my life. Can I give up now because there's no tobacco? I thought about it for a long time before I came up with this idea.'

'Thoo thoo thoo!' A shower of spittle falls on the yard and lies there like stars. Paban grins from ear to ear. The thought that he has fed cow dung to two young braggarts tickles him.

'Death lurks at his door,' Nibaran grinds his teeth at his father and announces to the world at large, 'but his greed grows by the hour. He has taken leave of his senses.'

Ghanai and Nitai let loose a stream of abuses and the children giggle from behind the door. But Paban remains unfazed.

'Eyi, chhonra!' he snaps at his son. 'Why do you talk of death? Is it in my hands? I'll die when my time comes, not a minute sooner or later.'

'If I ever catch you messing with cow dung again, I'll—I'll—'

Surendra puts an end to the battle by holding out a bidi. 'Here, thakurda, have a real smoke.'

Paban's face glows in delight. He takes the bidi in his shaking hand and cries, 'May you live a long life, son. May Ma Lakshmi shower her blessings on you. May all the wealth of the world fall to your lot. And all the sons too...' He lowers his voice, his eyes grow crafty. 'Can I have another one? For tomorrow morning?'

Surendra gives him another bidi which Paban promptly sticks behind his ear.

'Thakurda,' Surendra says casually, 'have you come across a ghost lately? You've seen many—I've heard you talk about them!'

'Of course I've seen many. I've seen them with my own eyes. A petni used to stand under that peepul tree every evening and make eyes at me. Once, she followed me all the way from Hijalmari Lake. I had caught a big catfish and the greedy slut caught a whiff of it, god knows how. "P - a - n - b - a - n!" she kept calling out to me in a nasal voice. "G - i - n - v - e m - n - e t - h - n - e f - i - n - s - h." When I turned around I saw not one but three of them. I dropped the fish and ran for my life.'

'You keep telling me these stories but you haven't caught one for me.'

'The trouble is, I don't see very well these days. My eyes aren't what they used to be. Still, once in a while … Why, only the other day I was sitting here and smoking. It was dusk and the light was failing. Suddenly I saw a woman coming from a corner of the cowshed. She was wearing a red Benarasi sari and held a lamp in her hands. She walked right past me and went towards the pond. I saw her clearly. I even spoke to her. "Ma go!" I called out. "Who are you? Where are you going?" But she neither looked back nor answered.'

'It must have been Nibaran kaka's wife.'

'Aa molo ja!' Paban flares up. 'Don't I know my own daughter-in-law? Besides, where would she get a Benarasi sari, she who doesn't have a rag to cover herself? This woman was beautiful and loaded with jewels. Nibaran kaka's wife, hmph!'

'Why didn't you run after her and catch her?'

'Do I have the strength to run? My legs start tottering and trembling the moment I stand up. But I did call out to her. I called again and again. She didn't look back. After a few seconds she vanished. Hyaan re, Suren, are you really offering ten rupees for a ghost?'

'Yes, Paban thakurda. I'm carrying the money with me.' Suren puts his hand inside his pocket and it makes a jingling sound. 'I'll give it to you the moment ... You needn't even catch the ghost. Just show it to me from afar and you'll get your money.'

Paban fixes his rheumy gaze on his son. 'Why don't you catch one, you useless fellow? The jungles are chock-full of them, but will you move your lazy bum and go looking? Ten rupees for a ghost. Where will you get a better deal? Ten king-sized yams sell for less than ten rupees.'

'Shut your yapping mouth,' Nibaran snarls at his father. 'Can anyone catch a ghost? Of all the nonsense ... I have never even seen one, let alone...'

'If you have eyes to see, you can see,' Paban says. His voice suddenly sounds chastened and subdued. 'There are seventeen different kinds in seventeen different colours in this very village. And is ten rupees an amount to scoff at?'

The hedgehog creates a diversion now. It lets out a desperate squawk and flings off all its quills.

'What's that!' Nibaran exclaims, startled.

'That's a porc,' Binod tells him. 'I saw it scurrying across the path that leads to Olai Chandi's shrine and caught it with the end of my spear. But the bugger has the span of nine cats. It's still alive.'

The children run forward to get a closer view of the hedgehog. The boy is stark naked and the girl is only wearing a pair of torn drawers. She is thirteen and conscious of her budding breasts. She keeps her arms crossed over her chest. 'Jah! Jah!' Nibaran hollers at the children. 'Get back in the house.' The girl obeys and walks away slowly, her eyes darting back to the hedgehog. The boy refuses to budge.

'What will you do with it?' Nibaran's eyes are gleaming greedily.

'Cook it into a curry and eat it.'

'You'll get good money if you sell it. People buy porcupines to keep in zoos.'

'Only if they are alive. And catching a live porc is easier said than done. With a length of banana husk maybe. But how would I get hold of one at a moment's notice? I saw the creature crawl past and flung down my spear. It went right through its belly. The son of a bitch is still squawking and squirming but it won't last much longer.'

'Porcs are thieving rascals. They creep into my yard at night and nibble at my yams.' Nibaran lets loose a stream of expletives. 'I hear the noise—*jhum jhum jhum*—and come out as quietly as I can but they are too clever for me. I never see them.'

'It's easier to catch a porc than a ghost,' Paban grumbles, 'but my worthless son can't even do that.' He sighs in self-pity. Hedgehog meat is delicious ... soft and red and layered with fat. Saliva trickles into his mouth from under his tongue. He sucks in his cheeks and swallows. A-ha-ha, it's been a long time since he's eaten it. Binod's house is only two miles away. If only he could walk that far, he would go there tomorrow afternoon and say, 'I've come for a taste of porc.' Surely Binod wouldn't grudge him a small piece and a ladle of broth.

A lot of time has passed. 'Let's go.' Surendra gets up. 'Tell your neighbours about my offer, thakurda, and keep your eyes peeled. Ten rupees per ghost. You don't even have to catch it. Just show it to me from afar and you'll get your money. But it has to be a genuine piece. No tricks! Remember that.'

'Why do you want to buy ghosts, Suren?' Paban asks, puzzled. 'Is there really such a thing as ghost fat?'

'Wait and watch. Wait and watch.' Surendra smirks. 'I'll turn doctor and cure many maladies. But first I must catch a ghost.'

'What if the ghost catches you instead and snaps your head off? Ghosts have a lot of anger pent up in them, a lifetime of hate and anger. One never knows what they will do.'

Surendra roars with laughter. A few days ago he would have slapped his broad chest and declared that he feared nothing in the world, neither a ghost nor its ancestors. They wouldn't dare come near him, let alone harm him. But Father Pereira has told him to keep a leash on his tongue so he doesn't indulge in loose talk any more.

'Don't laugh, Suren.' Paban's voice is stern. 'Your father was attacked by a ghost. I saw him with my own eyes, lying by the canal, his neck twisted like a chicken's, the whites of his eyes showing. His face had turned blue with fright.'

'That was years ago,' Suren answers with a toss of his shaggy head. 'In fact, that's one of the reasons why I want to start this business. I'd like to catch every bastard of a ghost that harms us mortals and make medicine out of them. Binod's mother saw a petni and was so frightened she fell into the river and died. Nitai's father was chased by a will-o-the-wisp across Hijalmari Lake. Ghanai's father has been possessed thrice and he nearly died of convulsions the last time. How can I ignore these things? Anyway, remember what I said.' Turning to his companions, he urges them to make haste and move towards Malo Para. Enough time has been wasted already.

But just as the party is about to leave they realize one of the lanterns is missing.

'Arre!' Nitai exclaims in surprise. 'They were both here a moment ago. I placed them on the ground myself.'

'You brought one lantern, not two,' Paban says in a solemn voice.

'Eyi!' Binod moves towards him aggressively. 'Don't lie, Paban thakurda. You know very well there were two.'

'Then where is the other one? Look under the peepul tree. You may have left it there by mistake.'

'There's no mistake. Nitai had one in his hand when we came here and Sukhen had the other one.'

'Where could it go?' Nibaran mutters uneasily. 'Surely a ghost didn't spirit it away.'

'One of your children has taken it,' Surendra says with conviction. 'They came to see the hedgehog and when no one was looking...'

Nibaran peers into the shack. 'There's nothing here. It's pitch dark inside.'

'No tricks, Nibaran kaka,' Surendra admonishes the older man. 'We'll search the shack, and if we find—'

'You'll search the shack!' Nibaran says indignantly. 'Don't you know your kaki is sleeping inside? Do you think we are thieves?'

'Then where is the lantern?'

'How should I know? What will we do with a lantern, you piece of shit? Can we afford a drop of kerosene? There isn't a grain of rice in the house. Kerosene! Hmph!'

'If we had money for kerosene,' Paban's quavering voice rises in his son's support, 'would I be smoking mango leaves and cow dung?'

'Call your children, Nibaran kaka. I want to question them.'

'Genu! Paanti!' Nibaran calls out, his voice loud with paternal authority. 'Come here at once.' The boy comes out of the shack. There is no sign of the girl. 'Have you taken the lantern?'

'I haven't taken it.'

'Where's your sister?'

The boy points a finger at the jungle behind the house. 'There,' he says.

'What's she doing there?'

'She's gone with Ma.'

Nitai lets out a squeal of laughter. 'Oh, Nibaran kaka! Have your wife and daughter gone in search of a ghost?'

'Shut your foul mouth, Nitai!' Paban glares at the midget. 'Don't talk nonsense. Why should a pregnant woman go looking for a ghost in the middle of the night? There are dozens of petnis lurking near the shithole. A glance from one of them and the child will shrivel and die in the womb.'

'Then what is your son's wife doing there?'

'Your kaki is afflicted with the dropsy,' Nibaran mutters with a glum face.

'Oh!' Nitai nods, in instant understanding. 'But she should have told us she was taking our lantern.'

'Who's taken your lantern, you scum? Wouldn't we have seen her if she did?'

'Arre, what are you trying to tell us, Nibaran kaka? That our lantern has vanished into thin air?'

'Let's take a look,' Surendra says decisively.

Paban and Nibaran don't move but the others walk in the direction pointed out by the boy. When they have gone a few yards, they catch sight of Paanti standing under an amloki tree. She is shivering in the cold. Her goosepimpled arms are folded tight across her breasts and her hands are buried in her armpits.

'Don't come any closer,' she cries out in panic. 'Ma is there, she's...'

The men see a faint glow of light behind a bush and quickly avert their gaze.

'Why didn't you tell us before taking the lantern?' Surendra snaps at the girl. 'We're waiting under the peepul at Panchlar Modh. Bring it to us when your mother's done...'

The girl sways her head obediently.

'And if, by chance, you come across a ghost or petni,' Nitai grins wickedly, 'be sure to holler. We'll run back and catch it. You'll get ten rupees.'

Paban is talking to his grandson. 'Choudhury babu caught a ghost once,' he says with a pull at his hookah, 'a living skeleton. It struggled and flapped and thrashed about with a terrible clanking of bones but Choudhury babu managed to throw a noose around its neck and drag it home at the end of his rope. If only we had such luck! What can't one buy with ten rupees? Seven seers of rice...'

'Have you really seen a ghost, thakurda?' Genu stares at his grandfather with curious eyes.

'Yes, child. Not once, many times.'

'Can you show me one? Just one, from afar?'

'If your destiny wills it, you will surely see one. But it's

better if you don't.' Throwing a burning glance at Surendra's
retreating figure, Paban hawks and spits venomously. 'The
bastard is riding on a high horse ever since he got himself
some money,' he mutters bitterly. The ball of phlegm he
has thrown up is specked with cow dung.

After a while, the *jhum jhum* of anklets signals the return
of the group. But this time they don't stop. The light from
their lanterns fade as they move towards Panchlar Modh
and Paban's house is engulfed once again in the darkness
of a moonless night.

The return of Surendra had created quite a hullaballoo in
the village. Nobody knew what to make of him. After his
father's death, their family line had vanished. All that
remained was the little boy who grew like a weed until he
turned thirteen, when he was employed by the Choudhurys
from across the canal to graze their cows and do odd-jobs
around the house. One day the boy found a pair of slippers
lying in the middle of the stairs and, instead of picking
them up with his hands, he nudged them into a corner with
his feet. They belonged to Mejo babu, the second son of the
house, and as luck would have it, Mejo babu caught him in
the act. The boy was beaten black and blue and then kicked
down the stairs and into the courtyard. Surendra left the
village that very night and didn't return. Needless to say,
no one bothered to find out where he had gone, or whether
he was alive or dead.

And now he was back, a hulk of a man. People said he
worked at a factory in the town and was flush with money.
And that was undoubtedly the truth, for he wore brightly
coloured shirts and smoked more cigarettes than bidis.

One day he was seen outside the Choudhury mansion, spitting at the wall. Not once, not twice; he spat thrice, each time with added venom. No one had dared do such a thing before. But Surendra wasn't caught and punished, for the simple reason that no one lived there any more, barring a doddering old steward, and what could *he* do but look on helplessly? The sun had set on the zamindari. The guards and servants had all gone. They hadn't been paid their wages for months. Why speak of wages, there wasn't even enough rice to go around.

Surendra was now firmly ensconced in the village. He got the dilapidated remains of his parental home repaired and stayed there over weekends. He had found himself a group of followers—young men, idlers and wastrels mostly, who banded together under his banner. And why shouldn't they? He fed them better than they had ever eaten in their lives and he was generous with cigarettes and bidis. They had a lot of fun too. Last week they got together and started cleaning the ancient lake, choked with water reeds and hyacinth, that lay in the eastern end of the village. Cleaning! Hah! All they did was jump into the water and have the time of their lives. It was a dangerous game. Everyone knew that a ghost, an ancient yaksha, haunted the lake and caught people by the throat and dragged them down. One of the boys nearly lost his life. When he came up, his face was blue and his limbs rigid. But did the idiots learn their lesson? No, they were going in again next week.

Another of their pranks was this offer to buy ghosts. The villagers were no fools. They knew why Surendra was doing this. And whatever these youngsters might think, ghosts were a reality in the villages of Bengal. If not, why had people believed in their existence for generations on end? But the ghosts were a handful. They appeared easily before simple innocent folk and kept away from the likes of Surendra. Even they were afraid of the hulking bully with his gruff voice.

Surendra began to increase his rate. Every night of the new moon saw him announcing a fresh one. First it was ten, then twenty, then fifty, and now it was a hundred rupees. A hundred rupees per ghost! And one didn't have to catch it either, just showing it from a distance was enough. But there had to be two witnesses. A hundred rupees! Mouths watered at the thought and muttered curses at the same time. The arrogant, abominable, disgusting son of a pig was thumbing his nose at starving people, making a mockery of their need for money! Even a man's life wasn't worth a hundred rupees, and he was offering it for a ghost! Why didn't the buggers catch him and wrench his head off his neck? It would serve him right, the smirking scoundrel.

When Surendra first came back to the village he had told Nitai and the others that there was no such thing as a soul or spirit. People died and that was that. The villagers were shocked. That he could even think such a blasphemous thought sent shivers down their spines. No soul! Where did human beings come from, then? And where were they headed? At first everyone was convinced that Surendra had turned Christian. If that were so, they could ostracize him and throw him out of the village. But last year Surendra had performed Durga Puja, that too with a lot of fanfare.

There had always been one Durga Puja in the village—in the house of the Choudhurys. But over the years it had lost its lustre. The babus had been absconding for a decade now, and why not? What was left for them here except that dilapidated mausoleum of a house? But the rule being that a Durga Puja once begun cannot be discontinued, some members of the community had got together and were performing it with their own money, needless to say on a very low budget.

Last year, Surendra and his gang raised a question. If the villagers were paying for the puja themselves, why should it be performed in the house of the zamindars? They weren't contributing a paisa but were reaping all the merit! It ought to be held in a central part of the village and everyone should be encouraged to participate. The elders understood why Surendra was hell-bent on taking the puja out of the Choudhury mansion. He was still seething with rage at the way he had been treated and wanted the wrath of the goddess to fall on the family. Arre baba, weren't they suffering enough already? The doughty, arrogant, intrepid Mejo babu was an old, broken man. One of his sons was in jail and another worked as a railway guard at Howrah Station.

Surendra won his case and Durga Puja was held in the park adjacent to the primary school building. Bill receipts were printed and donations collected. The gentlemen who had financed the puja earlier were quite happy at this development. Those who had contributed twenty-five rupees all along now paid five. Surendra didn't turn a hair. He and his band put up a large pandal and brought Ma Durga to it triumphantly, on their shoulders. How vigorously they danced on the night of Maha Ashtami! Surendra, with his huge black buffalo body, shaggy head and hibiscus red eyes was a sight to behold. Holding two flaming censers high over his head, he leaped and pranced about like one possessed. At one point he came down with a terrible crash. It was a wonder he wasn't blinded by the burning coconut husk on which he fell. Having fallen, he didn't get up again. His followers kept calling out to him and pulling at his arms and legs but he remained sprawled on the ground, still as a corpse. Then someone brought a pot of water and was about to pour it on his head when he sprang up, laughing, and started dancing again. Of all the tomfoolery! Drunken louts, every one of them!

Mejo babu's second son, the one who was presently serving a jail sentence, had come to the village just before Durga Puja last year. He brought two friends with him. The Choudhurys had always driven down in a car but these boys came on a motorcycle. Not that there is anything demeaning about a motorcycle. The sound it makes has a nice zamindari ring to it. The steward got a couple of rooms cleaned and the young men took up residence in the family mansion. The steward must have filled his master's ears with a lot of malicious reports against Surendra because the next morning Chhoto babu was seen standing outside Panchu's grocery shop asking, 'Can you tell me where Suren lives?'

'Which Suren?' Panchu enquired cautiously.

Now there'll be hell to pay, the villagers thought, eyeing the fair, handsome youth. It was true that the zamindars had lost all their money. It was also true that their foot soldiers and guards had left. It was no longer possible for Chhoto babu to send for Surendra and give him a shoe beating in the middle of the village maidan. Still, blue blood was blue blood...

It being a Sunday, Surendra was in the village. The three young men rode off in the direction of his house with a great roar of engines. What transpired after that, no one knows. But after about half an hour, the zamindar's son and his friends were seen coming out of Surendra's house, laughing and talking with him. At one point Chhoto babu put up his hand to pat Surendra's shoulder but it was too high and he couldn't quite reach it. Then Chhoto babu—and Nibaran saw this with his own eyes—brought out a packet of cigarettes from his pocket and Surendra took one as though it was the most natural thing in the world.

'Kaliyug! Kaliyug!' the elders exclaimed in horror. 'Ghor Kali!' In what other age could such a thing even be thought of?

The primary school stood smack in between two villages. The government employed teachers who worked for a couple of years and then left in search of greener pastures. The only one who had stuck on was Jogen master. He was of a poetic temperament and liked to sit by the river every evening and look at the sunset. One day he caught sight of Surendra at the weekly haat and accosted him in front of a lot of people.

'Hyaan re, Suren,' he said, 'is it true that you're going around saying there's no such thing as a soul?'

Jogen master had never taught Surendra so the latter had no reason to be overtly respectful. He didn't even bother to hide his bidi. But he did scratch the back of his neck and mutter uneasily, 'I'm an ignorant peasant, mastermoshai. What do I know of such things? That's for learned men like you to ponder and debate. I can only say that I've never seen one.'

Jogen master was taken aback for a moment but he pulled himself together and said gravely, 'You've never seen air either. But can you deny its existence?'

The villagers smirked and waited for Surendra's reply.

And pat came the answer: 'I can't see air but I can hold it in my hand.'

'You can hold air in your hand?' Jogen master was stumped. 'What are you saying, Suren? Try holding a bit of air in your lungs. After a few seconds it will struggle like a trapped bird and nearly kill you—won't it?' He glanced around him for affirmation and everyone nodded.

But Suren was unfazed. Walking up to a balloon seller who stood nearby, he took a balloon in his hand and blew on it till it swelled up like a gourd. Pinching the end between his thumb and forefinger, he waved the balloon about and cried out, 'Look, mastermoshai, I hold air in my hand. Just teach me how I can do the same with a soul and I'll change my views.'

'Don't even think of trying that, son.' Jogen shook his head pompously. 'The atma, the spirit, is beyond the reach of the senses. *Nainang chhidranti ong bong khong*—which means that no one can pierce a hole in a soul. You can neither burn it with fire nor drown it in water. It is immortal, eternal.'

Hole in a soul. Surendra's lips twitched. 'What happens when one burns a corpse, mastermoshai?' he asked. 'Does the soul fly out of the mouth? Whoosh! Like this?' Surendra released the air from the balloon. 'Where does it go?'

'It merges and becomes one with the paramatma—the larger soul—which is God.'

'Oh!'

'Don't you believe me?'

'Why shouldn't I believe you? You are a learned man. You know what you are saying.'

The people crowding around smiled and nodded. They

were pleased that Surendra had to concede defeat. But they were surprised too. They had expected him to stick to his guns and keep arguing for hours. The balloon business had been a bit of a setback for Jogen master. But all's well that ends well.

Now a pleased Jogen master patted Surendra on the back, as he would an obedient pupil, and said smiling, 'I hear you've started a business, Suren. People tell me you're buying ghosts.'

'Yes, mastermoshai.' Suren bowed his head meekly. 'I've got a large order from an industrialist in the city. He is offering me two-hundred-and-fifty per ghost. I'm willing to shell out one hundred to the catcher. That leaves me with a neat profit of one-hundred-and-fifty per piece. It's like any other business. Onions, for instance. The wholesaler buys onions at twenty-seven rupees a maund and sells it at retail for thirty-five rupees in the city. I'm doing exactly the same.'

Jogen master burst out laughing. Surendra joined him, as though what he was saying was the absolute truth and awfully funny at the same time.

'Have you found any?' There was a twinkle in Jogen master's eye.

'No.'

'Ha ha ha! You're nothing but a child, Suren!' Jogen master stopped laughing. His face turned grim. 'I advise you to give up this nonsense, Suren. It's a dangerous game you're playing. One doesn't know how it will end.'

Surendra lit a bidi. 'I'll go over to your house one day, mastermoshai, and we will discuss this issue at length. It's not possible to do so in the middle of the haat. You know, don't you, that my father was strangled by a ghost?'

'Yes, I've heard something of the sort…'

'My father had sold some paddy that day and he had money in a pouch tucked into his waist. His body was found but not the money. Who took it? Whose need was greater? The ghost who killed him or the bigger ghost you were telling me about—the paramatma? I have to find out. I'm sure you will be able to guide me in the matter. You see, not one man from the village came forward that day to give evidence.'

The old canal was choked with hyacinth, weeds and algae. It was as good as dead. With no means of irrigation, the jute and paddy fields gasped for water every summer, and gave up the ghost just before the rains came. But things were looking up now. The government was dredging and widening the canal and had leased out the work to Rehman Sheikh of the adjoining village of Sonamuri. What a blessing it would be if the canal started to flow again.

The eager anticipation of the villagers maddened Nibaran. He wanted to kick himself. Only last year he had mortgaged his two-and-a-half acres. What else could he have done? He was fatally ill and needed money for his treatment. If it had been anyone else—his wife, father or one of the children—he could have let them die. But how could he let himself die? He was the only able-bodied male in the family, the only earning member. What would become of the others if he was no more? He felt particularly incensed with his father. Why couldn't the old fool die and get off his back? He was in his dotage, incapable of bringing in a paisa. And he ate—my god, how much he ate! The older he got, the more greedy he became. His other sons had refused to keep him. But Nibaran was a dutiful man, he couldn't do the same. His heart welled over with self-pity at the thought.

Nibaran had an understanding with the new owner. The sharecropping rights would be his, and after the paddy had been harvested he would plant cauliflowers. But with most of his produce going elsewhere, how in the world would he feed his family and set aside enough money for the interest and instalments on the mortgage? When, if at all, would he redeem his land? His heart burned at the thought. Particularly now that the government was widening the canal and making irrigation possible. Why, oh why, hadn't they thought of it earlier, when he still had his land? Nibaran was a thatcher but over the years his calling had died a natural death. With crops failing every year, people barely got two meals a day. Who had the money to put up a new thatch? The few who could afford it preferred to use tiles, for which they sent for masons from the city.

Fifty or sixty men were required each day for the canal work. At first Rehman saheb brought them over from Sonamuri. But that, the men of Surendra's village declared, was unacceptable. The canal flowed through both villages and their inhabitants were equally needy. Why should one lot of people be preferred over another and allowed to reap the benefits? There was a big hulla-gulla only the day before yesterday, but Rehman saheb, who was a fair, just man, resolved the issue. Twenty-five men from each village would be employed at four-rupees-eight-annas a day. They would also be given a midday meal. But since the number of able-bodied males from the two villages exceeded more than fifty, they would have to take turns. No one would be employed for two days in succession. Nibaran had worked yesterday. Today he sat idle. A thatcher had become a coolie, a landowner a sharecropper. But what choice did he have? Prestige wouldn't fill his belly. Food, after all, was next to God.

Even on the days that Nibaran wasn't working, he liked to sit by the canal and watch the activity around him. Today, on his way there, he thought of Surendra. People who left the village and made their fortunes in the city never returned. Why had Surendra come back? Stout and healthy as an ox and flush with money! Nibaran's blood boiled. The scoundrel wouldn't part with a paisa when it came to a needy man like Nibaran but he was offering one hundred rupees for a ghost. What couldn't Nibaran have done with a hundred rupees? Surendra had not one but many hundreds jingling in his pockets. But what good was that to Nibaran? The world was grossly unfair. Some people had so much money they didn't know what to do with it. Others starved to death from want.

People saw ghosts all the time but Nibaran, curse his luck, had never seen one. Of late, he had taken to sneaking out of the house after dusk and walking through the jungle behind. Sometimes he thought he saw something—a flash of white, like a woman in a widow's thaan—slip past. But when he looked again he realized it was only a wood-apple tree or a banana clump swaying in the breeze. Every time that happened he got more incensed with Surendra. Damn the swaggering bugger! Damn him!

Nibaran stood on the canal's embankment and breathed in a lungful of air. A wave of nausea swept over him. Too much air on an empty stomach made him queasy and he felt a strange sinking in his heart. The fifty men busily digging and scraping seemed to belong to a different planet. They would soon get their meal and at the end of the day they would get four-rupees-eight-annas. And Nibaran would get nothing. His pregnant wife was racked with stomach pains so severe, he often saw her hunched against the wall, crying bitterly. She needed food, nourishing food, a little milk perhaps... They hadn't seen milk in months. All they were eating these days was rice starch and boiled kolmi greens picked from the edges of the pond.

The sun was about to set and the sky was turning russet and gold. There was something magnificent about the sky at this time of the day. *The Palace of the Omnipotent*, that was what it looked like. Nibaran gazed at the scene in front of him. 'Great God,' he muttered in prayer, 'you've sent me so much suffering in this life, so much sorrow and affliction! Dole out some good fortune in the next. A little happiness. Enable me to provide my family with two square meals a day, to put some jaggery and candy in my children's hands from time to time.'

A small group of people had gathered on the right side of the canal. Wondering what was going on, Nibaran made his way there. And then he heard something that made his heart jump. His eyes burned with fierce elation. He felt as though he had finally been given a chance to avenge his humiliation. Pushing his way into the centre of the clamouring, gesticulating crowd, he roared, 'Cut the crap and tell me the truth. Has anyone actually seen it?'

'I haven't seen it with my own eyes,' Charu from Sonamuri snapped back, 'but do you think I'm making it up?'

'Is she still there?'

'Of course. Bhanu saw her only a while ago. She was rolling on the ground and...'

'Is that true, Bhanu?'

Bhanu was so honest he was almost a simpleton. He scratched his bald head (his hair had started to fall out from the age of twenty) and said, 'Yes, I saw her. She was tossing from side to side and there was froth coming out of her mouth. The ojha is at work exorcising the ghost. Baap re, the incense he lit made my eyes burn so much I had to run—'

'Ojha!' Nibaran exclaimed. 'Are you all fools? Why did you send for the ojha? You should have informed Surendra. That son of a bitch has grown too big for his own good. Let's cut him down to size. We must force the hundred rupees out of him.'

'But Surendra is in town!'

'Go to the town then, and drag him here by his hair. Ghosts aren't going to oblige him by appearing only on weekends.'

'He comes back to the village some nights,' a weak voice piped up from the crowd. 'I've heard he keeps a woman here.'

'Good! Let's pounce on the blackguard and make him pay up.'

Surendra's house stood in one corner of the village. The land around it had been in the family for generations but was no longer so. His father had been a sturdy, hard-working man who raised enough crops in his meagre fields for his wife and son to live in comfort. After his death, of course, it was a different story. The land disappeared, Surendra had no idea how. But the house remained. Rural traditions, though strange, were rigidly upheld. People were always finding ways and means of impinging on another's land and claiming it as their own. But houses were left alone, even if they lay unoccupied for generations.

You might help yourself to the things inside, you might even pull out a door or window and use it for firewood. But you would never, ever move in. The deity of the house would be offended and bring harm upon you.

Surendra had been given living quarters in the vicinity of the factory that employed him. It had proper drains, running water and several other amenities. Yet Surendra preferred to spend as much time as he could at his house in the village. The earth of his forefathers called out to him. Not that he was very happy there. He spent night after night crying into his pillow. It was a strange sight: a huge, hefty man with enormous tears rolling down his cheeks. But no one saw him this way, for he wept alone. And it always started with memories of his mother; his poor, helpless, suffering mother whom he had so cruelly abandoned. The incident in the house of the zamindar had driven him mad with rage and humiliation. He was possessed by one thought only: to get away from this cursed life and make a better one for himself. He didn't think, even once, of the woman he was leaving behind. She died of grief and starvation, he heard later. And, what was most hurtful, she had been stricken with cholera and no one had come near her. Three days after her death, when the corpse had started stinking and polluting the air, scavengers were sent for to drag her body to the cremation ghat.

Now Surendra was back. He had money in his pockets, strength in his limbs and determination in his heart. He would avenge his mother's death. But the realization that he would never see her again made him break down and cry.

Surendra often thought of getting married to a girl from

his village. The very act might exorcise the demons he was grappling with and enable him to make peace with the people he hated and longed to punish. But where would he find a suitable girl? No one took his fancy. They were, without exception, dark and ungainly. Besides, they were severely malnourished. Many of them had crossed puberty quite a few years ago but their breasts were still as flat as boards.

'Surendra! Surendra!' a gruff voice called from outside the door. It sounded like his father's voice. Surendra's lips twisted in a smile. Some of the village boys, idlers and no-gooders, often tried to frighten him and drive him away. They threw stones at the tin roof in the dead of night, and once they tried to push a wet cat into his room through the bars of the window. Surendra had caught them in the act and given them a sound thrashing.

'Surendra! Surendra!' The voice was urgent now. Surendra opened the door and looked out. There was no one there. Everything was dark and still. Suddenly the silence was shattered as a gaggle of bats rose from a tree and flew towards the moon, shrieking. It was a crescent moon, three days old, hanging pale and faint in a hazy, starless sky. There was that voice again. The sound was louder now but the caller was invisible. Surendra shrugged his heavy shoulders. It was an illusion. Such things happened when you lived alone. It was time he found himself a wife. He turned to go back inside but before he could, something caught his eye. A row of silhouettes appeared on the horizon. A group of men were moving rapidly towards his house, calling out to him.

'What's the matter?' Surendra's brows furrowed.

'We've come for you, Suren-da.' Nitai, who was running

ahead of the others, jumped up and down in excitement. 'A petni has taken possession of a young woman in Sonamuri. She is Sarbananda Das's daughter-in-law, Shanti.'

Surendra snorted derisively. 'Hmph! How much bhang have you poured down your gullet, you fool?'

'Arre, na na!' A few others came forward. 'It's the truth. Shanti bouma is lying in the yard, writhing and frothing at the mouth. The petni is making her say all sorts of things. Obscene rubbish!'

'What kind of obscene rubbish?'

'You'd better hear that for yourself.'

'Why? Can't one of you tell me? Has anyone actually seen her?'

'Of course.' Nibaran came forward. 'Charu and Bhanu have both seen her. The ojha is trying hard to drive the petni away but the stubborn bitch refuses to go.'

'Where's Sarbananda's son Bibhuti?'

'He doesn't live in the village. He works in Durgapur.'

'Why hasn't anyone from the family come to call me?'

'*We've* come to call you. Isn't that enough? Do you think we are liars?' Nibaran said aggressively.

'Let me talk straight with you, Nibaran kaka. Sarbananda's house is two, two-and-a-half miles from here. I have no intention of walking all that way in the middle of the night only to find that I've been duped.'

'Could it be something else that's stopping you?' Nibaran sniggered. 'Are you afraid it might be true?'

Surendra laughed. These men, though old in years, spoke and behaved like children. They had cow dung for brains. 'Where business is concerned, Nibaran kaka,' he answered pleasantly, 'there's no room for fear. Can a coward prosper? I've made it clear that I buy only genuine stuff. No shady deals for me.'

'Why don't you come with us and check it out for yourself?'

'Very well, I'll come. But you must give me your word that there's no tomfoolery. Your lives won't be worth much if there is. I'll make mincemeat out of the lot of you and I'm a man of my word, remember that.'

Surendra went into the house with Nitai at his heels. He picked up a satchel from a hook on the wall and began to stuff it with things: a small tin box, a torch, a roll of bandages and an empty bottle of native Scotch.

Nitai looked at him curiously. 'What will you do with the empty bottle, Suren-da?' he asked.

'Can't you guess?' Surendra grinned. 'I'll use it to trap the petni. As soon as she leaves Shanti I'll hold out my bottle and whoosh … she'll fly into it. Then all I'll need to do is jam the cork tight. Shaala! You too, Nitai! Even you come to me with this tale of bhoot-petni. Shame on you!'

'Have you brought the money?' Nibaran asked anxiously as soon as the two stepped out of the house. 'You promised a hundred rupees per spirit, remember?'

'Why are you so worried about the money, Nibaran kaka? If anyone gets it, it will be Sarbananda Das, not you.'

Nibaran winced and fell silent. But his chest heaved in exultation. 'Spawn of a pig!' he mouthed soundlessly. 'Even if I don't get a paisa I'll still be thrilled to see you lose yours. To see your face dark and swollen, your pride crushed. Haramjada!'

Sarbananda Das had been quite well off at one time. Things were different now. He had lost most of his land in mortgages. But his son worked in the city and sent money every month. And he still had his house, a nice big one surrounded by areca palms. It had a central courtyard and four rooms, one on each side. A path shaded with palm trees led to a pond at the back. A shaggy rose-apple tree grew in a corner of the yard which, Surendra noted as they entered, was crowded with screaming, gesticulating people. The air was thick with acrid smoke rising from a censer. It was dark but for a weird white light coming from a petromax around which a swarm of insects buzzed and scorched their wings.

Shanti lay in the middle of the yard, water streaming down her hair, her clothes caked with mud. Her eyes were closed and her lips and chin were dappled with froth. She lay rigid for a while and then, all of a sudden, she was seized by convulsions. Her arms and legs twisted and flailed the air and she banged her head against the earth. This went on for some time before her body went rigid again. Sarbananda stood on one side, feeding incense into the smoking censer. The ojha sat at her head shouting mantras and circling a besom so menacingly that the sticks snapped and flew out in all directions. Subal, the ojha, was the son of the late Mahadev Ojha, renowned for his exorcising skills in twenty villages. People would look at Mahadev Ojha and tremble in awe and fear. He used to wear his hair in dreadlocks that fell to his waist. His hefty flanks were wrapped tightly in a blood-red loincloth that matched the colour of his eyes. These eyes, flaming with ganja, were the only feature visible on a face from which thick black hair sprouted, concealing brows, cheeks and chin. Mahadev Ojha, it was rumoured, could make bhoots and petnis dance at the end of his stick. He had died six months ago, in a miscalculated attempt to trap two demons

within his body and become their master. It had been a
tragic death and a severe loss to the community.

Mahadev's son, although he had followed in his father's
footsteps, was nowhere in the same league. He was young,
about twenty or twenty-one, with a soft, well-fed body and
a head of sleek, oiled hair. But he knew all the mantras.
And he had another great talent: he could touch his nose
with his tongue.

Subal was taking great pains with the job assigned to
him. He was reciting the mantras with a lot of feeling and
each time the woman moved, he brought his besom down
on her supine body with all the force that his plump,
pampered arm could muster. Mahadev Ojha, it was said,
could draw blood in streams with the ferocity of his beatings.
Subal lacked his father's physical strength but made up for
this deficiency with the most obscene curses and abuses,
which he now shouted at the top of his voice. 'Abagi!
Haramjadi!' Twisting Shanti's hair with one hand and
beating the besom on her breast with the other, he shrieked,
'Jah! Jah! Get off the girl before I kill you. Harlot! Wanton
tart!'

Surendra elbowed his way to the centre of the crowd.
His enormous body, dark as a monsoon cloud, towered
over Subal's. With his clenched teeth and hard jaws, he
looked like a messenger of Death. His first impulse was to
kick the bastard Subal out of the yard. How dare he raise
his hand on a woman? He even lifted a leg, as huge and
powerful as Bhima's club, but he put it down again. Father
Pereira had told him to use physical force only in self-
defence. 'Animals fight and kill one another,' he had said.
'You are a human being, Surendra. Always remember that.'

Surendra sank down on his haunches beside Subal.

'Wait a minute, karta,' he said affably. 'Let me take a look.' If it had been Mahadev Ojha instead of his son, there would have been hell to pay. No one had ever dared to interfere with his work. Surendra's massive bulk and menacing voice wouldn't have made him bat an eyelid. He had enough brawn in him to take on a dozen Surendras. But the boy, his son, was a worthless nincompoop.

'It's my case,' he whined feebly. 'Why should *you* take a look? I'm almost through. I'll have the bitch flying out in a matter of minutes.'

'Move, move! Make room.' Surendra brushed him off as he would a fly. Turning to Sarbananda, he asked, 'What happened?'

Sarbananda gulped. 'Th—th—that... that,' he stammered and stuttered, 'that ... rose-apple tree.'

Now Subal took up the tale. 'What happened is this,' he puffed out his chest and announced ponderously. 'The woman rose from her bed at the crack of dawn to take a piss. The sun hadn't risen yet. As soon as she stepped into the yard she saw three koi fish twisting and flapping in the mud in the yard. Her father-in-law had bought half a dozen from the haat last evening and she had kept three of them alive in a pot full of water. Some creature, probably a cat, had turned the pot over and the fish escaped. Now cats, as we know, are scared of koi fish because of the sting. Relieved that the fish were still alive, she picked them up and put them back into the pot. She wiped her hands on her sari and went out to, er, do whatever she had to do. She was about to go back to bed when...' Subal stopped dramatically and looked at the people around him for approval. They had heard the story fifty times already but where was the harm in hearing it again? They nodded encouragingly as

Subal continued, 'There were two evil spirits sitting in that tree. That's what they do, they lurk about in the dark waiting for an opportunity. The silly girl hadn't washed her hands after touching the fish. What's worse, she hadn't washed her feet after her piss. What do you expect? The two shit-eaters pounced on her and she fell flat in the yard, twisting and turning and—'

'Wait!' Surendra interrupted. 'Was anyone awake at that hour? Did anyone see her pick up the fish or take a piss?'

Subal's face turned dark and sullen. 'I don't need an eyewitness. I diagnosed the case as soon as I saw the woman. It's as clear as day. The pot is still there in the veranda. Go and take a look. There are three koi fish swimming in it.'

'Hmph!' Surendra grunted.

'You want proof?' Subal rose to the occasion. 'You shall have it.' Bringing down the besom heavily on Shanti's breast, he thundered, 'Tell me the truth, you dung-eating bitch! Didn't this woman take a piss even before the sun was up? Didn't she? Come on, own up before I kill you.'

'Oooh!' Shanti moaned.

'Hear that?' Subal turned to Surendra triumphantly. 'She's saying yes.' Bringing the besom down again, he shrieked, 'And didn't you swing the branch of the rose-apple tree and hit her on the head? Confess, haramjadi!'

'Oooh!' Shanti moaned louder. 'Hit … hit…'

'Listen to the harlot's confession.' Subal threw a meaningful glance at Surendra and continued to strike Shanti. 'Now the fight is between you and me, you spawn of the devil.' He gnashed his teeth. 'I'll get the better of you for sure.' Surendra sprang to his feet, yanked the besom out of Subal's hand, and flung it out of the yard.

Shanti had come from the village of Rasapagla as Bibhuti's bride. Sarbananda had seen her on a visit to his maternal uncle and liked her so much that he offered his graduate son for her. Not only was she extremely pretty, she had been to school as well and would make a fit bride for Bibhuti. Shanti was a modern girl. She had lived with her husband in Durgapur and worn her hair in braids for many years after her wedding. It was only a few months ago that Bibhuti had brought her to the village because running an establishment in the city had become too expensive. Since then, she had been living with her father-in-law and Bibhuti visited them from time to time. She was very young, only twenty, but already rumours ran rife that she was barren.

Surendra fixed his eyes on Shanti. She lay on her back, her long neck turned to one side. Her wet sari clung to her body, accentuating its contours, exposing their burgeoning beauty. Her eyes were open but they were empty, devoid of expression.

'There were two of them,' Subal said. 'The male one is still sitting in the tree. The female has entered the woman. They are a couple and will only leave together.'

Surendra walked towards the rose-apple tree. 'Where is he sitting?' he demanded. 'Show me.'

Subal shuddered and yelled out: 'Don't go near. He's still there. I can see him clearly. There, on the topmost branch! It's swaying under his weight. See! See!'

It was true. The branch was swaying gently.

'Let him go if he wants to,' someone called out from the crowd. 'Why stop him?'

Surendra rolled up his khakhi pants to his knees and scaled up the tree. Standing in a fork, he called out to Subal in a rough voice, 'Where? Where's the son of a bitch?'

'Higher!' Subal replied. 'Right on top.'

Surendra realized he was being tricked. Rose-apple wood is brittle and if he climbed any higher the branch would split beneath his weight. He would fall to the ground and the crowd would jeer. He took off his belt and made a noose which he flung around the branch, snapping it off the trunk. Gripping the branch with one hand, he climbed down the tree and waved it under Subal's nose. 'Here! Catch your bhoot. He was sitting right here among the leaves.' Subal's eyes rolled in terror and he ducked his head quickly.

Shanti sat up. Giggling a little, she beckoned to Surendra. 'Come,' she said invitingly.

'She's calling him!' a shrill cry rose from the crowd. 'The petni is calling him.'

Shanti picked up the end of her sari, which was trailing in the mud and water of the yard, and covered herself decorously. 'Come,' she said again, 'come to me.'

Surendra took a couple of tentative steps towards her. 'What is it?' he asked.

'Come closer.' Shanti patted the ground next to her. 'Sit here by my side. There's no need to be bashful. You're my beloved, my paramour, aren't you?'

Surendra obeyed with a puzzled frown. 'What do you want?' He threw her a baleful glance.

'I can't say it in front of all these people. I'll whisper it to you.' Leaning forward, she took his head in her hands. *Phss! Phss! Phss!* She hissed a few words and then suddenly clamped her teeth around his ear and bit it hard—so hard, the blood started streaming down his neck.

Kaan-kaata Suren! Kaan-kaata Suren! the crowd roared in glee.

Shanti's giggling gave way to a loud cackle—a strange sound, harsh and metallic like the clanking of knives. 'Will you marry me, Surendra?' She looked at him eagerly. 'We'll have such fun together. We'll hide in the jute fields and make love.'

The people standing in the yard were shocked. Shanti was such a shy, well-behaved girl. How could she utter such shameful rubbish, that too in front of her father-in-law? But of course, it wasn't she who was responsible. It wasn't even her voice—it was the petni's.

'Play with me.' Shanti flung herself against Surendra's chest. 'Make love to me. See how big my breasts are!'

Surendra lost his temper. His eyes blazed. At that moment he forgot everything Father Pereira had taught him. Seizing Shanti's hair with one hand, he slapped her hard on her cheek. Shanti fell back under the force of the blow and lay on the ground like a wilted stalk.

A voice called out from the crowd, Nibaran's voice: 'Eyi, Surendra, it's time to pay up. Don't let him off, Sarbananda-da. Catch him. Let's see his money.'

'Yes! Yes!' the others echoed. 'Let's see his money.'

'What money?' Surendra looked up.

'The money you promised for a spirit. We've shown you a petni. You've seen it with your own eyes...'

'No, I haven't.'

'Liar! You have the gall to deny it? This is a ploy to save your hundred rupees, isn't it? Do you think we'll let you? We're not fools. Give it! Give it!' The crowd advanced upon Surendra threateningly, the weak, starving, faint-hearted Nibaran taking the lead. He wouldn't get a paisa but the thought of Surendra being forced to part with a hundred rupees filled him with a fierce elation. Nitai, a member of

Surendra's own gang, stood trembling in one corner. The whole affair had left his heart pounding like a drum.

Surendra swung a mighty arm and waved the men away. With his legs planted firmly apart, he drew a huge knife out of his pocket. Its blade glittered, menacing and deadly, in the dim light of the yard. 'Don't you dare come nearer,' he growled. 'Don't you dare try any tricks with me. I can turn this yard into a river of blood and I'll do it without a twinge of remorse.'

His words led to a stampede. People fell over each other as they tried to flee, to escape the wrath of the man who stood in front of them like a gigantic mountain crag, flashing and circling the lethal weapon in his hands. No one had any doubt now that he was a hardened criminal, a murderer who was out to get their blood.

'I am a man of my word,' Surendra said quietly. 'I promised to pay a hundred rupees for a genuine ghost. But I'll be damned if I part with a paisa for fake goods. This woman isn't possessed, she's hysterical.' Picking up the rose-apple branch, he thrashed it fiercely on the ground in front of Subal. 'The male ghost is sitting here, isn't he?' he sneered. 'Then get the bastard out—if he hasn't run away after seeing me, that is.' Flinging the empty bottle of Scotch on the ground, he continued, 'Snake charmers play flutes and lure snakes into their baskets. Ojhas claim to do the same with ghosts. Come on, cajole your ghost into entering this bottle and fit the cork tightly. If the bottle jumps about by itself I'll know you're telling me the truth.' He took out a wad of notes from his pocket and waved it in the air. 'You'll get your hundred rupees right away.'

'Jah! Jah!' Subal waved dismissively for want of anything better to say.

Surendra knelt on the ground, took Shanti's wrist in his hand and started to feel her pulse.

'Eyi!' Sarbananda shouted. 'Why are you touching my daughter-in-law?'

Surendra turned his eyes, large and menacing, on the old man. 'Chup!' he thundered. 'Do you know what she whispered in my ear just now? Shall I repeat it in front of all these people? If you want to be driven out of the village with lime on one cheek and soot on the other, be my guest. Just let me know and I'll let the cat out of the bag.'

Sarbananda collapsed like a deflated balloon. His face turned ashen and a muscle in his cheek started to twitch. But Subal wasn't about to let go so easily. 'You are witnesses!' he appealed to what was left of the crowd. 'You saw how he snatched the case away from me. I was called first, wasn't I?'

'You've been babbling useless mantras for hours now,' Surendra said peaceably, 'but have they worked? Have you succeeded in driving out your petni?'

Subal elbowed him aggressively and answered, 'You move aside. I was about to begin the *bhoot damor tantra*, the most potent of them all. I'll have the slut out in a minute.'

'Have you heard of the *torhol tantra*? It's the grandfather of all tantras. Watch me put it in action and observe the results.' Opening his tin box, Surendra took out a hypodermic syringe and an ampoule. Slicing the top off the ampoule with an expert flick, he drew the fluid into the syringe. 'Don't be afraid.' He turned to Sarbananda. 'This is called an injection. I learned to give injections from the famous doctor, Father Pereira. He took me in when I left the village, fed me and clothed me, and taught me all I know.'

Raising the girl's right arm, he pierced the needle into the smooth brown flesh. Shanti didn't twitch a muscle. The crowd looked on in horror. Surendra turned to Sarbananda and said, 'Your daughter-in-law is suffering from an ailment called hysteria. She will sleep for eight to ten hours with the injection I've given her. Take her inside and lay her on the bed. Give her nourishing food when she awakes. She will be perfectly well by then.' Clapping a hand on his ear, he exclaimed, 'Oof! It burns like hell! She bit me so hard.'

'How ... how can I take her inside?' Sarbananda stammered. 'She has the strength of a dozen demons in her. It took five men to bring her out...'

'Hmph!' Surendra grunted. He picked her up as lightly as a feather and asked, 'Where does she sleep? Show me her room.' Stepping onto the dalaan, he glared at Sarbananda, his eyes bloodshot with hate. 'You knew she was pregnant,' he hissed in a low voice, 'yet you subjected her to this ordeal. Chhi! And you call yourself a gentleman.'

Rain, rain, rain. It had been pouring for three days and still hadn't stopped. Who would have said it was winter? It was more like the middle of the monsoon. Nibaran was returning home at the end of the day, water streaming down his head, his legs caked in mud up to the knees. He hadn't touched a drop of liquor but he was reeling and tottering like a drunk. His starved, emaciated body felt drained and empty. Within his breast lay an ocean of despair.

He had taken a loan to buy cauliflower saplings and had planted them in the mortgaged field only five days ago. Two days later the rains came. Torrential, unseasonal rain.

He hadn't dreamed that such a thing was possible. Half his plants had been washed away. He had tried to save the rest but what good would they do him? His moneylender's share, according to the terms, was fifty per cent.

But that was a worry for the future. What would he do for the present? What would they eat? It had been Nibaran's turn to work at the canal today but the dredging had been suspended because of the rain. If it hadn't been for this capricious weather he would have got a free meal and four rupees eight annas. Four rupees eight annas felt like a lot of money now. So much happiness could be bought with it. Rehman saheb had announced that all those who had to go back today would get work as soon as the rain stopped. It might be tomorrow. It might be the end of the week. Until then Nibaran and his family would have to suck in their stomachs and wait.

Nibaran turned angry eyes to the sky and hurled his fist at it. Even the elements were against him. The cauliflower saplings, sweet and innocent as babies in their mothers' laps, had raised their heads imploringly to the clouds. But they had shown no mercy. The rain had come pelting down, lashing at their tender heads till they snapped and were washed away. The little green darlings had sobbed and wept. Nibaran had heard them but he had been unable to save them. His enemies were too powerful.

Suddenly his foot slipped and he stumbled and nearly fell. The knot of his dhuti came loose and a small bottle, tucked at his waist, dropped to the ground. The light was fading and he couldn't see where it had fallen. His hands fumbled in the mud and slush. Where could it have gone? Bitterness welled up in his heart. Everything, everyone was against him. God, man and nature. All, all were against him. Just then his bony fingers closed on the glass vial. But the discovery brought him no joy. He felt like flinging it away with all the force in his shrivelled arm...

The doctor at the health centre in Sonamuri was a fishing enthusiast. Every Sunday morning he could be seen sitting by a pond, his rod dipped in the water, for hours on end. One winter morning last year, Genu and Paanti had caught sight of him fishing in the stagnant lake behind the Choudhury mansion. With nothing else to do, they had hovered around and made friends with him. They even brought him home to see their sick grandfather. The doctor had examined the old man and given Nibaran a load of advice: the patient needed nourishing food, vitamin pills and a good tonic. Needless to say, the advice entered through one ear and went out of the other. His father was nearly a hundred years old, good for nothing except to eat. It was time he made his way to the burning ghat. Nibaran had hoped, even prayed, that those would be his last few days on the earth. Most old people went at the end of winter. O ma! The dying man sat up a few days later, fit as a fiddle, and lived for a whole year afterwards. But there was no possibility of history repeating itself this time, Nibaran was certain.

Nibaran had sat by the canal for two hours this morning hoping that the rain would stop and work be resumed. Suddenly he saw the doctor walk past him, his head shielded by an umbrella.

'How is your father?' he stopped and asked affably.

'Well,' Nibaran answered. What else could he say?

'Come to the Centre when you have time,' the doctor told him. 'I'll write out a prescription. He needs some medicine and a good tonic.'

Nibaran was silent for a moment. And then someone, somebody other than Nibaran, spoke from within him. 'We are very poor, doctor babu,' he heard himself say. 'We don't have enough rice to fill our bellies, how can we afford to buy expensive medicine?'

The doctor's heavy brows came together. He fixed his large dark eyes on Nibaran's face for a whole minute, then, opening his black bag, took out a little glass bottle. It had some strange objects in it that looked like black and yellow worms. 'Give him one of these after each meal and come and see me tomorrow or the day after. I'll see what I can do.' He snapped his bag shut and said, 'One must never give up hope.' And leaving these words ringing in Nibaran's ears, he walked away.

Now, standing in the pouring rain, Nibaran's lips curled in a smile. An enigmatic smile that expressed nothing—not sorrow, not mockery, not hate, not anger. Not even self-pity. The doctor had told him to give his father one capsule after each meal. Each meal! The fool didn't know that the medicine he had given Nibaran was worth nothing to him. Even if he flung the bottle away he wouldn't be poorer. Yet … yet why had he searched so feverishly in the dark sticky mud when he thought he had lost it? He looked around him, as though seeking an answer.

He started walking again. The place he hated most in the world was his home but his footsteps moved involuntarily towards it. When he was within a few yards of his destination, he bent down to wash his feet in a little puddle of rain water. Looking up, he got the shock of his life. A ghost, grey-white and shadowy, was leaning against the pomelo tree that stood like a shaggy sentinel outside his shack. Nibaran's heart jumped so hard it stuck in his gullet. The ghost was old and emaciated. Nibaran could count his ribs even in the deepening gloom. He held out a skeletal arm and said in a cracked, nasal voice, 'You're back, Nibaran!'

A-a-a-a ... A shriek ripped out of Nibaran's throat and he turned tail and fled. After a few seconds, he stopped running and came back. 'Doos shaala!' he muttered beneath his breath. There was no such thing as a ghost. It was his father. But he had left the old man so weak and frail this morning, he could barely raise his head. And look at him now, standing outside the shack in the wind and rain. The bastard had the tenacity of a koi fish. He simply refused to die.

'What are you doing here?' Nibaran's voice was harsh, intimidating.

Paban's chest went up and down, up and down, like a pair of bellows. 'This ... this stormy weather...' he mumbled. 'You hadn't returned ... I was worried.'

Nibaran sighed. No chance of him going this winter, he thought bitterly. His heart swelled with self-pity. God! How much longer must I carry this burden?

'Have you brought anything?'

'What thing?' Nibaran's brow was puckered in a frown.

'Rice, flour ... anything?'

'Who will give it to me? Your father? The work on the canal has stopped and the cauliflower saplings have been washed away. I am ruined.'

'You've brought nothing?' Paban's voice sounded even more nasal, like a child who is about to cry. 'Nothing at all?'

'I've brought some medicine for you.' Nibaran drew out the bottle from the folds of his dhuti. 'Doctor babu gave it. Your grandchildren told him you were sick.'

Paban wasn't interested in medicine. 'We've eaten nothing all day,' he whined. 'The fire wasn't even lit. And now you come home empty-handed.'

An image of their future flashed in Nibaran's mind. 'There is no hope for us in this village,' he said quietly. 'We'll leave tomorrow morning for the town. We'll sit on the station platform and beg.'

'Yes.' Paban was enthused in a second. 'Let's do that.'

'Can you walk that far?'

'Why not? With a little help, I—'

'If you can, well and good. If not, you must stay here and guard the house.'

Nibaran entered the shack. His children lay sleeping on the floor. Their mother lay on her back, her eyes wide open. Her limbs were as thin as jute stalks, her belly swollen with child. 'I haven't brought anything today,' he announced. The woman neither moved nor spoke. Not a muscle twitched on her gaunt, grey face. 'Is there any food?' Nibaran asked cautiously.

'No.' She turned over slowly on her side.

'Why haven't you kept something for me, haramjadi?' Nibaran shouted at the top of his voice. 'What am I to eat? There was a handful of flour in the bin yesterday. I saw it!'

'I saved it for you till the evening.' The woman's voice was flat, toneless. 'Then, I don't know when, the children stole it. They mixed it with water and ate it.'

Paban pushed his torn kantha aside and sat up at these words. Glaring at his daughter-in-law, he took his son's side. 'They ate it all,' he whined. 'I begged and begged her to give me a little. Just a little. "My fever's gone," I said, "I'm hungry." But would she listen? "And even if you don't," I said, "keep some for Nibaran. The poor boy has

been slaving all day. He'll come home tired and hungry."
But they filled their stomachs, the three of them, and left
nothing for us.'

The daughter-in-law, who lay with her face to the wall,
now turned and looked at Paban. 'Death's head!' she hissed,
rage, hate and bitterness raining out of her eyes. 'Your
tongue should fall out of your mouth for telling such a lie!
The little ones couldn't bear the pangs of hunger and ate
the flour. Have I touched a morsel to my lips? Even with
this enemy draining the life out of me?' She struck her
stomach with the palm of her hand. 'I haven't eaten for two
whole days. I've given the rest of you everything I had. And
you living corpse, didn't I hear you creeping about in the
kitchen looking for something to fill your maw? Would you
have kept any for your precious son if you found it? Why
don't you die, you carcass? Die! And give my bones a rest.'
She sank back, breathless and panting with the effort of her
outburst.

'You see!' Paban appealed to his son. 'Listen to the way
she talks to me!'

But Nibaran didn't take his father's side. Nor his wife's.
He felt like kicking them all, hard on their bellies, and
throwing them out of the shack. All of them—his father,
his children, his wife, even the malicious creature lurking
in her womb. *He* was the one who needed food. Whatever
was in the house should have been kept for him. If the
skies cleared tomorrow he would get work. But weak and
famished as he was, where would he find the strength to
dig and carry tons of earth and stone? If *he* lived they would
all live. But did anyone understand this simple logic? He
was surrounded by monsters with slavering jaws wide as
the gates of hell.

The woman was still muttering her protest against her father-in-law's words. 'Chup!' Nibaran shut her up with a roar of command. Picking up the water pot, he poured half the water down his gullet and lay down. If the rain didn't stop tomorrow they would make their way to the station. God was partial to town folk. He didn't let them starve to death. That was his last thought before he drifted into a fitful, restless sleep.

The shack had two rooms, one big, one small. The door between them was left open these days. Nibaran stirred in his sleep. He felt the rain coming in through the window of the other room. His father slept there. The old bugger must be getting wet, he thought. Let him. If he was well enough to eat, he was well enough to get up and close the window. If the rain got heavier Nibaran would simply kick the door shut.

It is a moonless night, dark and silent. The only sound that can be heard is that of the drizzle on the tin roof, as light as the patter of crows' feet. The pregnant woman and her litter sleep the sleep of the dead. But Nibaran's pinched stomach keeps him awake. The sick old man can't sleep either. Nibaran hears a muffled groan.

'What's the matter?' he asks roughly.

'Nothing.' Paban draws a deep breath. 'Hunger is hard to bear,' he mutters.

'Here!' Nibaran flings the bottle of capsules at him. 'Eat.'

Paban fumbles in the dark and finds it. Pouring its contents into his mouth, he chews them noisily with his toothless gums. Nibaran hears the sound and his stomach turns and his eyes burn with fury.

'Oof!' Paban lets out a deep sigh. 'I haven't eaten rice in weeks. I long and long for some hot rice and a whiff of tobacco. "Bou," I begged her, "give me a stick of fire to light the chillum." She didn't give—'

'Will you shut your mouth?'

The old man is silenced.

Hours pass. Nibaran is still wide awake. A sliver of light creeps in through the window, trembles on the wall for a few seconds and disappears. A faint sound is heard in the distance. *Jhum jhum jhum!* Nibaran raises his head. He hears them coming. Kaan-kaata Suren and his gang. They've eaten well. They can afford to make merry even on a night like this. Death be on the rotter's head, Nibaran thinks viciously. So many good folk die. Why does this one live? Only to torment the weak and famished ... They are coming closer now. Nibaran can hear snatches of their song:

> Sons or daughters, distant kin
> Young or old, white, black or brown
> The price placed on the spirit's head
> is hundred taka—ten times ten

Khokh-khokh-khokh! Nibaran hears his father cough. 'Baba, o Baba!' he calls softly into the darkness. 'Are you in pain?'

'No.'

'Have you really seen a ghost? Tell me the truth.'

'Yes, I've seen many.'

'Does everyone turn into a ghost? Or only some people?'

'Only some. Those who die unnatural deaths. Those who die with unfulfilled longings and desires buried in their breasts.'

Nibaran springs to his feet. So suddenly, the old man is

startled. He can't see very well in the dark, just a dim shape standing at the door. His son.

'What is it?' he asks. 'Are you going out for a piss?'

'No. If *you* die, Baba…'

'Yes,' Paban pre-empts the question, 'I'll become a ghost. Send for Surendra when that happens. I'll enter his bottle. I won't give any trouble. You'll get a hundred rupees.' He sighs. 'We must think of the children.'

Suddenly his voice changes. 'D-o-o-o-n-t!' the old man shrieks. 'Don't kill me now! O baba Nibaran, give me another two days, a little hot rice … Let me fill my belly before I die. My soul yearns for a bellyful of rice … hot rice … and a whiff of tobacco! O baba Nibaran, give me two days … hot rice … I long and long … O baba Nibaran, just two more days.'

THE CAVE OF THE SHADOW

NEAR A TALL mountain peak lay a stretch of level ground on which a tiny township had come up. Its name was Hi-la. It was a charming spot full of trees bending over with fruit, and vines and bushes starred with blossoms. Streams of sparkling water cascaded down the slopes. The houses were small and shrouded in greenery. In the distance, mountain ranges rose in waves, reaching out to touch the sky.

Xuan Zang was to spend three days in Hi-la. His weary body needed rest and what better place for it than this emerald paradise? The inhabitants, Chinese Buddhists for the most part, welcomed the erudite monk and begged him to stay with them through the monsoon months. But that was not possible. Xuan Zang had a destination and a timeframe before him. The monsoons in this part of the world were notorious for their frenzy. And once they started, they went on and on. He had to be on his way before they arrived. He needed to cross a large stretch of perilous mountain terrain which would take him at least a week. Three days, he told himself, glancing at the gathering clouds, and not a moment longer.

Setting out early on the fourth day, Xuan walked down the slope from Hi-la, keeping pace with his horse which was trotting beside him. A number of people stood on either side of the path, heads bent in obeisance. Xuan Zang's cavalcade consisted of seven men and several horses carrying provisions, pitchers full of water, bales of silk and other gifts presented to him by the various royals from whom he had received hospitality along the way. They were aware of his fame as a scholar and preceptor and had vied with each other to honour him. Several ancient savants too had acknowledged his superior wisdom and showered felicitations upon him.

Xuan Zang was a young man, not yet thirty, with a supple, power-packed body and jewel-bright eyes. His father was a follower of Confucius but Xuan had been attracted to Buddhist doctrines from his youth. His extraordinary powers of application and retention were manifest right from that time. By the age of twenty he had read every book on the subject. And he had made a discovery: there were several errors and contradictions in the Chinese translations. He realized that in order to obtain authentic and accurate knowledge he would have to examine the originals. He had heard from his teachers that the best education in Buddhist theology was to be acquired from the University of Nalanda in India. It also housed a fine library of Buddhist texts. Of course, all this was hearsay. No one had seen Nalanda with his own eyes.

Xuan made a decision. He would be the one. But the moment he announced his intention of travelling to India a storm of protest rose from his family and community. It was one thing to talk about Nalanda, even expatiate on its merits, but to think of going there was madness. It was like declaring one's intention of going to heaven. India was so far away and the journey so fraught with danger that most travellers died before reaching their destination. Between the two countries stood the highest, most forbidding mountain ranges in the world, the vast desert of Taklamakan, perilous gorges and glaciers.

But the more Xuan heard about the hazards he would have to encounter, the more enthused he became. There was an adventurous streak in him and a dogged determination that fired his resolution. Far better to die, he thought, than to live with an unquenched thirst for knowledge. Go he would, but not before making exhaustive preparations.

He began by studying Sanskrit. Without a working knowledge of the language of Brahminical India, his expedition would be pointless. He wouldn't be able to communicate with anyone. He had a natural flair for languages and an instinctive understanding of linguistic roots and principles which enabled him to pick up different dialects and tongues with ease. The next step was to get together everything he would need for the journey.

When his preparations were almost complete, a hurdle was placed in his path. The dynasty had changed in recent months and the new king issued a decree forbidding his subjects from leaving their birthplace. Movement, westward in particular, would come under severe censure. Xuan Zang sent applications requesting special permission but he was refused each time. Finally he decided he would flout the decree and leave in secret.

There was only one route to India. On either side there were watch posts at intervals with armed soldiers on guard. Xuan Zang hid himself during the day and travelled only by night. Wild animals prowled around him and it was dangerous but he went on doggedly, stopping only when his supply of water was exhausted. Since water could only be obtained from camps, where sentries kept a close watch, Xuan had to sneak in like a thief in the dead of night to fill his pitchers. At one of the camps he was caught. A shower of arrows came flying towards him and he was forced to surrender. He was dragged to the the chief vigilance officer, who asked him a few questions and then rose to his feet and folded his hands in obeisance. He had recently converted to Buddhism and had heard of the erudite monk's resolution to travel to Nalanda. Far from arresting the illustrious intruder, he actually gave him instructions on how best to negotiate the next lap of the journey. He pointed out the danger zones, telling him which outposts he needed to avoid and where he would receive favourable treatment. He gave him letters of introduction, fresh stocks of food and water, and a guide to make his journey easier.

One night, Xuan dreamt that he was standing on the tallest peak of the Sumeru mountains after a long, weary climb. On opening his eyes, between sleeping and waking, he thought he had reached Nalanda. His heart lifted. It was an omen. He would achieve his goal.

The frontiers of the Chinese empire were dotted with small principalities, the heads of which welcomed Xuan and offered him shelter. Some were not particularly hospitable but they didn't try to hamper his movements. At Turfaan, Xuan was almost forced to abandon his expedition. And this was due to an excess of love and reverence. The king and queen, Chinese Buddhists from the Mahayani sect, were as humble and devout as the lowest of their subjects and overwhelmed by the presence of the theologian in their midst. There were some Hinayanis in the kingdom, and strife and tension between the sects was not uncommon. King Kru Wen had an idea. He would organize a vast assembly of religious men and invite Xuan Zang to interpret the finer nuances of Buddhist philosophy.

The convention was a huge success. The wisdom and erudition of the young man left even the royal priests open-mouthed in wonder. Xuan felt gratified. He had never received such honour and adulation in his life. But he had no intention of resting on his laurels.

'Your majesty,' he said to his host a few days later, 'the time has come for me to bid farewell. I must be on my way.'

The king looked up in surprise. 'Already!' he exclaimed. 'But you've just come. You must stay a while longer.'

Xuan couldn't ignore the royal command. A week went by before he placed his request again.

'Impossible!' Kru Wen shook his head energetically. 'You cannot leave us so soon. Why do you want to go away? Aren't you comfortable here?'

'The question of discomfort doesn't arise, your majesty. I have never been taken care of so well in all my life. But I must go...'

'Why? Why undertake such a long, perilous journey? Stay in my kingdom as chief royal preceptor. Your presence here will cover me with fame and glory.'

'Forgive me,' Xuan replied politely but firmly. 'I left my land and kin on a mission. I have a goal before me. I cannot abandon it. I shall leave tomorrow.'

'No,' said the king just as firmly. 'I can't let you go. I've made up my mind and will not change it even if the peaks of Pamir turn upside down.'

Xuan was in a fix. Flouting the royal command openly was unthinkable. He considered sneaking away in the dead of night but rejected the idea. His spirit rebelled against any form of deceit and prevarication. But what was he to do? It was true that the king and queen had been exceedingly kind to him, and he was grateful. But he hadn't come all the way to Turfaan to spend the rest of his life in ease and luxury. His moral dilemma unnerved him and brought tears to his eyes. The king and queen wept with him but did not change their minds.

Xuan was forced to go on a hunger strike. Not a morsel of food or drop of water passed through his lips. He even gave up sleep. His host and hostess begged him to eat. They brought food for him with their own hands. But Xuan wouldn't relent. Days passed. His limbs became weak and thin, his breathing hard and laboured.

The queen was frightened. If their distinguished guest died, they would be held responsible. She pleaded with her husband to let him have his way. Yielding to her entreaties, Kru Wen gave his permission. Standing before Xuan with folded hands, he said, 'I tried to stop you from leaving us. But no more. Go where you will. But before you leave you must make a solemn oath. You will break journey here on your return and stay in my kingdom for at least three years.'

Xuan left Turfaan after a ceremonial farewell at which he was showered with gifts and honours. The king gave him letters of introduction to the heads of state he would meet en route, horses laden with water and provisions and a small band of men to guide him on his way.

Xuan made steady progress, stopping only for short intervals to rest and recuperate. Traversing the vast desert of Taklamakan, he made his way across the icy slopes of Tsien San, a perilous, blizzard-ridden mountain terrain that led to Tashkent. Beyond Tashkent lay the Bamiyan kingdom, a historic site dotted with stupas and monasteries.

It also contained two gigantic statues of the Buddha, the likes of which couldn't be found anywhere in the world. The people of Bamiyan were true Buddhists—pure of heart and clean living. Their king was a good man too. He welcomed Xuan Zang and accorded him the highest hospitality in the most luxurious wing of his palace.

Leaving Bamiyan behind, Xuan entered the kingdom of Kapila. And now he was assailed by a strange sensation. He felt he had reached his goal, the holy land he had dreamed of for so many years. Nalanda was a long way off but here in Kapila, even the voices of the common folk held Sanskrit intonations that fell sweetly into his ears. The names were different too and there were very few Chinese people.

Kapilavastu, once ruled by the great emperor Kanishka, had been visited by Gautam Buddha himself. There were relics everywhere. Some monasteries had preserved footprints, others, bits of bone and hair. Xuan knew that most of these were fake. Figments of the imagination, they represented a basic human need to cling to a glorious past no one had seen but held proudly in their hearts. At one monastery he was told that the Buddha had flown down there straight from the sky. Xuan didn't believe in miracles but he respected peoples' beliefs and sentiments and gave everyone a patient hearing. Strains of '*Buddham sharanam gachchhami/ dharmam sharanam gachchhami/ sangham sharanam gachchhami*' from the sanghams or temples of Kapila floated into his ears. He smiled. Foreign sounds but so beautiful! Even his name sounded foreign in the new tongue. Unable to articulate Xuan Zang correctly, people were calling him Huien Tsang. He didn't mind. He accepted his new name and responded to it.

Huien walked down the slope from Hi-la and came to the edge of a pretty little garden from which two paths led in opposite directions. The narrower one went further down into a deep forest, the other wound up towards the mountain range. This was the one Huien would take. He would have to cross the tallest peak in order to reach the other side. It would take him at least a week.

Huien entered the garden, where a group of men had assembled to bid him farewell. As in Hi-la, there was a clamour of voices begging him to stay a little longer. Huien folded his hands and promised to fulfil their wishes but only on the journey back.

'O venerable ascetic!' an ancient voice quavered. 'I have a question, an anxiety I would like to share with you if you allow me.'

Huien turned to the speaker and nodded encouragingly.

'We have been Buddhists for four generations now,' the old man said, 'and followed all the tenets faithfully. Except in one thing. Our climate, as you can see, is very cold and we can keep warm only by eating meat. Our children cannot live without it. We know that ahimsa is the main pillar on which our holy faith rests. Yet we cannot give up killing and eating animals. Does that mean we are guilty of committing a deadly sin generation after generation?'

'I have had this question put to me before,' Huien answered gravely, 'but to tell you the truth, I have no ready answer. I can only repeat what the great Buddha himself said on the subject. The matter was debated once in his lifetime, in Vaishali. A powerful chieftain had converted to Buddhism but hadn't given up his profession, which was hunting animals and selling meat. Some other Buddhists were his customers and ate meat regularly. This led to an altercation with another group, who were strict vegetarians. Both groups came to the Buddha for guidance. As you know, our All Merciful Sakyamuni didn't believe in force on anyone or in anything. He called all his followers together and this is the advice he gave: *Taking a life is wrong. Many of us disapprove of it but stopping others from doing so lies outside our power. What we don't see we don't know. But if we know or even suspect that it is being done for our hospitality and entertainment, it is our duty to follow the path of quiet rejection. Not words, not blows. Only silent non-cooperation.* So you see, he didn't ban the eating of meat altogether...'

'Is it permissible then,' said a voice in the crowd, 'to buy meat from those we know to be hunters if we have not seen them in the act of killing?'

Huien shook his head in the negative.

'Have you ever eaten meat, Acharya?'

'No. I have been vegetarian from childhood. Even in the harshest of winters I haven't needed meat to keep me warm.'

'Acharya,' a young man said, changing the subject, 'since you insist on leaving us, we pray for your safe journey. But before you go please give us some parting advice on how to live our lives and make them better.'

'What advice can I give beyond this that every man must live according to his innermost perceptions and understanding of the world? If he follows his conscience he cannot go wrong. If you ignite your soul as you would a lamp, its light will guide you. You will see your path clearly before you. But no more. I must be on my way.' Straddling his horse, Huien pointed in the direction of the mountain range. 'I shall take that route,' he said, 'but where does the other go? The one that is winding down?'

The men looked at each other, perplexed. No one had the answer.

Then an old man spoke. 'No one uses it, Acharya,' he said. 'It is a narrow track that winds through miles of impenetrable forest. At the end lies a ferocious river, and beyond that is the cave of the shadow.'

'Cave of the shadow!' Huien exclaimed. 'What's that?'

'Hundreds of years ago, Nagaraj Gopala and our great Sakyamuni met in that cave. They held a long debate that lasted several days. In the end the king conceded defeat. He acknowledged the Buddha's superior wisdom and touched his feet in reverence. Pleased with his humility, the latter gifted him with his shadow. It can still be seen on one wall of the cave.'

'What did you say?' Huien cried out, startled. 'The Buddha gifted his shadow to Nagaraj Gopala! And it can still be seen!'

'Yes, Acharya,' another old man took up the tale. 'It is still there. It is from the shadow that the cave gets its name.'

Huien was silent. His logic dismissed the story. Lord Buddha had embraced nirvana twelve centuries ago. How could his shadow remain on the earth? Besides, a shadow merely followed a form, be it human, animal or plant. It cannot be gifted away. Yet the story intrigued him. Was it pure fantasy? Or was there a shred of truth in it? He had to find out.

'Is there anyone here who has seen the shadow?' he asked. Two men, both octogenarians, raised their hands.

'You claim to have seen the shadow with your own eyes? Tell me the truth...' Huien stopped suddenly, ashamed of what he had just said. These were poor, honest mountain folk. They never lied. They didn't need to. The reasons for which city people dissembled and prevaricated simply did not exist here. He shouldn't have doubted them. Leaping off his horse, he walked towards the two old men and asked them for an account of their experience. They told him that as boys of ten or twelve, they had accompanied their fathers to the cave and seen the shadow. But they were the last to do so. An earthquake had followed soon after, devastating the area. The path to the cave was blocked by huge boulders and made inaccessible. It was surrounded by dense forest and the slender stream beside which they had grazed their animals in childhood had turned into a dangerous, current-filled river. No one went there now.

Huien Tsang made a silent vow. He would visit the cave and find out the truth for himself. There were many statues of the Buddha in different parts of the world but they weren't authentic representations. No image dating from his lifetime was extant so no one knew what he had actually looked like. It naturally followed that the Bamiyan and other sculptors had relied on their imaginations to create his likeness. The shadow, if such a thing existed, would be an exact replica of the Buddha. Huien's heart leapt up in excitement. There was no question of leaving without checking out the cave and seeing the shadow. And in the event of not seeing it, assuring himself that what he had heard was only an interesting story. It would take a lot of time and, from what he had heard, he would have to navigate dangerous waters. But he would do it.

The moment Huien expressed his intention, a chorus of dissenting voices rose from the crowd. It was too risky, they pointed out. The track became hair-thin as it penetrated the forest so there was no question of going all the way on horseback. Indeed, some parts would be difficult to negotiate even on foot. Danger lurked at every step. Apart from predatory animals like black bears and tigers, the jungle was infested with robbers. Why, only the other day, two hunters strayed deeper into the forest than usual and didn't return. One body had floated down the river in a shocking state of mutilation and the other had disappeared. It would be inadvisable for their distinguished visitor even to contemplate undertaking such a journey. He would never reach the cave. And even if by some miracle he did, the rains would start before his return and the other route, across the mountains, would become inaccessible. He would suffer an inordinate delay in reaching Nalanda.

Huien listened to everyone patiently. But the faint smile on his lips told them that he was not going to change his mind. He had been set upon by dacoits several times during his travels and once been taken prisoner by the king's soldiers. He had crossed the perilous desert of Taklamakan alone. He had walked through terrible blizzards that raged for days at a stretch. He had had two close shaves with death and once he had lost all his belongings and been forced to sleep on a slab of ice. What was a stretch of forest compared to all that? He would go to the cave, no matter what lay in wait for him along the way.

The porters carrying his luggage refused to accompany him. They had been told that they would take the route across the mountains and reach the other side before the rains came. If the worthy monk wanted to make a detour and delay the journey, they should be set free. Huien wasn't surprised. He had faced this situation several times on his journey. His royal hosts would send porters to carry and guard the valuables they had gifted him but the latter got restless as soon as they crossed their country's border. This, Huien realized, was human tendency. Most people clung to the security of the place they knew intimately, the security of home and family. Very few felt the urge to push frontiers and walk out into the vast unknown. It was these few who were continually changing the known world.

Huien didn't try to make the porters change their minds. 'Those of you who wish to go back to Hi-la are welcome to do so and those who wish to embark on the journey across the mountains, straightaway, may do that. I shall join you later. Another thing, please share the bales of silk and other gifts that your king has given me amongst yourselves. I have no need of them. But do it peacefully. No fighting and quarrelling.'

Without waiting for an answer, Huien turned his horse around and spurred him in the direction of the downward path.

On and on it meandered, alongside a river which, though flowing swiftly, was shallow enough to reveal the many-coloured pebbles strewn across its bed. Since it was the height of summer, the river had assumed the look of a slender stream, but with the onset of the monsoon, it would change its contours, transforming itself from a scrawny child to a grown woman, voluptuous, with a dangerous glint in her eyes. Huien had seen such transformations before and knew what they were like. He once had to wait on the bank of a river in spate for days, not daring to plunge in.

Steering his horse carefully down the narrow track, he looked around with curious eyes. Trees, bushes, vines and ferns grew thick and lush, broken by walls of mountain. It was obvious that the path hadn't felt a human footstep for some years now. Huge uprooted trees blocked it in places, heaps of boulders in others. Birds called out from the branches above his head but Huien knew they would soon fall silent. The monsoon would be here in a few days and winter would follow. The rain would turn to hail and sleet overnight and the birds and animals would flee downward to warmer climes. All one would see, for miles around, was a glittering landscape of ice and snow. All one would hear was the whistle of the wind and the howl of the blizzard.

Suddenly Huien heard a splash. And then another. He turned sharply and saw a lad of nine or ten running across the river towards him. Huien was surprised. He jumped off his horse and waited.

'Why are you here, child?' he asked as soon as the boy drew near. 'Do you bring a message for me?'

The boy didn't answer. He moved closer to Huien and looked up at him with bashful eyes. Huien was touched. The boy had crept up so close, his tender body was grazing Huien's hard, strapping one, almost as though he was seeking protection. Putting out his hand, Huien stroked the small head.

'What is your name?' he asked.

'Gangi.'

Gangi. The word fell like music in Huien's ears. It had a Sanskrit sound. It could be a tribal version of a name common in Brahminical India: Ganga. The mighty river Ganga was the cradle of the ancient Hindu civilization. Huien had read about it in many a Buddhist tract. The holy city of Kashi stood on one bank and a few miles further lay Sarnath. Sarnath, the great pilgrimage spot sacred to Buddhists! Huien would go there. He would see the Bodhi tree with his own eyes. It was a long way off. There were mountains to cross and dangerous terrain to get through. It would take him over a year. Yet the sound of the boy's name made his heart leap with anticipation. He felt as though he was close to his goal. Very close.

'What do you want from me, my child?' Huien ruffled the dusty hair.

'I want to go with you.'

'Why?'

'I want to go,' the boy repeated. He didn't have a reason. He simply wanted to be with Huien.

Huien's lips curved in a smile. Only a few hours ago a group of adults had begged him to abandon the venture. They had pointed out the dangers but not one of them had offered to accompany him. But this boy, a mere child, had shown that courage. In him Huien recognized a kindred spirit. They were two of a kind—the kind that felt the urge to push frontiers and explore the beyond.

'Do you know where I am going, Gangi?' he asked. He wouldn't snatch the dream from the innocent eyes. He wouldn't turn the boy away. But he had to be told the truth.

'I know.' Gangi swayed his head. 'To the cave of the shadow.'

'It is an arduous trek. There is peril at every step.'

'What is peril?'

'Wait till you're older. Not only will you recognize peril, you'll also know how to deal with it. You're too young now. I'll take you with me but on one condition. You'll have to obey me and do everything I tell you. Do I have your promise?'

Gangi swayed his head happily and Huien lifted him onto his horse.

The path was rugged and Gangi was heavy for his age. The horse's pace slowed down. Huien jumped off and started to walk. Minutes later, Gangi joined him. It was a beautiful morning. Above their heads, song birds trilled sweetly from green branches. The path, though narrow, was not inaccessible except in places where piles of rock had tumbled down the mountain slope. Huien and Gangi were forced to make detours by crossing the stream and crossing back. Children tend to run this way and that and Gangi was no exception. Leaving Huien's side from time to time, he leapt into the water and splashed about. The river bed was strewn with loose stones covered with slippery moss. Afraid that the boy would fall and hurt his head, Huien kept calling out to him. Gangi obeyed but only for a while before he was off again, chasing a piece of driftwood, picking blooms from a water lily clump or trying to catch a swarm of minnows with his hands. Huien was forced to pull him out several times. It wasn't just the stones he was afraid of. There were currents that could suck the child in and throw him into deep pools of icy, stagnant water. There was no way Huien could save him then.

But after warning Gangi several times to keep away from the river, Huien waded into it himself and splashed about. Although he was an adult and a revered erudite monk, Huien was a boy at heart. The two chased and pushed each other into the cool, crystal-clear water and laughed with pure joy. The sky, the trees and mountains hadn't seen such innocent faces nor heard such sweet human voices in years. They strained their ears to catch the peals of joyous laughter; they looked on with glowing eyes at the antics of the strange pair, so far apart in years yet so wonderfully in sync at heart. Huien had never laughed so spontaneously nor played with a child like this. He felt a weight slipping off his chest; a load of uneasiness, doubt and anxiety. He realized that knowledge and scholarship created pressures of their own which could only be dispelled by turning oneself into a child. That was when the mind became free, the heart felt pure and clear.

But the joy was short-lived. Suddenly Huien's eyes beheld a sight that made his blood curdle. Up ahead, on a huge hump of rock that rose like a giant turtle out of the water, stood a group of men. They wore loose black robes and had red bands tied across their foreheads. Swords dangled from their waists. Huien became himself in an instant. Pushing Gangi behind him, he stood quietly, waiting for them to make the first move. The expressions on the faces of the men, who were now running rapidly down the rock, told him that they were brigands—fierce, stone-hearted, devoid of conscience. Such men had no qualms about torturing children, even mutilating them in front of their parents, to gain information.

'Gangi,' Huien whispered urgently, 'listen carefully to what I say and obey me. Turn back and run as fast as you can. Don't stop till you reach home. And don't breathe a word about what you've seen to anyone. Not even to your parents. It is our secret and will rest with us. I will come back for you, believe me. I'll come back. Now run … run.'

Gangi obeyed. In a few seconds he became a speck in the distance and was swallowed up by the trees. Huien stood waiting. The brigands were five in number. Their leader was easily recognizable. His figure was larger and more menacing than the others, his face was as hard as granite. 'Eyi!' he shouted in a grating voice. 'Who are you?'

'I am a traveller,' Huien answered calmly.

'What is a traveller doing in this part of the world? This track leads nowhere.'

'I am making my way to Nagaraj Gopala's cave of the shadow.'

'Hmph!' The dacoit's brow furrowed. 'I've heard of this cave. But terrible dangers lie along the path, don't you know that?'

'I do,' Huien replied. 'I have been told that that the jungles here swarm with wild animals and poisonous vipers. But you are human beings like me. I perceive no threat from you.'

'You don't!' The man laughed out loud. 'Fool! You have read many books, I can tell that from the way you speak. But you are ignorant of one basic fact. The greatest danger to man comes from other men.'

Huien smiled. 'All I have with me now is a water pot and a basket with some dried fruit and rice cakes in it. You are welcome to take them. I have nothing else to lose.'

'You have a life to lose. We could kill you.'

'But why would you kill me when I've given you all that I have? You are not cannibals, you won't eat my flesh. Why waste it then? Please explain.'

'You're slick with your tongue, I see. But why should I bother to explain anything? It is much easier for me to slit your throat.'

'Please do so if that gives you satisfaction.'

'No one goes to that cave,' one of the brigands said thoughtfully. 'Why should they? There's nothing there. Unless … unless the man has heard of hidden treasure.'

'Yes, that's exactly what I've heard. Of course, my notion of treasure may differ from yours. I've heard that Lord Buddha's shadow can be seen on one wall of the cave. If I am able to catch a glimpse of the shadow I will feel more enriched than if I were handed the keys to an emperor's treasury.'

'Buddha's shadow!' The leader frowned. 'But he died long ago, didn't he?'

'He attained nirvana twelve centuries ago.'

'Nirvana! Centuries! We don't understand your bookish tongue. Just tell us in plain words, how many years?'

'Your father, grandfather, great-grandfather ... go back fifty generations. That's how long.'

'Fifty generations! Buddha died so long ago and you say his shadow can still be seen! Are you mad or drunk?' He roared with laughter. The others joined him. Sobering down, he observed solemnly, 'A man has only one shadow and it follows his physical form. Look, this is me standing here and that's my shadow. As I move away,' he accompanied his words with a sideways leap, 'my shadow moves with me. Can I make it stick in one place?'

'No,' Huien answered equally solemnly, 'you can't. For the simple reason that you are not Gautam Buddha. We are ordinary men. We cannot disrupt the laws of nature. But there are some among us who can. They have superhuman powers. That is why we call them saints.'

'O re!' the leader yelled at the others. His eyes, inflamed with power, rolled menacingly. 'This man is talking nonsense. Let's bind him and take him to the cave. We'll see what he does there.'

Two of the men sprang forward, tied Huien's hands behind his back, and started dragging him down the path that led to the cave.

'Nalanda! Nalanda! Nalanda!' Huien muttered all the way. That was his mantra. It helped him keep calm. He had delayed his journey in order to see the shadow, the dacoits would delay him further. But Nalanda was his goal. He would reach it come what may. And now that he thought about it, the situation had a positive side. It's all for the best, he thought. No fear of losing my way or being attacked by wild animals. The brigands will take me to the cave alive and well.

The jungle grew deeper and denser as they made their way. The track became a hairline and mounds of rubble could be seen between the trees. These, Huien realized, were the remains of the houses that had fallen during the earthquake. There was no sign of human habitation. The forest had claimed its own.

The stream widened and became a cataract falling sharply downward. A giant wall of mountains rose on one side. On the other was an impenetrable bank of trees and thorny bushes. Heaps of rock lay on the track, obstructing their path. The only way forward was to swing on a rope from branch to branch of the vast trees at the edges. Huien's hands were untied and he followed the others, his sturdy body swaying as they ventured down the perilous slopes.

It was late afternoon when the party reached its destination. The cave, a deep hole in the middle of a mountain slope, had a wide mouth and markings on the roof which, though indistinct, bore the mark of a human hand. Inside, it was spacious enough to accommodate thirty to forty people. A shiver ran down Huien's spine. Gautam Buddha had been here. Perhaps he had stood where Huien was standing now. His limbs trembled in anticipation mingled with doubt. Would he see the shadow or wouldn't he?

While the brigands were running round the cave,

inspecting every nook and corner for signs of hidden treasure, Huien walked straight to the end. The two elders of Hi-la had told him that fifty paces from the mouth of the cave stood a high wall of rock. When he reached it, Huien had to turn his eyes eastward. The shadow would be there. Huien obeyed their instructions to the letter. But where was the shadow?

A thump on his shoulder made Huien jerk his head back. The dacoit leader had crept up behind him. He asked Huien in a mocking voice, 'Where's your shadow, learned monk? Show it to us or face the consequences.'

'What consequences?'

'We'll turn *you* into a shadow, what else?' The man's voice rumbled like a menacing cloud. 'Stop beating about the bush and tell us truthfully why you're here. What are you after?'

'I've come to see the shadow,' Huien answered with a calm he was far from feeling. 'There's nothing else for me here.'

'Liar!' The hand closed over Huien's shoulder in a fierce grip. 'You've read many books and spout a lot of theology. But don't you have any common sense? Dead men leave no shadows. Don't you know that?'

'I heard two ancients say that they've seen the shadow with their own eyes. But whether at dawn or dusk I did not ask.'

'You're confusing the issue. If there *is* a shadow, it should be present at all times. Can it come and go on a whim?'

'I'm no judge of that. I shall sit here until dawn.'

'Then we will sit here too.' Turning to the others, he asked, 'What do you say?'

The men nodded in agreement. 'I spent a night in this cave some years ago,' one of them muttered, 'but I didn't see any shadow.'

Huien dropped to the floor of the cave. Facing the wall, he closed his eyes and started reciting shlokas from the *Srimala Devi Simha Naad*.

Dusk descends suddenly in the mountains. The light dimmed as the sun dropped behind a tall peak. The robbers sat in a circle close to their captive and took out their food and drink. Huien felt neither hunger nor thirst.

A few minutes later some heavy footfalls were heard. One of the men rose and peeped outside. Running back, he whispered urgently, 'There are some bears at the mouth of the cave. This is probably their den. What if they come inside and attack us?'

'Keep a pile of stones ready, each of you,' the leader whispered. 'Throw them as soon as they come near. Target their noses. They are most vulnerable when hit on the nose and will flee. We are five of us, we have nothing to fear.'

Minutes later a battle ensued, a battle between man and beast the like of which had never been seen before. The air was rent with curses, shrieks of agony and angry growls. Finally the bears were forced to retreat. The entire incident took place before Huien but he neither spoke nor moved.

Dawn broke, a bright, beautiful dawn. Slowly the cave filled with light. But where was the shadow? Huien's eyes remained shut and his lips continued to murmur shlokas.

'Hey! You monk!' The brigand leader gave him a shove. 'Where's your shadow? We may be sinners and therefore deprived of the holy sight. What about you?'

'Perhaps I too have committed some sin unknowingly. That is why I am deprived...'

'What will you do now?'

'I'll wait for it to appear. I'll stay here as long as it takes.'

'You've wasted our time. You deserve to be punished.'

'By all means. Do with me what you wish.'

'Mad!' the leader muttered beneath his breath. 'Stark, raving mad!'

Dropping to the floor, he settled down to breakfast with the others. Chewing on a dried deer leg, he pointed to Huien and observed thoughtfully, 'That man there … just think. He's been sitting in exactly the same position since yesterday. He hasn't moved an inch or drunk a drop of water. What is this? Just a sham? Or is there more to it? Is he human or is he…'

'Shall I prick him with my sword and find out?' one of the men offered.

'No.' The leader's eyes were grave. 'Leave him alone.'

'Look! Look!' another exclaimed. 'It's turning dark. It was so bright a minute ago!'

This was a common phenomenon in the mountains just before the monsoon. The sky would be flooded with light one moment and dark with clouds the next. The rain came pelting down. The wind whistled through the trees and thunder resounded from the surrounding hills. There was no question of leaving the cave just yet. Only a mad man would think of venturing out.

'This rain won't last long,' the leader said. 'We'll wait a while and then make our way back. Pilgrims try to scale the peaks during this season. We'll fall on some and rob them.'

'There's another cave like this on the mountain track,' one of the men suggested. 'We could hide in it and seize the opportunity when it comes and—'

'Do you remember the old man we captured last year?'

another interrupted. 'How he wept and pleaded? How he clutched our feet and begged us to spare his life? Arre baba, you're a doddering ancient, I said, with one foot in the grave! How much longer will you cling to life?'

The rain stopped. As suddenly as it had come. And light seeped into the cave from crevices of clouds. It was no ordinary light. It was a divine radiance...

The robbers picked up their belongings and prepared to depart.

Suddenly the leader gave a shout. 'Open your eyes, monk! Open your eyes! Look! Look!'

Huien's hands were folded and his lips were still moving in prayer. Opening his eyes slowly, he turned them to the east. A beam of light had appeared like a pathway between the clouds and in its centre was a rising peak that threw its shadow on the wall. Before Huien's amazed eyes, it took form, a human form. Believer or unbeliever, no one could deny the vision or pretend not to recognize it. It was a silhouette of Lord Buddha sitting in the lotus pose, rapt in meditation.

Around the shadow was dazzling sunshine, yellow as molten gold. Gradually, the light dimmed and the vision faded. But Huien's eyes continued to gaze on the wall as though he still saw it. Strangely enough, the brigand chief was equally affected. A hushed silence descended on the cave. It was broken by a rough, unruly voice.

'What's so wonderful about this shadow?' The youngest member of the gang dismissed the vision disdainfully. 'It is only the play of sun and cloud. It happens all the time. You can't call this a miracle.'

'Fool!'

The imprecation burst into Huien's eardrums like a clap

of thunder. He looked up, startled. The brigand chief's eyes, flaming with rage, were turned on the hapless youngster.

'The great Lord Buddha's form appeared in the play of sun and cloud!' he shouted. 'This in itself is a miracle. Don't you have the sense to see that? Will your shadow or mine appear anywhere after we are dead?'

Huien rose and touched the man's arm. 'I owe you a deep debt of gratitude,' he said. 'My eyes were closed in meaningless meditation. It was you who opened them, you who showed me the shadow.'

The others were getting restless. 'Come, chief,' one of them said. 'Let's go. We've seen the shadow. There's nothing more for us here.'

'Yes ... yes,' the brigand chief hesitated. 'We'll go. But ... but something is happening to me ... I feel a strange churning within me. I ... I...'

'Do you feel unwell? Are you in pain?'

'I don't know ... I feel as though a cascade of water is falling into my heart, cool and clear. Fresh breezes are blowing over me. Temple bells are ringing in my ears. No ... this isn't pain, it's something else. My limbs are growing heavy. My eyes are closing in sleep. Deep, restful sleep. I've never felt like this before. What is happening to me, monk? Can you tell me?'

'Yes,' Huien answered. 'What you feel is peace. Pure, unalloyed peace is flooding your heart, soul and body. You have lived a life filled with violence and strife. You have robbed and killed. You've tasted power and acquired wealth. But there is one thing you've never known: the peace and tranquillity that come from renunciation. The sighting of the holy shadow has touched your soul. But the effect might be transitory. It will vanish the moment you go back to your old ways.'

'It's getting late. Come, chief,' several voices spoke in unison. They held a trace of impatience.

The leader turned to his men and said quietly, 'You go. I shall keep the monk company.' Turning to Huien, he cried out in a strange, wondering voice, 'I can't let go of this feeling. It's … it's exquisite. What shall I do? Tell me, monk. What shall I do?'

'How can I tell you?'

'Then let me stay with you. I'll go wherever you take me.'

'I'm going far, very far. Can you come all the way with me?'

'I'll try. I'll go as far as I can. But you must help me. Give me a mantra. Oh, monk, teach me to live as you do.' Dropping to his knees, he clutched Huien's feet.

THE NIGHT OF THE ANGELS

Lal Mian

The power of Lal Mian's personality and the force in his arm were proverbial in the village. Proven beyond a doubt by the tremendous thwack on the ear he had given Hasem, years ago, deafening him and earning the boy the sobriquet 'One-eared Hasem'. Hasem worked in a tea stall that stood at the end of the Line and his odd behaviour created quite a bit of confusion in the minds of customers who didn't know his case. They wondered why the young man ignored their orders when he stood to their right and jumped to serve them when he faced the other way.

Lal Mian was also the first to use nylon instead of cotton thread for his fishing line. One morning, the villagers saw him sitting on the bank of Boro Shariker Pukur with a shimmering blue thread dangling from the end of his rod. This pond, though owned jointly by twelve co-parceners, was open to the villagers. Anyone could fish in it with lines. Only the owners were allowed to cast nets, that too for wedding feasts and other ceremonial occasions. The pond was huge, choked with lotus and teeming with fish.

One afternoon, Lal Mian felt a sudden tug in his line and began to turn the wheel as fast as he could. But the creature at the other end flapped and struggled so violently that the water churned and foamed as though it bore deadly currents. O re baap re, thought Lal Mian, is this a fish or a water demon? But if the creature was strong, so was Lal Mian. He had never lost a battle in his life and, with Gazi's blessings on his head, he wouldn't lose one now. He gave the line a tremendous pull and, in the process, tumbled into the water.

But Lal Mian wasn't one to admit defeat. A battle ensued, the like of which had never been seen before. As the opponents thrashed about and wrestled in the water, Lal Mian got entangled in his own thread. He didn't know what to do. He couldn't let go of the line and swim to the bank, for the powerful creature was pulling with all its might. The battle raged for over an hour. But Lal Mian won in the end. He caught the fish with his bare hands and brought it out of the water, clasped to his chest. The people standing on the bank looked on, open-mouthed. They had never seen anything like this in all their lives.

It was a king-sized katla, weighing eight kilos, with huge eyes popping out of a head as big and black as a rice pot. The incident set a record in the history of fishing exploits which hadn't been touched since. 'Arre! Ja, ja!' the village elders exclaimed contemptuously whenever one was reported. 'No one can break Lal Mian's *reckott*. We saw it with our own eyes. What do you youngsters know?'

However, both these achievements were highlights of Lal Mian's youth, when his body was as tough as beaten steel. Now, in the autumn of his life, his power lay in his brain. Woe upon you if you got into a fracas with Lal Mian. He would take you to court—he moved the courts as easily as he plucked mangoes from his favourite tree—and hound you out of your land. Why land? Even out of your home and hearth.

That night, Lal Mian was walking home, a dandified figure in a silk lungi, white mulmul shirt and rubber pumps on his feet. He held a three-cell torch in his hand which he flashed arrogantly this way and that. It had rained a while ago and the path was covered with mud and slush. But Lal Mian walked with long, confident strides. Stumbling and slipping were for lesser mortals. Lal Mian was a tiger. What could a little mud do to him?

The night was dark and still and the villagers fast asleep. As he walked past his guava grove he heard a cry—a baby's cry. Wrinkling his nose in distaste, he walked on.

Omnipresent Haseena

Rehman saheb worked in the settlement office in Kolkata and often brought friends home. He would stop at Adhbele on the way and pick up a large fish or a joint of beef from the bazaar. The evening would be spent in eating, drinking, music and merry-making. Rehman saheb's father had been a very religious man who prayed five times a day, gave alms to the poor and frowned upon earthly pleasures. Thirty-five-year-old Rehman saheb had to curb his natural inclinations when the old man was alive. But by Allah's grace his *intekaal* had come six months ago, leaving Rehman saheb free to enjoy life with the money that had been left to him. Though the way he was going, the villagers said, he would blow up his inheritance in a few months.

That evening, Rehman saheb brought four guests with him. His wife Najma was pregnant. His mother was old and feeble. Who would do the cooking? 'Call Haseena,' he told the little girl who washed the pots and pans. 'Tell her I want her.'

Haseena came running. She was an amazing woman, one of the wonders of Allah's creation. At thirty-one she looked seventeen. Her skin was dark but glowed like moonlight. Her limbs were strong and supple and she had the agility of a young doe. No one had ever seen her walk. She was running all the time. As for her talents, you couldn't count them on your fingers. She was a wonderful cook and could produce lip-licking dishes in the twinkling of an eye. If you needed water, she would run to the pond twenty times with heavy brass pitchers. Ask her to clean the house and she would sweep and swab and dust and wipe until the doors, windows, walls and floors sparkled. And all this with a smile on her lips. Haseena was a rich man's poor daughter, and because of this she was at everyone's beck and call. Whenever and wherever labour was required, Haseena was sent for. For she could do with two hands the work of seventeen.

That evening, as Rehman saheb sat with his guests in the room overlooking the pond, he called out to Haseena every five minutes. Now he wanted water, now more kebabs, now a matchbox. Haseena was cooking in the kitchen downstairs but sprang to do his bidding each time. Sprinting up and down the stairs, she served the guests, ran to the pond for water several times and even took time off to pound betel for Rehman saheb's old mother, who loved her paan but had no teeth to chew it with. Haseena was everywhere—in the kitchen, by the pond, in Rehman saheb's room—at the same time. And through all this the smile never left her lips.

'Here, Rehman bhai.' She thrust a hand from behind the door. 'You wanted a matchbox.'

'Why don't you come in?' Rehman saheb invited her. 'There's no need to be so shy.' Rising, he took her hand and pulled her into the room. 'She is a distant cousin of mine,' he introduced her to his guests. 'And also the daughter of a sworn enemy. I've been fighting a court case with her father for years. He is a shrewd and wily fellow but the girl is a gem. Can you guess her age?'

Everyone played this game with Haseena. A woman in her thirties would have crows' feet around her eyes and a few lines above her brow. But Haseena's face was as smooth as ivory and her expression as innocent as a child's. Her dusky form was swathed in a black sari. She was as starkly beautiful as a moonless night.

'Eighteen,' one of the guests replied.

'Seventeen,' said another.

'No no, she couldn't be that old,' said a third. 'She must be fifteen, sixteen at the most.'

Rehman saheb burst out laughing. 'Her eldest son is about fifteen. Isn't that right, Haseena? And do you know how many children she has birthed? Three. Or is it four? Eh, Haseena?'

'Three.' Haseena's eyes were on her hands.

The guests looked on in wonder.

'Mijanur!' Rehman saheb addressed one of them. 'You are neither married nor betrothed. Why don't you take this woman? Ki re, Haseena! Will you sit in a nikah with this friend of mine?'

Haseena swayed her head as far as it would go.

'You see how innocent she is?' Rehman saheb turned to his friends. 'She is just like a child. And very keen on finding a husband. A lot of men are interested in marrying her. But she has one condition. And everyone backs off when they hear it.'

Dusk in the Line

The village, though only seventy miles away from Kolkata, didn't have electricity and consequently no railway connection. But a mile-and-a-half away there was a main road along which a number of buses plied. The villagers, for some inexplicable reason, called it 'the Line'. It had a bus stop and a few shops.

The Line was popular with the men and they tended to flock there in the evenings after work. One could have a cup of tea and exchange gossip and news with friends, or pick up useful information such as the difference in the price of jute, potatoes and fish between Bashirhaat Market and Adhbele Bazaar. The most brightly lit and best-stocked shop belonged to Biren Saha. You could get anything you wanted, from needles to footballs. On the counter facing the road was a row of glass jars containing biscuits and sweets. Each time a bus came to a halt, Biren Saha looked up to see who had got off and what they had brought with them.

Three children stood at the entrance to the shop. The eldest was a boy of thirteen and the youngest a little girl of about seven. All three wore torn drawers and were naked from the waist up. Their mouths drooled and they licked the sweets and toffees in the jars with their eyes.

'Eyi!' Biren Saha rushed at them. 'What are you doing here? Shoo! Scoot!'

But the three stood where they were, still as statues. The girl had snot running down her upper lip and the younger boy scratched noisily at a scaly patch on his thigh. The eldest looked this way and that with restless eyes. His face was thin and dark but his expression was bright and intelligent. His name was Javed. Biren Saha made another rush at them but they didn't move an inch.

Customers edged past them as they entered and exited the shop, their noses crinkled in disgust. The sight infuriated Biren Saha. What a nuisance this was. Which shopkeeper liked to have three famished children staring greedily at his wares? Each time he got a break from serving his customers, he tried to drive them away. Finally, admitting defeat, he took out three toffees and said, 'Here. Take these and go.'

But the children didn't hold out their palms. They glanced at one another and didn't move. And then ... and then a powerful weapon was put into Biren Saha's hands, guaranteed to make them flee. A bus coming from Bashirhaat stopped outside his shop. Descending from it was Lal Mian.

'Oyi je!' Biren pointed a finger. 'There's Lal Mian!'

The statues came to life. They turned and ran like rabbits. Within seconds they had scattered in three different directions and were swallowed up by the gathering dusk.

Goni Chowdhury's Secret Sorrow

Those who till the soil have few ups and downs in their lives. Some years yield poor harvests and stomachs groan with hunger. Others are even worse and people learn to cope with starvation. Once in a while, the price of jute might go up and a few lucky ones manage to take their produce to the market in time, and make a little money. That is when thatches are repaired and children get two square meals a day.

But such was not the case with Goni Khan Chowdhury.

He and his brother Rahim had tilled their separate fields until one day a bright idea struck the former. He had made a small pile of money after selling his jute and instead of frittering it away, he decided to attend the water toll auction and bid for a *bherhi*. Bherhis or fishing dams were yielding gold these days. As a result, Goni Khan became the proud owner of a two-storeyed house with a radio and a gun proudly displayed in his drawing room. He wore a watch on his wrist and lit his cigarettes with a lighter. His five sons were doing well. Two of them supervised the farming and two the running of the bherhi. The youngest one went to school.

Goni was nursing a new ambition these days. He would bid for a ferry service at the next auction and invest in a fleet of boats. Though elderly, Goni Chowdhury was strong and healthy. Both his wives had died before their time and left him desolate. But he wasn't thinking of a third marriage. His sons had taken a load of responsibility off his shoulders and his daughters-in-law looked after him well enough. He had plenty of money, some of which he used in philanthropic work. The village mosque was so old and dilapidated it was falling about the mullah's ears. Goni Chowdhury donated money for its repairs. The madrasa had closed down and the teachers hadn't been paid for months. Goni Chowdhury settled their dues and got it running again. At his insistence, a tube well was dug outside the tomb of the Pir of Tentulgacchhi so that everyone who visited the shrine got clean water to drink. And at the function held after the death of the poet Kazi, he was invited to take the chair as president. Yet no one could say that his newly acquired wealth had gone to his head. No one could fault him for anything. He was a great man, merciful and compassionate.

Everyone looked on respectfully as he walked down the village path and offered him their salaams.

That evening, Goni Chowdhury felt a little feverish. He had been feeling this way quite often these days. He kept telling himself to see a doctor but what with one thing and another he hadn't found the time. Besides, he had peasant blood in his veins and felt foolish about running to the doctor every time a little something went wrong. His friend Ghias-ud-din had passed away that day and he meant to attend the burial. But he decided against it. Instead, he went upstairs and stretched himself out on the bed. But he felt restless and couldn't sleep. He went to the window and stood for a while looking at the sunset. Then he came back to bed and lay down again. The house was dark and still. His sons hadn't returned home and his daughters-in-law had gone over to the neighbours for a chat. He rose and went to the window again. From where he stood he could see his entire property—his pond, his orchards of mango and jackfruit, his fields of swaying paddy. Beyond the pond lay his brother's thatched hut. He sighed. Rahim had remained a peasant while he, Goni Khan Chowdhury, had become a king. All through his own efforts, his hard work and intelligence.

Suddenly he felt his chest contort with pain. What was the use of it all? What had he gained? Look at him now, he was sick and lonely with no one to sit beside him, no one to stroke his fevered brow and thread her fingers through his hair. His body was strong and healthy, packed with energy and vitality. Yet he kept it starving. Why? He missed the soft touch of a woman's hand. A few words of love. For some reason he didn't think of his dead wives. Another woman's face swam before his vision, soft and gentle; tenderness raining from large, dark eyes; magic in her smile.

Haseena's Story

When Haseena was sixteen years old and looked her age, she had climbed onto a bus one day and run away. Her body had started ripening from the age of thirteen and her burgeoning beauty enticing the men around her. Her sisters' husbands lost no opportunity to clasp her to their chests and stroke her hips and breasts in the guise of brotherly love. These early embraces sparked off a fire that heated her limbs and set her soul aflame with passion. So, when a tall, strong, upstanding lad beckoned to her from the Line, she couldn't refuse. Getting into a bus with him, she disappeared from the village.

Her father, the redoubtable Lal Mian, sent his minions in every direction and the guilty pair was traced in a few days. The boy's name was Jamaal-ud-din and he owned a fruit shop in India Ghat, a few miles away. Lal Mian beat his daughter until she fainted and nearly throttled the young man to death. Then, sighing over the evil destiny his daughter had chosen for herself, he got them married.

Lal Mian had only one son, a sickly boy, weak and infirm from birth. His other four daughters had married well and were settled in homes of their own. He decided to keep Jamaal as a live-in son-in-law. But the boy was stubborn and impertinent and didn't know what was good for him. He refused his father-in-law's offer and went back to his fruit stall. An infuriated Lal Mian vowed never to see his face again and even cut off all connections with his daughter.

For the first few years, Jamaal did quite well for himself. The fruit stall was only a façade for his real business, which was smuggling arms across the border. It was a risky venture but Jamaal was one of those who thrived on danger and enjoyed taking risks. He couldn't live a tame, safe, humdrum life. He had brains, a broad chest and fire in his eyes. He was born to conquer the world, he told himself, not to live on its peripheries.

Business started deteriorating during the Bangladesh war. Arms became dirt cheap. A musket was selling for a hundred rupees, an LMG for three hundred. The profits he made weren't worth the risk. He decided to get into the fishing business. But here he encountered another hurdle. His father-in-law, Lal Mian, and Goni Khan Chowdhury were bosom friends. Between them they owned all the bherhis in the vicinity and were chary of a third party stepping into their kingdom. They resisted attempts to smuggle fish from Bangladesh in their own interest, and being rich and powerful, had the police on their side. Jamaal-ud-din was forced to admit defeat and abandon the business. His anger and frustration led to brawls and scuffles in which he could have lost his life. But he didn't. He lost it another way.

On a dark winter's night he died of fever and an excruciating headache. This was a mysterious new disease. No one had heard of it and nothing could be done. Within a week everything was over. Jamaal had saved nothing. All he left behind were a young wife and three small children with starvation staring in their faces. But that was only one part of Haseena's troubles. The other, more deadly one, was that with Jamaal out of the way, human vultures had started swarming around her, eyes inflamed with lust, greedy tongues hanging out for a taste of her voluptuous body.

Lal Mian decided to bring Haseena back. He hated her for what she had done and would have gladly abandoned her to her fate. But if a daughter of his enrolled her name in a Hasnabad brothel, every finger would point in his direction. 'Look! Lal Mian's daughter has become a prostitute,' they would say.

Stomping into Haseena's house, he commanded roughly, 'Pack your things. You're coming home.' Throwing a glance at the three infants cowering in a corner, their eyes round with awe and fear, his face twisted with repulsion. 'You must leave these imps of Satan behind,' he told his daughter. 'I can't take them with me.'

Haseena flung herself at her father's feet. 'Abba!' she wept, deep, shuddering sobs rising from her chest. 'How can I leave them behind? I bore them in my womb. Who do they have but me?'

'Why?' Lal Mian looked surprised. 'Jamaal must have some relatives. Let them take charge. These brats have nothing to do with me.'

'Their father had no one but an old grandmother. She is sick and half-blind. She can't fend for herself, how can she take care of the children?'

'Then let them loose in the streets. Lots of children live in the streets...'

Haseena shook her head. Tears ran down her cheeks and fell on her breast.

Lal Mian was disgusted. 'Go to hell then!' he shouted angrily. 'Starve to death.' He returned without Haseena and promptly forgot about her.

A few weeks later, a pale, famished-looking Haseena arrived at her father's house, the girl astride her hip, the two boys clinging to her sari. Lal Mian raved and ranted and threatened to throw them out. This depraved creature wasn't his daughter, he declared. He didn't want to see her face.

'A-ha-ha-ha,' his second wife, Najma, tried to calm him down. 'Now that they are here we can't drive them away. We must think of something. Let them live in the shed across the canal, the one you built for storing your jute. It's empty...'

'What!' Now the full force of Lal Mian's anger fell on his wife. 'A daughter of mine live all by herself beyond the canal! At the mercy of hundreds of lustful devils waiting for a chance to tear her to bits!' He raved and ranted some more and then ordered his field hands to put up a small hut in a corner of his guava grove. Part of the land it stood upon belonged to Rehman saheb. When the latter objected to this sudden encroachment, Lal Mian promptly took him to court. The case kept him happily occupied for the next few years. Haseena got a place to live in but on one condition: her father would provide for her but not for her children. They were not of his blood. They had been spawned by his enemy.

Haseena was forced to fend for them by taking on work in the neighbouring houses. While she was out, the three, always together, hovered around the garbage dumps and dustbins of the village, looking for food. Whatever they found they crammed into their mouths. *How greedy they were! How disgustingly greedy!* The mistresses of the houses in which Haseena worked clicked their tongues in horror and told Haseena that she was not to bring them with her on any pretext. Who knew what they would do, what they would steal?

One evening, Lal Mian stepped off the bus to see the three standing outside a shop, their hands outstretched. *They were begging! His grandchildren were begging!* Lal Mian's heart nearly stopped in shock and fury. How dare these loathsome creatures, these worms of the gutter, besmirch his fair name? True, they were not of his blood. Their father had been the devil in human form. But their mother was his daughter. He made a rush at them but didn't get a chance to administer his legendary thwack on the ear. The children scampered away like mice. Lal Mian walked home, weighed down with shame and loathing. Entering the hut in the guava grove, he dragged Haseena out by her hair. If he saw those scum of her womb begging in the Line ever again, he threatened his daughter with flaming eyes, he would burn down the hut with all of them in it.

The children had to stop begging openly from that day on. But tortured by hunger pangs, they begged on the sly. The eldest boy was smart and clever. Clinging to the iron ladder at the back of a bus, he would ride all the way to Adhbele, beg for a few hours and then return the same way, assured that Lal Mian's eyes wouldn't reach that far.

But other eyes did. One afternoon, while Haseena was gathering coconut fronds from her father's garden, Ghias approached her. 'O Haseena!' He smiled. 'I saw your son Javed a while ago. He was begging at the Berha Champa crossing. You're lucky Lal Mian doesn't know. He would butcher you all if he did.'

Haseena dropped the fronds and looked at him with the eyes of a wounded bird. Running forward, she flung herself at his feet. 'Don't tell Abba, Ghias bhai,' she begged. 'Please don't tell him. Javed won't do it again. I'll make sure he doesn't.'

'Arre! Arre!' Ghias lifted her to her feet and in the process had a go at her breasts. 'Of course I won't tell him. You are so dear to me. Can I put you in harm's way? But there are others in the village who might. In fact, I came to warn you.'

The very next day, Ghias told Lal Mian what he had seen. This time there was no running away. Lal Mian entered the hut late at night and, pulling the sleeping Javed up by his hair, beat him till he was half dead. 'Haseena,' he addressed his daughter solemnly. 'Things can't go on like this. You must marry again. I've found a groom for you.'

Haseena nodded. She was ready to obey her father.

'He is my friend Rajab Ali's son Shamsher. Rajab Ali has a fleet of trucks and lives in Bajitpur. They're very well-off and will surround you with comforts.'

Haseena's lips parted in a pleased smile. But the smile vanished at her father's next sentence.

'As for the litter you have spawned, I'll get rid of it.'

'Get rid?' Haseena stared at him. 'Where ... where will you send them?'

'Leave that to me. I'll make suitable arrangements.'

'But they can't live without me. They've never...'

'Are you thinking of taking them with you? Have you lost your mind?'

'W—why? Won't the ... um ... gentleman from Bajitpur allow me to keep them?'

Lal Mian sighed. 'What man in his senses will take a wife with three little snails clinging to her legs?' he asked with a degree of patience unusual for him.

'Where will I leave them? They were born of my womb.'

'Arre, ja ja!' Lal Mian said dismissively. He looked at her as though he had never heard such absurd nonsense in his life. What did people do when their cats and bitches littered too often? Didn't they stuff the newborns in a sack and drown them in the canal? Or take them to the middle of a forest and leave them there? If these brats were simply taken to Sealdah station and pushed into the crowd on the platform they would never find their way back. And everyone could breathe a sigh of relief and go on with their lives. A lot of men wanted to marry this daughter of his. She was young and beautiful and had many good qualities. She would make a good wife. And she herself could live sumptuously. Saris, jewels—whatever she wished for would be hers. She could even start a new family. But these imps of Satan stood in the way.

Lal Mian sighed and looked at his daughter. She was weeping and shaking her head. No, she wouldn't sit in a nikaah with a man who wouldn't let her keep her children. She had carried each one of them in her womb for nine months. She could still feel the pull of her umbilical cord.

Shamsul, the Do-gooder

Between the two villages stood a primary school. The children of both studied here but till date only twelve had made it to the high school in town. The brightest of them was Badr-ud-din Sheikh's son Shamsul Haq. He was the only graduate in these parts and a fine young man, quiet, intelligent and well-behaved.

That evening, Shamsul was sitting in the tea stall when a sudden commotion—'Arre! Arre! Stop! Stop!'—followed by a loud screeching of brakes made him spring to his feet. Running out, he saw a little girl standing in the middle of the road, within inches of a giant bus, staring at it with bewildered eyes. Other people ran out too, screaming and shouting, not at the bus driver but at the child. For it wasn't the driver's fault. In fact, he had stopped the bus with commendable skill and presence of mind. It was the beggarly brat that had run across without looking right or left. The driver jumped off the bus and slapped the girl angrily. Then he relented and picked her up. Murmuring endearments in her ear, he caressed the tender cheek that had been marked by his large, rough hand.

'Who is she?' Shamsul asked one of the men.

'Lal Mian's granddaughter.'

'Why is she wandering about by herself so late in the evening?'

'That's what they do. She has two brothers. Look, there they are. They hang about in the Line until dark.'

'Haseena's children have the life force of koi fish,' said a voice from the crowd. 'Any other child her age would have been crushed to death. Remember the time Javed was bitten by a snake? Everyone thought he would die. But did he? Now if it was my son or yours...' The crowd burst into laughter.

A shadow passed over Shamsul's face. Children were god's gift to humanity yet their lives had such little value. A small girl had just been saved from a terrible death. And people were laughing...

Shamsul pushed his way through the crowd and took the girl by the hand. Stroking her tangled head, he said gently, 'You mustn't run about the streets like this. What is your name?' The child was sobbing, partly from fear and partly from the burning in her cheek. She mumbled something but Shamsul couldn't hear her. He stooped and brought his face level with hers and asked again, 'What's your name?'

The girl sniffed and muttered, 'Nahar-un-necchha.'

Shamsul lifted her in his arms and said, 'Come. Let me take you home.'

Her two brothers had been standing at a distance, looking

on with wary eyes. Now they sprang forward. 'Yes, yes,' they invited Shamsul enthusiastically. 'Come to our house. We'll show you the way.' Snatching the torch from Shamsul's hand, Javed ran forward, leading the party.

Haseena was sitting by a tiny kerosene lamp that exuded more smoke than light, stitching a torn blouse. She had taken off the blouse a few minutes ago and her torso was bare. Seeing a man accompanying her children, she quickly drew the end of her tattered sari over her breasts.

'You're Haseena, aren't you?' Since he lived in the same village, Shamsul knew her slightly. 'Why do you let your children wander about in the streets?'

Before Haseena could respond, Javed launched into a spirited account of the accident that could have, but for a freak chance, killed his sister. The children lived such drab, dull lives, they revelled in anything that had an element of spice and drama.

Haseena clasped her daughter to her bosom. She looked up at Shamsul and answered his question: 'What can I do? Where can I go? No one loves my children. Such is my destiny!'

Shamsul dropped to the ground beside her and heard her story. Time went by. The moon rose in the sky above the guava grove and clusters of stars sparkled around it. A sudden splash in the pond as a palmyra fruit fell into it brought them back to the present. Shamsul sighed. What cruelty and injustice were meted out to women in their society. Such grave disparities existed between the rich and poor, the powerful and weak. People had taken things lying down for centuries. But no more. The time had come to deal with it. He would start by doing his bit.

'There's no point in waiting for things to change,' he

told Haseena. 'It will take years. But you cannot go on like this. You need to take care of your children's future. Just because Nahar was saved today, just because Javed didn't die of snakebite last year, doesn't mean they'll have the same luck every time. You must educate them, discipline them. Only then will they be able to take care of you one day.'

'That one,' Haseena said, pointing a finger at Javed, 'studied till Class Two. After that...' she sighed, 'there was no money to send him to school.'

'You mustn't refer to your child as "that one". It is demeaning. And why are you working with needle and thread in such poor light? You'll ruin your eyes. You should do your stitching during the day.'

Shamsul started visiting Haseena from time to time. It was always after dusk for he held a job at the post office and had to work till late in the evening. He always brought something with him—books and pencils for Javed, a frock for Nahar.

Tongues started wagging and rumour and gossip ran rife. One day, as he entered one of the shops in the Line, Shamsul was shocked to hear a group of men talking about his relationship with Haseena.

'O Shamsul Mian!' one of them called out in a hearty voice. 'How are you and Haseena bibi getting along? She has magic in her body, doesn't she? But you'd better be careful. The news shouldn't reach your wife's ears.'

Shamsul's face turned white. He had been married for only a year-and-a-half. His wife was beautiful and college-educated. How could people even dream that he was having an affair with an illiterate village widow? He refuted the rumour forcefully. But would anyone listen?

The men wagged their heads and smiled snidely. 'Since when has the presence of a wife stopped a man from looking at another woman? If the world were so clean, so pure ... anyway, just make sure the news doesn't reach Lal Mian. He'll force you to marry his daughter and you'll be landed with the widow and her three children.'

Shamsul explained at length that all he was trying to do was help a family in distress. But no one bought his arguments. As a result, Shamsul stopped visiting Haseena. He was the seventh one to be prevented by the men of the village in his efforts to make Haseena's life easier.

The Mango Grove

Much to her dismay, Haseena suddenly found herself face to face with Goni Khan Chowdhury. It was early in the morning and the latter was walking in his orchard, inspecting his trees. Quickly hiding the bunch of raw mangoes she had picked under her sari, Haseena stooped and touched the old man's feet. Goni Khan's eyes were as sharp as needles and the movement of her hand hadn't escaped him. Lifting her chin, he murmured a blessing. 'May Allah take care of you and your children. May you prosper and be happy. How many mangoes have you taken, daughter?'

Haseena's heart thudded violently. 'O chacha!' she pleaded in a piteous voice. 'I didn't pluck even one from the tree. I just took a few windfalls. Believe me, chacha!'

'Tch tch tch!' Goni Khan clicked his tongue kindly. 'Even if you did, so what? No harm done. You needed mangoes, you took some. The matter ends there.' While caressing Haseena's chin Goni Khan had seen her eyes—

deep and dark like ancient lakes that held worlds of mysteries in their depths. His heart softened towards her. 'Let me see what you have taken,' he said. 'Don't be afraid.'

Haseena brought the bunch out slowly. Through the tear in her blouse, Goni Khan caught a glimpse of her breasts. Rich, swelling hills, lustrous as moonlight. His heart softened a little more. 'Only five!' he exclaimed. 'That's nothing, you should have taken more.'

'The children were clamouring for mango chutney so I thought I'd make some. "You mustn't steal," I told them sternly, "I'll take what I need from chacha's garden."'

'You're absolutely right. Take as many as you like. In fact, come to me whenever you need anything. There's no need to feel shy. Do you want some more?'

These mangoes were of the Golapkhas variety. Dwarf trees especially grafted for a combination of rich taste and scent. Crisp and sweet even when raw, they weren't cooking mangoes. Goni Khan knew Haseena was lying but he stretched out his hand and plucked another ten or twelve big fat ones from the low branches and said, 'Here. Spread out your anchal and take these.'

Haseena's sari was in tatters. Obeying Goni Khan would mean exposing her bosom. She blushed and looked down at her feet.

Goni Khan smiled sweetly at her. 'There's no need to feel embarrassed. Am I not your chacha?'

Haseena slowly unwrapped the end of her sari from her shoulders and held it out. Goni Khan dropped the mangoes into it. His rheumy eyes glistened. 'Happy?' he asked, taking her hand. Haseena swayed her head. Goni Khan's hands grazed her shoulders and cupped her breasts. 'Come,' he whispered. After that it was a matter of seconds before he pushed her down gently and lay on top of her. The mangoes fell out of Haseena's torn anchal and rolled across the grass. Haseena moaned in protest but no one heard her. It was barely dawn and no one was awake, not even the birds.

It was over in a few minutes. Goni Khan Chowdhury's heart pounded with contrary emotions. Swelling in triumph one moment at the proof that even in his old age he hadn't lost his virility, sinking fearfully the next. What had he done? How could he have succumbed to temptation so easily? He was an elderly man, a family patriarch, rich and respected in the community. Moreover, he was Lal Mian's friend. What if the girl reported the matter to her father?

Mixed with fear was regret. He shouldn't have done what he did. He shouldn't have lost his head. Was it in the nature of men to think they had the right to the bodies of defenceless women? If the girl's husband, the fiery, iron-chested Jamaal, were alive today would he have dared? Chhi chhi chhi, if his sons came to know ... if other people... Why, the girl was young enough to be his daughter! He would be shamed before everyone. He wouldn't know where to hide his white head.

What's done is done, he thought, deciding to take the bold way out. If it came to it, he would marry the girl. With her as a bedfellow he would be able to keep his virility for another twenty years! But Haseena had three children. Ore baap re! His sons would be furious. Their inheritance would be threatened. No, no, he couldn't think of it.

Haseena was sitting on the grass, chin resting on her knees. Her eyes were forlorn and the ever-present smile had left her lips. 'O Haseena!' Goni Khan touched his ears and bit his tongue. 'Please ... please don't tell anyone. I'll

give you whatever you want. I'll look after your children.
But you must swear in Allah's name that this secret will
rest with you and me alone. I'll go to hell if...'

'No, chacha,' Haseena mumured through pale, dry lips.
'I won't tell anyone. Forgive me. I am an ill-fated woman
and such is my destiny.'

'I'll take care of you. Only ... only remember my position.
Don't shame me. This mustn't reach anyone's ears.'

'Don't worry, chacha. No one will know.'

Goni Khan hurried out of the grove.

Haseena didn't move. She remained sitting where she
was. So many thoughts came to her, so many memories.
Her husband Jamaal, her three children. She had betrayed
them. She had committed the grievous sin of adultery for
which Allah would surely punish her. But what else could
she have done? Goni chacha was such an important man.
He held such a high status in the community. How could
she, a petty, insignificant woman, deny him what he wanted?
Wouldn't that reek of audacity and arrogance? There was
no question of telling anyone. The only thing she would
gain for herself if she did was the reputation of a whore.

A similar incident had occurred a month ago. Rehman
saheb's friend Mijanur, who could well have been named
Majnu, so handsome and romantic was he to look at, had
taken her by the hand one afternoon and whispered, 'I am
still unwed because no woman has caught my fancy. But
ever since I saw you I wanted to marry you. I have told my
mother and she has no objection. But she doesn't want you
to bring your children into the house. Now I love your
children and would like to be a father to them. I'll work on
my mother and make her change her mind. Only, I need a
little time.'

Haseena looked around fearfully. Rehman saheb was taking a nap downstairs. She and Mijanur were alone in the room overlooking the river. He had asked for a glass of water and she had brought it to him.

'Why are you standing behind the door?' Mijanur smiled at her. 'Come closer. Tell me about yourself.'

What a deep, rich voice he had, so gentle and kind. What a nice man he was. She had seen him bathing in Baro Shariker Pukur that morning. On his way back, he had picked up little Naharunnissa and pinched her cheeks lovingly. Haseena's heart had melted with gratitude. No one in the village cared to touch her children, let alone caress them. All they got were curses and abuses.

Mijanur drew her into his lap and kissed and caressed the mother exactly as he had the daughter. Haseena blushed and tried to rise.

'Why do you pull away?' Mijanur asked in surprise. 'Don't you know how much I love you? You're so-o-o sweet.'

At these words a spurt of laughter bubbled up from Haseena's breast and reached her lips. She had received many compliments from men. She had been told she was as beautiful as a piece of statuary, that she sparkled like gold and gems. She was an enchantress by day, a tigress by night. But no one had ever told her that she was sweet. Perhaps that was how city folk talked. Their language was so polished and refined. Mijanur's kisses were like fire, his arms so powerful she seemed to melt into them. She felt a delicious languor steal over her limbs. Still she struggled. 'Let me go,' she whispered. 'Please let me go. If someone sees us it will be the end of me.'

'No one will see us.'

Like today, that day too Haseena had resisted but not forcefully enough. How could she? Mijanur saheb was such an important man. A big officer in the city, and so learned. He who could have his pick of pretty women had chosen her, Haseena, to love and caress. How could she withhold herself from him? Especially after he promised to marry her. 'What are you afraid of, Haseena?' he had said. 'I have promised to marry you and look after your children. It's only my mother, but I know I can persuade her in the end. All I need is a little time...'

Sitting on the grass in the orchard, Haseena sighed. Then she stood up and plucked a few more mangoes from the Golapkhas trees. This time there was nothing furtive about her. She chose the largest, glossiest ones and tore them off the boughs boldly and confidently. And she took her time over it. As though the orchard belonged to her.

Shadow of the Moon in the Pond

Haseena woke up with a start. She had heard the yelp of a jackal close to her hut. Jackals were foolish creatures. They couldn't resist calling out even when they were creeping into people's yards trying to steal a hen. The cry would alert the stray dogs in the village and a chase would follow. Vociferous barking interspersed with the jackal's 'hukkah-hu' would shatter the silence of the night.

Haseena rose and walked over to the window. 'Hoosh! Hoosh!' She tried to drive the creature away. As she did so, her eyes fell on the pond just beyond her hut. A large, misty, frost-white moon was swimming in it. Haseena's heart lifted. Ever since she was a child she had loved seeing the moon's reflection in water. The sight drew her to it like a magnet. The night was still and silent. Not a breath of wind stirred the fronds of the coconut palms fringing the pond. The water, pale green by day, was midnight blue. The huge lotus leaves floating on its surface gleamed dull silver as the playful moon darted in-between them in a game of hide-and-seek. Haseena's eyes misted over and an old, familiar tug, whether of joy or pain she couldn't tell, wrenched her chest. She stood at the window for a long, long time, weeping silently.

Finally she turned and glanced at the children lying sprawled on the floor of the hut on tattered kanthas. Her children—Javed, Siraj and Nahar. A cloud of mosquitoes hovered above them which they shooed and slapped away even in their sleep. The mosquito net Jamaal had bought was full of holes now. She had no money to buy another one. With the moonlight on their faces, they looked as tender and innocent as any other children their age. Looking at them now, who would call them greedy, thieving brats full of guile and cunning?

Haseena hardly saw them during the day. She went about her daily chores—gathering firewood, making dung cakes, washing floors and vessels for other people. The children ran about like stray dogs, sniffing at dumps and dustbins. But they were careful never to go near the main house. They were afraid of Lal Mian's second wife. If chhoto bibi caught them within a hundred yards of her domain, she would chase them out with her broomstick. Sometimes they left the village and wandered here and there. Why, only last month Siraj was knocked down by a bull in Baanpur Haat! Baanpur was six miles away. Even little Nahar had walked all the way there and back. Haseena kept telling them not to go so far but would they listen?

They came home only after dusk, clamouring for food. Haseena could never give them as much as they wanted. Whatever little she had, they shared amongst themselves and ate it in the twinkling of an eye. After feeding them Haseena spent an hour playing with her children. At these times she was like a mother cat frisking and gambolling with her young. They tumbled all over her, pulled at her sari and chased her around the room. Even Javed, who was a big boy, loved playing with his mother. Then, worn out by the rigours of the day, they fell asleep with their heads in her lap.

Haseena stroked her children's faces as they slept in the moonlight. She felt like waking them up and playing a game with them. She was never as happy as when she played with her children. Haseena's body was like a river surging with youth and desire. But she refused to go to a new husband and enjoy the pleasures of matrimony if she couldn't take her children with her.

She got up and stood by the window once again. The moon was still playing by itself in the dark waters of the pond. 'Happy moon!' she whispered. 'Lucky moon! You don't have to struggle day after day to put a few handfuls of rice in your children's mouths.'

Sukhendu Babu

Lal Mian lost his case in the lower court. The judge decreed that the land on which Haseena's hut stood belonged in part to Rehman Sheikh and would have to be demolished. Lal Mian, of course, was not one to give up so easily. He decided to appeal to a higher court. But his indignation against his daughter welled up afresh. It was because of her, only because of her, that he had been humiliated. He who had never lost a court case in his life had to suffer this indignity in his old age. Sending for Haseena, he told her sternly that if she didn't obey him and marry the man he had chosen for her he would withdraw his support. Which father had to fend for a daughter who was neither sick nor disabled? Haseena was young, reasonably attractive and healthy. What earthly reason did she have for refusing to sit in a nikaah? Why should he, Lal Mian, take on her responsibility? Times were hard enough for him as it was...

Times were indeed hard. The price of jute was falling by the day. The fisheries were yielding only a fraction of their usual produce. A canker called 'majra poka' was devastating the paddy. All the villagers were affected. Even Rahim chacha, who had such a sunny disposition, was going around with creases on his brow. He looked at the stretch of dun-coloured straw that had once been his paddy field and sighed. *Ha Allah!* The fruits of his labour were like his children. How would a father feel if he saw his offspring lying dead around him?

Only those families that had one or two earning members fared relatively better. They had the comfort of a fixed sum coming in every month. Rehman saheb's was one such. He still had friends coming over on weekends, with Haseena doing the cooking and serving. On these occasions, Haseena's children ate well, for she always brought back a large thaala piled high with saffron-tinted rice and spicy beef curry. For the last few months, however, Rehman saheb was staying in his wife's paternal village, where she had gone for her delivery. As a result, Haseena had lost touch with Mijanur.

That Saturday, Rehman saheb decided to return home.

He brought with him his Hindu friend Sukhendu, a well-known contractor in these parts. And, as usual, he sent for Haseena. Rehman saheb had a purpose in bringing Sukhendu. He had co-partnered with Goni Khan Chowdhury in bidding for a ferry service to the Sunderbans. Since this kind of business was a first for him, he wanted an influential man like Sukhendu on his side. Sukhendu knew all the important men in the locality and, being Hindu, was on familiar terms with them. He addressed the wife of the SDPO as 'Boudi' and had established a pleasant, bantering relationship with her. Whenever he came to the ASP's house, he touched the feet of his old mother and enquired politely after her health. Half his work got done that way. It was far more effective than offering a bribe.

Sukhendu babu was about thirty, with a tall, hefty frame and a plain but pleasant face. That he was a boozer and a libertine was written all over him. And indeed, he liked nothing better than to gorge on wine and women. Yet he was a good man in other ways. He was not a wily schemer and bore no malice towards anyone. On the contrary, while in his cups, he often made extravagant offers of help to all and sundry. 'Just leave everything to me,' he would announce expansively, 'I'll take care of it.' And strangely enough, more often than not, he did. He had got to know Rehman saheb just a few months ago and had invited himself to the biryani and beef kebabs of which he had heard such praises. 'Rehman bhai,' he had said wistfully, 'we can't cook meat the way you Muslims do. Whenever I am in Kolkata I make it a point to eat my fill at Amenia. In my own house, baap re baap, my old grandmother guards the kitchen like a dragon. Even chicken has to be cooked and eaten on the sly.'

Rehman saheb was lavish with his hospitality. Dozens of whisky bottles were kept ready along with the biryani and kebabs. Unfortunately, Sukhendu got so drunk by the time they were served that he could barely sample the food. His eyes were glazed with whisky fumes and his tongue felt stiff like leather.

'Send for some water,' he told his host. 'I've been drinking neat for hours. My mouth is as dry as salted fish.'

Rehman saheb sent for Haseena and ordered a jug of water. When it was brought, he said with exaggerated solicitude, 'You've pumped it from the tube well, I hope. Sukhendu babu won't drink pond water.'

'It's all right.' The words slurred in Sukhendu's mouth. 'As long as it is water ... give it to me.'

Rehman saheb took Haseena's hand and drew her forward. 'Take a good look at this girl, Sukhendu-da, and tell me how old she is.'

The same old game...

Sukhendu burst out laughing when he heard Haseena's real age and said, 'She doesn't look it. By god, she doesn't!' His eyes glittered with lust. Two fiery tongues sprang from them and darted all over her body, licking, slurping. Good stuff, he thought. How much would she cost? The next moment he gave his head a vigorous shake and, lighting a cigarette, tried to dispel the whisky fumes. Baap re ... he told himself fearfully. A Muslim girl from a good family. They'll have my head if I'm caught even thinking of such a thing. Riots broke out at the drop of a hat these days. Na, baba, na. He would steer clear of this woman. Goni Khan had promised to take him to Lucknow this winter, where he could have his fill of tawaifs and baijis. They were khandani too, but had no such taboos. Besides, Lucknow was miles away. Not a word of his indiscretions would reach his friends and family.

Rehman saheb was a little surprised by Sukhendu's lukewarm response and hastened to fan the flames. Smiling at Haseena, he said, 'The arrangements for your nikaah were more or less complete but poor Mijanur got transferred. Bank jobs are like that. Here today, there tomorrow. They've sent him to Darjeeling. Did you know that?'

Haseena shook her head. She felt no sense of betrayal. At least he said he would marry me and take care of my children, she thought. How many men do even that? She sighed. Little Nahar was ill. Her limbs were burning with fever. But Haseena could neither give her proper food nor medicine. *Hai Khodatallah! Take care of her! Shield her from harm!*

'I'm looking for another groom for you, Haseena,' Rehman saheb's voice broke into her thoughts. 'The only problem is that brood of yours.'

'Brood!' Sukhendu, whose head was lolling on his chest, looked up with a start. 'What brood? Whose children?' Rehman saheb recounted Haseena's history. In a flash, Sukhendu's philanthropic side sprang to the surface. His brow puckered and he muttered thoughtfully, 'It is indeed a problem. Who will marry a woman with three children? But I could ... I could try. Provided, of course, you all are willing to...'

'Willing to do what?'

'Look, isn't it better to send the children to an orphanage? The royals have all been pensioned off and their palaces acquired by the government. Only last year the Putia palace was converted to an orphanage.'

'Is that so?'

'Of course.' Sukhendu lost his temper. 'I supplied the furniture, wouldn't I know?' Calming down, he continued, 'It will be better for the children in every way. They'll get nourishing food, an education...'

'Free of cost?' Rehman saheb stared at his guest.

'Of course. The government pays for everything.'

Rehman saheb turned to Haseena. 'It's an excellent idea. Just think of it, Haseena. They will get good food to eat. They'll go to school...'

Haseena stood silent, her eyes on the floor.

A sudden thought struck Rehman saheb. 'Sukhendu-da,' he asked, 'will they take Haseena's children?'

'Of course they will. Why shouldn't they?'

'Let me be frank with you. These are Muslim children. Will they...'

Sukhendu gave a snort of laughter. 'Arre baba, an orphan is an orphan. A child without parents. Where does the question of religion come in?'

'Na na...' Rehman saheb was quick to change the drift of the conversation. 'I was just thinking, they are quite big ... the eldest is thirteen.'

'Leave all that to me.' Sukhendu lifted his hands in the air as though granting a boon. 'I'll manage everything.' He turned to Haseena, his drunken eyes licking every inch of her body. 'Just tell me what you want,' he said pompously, 'I'll give you ... I'll give you everything.' Inwardly he felt a stab of resentment. What a prize, he thought, and so completely wasted. But perhaps, with the children taken care of, out of gratitude, she might come ... it would be heaven. But—and here his heart drooped a little—supposing she doesn't? To hell with her! The whisky sprang into his head again. There's always Lucknow with its wealth of exotic attar and garlic-scented Muslim women!

Only to Come and Go

As was to be expected, Sukhendu forgot his lavish promises the very next day. But somehow, though the conversation had taken place in the privacy of Rehman saheb's house, it became common knowledge. The village was agog with excitement. Haseena's children were being sent to the erstwhile royal kingdom of Putia. Many hadn't even heard of Putia, let alone the fact that the palace now housed an orphanage. But everyone approved. Haseena's children would be taken care of and it wouldn't cost any of them a paisa.

For some strange reason, the plan enthused Goni Khan Chowdhury's sons the most. It was terrible, they said, the way the children wandered about like stray cattle. Something should have been done for them long ago. They went around collecting opinions from the rest of the villagers and got a favourable response. Even Shamsul Haq endorsed it. Sitting in the tea shop in the Line, he declared that this was the best solution.

As for Lal Mian, he was so excited he was ready to pack them off that very minute. Once the brood was out of the way, Haseena could breathe a sigh of relief and get on with her own life. He was her father, wasn't he? He would ensure that she found a good husband who would provide for her well. The pressure on Haseena was mounting by the day. Even Shamsul the do-gooder came to her and said, 'Your first consideration should be the welfare of your children. Just think, they will get an education and in time become respected citizens of the country. Isn't that better for them than living with you and growing up like savages?' Haseena was forced to agree. What he said was true. So many people were saying the same thing. They couldn't all be wrong.

Having obtained her consent, the next thing to do was to go to Sukhendu babu and make him redeem his promise. Sukhendu did help a bit, but most of the work was done by two of Goni Khan's sons.

The fateful day came. Haseena woke the children early, bathed and fed them, and dressed them in the new clothes that had been bought for them. Goni Khan's sons, accompanied by Ghias, took them to the orphanage. On reaching the office, the men got busy with completing the formalities. The children stood staring at everything around them, eyes round with wonder. Suddenly, Haseena came rushing in, as though blown by a hurricane. Her hair and clothes were wild and dishevelled and she was shrieking like a mad woman: 'Ogo, babu! Let them go. They are not orphans. They have a mother. I'm their mother. I've borne them in my womb. They've never lived away from me.' The children ran to her, sobbing, and clung to her sari. The clerk looked up from the counter and shook his head gravely. 'This is called *Universal Motherhood*. If only I had a camera...'

The children had travelled by bus on the way to the orphanage. They came back walking. Javed ran ahead and caught a grasshopper.

'Let it go!' Haseena screamed at him. 'Set it free, haramjada!'

Javed obeyed. The grasshopper flew off but one of its wings was left clinging to the boy's palm.

Siraj jumped into a pond and came up with a bunch of lotus stems in his hands. He was grinning from ear to ear. Lotus stems made a tasty chacchari.

The Night of the Angels

It was the night of Shab-e-Baraat. Haseena lay on her back, staring at the rusty sheet of tin that served as a roof. It had been a wonderful day. She couldn't remember a happier one.

She had been sent for by Ghias's grandmother, who was the kindest, most beautiful woman she knew. Even at eighty, dadima was like a ripe fruit, pink and plump. One look at her told you what an exquisite beauty she had been in her youth. She was also very religious and the only woman in the village who had read the holy book. She could read Urdu and enunciate the ayats properly. Shab-e-Baraat was observed in every house but Ghias's celebrations outshone them all. The scale of pomp and ceremony set a new record each year.

Work, work, work! The women of the house, Haseena among them, rose at dawn and started to pound the rice—mounds and mounds of it, which then had to be sifted through a fine cloth, kneaded with warm water and rolled into rutis. Rutis were baked in hundreds in Ghias's house. Dadima had a rule: no one who came to the house would go back empty-handed.

Haseena kept slipping out of the kitchen and running up to the old lady's room, where dadima sat on her prayer carpet, reading from the Holy Quran set up on a small pedestal. She had scripted this copy herself in her neat, pearl-like hand. Her face glowed with an unearthly light while she read, and Haseena gazed on it as though she had never seen anything so beautiful in her life. 'O dadima!' she interrupted once, 'please read a little louder. I want to hear it too.'

'Why don't you come closer then?' The old lady smiled at Haseena. 'Come sit by me, child.' She began to explain the ayats to the girl, who sat, eyes closed, as though in a trance. A divine contentment stole over her. She felt as though there was no sin in the world, no sorrow or bitterness. Only joy and harmony. Only peace and love.

Frantic calls from the kitchen forced Haseena to return to her tasks. But though her hands worked with their customary efficiency, her heart was elsewhere. She longed to go back to dadima's room and hear Allah's tidings in her quavering voice. When she was young, her mind had been restless and she hadn't cared to listen to the Quran, let alone follow its teachings. But now she had crossed thirty. She made up her mind to change herself. She wouldn't allow any man to come near her any more. She would always tell the truth. She wouldn't steal from people's kitchens and orchards even if her children went hungry. Ghias made several attempts to get her alone for a few minutes that day. But Haseena ignored him. She would keep herself pure and holy. For tonight was the night of the angels.

She went through the day wrapped in a cloud of peace and happiness. The poor and the destitute came flocking to the door and Haseena gave them food with her own hands. Could anything be more wonderful? At the onset of dusk, when the fireworks started, Haseena saw her children standing in a corner of the courtyard, looking on with wonder in their eyes. They weren't driven out like stray dogs today. Not only were they allowed to enjoy the spectacle, they were even given a sparkler each.

After the festivities were over, Haseena walked back home. She carried a paraat in her hands with forty rutis in it and a large earthen pot of mutton curry. Ghias's family didn't eat beef. Only the best goat meat came into the house. It was richly cooked with big lumps of potatoes. More than the meat, Javed loved potatoes swimming in gravy.

Haseena walked down the village path, the children skipping next to her, slurping and licking their lips in anticipation. They couldn't wait to reach home and fall on the delicious food.

The destitutes were still walking up and down the village. They came from far and near and would visit every house in the village. Stopping a small group, Haseena gave three of her rutis to each of them. Her heart leapt with joy. She had distributed food all day. But that hadn't been hers. *This* was hers, earned with her own hard labour. 'Eat,' she said, smiling at them. 'Eat your fill.' The day had brought her more happiness than she could hold. Her chest tightened. With joy? Or was it pain?

Now, as she lay staring into the dark, a wave of rapture passed through her. She had obeyed Allah's command. She had fed the hungry and comforted the comfortless. Her children too had eaten well. Tired and spent, but smiling in bliss, they had fallen asleep around her. But for her there was no sleep. She would stay awake. Tonight an angel would come down from heaven and write her destiny on her brow. She had to keep herself pure and holy, harm no one, think no evil thoughts. She wouldn't sleep tonight. What if an evil thought came to her in a dream? How long could she go on like this? Would her destiny never change?

Haseena's eyes turned to the tiny window of her hut. A vast sky lay beyond it. She saw an angel bathed in celestial light, flying down from heaven. His luminous wings cut through the air, leaving a trail of silver vapour. He would come to her, she knew that. But when? Haseena's eyes were wide open, straining into the dark. She waited.

A light drizzle was falling, clouding the waters of the pond. The moon wouldn't play among the lotus leaves tonight. As on all nights of Shab-e-Baraat, the falling rain dimmed all sights and sounds. The earth waited, with bated breath, for the coming of the angel...

Suddenly, a ripple of pain passed through her belly, contorting it. She felt a wave of nausea, sharp and pungent, rise from her stomach and reach her throat. Running outside, she retched and vomited by the door of the hut. Again and again. Haseena began to cry; soft, moaning sobs. She knew what it meant. She hadn't been herself for the last few days. Lethargy, queasiness and depression were weighing her down. She had guessed what it was but didn't want to admit it. Now she could deny it no longer. Another ... another deadly foe was growing like a canker within her. As the thought crossed her mind, she bit her tongue. Chhi chhi chhi! She shook her head. Can one's own child be an enemy? Even such a thought is sin.

NAMELESS

I WENT TO see the forest but ended up seeing much more. I saw flowers, exotic blooms I'd never seen before and whose names I did not know. But I don't remember them. What I do remember is a face, the face of an adolescent boy. I think about him often and marvel at the strangeness of life.

The setting in which I saw him was charming, the kind one sees in films. Or perhaps memory improves upon the real. Because what I remember is truly beautiful.

It was a small clearing in the densest part of the jungle. Surrounding it were hills through which one could see a tiny valley. A reddish stream rippled past. Green woods, blood-red river—a poet might have described it thus. Except that it wasn't a river, it was a thin thread of water twisting and turning over red rocks and earth as it went along. Washing them and imbibing their colour. And it wasn't really red, it was deep saffron.

The time was afternoon and the sun's rays were bright gold. Yet they were neither hot nor glaring. After two days of dark clouds and incessant rain, the light was mellow and comforting to the eye. The heart sang with happiness on days like these.

We had crossed the river and climbed one of the hills to

see a temple where, it was rumoured, human sacrifices take place. Human sacrifice in this day and age? I rejected the idea rightaway. Impossible! In the distant past perhaps … The place wasn't even that far from Kolkata. Two hundred miles or so, in Medinipur. We talked to a few people but got nothing out of them. Neither a clear 'yes' nor a 'no'. Some of them looked up at the sky and murmured vaguely, 'Might be true. Who can tell?'

The temple was small and unpretentious, without a soul in the vicinity. There was a wooden contraption at the entrance in which the sacrificial head—of goats and buffaloes in all probability—was placed before being axed. The earth below was splattered with fresh blood.

On the way back, my friend, the chowkidar from the bungalow who was acting as our guide, and I sat by the red stream to rest. On our way to the temple I had noticed a few goats grazing next to the stream and a boy, about twelve years old, minding them. His body was bare but for a pair of dirty shorts. Now he came splashing through the stream to our side and, crouching under a tree, looked at us with curious eyes.

'He has a lovely face, doesn't he?' said my friend.

I nodded and beckoned to the boy to come closer but he neither moved nor spoke. He didn't take his eyes off us either. 'Call him,' I said to the chowkidar. 'Tell him we would like to speak with him.'

The chowkidar barked out a command and the boy's face lit up in a smile. But he remained sitting where he was, staring at us with bright, laughing eyes. The three of us called out to him several times but he paid no attention. Quite a stubborn lad, I thought.

'Do you know him?' I asked the chowkidar.

'Of course,' came the prompt reply. 'He is Mahadev Mahto's bhaatua.'

Bhaatua? What was that? I didn't ask the question at the time. I came to know the meaning later.

'Eyi! What's your name?' I shouted at the boy. 'Why don't you speak when you are spoken to?'

Still no response.

'It could be because we are from the city,' my friend observed. 'Perhaps he feels threatened in some way.'

'Why should he feel threatened? Will we eat him up?' I turned to the chowkidar. 'What's his name?'

'He is nameless, sir,' the man replied. 'He is mute. That's why he wasn't given a name. People call him "Boy" or "Dumbo".'

I wanted to talk to the sweet-faced goatherd but how could I? He was mute. And his affliction had made him wary of strangers. He wouldn't come near us. The thought saddened me.

The long walk had made us hungry and we rose to leave. The boy rose too. Splashing and leaping across the stream, he stood behind a tree on the other bank. And, until we left, he didn't take his eyes off us. He kept peeping from behind the tree as though he was playing hide-and-seek.

On our first arrival we had thought that the forest was dense and deep and totally uninhabited but that wasn't true. There were pockets here and there where people lived in clusters, did some farming and reared animals. There were no tigers here. But there were other, larger animals.

That evening a group of men crowded at the gate of our bungalow. Excited voices wanted to know if we had guns with us. I smiled to myself. They had seen our jeep and thought we were big game hunters. I could not vouch for my friend but I had never touched a gun in my life. They explained that they needed guns to scare off some elephants who were causing a lot of damage. Every year, during this season, elephants came down from the mountains to graze on the corn and paddy the foresters grew. This year, owing to a severe drought, they hadn't yet begun sowing their crops. Deprived of food, the angry elephants had turned rogue. The beating of tins and the flinging of flaring torches were not frightening them away as they had in the past. That was why the men wanted guns.

One goes to the forest in the hope of seeing wild animals. The thought of elephants herding nearby filled us with a sense of adventure. My friend and I were ready to go out that very moment but the chowkidar stopped us. 'Wait till the morning, sir,' he advised, 'don't go out in the dark.' While we were staying in the bungalow we were his responsibility. We understood this and decided to heed his warning. Instead of going into the forest, we climbed the hill at the back and stood on a rock. With luck, we thought, we might catch a glimpse of the elephants. Even if we didn't see them, we might hear their trumpeting. But the night was dark and silent. We saw nothing and heard nothing. We waited for a while and then returned to the bungalow.

A knot of people were still huddled at the gate but they left after a while. 'A man has been sent to the police station at Banspahari,' the chowkidar informed us. 'There are three elephants on a rampage and they are refusing to budge. If the government doesn't take swift action, they will tear down every house in the village.'

'One man!' I exclaimed. 'One man walked alone to Banspahari! He must be very brave. Who is he?'

'He is Guru Mukhiya's bhaatua. His name is Ganai.'

'But the night is so dark. What if he comes up against the elephants? They'll trample him to death.'

The chowkidar shrugged.

But this story is not about elephants. It is about the strange phenomenon called 'bhaatua'.

'What is a bhaatua?' I asked. 'I keep hearing the word. What does it mean?'

A bhaatua, the chowkidar explained, was a slave who was under a bond to perform any kind of labour his owner demanded of him in exchange for 'bhaat' or boiled rice. Anything from working in the fields to walking through the jungle on a dark night to deliver a message. He had no right to refuse. What was stranger was that the bond was passed on to the next generation. A bhaatua's children were also bhaatuas, and their children after them.

'What about the wives?' I asked.

'They are also bhaatuas. Someone else's, perhaps.'

'Does that mean they have no homes?'

'How can they have homes, sir? A bhaatua is on duty twenty-four hours a day. Ganai had a hut and a strip of land. He sold them to provide dowry for his daughter. That is when he became a bhaatua.'

'And the boy we saw this morning? How did he become a bhaatua?'

'He is Ganai's son, sir.'

I was stunned into silence. No home, no household. A family whose members saw each another once in a while. What did they talk about when they met? What did they share? I thought of the boy grazing goats by the red stream. He didn't even have a name. He was a bhaatua and he was mute. Even then, didn't he deserve a name? Even animals like dogs, cats and cows are given names by their owners. But this boy with the sweet face and sunny smile was nameless. What was he thinking about, this mute, nameless slave, as he sat crouching behind the tree looking at us with his bright, laughing eyes?

NOT OF THIS WORLD

RASHID KHAN GLANCED at the fifty-rupee note in his hand. The couple had refused to take it. The boy had shaken his head and folded his hands. The girl had held her ears and bitten her tongue. 'We are not supposed to touch money on all days,' she had said.

Rashid Khan sat back in his chair and watched them sipping tea from clay pots, slurping with relish. Earlier, the orderly had offered them tea in cups and saucers but they had waved him away. 'Forgive us,' the girl had said humbly. 'We don't eat or drink out of household vessels.'

Rashid Khan's brows puckered in thought. Why were they refusing his money? Was fifty rupees too little? Were they expecting a hundred? The girl had said they weren't supposed to touch money on all days. *All days!* What did that mean?

The police tent, a colourful one called 'Swiss Cottage', was pitched in one corner of the fair grounds. While taking a round an hour ago, Rashid Khan had noticed the pair of bauls. They were quite young. The boy appeared to be around twenty-three or twenty-four and the girl a couple of years younger. The boy's dhuti and the girl's sari were dyed a dull orange with ela mati, the reddish clay of Birbhum, and they wore their hair knotted high on top of their heads. The innocence of youth clung to their faces.

186

Since the scheduled three days were over, the fair was officially closed. It was in the process of breaking up and the stall owners were preparing to depart. But the ground was still full of people and the air fit to burst with a cacophony of amplifiers. It was impossible to hear any singing in the open, so Rashid Khan had invited them to his tent. Chatting with them along the way, he learned that they didn't belong to any particular sect or brotherhood, nor were they the disciples of a famous baul. They were wayfarers who had met one another and decided to make up a couple. They spoke in a quaint singsong voice using a lot of allegory and metaphor.

On being asked where they came from, which village, the girl cried out, 'No village, go! No village. I am a daughter of the desert.'

The boy murmured, 'From the sea. I came floating on the waves.'

'And who taught you to sing?'

'The wind,' the girl replied. 'So many songs come wafting on the breeze and enter our ears. There's music even in the tears and laughter of humans. People sing even as they weep—don't they, babu?'

'That's true.' Rashid Khan nodded. Rural people have a tendency to speak in riddles, he thought. It was quite interesting.

But why were they refusing his money? He had seen plenty of bauls before. Bauls were not nomads. They were minstrels who lived in akhras and made a living by singing. They had wives and children like other men. They were far from indifferent to money and the comforts it could buy. Only the other day a baul had come to him for monetary help. He was sending his son abroad, he said, and needed money for the passport. Bauls expected and took money whenever and wherever they performed. And haggling for more wasn't alien to their nature, either. Of course, they did so discreetly with exquisite humility. Even the bauls who sang in trains...

Rashid Khan hated dispensing charity. If anyone came to him with a mourning cloth around his neck and asked for help with a father's funeral, he refused outright. 'Don't you know,' he told him severely, 'that a dead man's soul remains imprisoned in this world if his son has to beg or borrow for the funeral rites? Such a spirit is never set free.' Yet if he heard a beggar sing, be it in a train or in the street, he was happy to shell out twenty or even thirty rupees. He didn't see it as almsgiving. It was a fee to a deserving artist.

Draining the last of their tea, the pair rose to their feet. And then something came over Rashid Khan and he did the strangest thing...

Ordinary people, Rashid Khan's friends among them, are of the opinion that the police have learned the art of taking but have absolutely no notion of giving. No one ever got anything out of a policeman. Rashid Khan was aware of this. A tiny smile flickered on his lips as he drew out his purse, put the fifty rupees back, and pulled out a five-hundred-rupee note. 'Take this.' He held it out to the pair. 'It will come in useful.'

But wonder of wonders! The boy shook his head and the girl moved back a few steps.

'Forgive us, babu.' She brought her palms together. 'We can't touch any money today.'

Surprised and annoyed, Rashid Khan cried out sharply, 'What do you mean? Is today a special day? Are you under a vow or something?'

'Na-go!' The girl laughed, a sweet laugh like the tinkling of bells. 'We don't believe in vows and rituals. We are happy today, that's why we won't touch money.'

'You are happy today.' Rashid Khan smiled. 'That's good. But you still need to eat and drink.'

'Hunger and thirst can't come near us when we are happy.'

'Very well, but what about tomorrow? Suppose you are unhappy tomorrow? Hunger and thirst will assault you with a vengeance. What will you do then?'

'With your blessings, babu,' the girl replied with a smile, 'we'll be happy tomorrow too.'

Joining their palms together, the two took their leave. Rashid Khan stared glumly at the five-hundred-rupee note in his hand. Then, rising to his feet, he called out in a loud voice, 'Nitai! Nitai!' Almost instantly, a middle-aged man in a dhuti and a half-sleeved blue shirt stood before him. The man's eyes were as narrow and pointed as his moustache. He was an informer and held a part-time job in the police department. 'Follow the boy and girl who just left my tent,' Rashid Khan commanded. 'But be discreet. Take note of what they do, what they eat and where they sleep. And also the people with whom they associate. What time is it?' Glancing at his watch, he added, 'Seven forty-five. Keep your eyes glued to them till midnight. Then come to me with the details.'

Nitai's tiny eyes twinkled. 'You've hit the nail on the head, sir.' He grinned ingratiatingly. 'There are a lot of pickpockets and petty thieves about and many of them are going around disguised as bauls. They dress like them and talk like them. Your eyes are extraordinarily sharp, sir.'

'Is that so?' Rashid Khan frowned. 'Have you identified any?'

'Of course. I gave information about one such rascal only yesterday and the police nabbed him. Do you remember the dacoity case last year, sir, when one of the dacoits jumped off the police van and disappeared? That's the one. He was lurking in the fair grounds in a baul's robe. I pointed him out from a distance.'

'Is this pair from the same gang?'

'I can't say for sure, sir. They are newcomers. I haven't seen them before. But I've heard that the principal rings are recruiting young, innocent-looking boys and girls.'

'Go,' Rashid Khan barked out. 'Don't waste any more time. You might lose sight of them.'

After Nitai's departure, Rashid Khan got busy. There was enough work for the police force even after the fair had ended. Five cases of chain-snatching had been reported, of which three perpetrators had been caught. The other two were still at large. A little girl had disappeared and one of the stall-owners had been robbed of thirty-seven thousand rupees. As he worked on these cases, Rashid Khan forgot about the boy and girl. Well, he forgot them, yes, but not entirely. They lurked in some deep layer of his consciousness and occasionally their faces rose to the surface.

At about nine-thirty he dismissed his underlings. He liked to be alone at this hour, enjoy a few pegs of whisky and listen to good classical music on a CD. The dynamic police officer had another side to him—he was a discerning lover of music and wrote poetry as a hobby.

Rashid Khan preferred touring his district to sitting at his desk in the headquarters. He loved travelling and was lucky that he could do so without any major disturbances on the home front. He was a common sight in the circuit houses and dak bungalows of Birbhum. Where such resources were not available, he was quite happy to pitch a tent for the night. Sometimes he brought his friends along. Two poets had accompanied him on this trip. They had left just before dusk.

Rashid Khan made do with very little sleep. He could stay awake for nights on end if he needed to. And no matter how much he drank, he never got sodden. If anything, whisky sharpened his faculties and alerted his senses. The most delicate, most refined nuances of the music and poetry he heard while intoxicated entered his ears and touched his soul...

'Sir! Sir!' Nitai's voice came softly from outside.

Rashid Khan glanced at his watch. It was fifty minutes past twelve. 'Come in,' he said.

Slipping into the tent, Nitai sat down and gave a detailed account of all that he had seen and heard. It wasn't much. To prove his veracity, he took out a little notebook and checked the jottings he had made.

8.25. The duo drank water from the well in Rathtala, after which they resumed their walk. On the way they came across an accident, a collision of lorries, but they didn't stop or speak to anyone.

9.10. They rested under a tree for a while.

10.45. They started walking again. Taking a side road, they went to the old Shib Mandir at Bankipur. Quite a few people were sleeping in the vestibule of the temple but the pair didn't join them. They sat some distance away.

Nitai had kept a watch on them till five minutes past twelve, just as Rashid Khan had instructed. He hadn't seen them eat or drink anything. Nor did they smoke ganja or any other narcotic. Their bundle might have contained puffed rice but Nitai couldn't say for sure since they hadn't opened it.

'Did they go to sleep in the vestibule?'

'No, sir. They sat facing each other all the while that I was there. They weren't talking but I think they were singing in low voices.'

'What were they singing? Could you identify the song?'

'No, sir, I didn't go that close. But something rather strange happened. A night bird—you know, the one that calls "Chokh gelo!"—cried out suddenly and the girl responded with exactly the same cry. Then the bird called again, as though in reply.' Nitai was silent for a moment, his brow knitted in thought. 'You know what I think, sir?' he said. 'I think, in fact I'm positive, that it was the girl who lured the boy away from his home, not the other way around. Now if one of them is Muslim and the other Hindu, there'll be hell to pay. The public, as you know, is dead against these mixed religion love affairs. Once, in Bakreswar, a girl from the cowherding community ran off with a Muslim boy and—' Rashid Khan put up a hand to stop him.

'Shall I follow them again tomorrow, sir?' Nitai asked after a while. 'What if there's a religion or caste factor?'

'Discuss that with Binod Chatterjee,' Rashid Khan said curtly. 'You needn't come to me with further reports.'

Rashid Khan lost interest in the couple. The complications of caste and religion didn't concern him in the least. It was their refusal to take the five-hundred rupees that had aroused his curiosity, that was all. Of course, there could be a simple explanation. It was possible that they came from good families and had money of their own. Their singing was mediocre, nothing to write home about. Besides, Rashid Khan wasn't particularly fond of baul songs. He found them rather monotonous after a while. His passion was Hindustani classical music. He dismissed the boy and girl from his mind. There was no need for him to bother his head about them any more.

A few days later, he saw them again, on Ahmedpur Road. It had been a close, dark morning without a trace of sunlight. Now the rain was splashing down in curving sweeps. Thunder rumbled with a terrible roar and there were flashes of lightning.

'Stop!' Rashid Khan yelled at the driver of the jeep. 'Stop at once!' Through the haze of driving rain, he had caught sight of the pair walking down the road. Their movements were fluid and graceful—they looked like swans gliding across a lake. Humans can't be this much at ease, he thought wonderingly, even when walking through spring breezes under a moonlit sky. Poking his head out of the window, he shouted, 'Eyi! Why are you walking in the rain? You're soaked to the skin.'

The couple looked up with eager faces. 'Nomoshkar, babu,' they called out, recognizing him.

'Get into the jeep,' Rashid Khan commanded.

'Why, babu?' the boy asked in surprise. 'We are enjoying walking in the rain.'

'Nonsense. The sky is pouring buckets. You'll catch your death.'

'But the trees are getting wet too,' the girl answered. 'And look at the cows in that field. They won't get sick.'

'Ha ha ha!' the other policemen in the jeep guffawed at this.

But Rashid Khan did not laugh. 'Are they human beings?' he asked solemnly. 'Do they wear clothes like you?'

'We've been calling out to the rain all morning,' the girl said. 'Come, come, we called her over and over again. And now that she is here, can we run away? Won't she feel hurt and offended, babu?'

There was another burst of laughter from the policemen. Rashid Khan turned to them and said, 'These two are young and foolish. They're enjoying getting drenched in the rain. Let them be. They can get as wet and cold as they wish.' A VIP was coming from Delhi to Santiniketan and arrangements had to be made for his security. Rashid Khan couldn't afford to waste any more time. 'Let's go,' he ordered. Leaving the pair behind, the jeep shot ahead in the direction of Bolpur.

Rashid Khan saw the boy again, a few days later, on his way back on the same road. Dusk was falling and the shadows of twilight had gathered around the chhatim tree under which he sat strumming the single string of his ektara and singing softly to himself. Rashid Khan stopped his vehicle and climbed out. He had dismissed the pair consciously from his thoughts but a slight trace of curiosity remained. How did they make a living? What did they eat and how did they come by it? Surely they must have some practical strategy? He had to find out. The boy saw the police officer but did not stop strumming or singing. Rashid Khan looked around for the girl but couldn't see her. He thought they were inseparable. Where was she?

'O he!' he called out affably. 'Where is your companion? The daughter of the desert?'

The boy stopped singing and brought his palms together. 'She isn't here,' he said softly. 'The men of the desert have taken her away.'

'What do you mean?' Rashid Khan asked sharply. 'Have her own people found her? Has she gone away with them?'

'Na go, babu!' the boy exclaimed. 'Not her own people.

These were strangers. The men of the desert are cruel, pitiless. They have no heart.'

'Stop talking in riddles,' Rashid Khan snapped at the boy, 'and tell me what happened in plain Bangla. Was she taken against her will? Who took her?'

'Four or five men were here. They looked as though they had risen from hell. They wielded sticks and knives. They carried her away by force.'

'Carried her away! And you did nothing?'

'God hasn't given me the strength to fight against so many,' the boy answered in a voice curiously devoid of pain or passion. 'You could have stopped them if you were here.'

Rashid Khan realized he wasn't being fair to the lad. What could he have done? Had he shown resistance he would have been lying under this tree, a corpse, or at best a mass of broken bones.

'When did this happen?'

The boy thought for a minute. 'The whole of today has passed,' he said in the same strange, faraway voice. 'And the night before. All of yesterday too. They came at dawn just as the sky was turning pearl and gold...'

'Why didn't you inform me?'

'How could I leave this place, babu? She'll come back here, and if she doesn't find me, she'll...'

Rashid Khan's jaw hardened. *Come back.* There was little hope of that. There had been a spate of kidnappings and rapes recently. And not one of the victims had returned. The girl might not be particularly good-looking but she wasn't crippled or disabled. The bloom of youth and health shone in her skin, eyes and hair. She was meat to her captors, a lump of succulent meat. They would swallow her whole. Besides, raping a woman wasn't enough for the devils these days. Killing their victims or transporting them to far-off destinations was the latest trend. The sons of bitches didn't even draw the line at children. Reports came in every day of five- or six-year-olds being raped and killed. What pleasure did men derive from such acts? Rashid Khan shook his head. No pleasure. Those who had the sensitivity to experience pleasure could never indulge in violence and bloodshed. These were sick people, perverts and parasites who were feeding on a healthy society, infecting it.

What fools these two were, what gullible fools! Even travellers and wayfarers didn't dare sleep in the open these days. Rashid Khan felt his anger returning. Why was the boy such a worthless ninny? Was life only about spouting metaphors and similes? Shouldn't he have bestirred himself and tried to look for his partner? He hadn't even had the sense to inform the police. Instead, he had wasted two whole days singing and strumming his ektara. 'You should have reported the matter to the police,' he told the young man severely. 'Is it enough to sit here doing nothing?'

'I couldn't leave this place, babu.' The boy lifted large, shining eyes to the police officer's face. 'She'll come here to look for me. I know it. We'll be together again.'

'How can she come here? You think she can elude her captors? They must have tied her down with ropes.'

'She has to come back. There is no other way. If she can't break her bonds, she'll drown in them but return she must.'

'Suppose she doesn't?'

'I've told you, babu. No bonds can keep her away from me. Her body might lie there but not she. And if such a thing were to happen, I will know. The wind will whisper it in my ear. And then I shan't sit here any longer. What would be the use? I shall open this cage and set the bird free.' He touched his chest.

Rashid Khan snorted in impatience. A modern Romeo and Juliet, he thought contemptuously. Then, turning to one of the policemen who had accompanied him, he asked roughly, 'Why are you in the police force, Binod babu? A girl is picked up every other day and you do nothing!'

'But sir!' Binod Chatterjee protested. 'No FIR was lodged.'

'Damn the FIR. Aren't you aware of the general situation? Shouldn't you have taken some precautionary measures? Isn't that the job of the police? Listen, I give you forty-eight hours to find the girl, not a minute more. Look for her body first. If they've killed her, you'll find it in the vicinity. If you don't, well and good. It means they've kept her hidden prior to smuggling her out of West Bengal. Get hold of these gangs. Don't pretend you don't know them. I know you do. Raid their hideouts. Alert the railway police. Send messages to the SPs of Bardhaman and Murshidabad. I'll talk to them tonight.'

The police are helpless most of the time. So they say. But the truth, perhaps, is that they cannot do what they do not wish to do. If they have a mind, they can achieve the unachievable. In a remarkably short time, too. The missing baul was found within forty-eight hours. Not dead, alive. And seven other girls with her.

The news was conveyed telephonically to Rashid Khan at the PWD bungalow of Bolpur and the girl brought to him. He gazed at her face for a few minutes. It was thinner than before and her eyes had sunk in their sockets. There were no visible injuries on her face or body but her sari was soiled and torn at the shoulder and her open hair was tangled and caked with dust.

'You've suffered...' Rashid Khan's voice was tender, compassionate. He was about to add a few more words of comfort but the girl forestalled him.

'No,' she said quietly, 'not all that much.'

'Did they ... er...' Rashid Khan stammered a little in embarrassment, 'did they hurt you ... or ... or...?'

'If one can think of one's body as separate from oneself,' the girl said softly, 'if one can think, *this is not mine*, if one can convince oneself of it, then no matter how grave the injury, how severe the torture, there is no pain. The body becomes a mere vessel. It feels nothing.'

'This is high philosophy.' Rashid Khan smiled but his voice remained tense and worried. 'Where did you learn all this? You're so young...'

'I haven't learned anything.' The girl raised her eyes, now weary and circled with dark shadows, to Rashid Khan's face. 'I only listen to my heart. I try to understand what it is saying. It tells me all I need to know.'

'When they carried you away ... when they forced you to ... how did you feel? Weren't you afraid?'

'Terrible things happen in the desert, babu. So many people get hurt, so many lives are lost long before their time. Yet joy and laughter remain.'

Rashid Khan pushed back his chair and rose to his feet. He had just remembered her companion. The boy had said that he would wait under the tree until she came to him. And if the wind brought news of her annihilation, he would set his own soul free. All sorts of news, true and false, are carried by the wind. What if the boy had done something rash already? Then the girl too … *A real-life Romeo and Juliet!* Rashid Khan thought wryly.

Sending for his jeep, he ordered the driver to take Ahmedpur Road. The girl sat beside him but he didn't exchange a word with her. A line from a song by Rajanikanta Sen kept playing in his head: *When I leave this desert of thirst…* There was nothing profoundly original in the girl's use of the desert as a metaphor for the everyday world and in the boy's assertion that he had come floating on the waves of the sea … both ideas were rooted in baul philosophy. Bauls sang freely of *bhava samudra*, the ocean of existence from where all life comes and to which all life must return. The desert of thirst lies in-between…

Rashid Khan wondered what the reunion would be like, what they would say to one another. In his mind's eye he saw the daughter of the desert glide swiftly, like a bird in flight, towards the son of the ocean and fall into his arms. He saw them clinging to each other, weeping silently, unceasingly. The girl had said there was music in human tears.

But nothing of the sort happened. The jeep stopped on the other side of the road and the girl got off. Walking slowly across, she stood quietly near the spot where the boy sat, his back resting against the trunk of the tree. It was obvious to Rashid Khan that he hadn't moved from this position in the last four days. He had sat as motionless as the Buddha under the Bodhi tree. The moon, rising from a cloudless sky, chequered his form with light and shadow.

Where is that flower, the girl murmured softly, *whose honey no bee has ever tasted?* There was wonder in her voice. The boy didn't move from his place at the sight of his beloved nor did he betray any emotion. His face was statuesque, devoid of expression.

The river's water has ceased to flow, he answered, *but the river remains where it was.*

A curious feeling came over Rashid Khan. They aren't talking, he thought to himself. They are singing. Their voices rose and fell like the swell and ebb of sea waves. A distinct lilt and cadence. A hint of a primary tune that was wild and wonderful.

A new moon has risen, the girl sang softly, as though to herself, *and the flute of the beloved is playing…*

The ant is drunk on honey, the boy answered in the same soft, lilting voice, *and has lost all sense of direction.*

The boatman from an alien land now sleeps within his boat…

The eyes of the mind see everything. But the eyes have not seen the mind…

Rashid Khan's eyes nearly sprang out of his head. What was this? After all that had happened, how could the two of them sit here singing like the hero and heroine of a Hindi film? Was it all pretence? Playacting? An attempt to be different from other people? But even as he thought this, he knew he was wrong. This wasn't a dialogue from a play nor was it singing in the regular sense, for the lines did not match either in rhythm or in meaning. They were conveying something to one another, he was sure of that. Were they using a secret language whose code was known only to them? There was a primitive passion in the exchange, an intense yearning. Like two birds calling out to one another…

Suddenly a surge of love, such as he had never felt before, rose within him. Tempestuous, chaotic, it swamped his heart and flooded his soul. His limbs quivered.

The boy and girl were not like any humans he knew. They were not of this world. Like migratory birds, they were roosting in the harsh sands of the desert for a while.

They could spread their wings and fly away whenever they wished. They could bridge the few feet that lay between them and touch each other. Any moment now. Until then ... Rashid Khan shut his eyes. He couldn't bear to see them go. How long would it be before they vanished? Ten seconds? Rashid Khan started counting. *One ... two ... three ... four...*

SHAH JAHAN AND HIS PRIVATE ARMY

ONCE, THERE WAS a major ruckus in Gajipur Haat. Quarrels between pumpkin sellers and sweet-potato sellers over space rights were not uncommon and they often turned into nasty clashes. Things were not so bad that day. Truth be told, there was more smoke than fire. Some shoving and pushing and a lot of curses and abuses. One or two men raised their lathis. But the only blow that fell was on poor Haju, who sold neither pumpkins nor sweet potatoes. In fact, he had nothing to do with anything.

At the sight of blood gushing from the crack in his skull, both parties were stunned into silence. They stood shamefaced for a few seconds and then ran to him with exclamations of sympathy. Taken aback at the sudden assault, Haju sank to his haunches, gripping his head with both hands. He didn't utter a word of reproach or a moan of pain. His eyes turned this way and that like a trapped animal's. As though it was his fault, which it was. As soon as the first wave of commiseration died down, there were angry voices from the crowd: 'Why did *you* have to get into this, haramjada?'

But that was Haju. Always getting into trouble. Bad luck tailed him like a shadow. Only the other day, an ox had strayed into the haat and someone had twisted its tail and given it a shove. Maddened with pain, the animal had rushed headlong towards Haju and tossed him in the air. Everyone else escaped without a scratch. Another time, he was bitten by a water snake while pulling out some lotus stems from the pond. No one in Gajipur had ever been bitten by a water snake before.

Why was Haju wandering around the haat? What was his business there? He wasn't selling or buying anything. No one had the answer, least of all Haju himself. But there he was, every market day, long arms dangling from a frame as tall and thin as an exclamation mark. He wore a green-and-black checked lungi and vest and shaved only occasionally, once a fortnight perhaps. He gazed for hours at something or the other—a known or unknown face, a tree, a bird, a basket of pumpkins ... But his eyes were blank, devoid of all expression.

Gajipur Haat was not a nice place. A lot of money changed hands on market days; consequently, human vultures lay in wait, ready to ignite passions and spark off communal clashes. The traders were mostly Hindu but the moneylenders were Muslim. The new MLA was Sheikh Anwar Ali but the old one, Bishnu Sikdar, still wielded a fair amount of clout. A precarious peace was maintained but the tightrope could snap at any moment and all hell let loose.

In such a situation, only the shrewd and self-centred could flourish. Power, be it of muscle or money, was a must. Haju had neither. Let alone wield power, he hadn't even learned the primary lesson of 'give and take'. He had nothing to give to anyone nor did he want anything. As a boy he was often seen standing under a date palm tree in an empty field, staring at the sunset. He stood for hours, as though he was seeking something, as if he was trying to read a message in the changing hues of the sky. The village elders told his parents that the boy was not meant for this world. He would become a fakir some day. But Haju didn't become a fakir. He had a nasty fall from the same date palm and broke his leg. He didn't stand under it after that. He sat by the canal and gazed at the reflection of the setting sun in its waters...

Haju's uncle's friend, Mojammel, gathered some marigold leaves, pounded them into a pulp and applied it on his wound. Thrusting a bidi into Haju's hand, he whispered, 'Look around carefully, Haju. Can you identify the man who hit you?'

'No, Mojammel chacha.'

'Who says you are useless?' Mojammel sniggered. 'The fight stopped because you got hit on the head, or who knows where it would have ended? Go home now. Tell everyone I was the culprit.'

Haju lit his bidi and staggered off in the direction of the village. His head was throbbing and a trickle of blood was still flowing down his neck and onto his vest. Mojammel's words made no sense to him and were quickly forgotten. Haju crossed the canal, reduced in the winter drought to a streak of pebbles, and stepped into a field. He walked across slowly, the sun beating down on his head, his eyes fixed on his own shadow. Haju knew he was slower and duller than other people. No matter what he was asked to do—weed the fields, draw water from the well or even do odd-jobs around the house—it remained undone. He would stand in one place, staring at the spud or bucket in his hands as though he was immersed in thought. But the truth was, he was thinking of nothing. His mind was blank.

His father and uncles had tried to discipline him. He had been kicked and cuffed many times, been called shiftless and worthless. But none of it bothered him. He told himself that all men were not cast in the same mould. Khodatallah had made him the way he was. What could he do?

Despite his deficiencies, he was married soon after crossing puberty and had four sons in quick succession. But though he was physically a husband and a father, spiritually he was neither. He didn't consider his wife and children his responsibility and they treated him like dirt. His wife Sayeeda was a garrulous woman with a tongue as sharp as a blade. She harangued her husband all day long, nagging and reproaching him until foam flecked the corners of her mouth. But none of it made a dent in Haju's consciousness. Everything she said slid off him like rain water from a yam leaf.

Before entering the house, Haju washed his feet in a pond, rubbing one foot over the other slowly, painstakingly, as though he had all the time in the world. And indeed he did. All he had to do after he got home was to sit on the dalaan with his back to the wall and wait for his wife to serve the evening meal. If there was anything that enthused Haju, it was food. Lately, though, he had had to go hungry quite often. Things were different when they all lived together. From the huge rice pot that bubbled in the kitchen, a few handfuls were always set aside for the worthless member who did nothing to deserve them. His mother had been alive then and, like any mother, she was fiercely protective of her weak, mentally deficient son. But after Amma was put into the earth, everything changed. His brother moved out with his family. Now there was only Sayeeda between him and starvation...

It was she who saw him first. 'There's blood on your head!' she exclaimed.

'Yes. Blood.'

'But how? How did this happen? Did you have a fall?' Her voice grew louder and more menacing the closer she approached. Her strong, tightly packed body gave no indication that she had birthed four children. She had to do the work of two able-bodied men and the harder she pushed herself the stronger her limbs became, and the sharper and more shrewish her tongue.

Haju's eldest son came up to them and stood next to his mother. He was thirteen and worked as a cowherd in a house nearby. As a result, he took himself very seriously and made it a point to taunt and belittle his father whenever he got the chance. At the sound of their voices, other members of the extended family flocked into the yard with excited questions and exclamations. But none of it affected Haju. He knew how it would go. He would be scolded and threatened, jeered and ridiculed. And when the shadows of dusk gathered in the yard and night birds called and jackals howled, silence would descend. The crowd would disperse. People would go about their business and Haju would be forgotten. He was prepared to wait patiently till then.

But today destiny had something else in store for him. Although he hadn't uttered a word, it wasn't long before the truth came out: Haju hadn't had a fall, someone had hit him with a lathi. But who? And why? The people in the yard looked at one another in shock and bewilderment. He was such a good man, incapable of doing anything wrong. Why was he always getting into trouble? Some clicked their tongues in sympathy, some cursed the offender in loud voices and others shook their heads in wonder. What a strange world they lived in, where the good and innocent suffered and the wicked flourished like the green bay tree. The noise and clamour washed over Haju in waves but the expression on his face remained unchanged. Pressing a hand to the side of his head where the dried blood had caked his hair, his answer to all the questions was a steady: 'I don't know how it happened. I felt something hit my head and I fell. It doesn't hurt too much, it's only a little blood.'

Sayeeda's elder brother Eklas pushed his way through the crowd. He was a practical man, a man of the world. He knew that in today's day and age being good didn't get you anywhere. If anything, it landed you in all sorts of trouble. Though he lived and worked in Kolkata, he knew all there was to know about rural politics and kept a sharp watch on the goings-on of his village and the ones around it. He had stopped briefly at his sister's house today on his way back to the city and heard the whole story. Suddenly he had an idea. He would take Haju to Kolkata and get him to start earning a living. He would make a man of him.

No one paid any heed to the proposal at first. Haju in Kolkata? Someone who couldn't fend for himself in his own village was doomed in the city. He was such a numbskull he would come under a bus or a car the very first day! As for earning a living, had he learned any skills? Could he *do* anything? But Eklas waved everyone's objections away. When a fire broke out, he told them ponderously, even dolts and idiots ran to save their lives. Self-preservation was a primary instinct. Fires (metaphorical ones) raged in the city day and night. Even the dullest, the most laid-back, learned the art of survival. All his years in the village hadn't changed Haju one bit. Why not see if the city could do something for him? If nothing else, he could sit at home and roll bidis. He could earn five to seven rupees a day from just that. No one starved in Kolkata. Turning to his brother-in-law, he asked, 'Ki re, Haju? Will you come to the city with me?'

'Yes.' Haju nodded meekly. He had heard the word 'city' but had no idea of what it meant. He knew only his own village and the eight or ten surrounding it. He had never ventured beyond Murshidganj to the left and Suleimanpur to the right. It might be nice to see what the rest of the world was like.

Early next morning, Haju set off with his brother-in-law. 'Don't worry,' Eklas told his sister as she packed some bundles of clothes and provisions. 'I'll look after him. Trust me, he'll be sending you money orders in a couple of months.'

The two set out on the seven-mile walk past the canal to Aronghata, from where they would board the bus to Kolkata. It was a pleasant morning, not too warm, with a fine breeze. Eklas was even more garrulous than his sister and talked continuously. But very little of what he said entered Haju's ears. He walked slowly, a faint smile on his lips, his eyes fixed on the reflection of the sky in the waters of the canal, as though he had never seen anything like it before, as though it was the most splendid sight in the world.

As they approached Suleimanpur, Eklas got a shock. 'O re baba!' he exclaimed. 'What's this?' A procession of a hundred-and-fifty men was coming their way. As he glanced to the left, the doughty city man's heart began to pound like a pestle. There was a crowd standing on the bank, evidently waiting for the approaching men. Some waved flags, others wielded lathis, axes and spuds in their hands. And all were shouting slogans.

'O Haju!' Eklas cried out, his voice trembling. 'There's trouble brewing. We'll get caught. Quick, run as fast as you can.'

Haju hadn't even learned to walk fast, let alone run. His footsteps faltered and became slower as he gazed at the procession, eyes wide with curiosity. The long line had left the field and was climbing onto the embankment now, winding and unwinding like a giant snake. There was a bamboo bridge nearby, which they would have to cross before meeting their opponents on the other side of the canal.

Eklas hurried ahead as fast as his short, fat legs would carry him and then turned and looked back. His companion was standing exactly where he had left him...

Haju stared at the bridge. He hadn't seen it the last time he came to Suleimanpur. Or had he? It was a complex question and he tried to think it through, his brow furrowed in concentration.

Eklas rushed up to him and, seizing his vest, yanked him away roughly. 'Why don't you hurry, you dolt?' he scolded. 'Do you want to get hit on your head a second time?'

Eklas ran all the way, dragging the reluctant Haju along, until they reached Aggarwal Cold Storage, which stood at the far end of the village. Here the two sank down on their haunches to recover their breath.

'Allah knows what's going on there!' Eklas puffed and panted. 'Five or six corpses must be lying on the ground by now.'

The words had barely entered Haju's ears when the scene rose before his eyes, clear as crystal. He saw a field waving with golden paddy crushed and trodden in places, crimson with clotted blood. Seven men lay on the ground—some on their backs, some twisted into unnatural shapes, some crouched on their knees clutching their stomachs.

'Do you know why men kill each other, Haju?' Eklas asked presently.

Haju turned his eyes on his brother-in-law. Large, unblinking, bovine eyes full of patience and sorrow. Sayeeda said her husband's eyes looked like that when he was deep in thought. Eklas's question startled him. 'No.' He shook his head slowly. 'I don't know.'

'Why don't you know? You would if you used your brains.'

'I try to. But Bara Mullah says I don't have any. He says I have cow-dung instead of brains.'

'Heh heh heh! Lesson number one, Haju: men kill each other to save their own lives. If you hit someone, they'll hit you back. That's called survival.'

'But I never hit anyone. Yet people hit me.'

'That's because you're a blockhead. Anyway, we're on our way to Kolkata. Once we are there, I'll make a man of you.'

After drinking their fill of water from the tube well outside the cold storage, the two proceeded to Kolkata. Eklas lodged with a dozen Muslim men in a double-storeyed earthen house on Dargah Road near Maula Ali. They had a common kitchen and everyone was allotted a share of the housework. No one objected to Haju's presence. Among so many mouths, one more was not difficult to feed. But since he wasn't going out to work like the others, they assumed he would do the cooking and cleaning. But what did Haju know of cooking? On the first day, not only did he burn the rice but both his hands too. The men came home to find him staring at the fire as if he could see something extraordinary in it while the acrid smell of burning rice filled the house.

Next, he was given the task of scouring the utensils and washing the clothes. Again the men came home to find him sitting in the yard, surrounded by pots and pans and piles of dirty laundry. His glazed eyes were fixed on the water running out of the tap at full force, turning the yard into a lake of mud.

The eldest and most respected member of the group was a man named Saifullah. He was a chaprasi in the Small Causes Court and took himself and his position very seriously. He was so infuriated by this sight that he rushed at Haju and gave him a resounding thwack on the left ear. 'Shaala!' he thundered. 'Imp of Satan! What do you think you're doing?'

Eklas was standing nearby. His face was solemn and he pronounced in a sombre voice, 'I brought him to the city to make a man of him. He needs a few cuffs and blows to teach him what's what.'

Well! Haju did learn what was what—to some extent, anyway. For the rest of the evening and late into the night, he washed the clothes and scoured the pots with Eklas and Saifullah standing guard, ready to land a blow on his back the moment his hands slackened. And it wasn't just those two. All the inmates, some of them younger than Haju's eldest son, felt free to yank him by the hair or give him a shove on the neck whenever they thought fit. Every member of the house took turns to lecture him on his deficiencies and beat him when he failed in his duties. Haju didn't mind in the least. He adapted himself quickly to his new life and, as a matter of fact, liked it very much.

The afternoons were the best. Everyone was away at work and he could spend hours sitting in the veranda staring at the street. So much went on there, so many people walked past. Pedlars hawking their wares, men in caps and lungis on their way to the dargah, women in burkhas sitting in cycle-rickshaws. From time to time, the call of the muezzin came to his ears, loud and clear over the microphone. He felt a tingling in his spine every time he heard the strange, alien sounds. He had heard them innumerable times but never over a microphone. The deep resonant tones shook his soul. He felt as though Allah was calling out to him. To him, Haju. He unrolled his prayer mat and went down on his knees, tears of happiness glistening in his eyes. And once he began his namaaz, he went on and on, losing all track of time. It was only when Naim or Kader grabbed him by the shoulders and yanked him to his feet that he became aware of the present.

Eklas had promised his sister that Haju would start earning in a few months and send his wages home. He was a conscientious man and intended to redeem his promise. He told himself that he hadn't brought Haju to the city to live on people's charity. He had to get him to start making money. In the basti nearby there was a bidi-making business from which many people—old, young, crippled and able-bodied—earned their living. Eklas managed to find an opening for Haju there. The work was simple. He would be given a tray with all the material and he would have to sit in one place, legs stretched out comfortably, and roll the leaves. No hustle-bustle, no pushing and shoving, no taunts and curses from the employer. Payments were made based on the number of bidis presented at the end of the day, and the rate was six rupees per thousand bidis. Most of the workers made seven or eight rupees quite easily, some even nine or ten. Even if Haju managed to roll only five hundred a day to begin with, he would still be earning three rupees, wouldn't he?

Haju rolled five bidis the first day, seven the next. The others looked at him from the corners of their eyes and sniggered. 'Have you fallen asleep? O mian!' But Haju wasn't asleep. He sat for hours, eyes fixed on the tray, observing the veins on the tobacco leaves and inhaling the sweet, pungent aroma of the spices. The sensations were so heady, his hands refused to move from his lap. The employer complained to Eklas. The man did nothing but stare at the tray all day long. What was the use of keeping him on when there were so many others eager for the job? The long and short of it was that Haju was incapable of doing what others did with the greatest of ease. But as we all know, Khodatallah allots each of his created beings a task before sending him into the world. Haju was soon to find his.

A relative of Saifullah's, a man named Imtiaz, was a frequent visitor to the house on Dargah Road. He was a genial, mild-tempered man with a soft, plump body and a dark, curly beard. He worked as assistant to the chef in a big hotel nearby. Whenever he came over, he brought a large dekchi filled to the brim with biryani, korma, kebabs, minced mutton and peas. No one knew if he stole the stuff or if it was given to him from the leftovers. And no one cared to know, either.

Haju hadn't even heard of these delicacies, let alone tasted them. He ate everything he was given with relish. Imtiaz was fond of him and refilled his enamel thala each time he found it empty. He also took Haju's side when someone bullied or abused him.

'Aha re...' He clicked his tongue sympathetically. 'He's such a good boy. He hasn't learned the first lesson in self-protection. What harm can he do anybody? Where in the world will you find another like him?'

'That's true.' Saifullah wagged his salt-and-pepper beard solemnly. 'If thieves break into the house when the rest of us are away, our Haju won't utter a word. All he'll do is stare at them. He's so good he loves everybody, even thieves and dacoits.'

Imtiaz burst out laughing. 'We live in such troubled times, Dulha bhai,' he said affably, 'that it is difficult to distinguish between thieves and genuine visitors. I don't blame Haju. Anyway, I've thought of something. I can get him employed at my hotel—if the rest of you agree, of course.'

Everyone sat up, startled. Employment! For Haju! In a grand hotel that sahebs and mems frequented! Where big officers from Delhi and Bombay came to stay! They had seen the hotel from a distance and been struck by its size and splendour. Once, Kader had gone to meet Imtiaz there and been driven away by a magnificent personage in a red-and-gold uniform and an enormous turban. No worker was allowed to enter or leave the hotel during duty hours, he was told. They had all applied to Imtiaz for jobs. Apart from the excellent salaries, a lot of money was to be made by way of tips. But Imtiaz hadn't obliged any of them so far. And today he was offering one to Haju, of all people.

Voices rose in protest. Saifullah held up his hand to silence them. 'What you propose is out of the question, Imtiaz,' he said in a pompous tone befitting his age and position. 'You'll land yourself in serious trouble. The man is such a dunce he can't even roll bidis. What work can he do in a hotel? He'll break half the things he's entrusted with and who knows what he'll say to whom? You might end up losing your own job. Forget Haju. He is one of Allah's castrated goats sent out into the world only to graze. Let him be. We'll continue to feed him as we have been doing.'

But Imtiaz wouldn't change his mind. 'He's ideal for the post I'm offering,' he said. 'He won't handle anything so there's no question of breakage. He won't need to speak with anyone either.'

'Why don't you give it to me then?' Kader muttered in a sullen voice. 'I've told you, our factory is heading for a lockout.'

'You're not fit for the job. Everyone can't do everything, can they? It's tailor-made for Haju. All he has to do is stand in one place and salute.'

'He won't be able to do even that. He'll forget.'

'That won't matter. No one will notice.'

'Ki re, Haju?' Eklas turned to his brother-in-law in delight. 'Would you like to work in Imtiaz bhai's hotel?'

Haju tilted his head sideways as far as it would go. The word 'hotel' had set his pulse racing. The rich aroma of ghee and spices rose like a cloud before his nostrils and he inhaled deeply. So many delicious dishes were cooked in the hotel. Koftas and kebabs, sharp curries and roasted meats, sweet chutneys and desserts.

Imtiaz bought Haju a couple of shirts and trousers from Entally Market and took him to the hotel. Haju got the job and he loved it. It was wonderful. There was no running around, no cuffs and blows, no one taunting him. It was so much easier than rolling bidis. All he had to do was stand near the door inside the men's toilet located on the ground floor of the India International Hotel and salute each time someone pushed the door open and walked in. Haju marvelled at the beauty of the place with its milk-white tiles, gleaming mirrors and shining taps. He forgot to salute quite often, but it didn't matter. No one noticed. Intent on their own business, most of the gentlemen didn't even cast a glance in his direction. But Haju's eyes took in every detail of their fine appearance and smart clothes. Even the sound of the urine clattering into the commode fascinated him. Each man's piss has a different sound and smell, he thought, and his eyes were glazed with wonder at the range and diversity of Allah's creation. There were so many different people in the world, with so many different habits. Some scrubbed their hands meticulously with soap, others walked out without even washing them with water. Some took no notice of him, others pressed a twenty-five paisa coin in his hand with a smile. Haju felt himself especially blessed for being given this new experience. Even Mian Know-all Saifullah hadn't a notion that such a place existed.

Haju's duty hours were from one in the afternoon till eleven at night with a half-hour tiffin break. The toilet was used only occasionally in the earlier hours and Haju was quite happy inhaling the smell of naphthalene and staring at the walls and floor and at his own face in the vast mirrors. It got busy from the late evening. The smell changed. As the chatter and laughter from the bar grew louder and merrier, the toilet started humming with activity. Though Haju had never touched liquor in his life, he had seen its effect on people. Toddy was sold and consumed freely in Gajipur and the traders often got into drunken brawls. But the kind of drinking that went on here was different. It was more civilized and subdued. Yes, he had seen some gentlemen swaying on their feet and some having difficulty zipping up their pants. One or two even threw up. Haju stood with his back to the wall, stiff as a ramrod, lapping it all up with his eyes. He never came forward to help. Imtiaz had warned him strictly never to leave his post, no matter what happened. He was not to move unless someone called out to him and never to speak unless he was spoken to.

One night, at about ten o'clock, two young babus pushed the door open and tottered in. Their hair and clothes were in disarray and their eyes as red as hibiscus flowers. By now, Haju recognized most of the guests who frequented the hotel. These two were new. He stared with avid curiosity, and though he understood very little of what they were saying, he listened intently to their conversation. The two young men were poets. Poets, of course, never had the money to drink and dine at a hotel like the India International. If at all they came, it was as someone's guests. These two had been invited by a rich businessman who fancied himself as a connoisseur of the arts and took pride in sponsoring artistes and litterateurs. Suddenly one of the poets looked directly at Haju and declared in an angry voice, 'I find this intolerable. It makes my blood boil!'

'What?' The other looked at him, puzzled. 'Who are you talking about? That short, fat bloke with the pretty girl? I agree. I shall beat him to a pulp when I see him next.'

'No,' the first one said. 'I'm talking about the attendant in this toilet. What sense is there in making a man stand and watch others urinate? It's disgusting.'

'It's a British legacy. The most nauseating way of dehumanizing the native that the rulers could come up with. And look at our own people! They take pride in aping and perpetuating it.'

'Is this system prevalent in England?'

'I doubt it. These repulsive traditions were created only for the colonies.'

'Well, can we deny that the Bengal of today is a colony of the Marwaris?'

The two men washed their hands and splashed water on their faces and on the napes of their necks. Haju stood like a statue, his back to the wall. Suddenly one of them turned to him and barked out two questions: 'Ghar kahan? Mulk kahan?' Haju stood where he was, his eyes large and blank like that of a cow tethered to a post. He didn't understand a word of what the man had asked. People high on alcohol have a certain stubbornness to them. No matter how inconsequential, the man had asked a question and he had to have an answer. Tottering up to Haju, he grabbed him by the chin and asked sternly, this time in Bengali, 'Why don't you answer me? Where do you come from? Which village?'

Now Haju mumbled in a trembling voice, 'Gajipur, saheb.'

'Which district?'

'Medinipur.'

'What's your name?'

'Haju.'

'Haju! What kind of name is Haju? You must have a proper name. What is it?'

Everyone had called him Haju since he could remember. But he did have another name. 'Shajaan, saheb,' he mumbled.

The man looked puzzled. 'Peculiar man,' he muttered.

'With a peculiar name. No one is called Shajaan ... Hindu or Muslim?' He fixed a stern eye on Haju.

The man's looks and voice intimidated Haju. His limbs trembled with fear. 'We are Mocholman, saheb,' he croaked.

'O Hari!' The other man threw back his head and laughed. 'Don't you understand?' He poked his friend in the ribs. 'His name is Shah Jahan.' Leaning towards Haju, he bowed his head in mock servility and exclaimed, 'Your majesty! Emperor Shah Jahan! Why aren't you in your fort at Agra? Has someone whisked you away from there and kept you imprisoned in this urinal?'

'Let's go.' His companion grabbed his shoulder and pushed him towards the door. 'I don't know why we put up with such loathsome practices.' He said the words so forcefully spittle flew out of his mouth in every direction. 'We should kick the manager out of the hotel.'

'Heh heh heh!' Laughter rumbled out of the other's throat, thick and gurgling like oil. 'You always have these elevated ideas after half a dozen pegs. By tomorrow morning ... whoosh! They'll have flown out of the window. As for kicking the manager, what good will that do us? The doors of the hotel will be shut in our faces forever.'

'Still...' the other persisted. 'I'll kick the manager someday or the other, wait and watch. I'm biding my time. A mighty kick on his mighty rump! Ha ha ha!'

As he reached the door, the other man stumbled and fell on Haju. 'Your humble slave begs your forgiveness, your majesty!' The words slurred in his mouth. 'You were the Lord of the Realm! Ruler of Hindustan! Today you are a prisoner in this urinal. But such is life. Goodnight, sleep tight.'

None of this made any sense to Haju. Nor did it disturb

him in the least. Alcohol had peculiar effects on the best of men, he knew that. Some laughed a lot and sang snatches of lewd songs. Others became quarrelsome and aggressive. He was grateful that these two hadn't cuffed and kicked him or dashed his head against the wall.

But the episode didn't end there. After a while another babu walked in. As he unzipped his trousers, he looked askance at Haju and said with a merry twinkle in his eye, 'I hear your name is Shah Jahan. Is that true? Heh heh heh!'

Apparently, back at the bar, the two poets had got into an argument with some others regarding the propriety of keeping an attendant in the toilet. Completely drunk, they became so vehement and loud that they had to be physically removed and sent out of the hotel. In the process, Haju, whom no one had even noticed before, became an important figure. The quarrel was about him and his name had leaked out. Now people started calling him by name. 'Eyi, Shah Jehan,' one said, 'pass me the towel.' 'Where's the soap, Shah Jahan?' another asked. Of course, none of this had any effect on Haju nor did it improve his prospects in the least. In fact, most of the time he didn't even realize it was his name they were taking. Genteel folk pronounced their words differently. And after a few drinks they became even less intelligible.

Anyway, Haju was a success at his job and he enjoyed it, especially the afternoon hours. Barring Saturdays and Sundays he was left alone, undisturbed, from three to six. He could even go out if he wished. Hardly anyone came. But he didn't go anywhere. He stood at his post, staring at everything and marvelling over and over again at the beauty and glamour of his surroundings.

One afternoon, he saw a line of red ants crawling up the

wall. Slowly, steadily, following one another like perfectly disciplined soldiers. Not one moved this way or that. Entranced by the thin streak of red on the dazzling white of the wall, it didn't occur to Haju to wonder where they had come from or where they were going. Instead, another scene rose before his eyes. The procession he had seen in Suleimanpur on his way to Kolkata with Eklas. The long line had moved just so along the embankment and across the bridge. Haju dipped his finger in water and drew a line on the wall, leaving a gap in the middle. The tiles were slippery so he widened the line with more water. The wide line was the canal, the gap the bridge. The ants came up to the canal and stopped short. Only one or two ran back the way they had come—as though in panic, as though they needed to take fresh orders from their commander-in-chief.

Haju looked on in wonder. Why weren't the ants crossing the bridge? 'Good. Very good,' he found himself whispering. 'You've taken the right decision, sons. Where's the sense in occupying another's territory? Why fight and kill each other for nothing? Is there a lack of space on Allah's earth?' He ran his finger along the wall and widened the canal. And now, before his amazed eyes, the ants changed direction. The procession turned to the left and moved in an orderly line. Silent, disciplined soldiers, every one of them. Haju's heart gave a tremendous leap. They had heard him! They were obeying him! He began to draw more lines on the wall and called out encouragingly, 'This way, sons. This way ... this way...'

FLESH

THE SKY WAS cloudy that morning. The children's hearts sank. What if it rained? *God! Don't let it rain. Please ... please god!* But the clouds massed thicker and darker over the banyan tree that stood sentinel at the mouth of the burning ghat.

The name of the village was Chhoto Saturhi. In the tiny yard of Bibhupada Gorhai's thatched hut, three children were looking up at the sky and trying to drive away the clouds. 'Berry on a lime leaf/ Go back rain/ From where you came,' they sang over and over again. The clouds heard the children and wanted to humour them. But to come so close and return without dropping even a mild shower ... well, even clouds had some self-respect.

Suddenly, the heat and suffocating humidity of the morning was blown away by a violent gust of wind. It whistled in the trees, setting branches waving wildly and fan palms lashing their fronds. The clouds began to rumble and growl and then let out a menacing roar. Huge drops of rain pelted to the ground. Harder and faster.

But it was all over within minutes. A laughing sun shone bright and clear. Laughing? Yes, at the folly of humans. They were such strange creatures. Only two months ago they were looking up at the sky day after day, eyes wide with anxiety and distress. *Would the rains never come?* So much weeping, so many prayers, so many frogs killed and turned to face the sky! And now—the clouds moved away. But they bided their time. They would return.

The children were feverish with excitement. Their parents had promised to take them out that day. It was terrible weather, mud and slush lay thick on the ground. But at least it wasn't raining. Impatient to be off, they tugged at their father's hand. But Bibhupada was waiting for his wife. Why was Surobala taking so long?

'Koi re!' he called impatiently. 'If we don't set out now ... we must reach by afternoon or else...'

'Ma!' the little girl cried. 'Come quickly. Come na...' She was seven and her brothers nine and six. The little one's head was tonsured. It had been teeming with lice a few days ago.

Surobala came out of the hut carrying a bundle on one hip. Lifting the latch, she secured the door with a tiny lock and handed the key to her husband. She was about thirty, tall and thin. Her face was unremarkable except in one thing: it was a frozen face. Immobile. Joy or sorrow, anger or revulsion, love or hate, triumph or defeat—it registered nothing. 'Let's go then,' she said.

Bibhupada's expression changed. Only a moment ago he was calling out to his wife to hurry but now he stood undecided. 'Are you sure you want to?' he muttered.

'Yes. I've made up my mind.'

'The children ... taking the children ... is it...?'

'Yes. We'll take them along with us.'

'We want to go!' the children, alarmed at the prospect of being left behind, cried out together. 'You have to take us with you.'

Bibhupada's hut stood by itself at one end of the village. A few other huts could be seen some distance away, straggling haphazardly along the edge of the canal. The shortest path in and out of Chhoto Saturhi skirted the entire length of the burning ghat. The children kept away from it as a rule, frightened by the skulls and bones that lay scattered around. Those who couldn't afford to buy wood to cremate their dead simply touched the corpse's mouth with a knot of flaming grass and left it to rot or become a feast for jackals and vultures. Today, of course, their parents were with them. They were going out—mother, father and three siblings—together for the first time in their short lives. The boys had been to the weekly market once or twice with their father but the girl and her mother always stayed at home.

As they walked past the banyan tree, they saw an ascetic, coated with ash from head to foot, sitting in its shade. A trident was planted in the soft, wet soil by his side. Surobala went up to him and touched her head to his feet. He raised his hand and murmured a blessing. His eyes were hopeful but Surobala had nothing to give him.

'Ma,' the girl asked as soon as she rejoined the group. 'Why do sadhus cover themselves with ash?'

Surobala glanced at her husband and he provided the answer. 'That's because they are followers of Shiv Thakur. And Shiv Thakur has told them that they can't be his chelas if they don't do so.'

'Why does Shiv Thakur have a snake on his head, Baba?' the littlest one piped up.

This time Bibhupada didn't have an answer. 'A snake?' he mumbled. 'Because … um … just like that. No special reason.' Then he said loudly, 'Come on, walk faster. There's no time for dawdling.' The children ran ahead, so far that their father had to yell out to them to stop.

They passed Rath-tala, from where the chariot of Jagannath made its customary journey to the sea every year. This was a prosperous area with several affluent families living in it. Dol, the festival of colours, and Durga Puja were also celebrated here. Bibhupada's destination was still a long way off and although they could have walked the whole way it would take several hours and they wouldn't be able to return before midnight. Bibhupada approached one of the van-rickshaws that stood waiting for passengers. The driver, a rough-looking man, stood next to his vehicle, taking leisurely sips from a glass of tea. 'How are you, Gobindo-da?' Bibhupada bared his teeth ingratiatingly. 'Will you be on your way soon?' His body contorted with self-abasement.

Bibhupada had spoken to Gobindo the previous day. The latter was to go to Sanatanpur to pick up ten pots of palm gur and he had promised to take Bibhu and his family along if no other passengers were available. But it seemed as though he had forgotten. 'Well,' he drank the last of his tea and said thoughtfully, 'I don't see any other passengers and I must be on my way but...'

'But?' Bibhupada hung onto his reply.

'I can't take you for free, you know. After all, pulling an empty van is one thing and pulling it when five people are sitting in it is quite another.' Bibhupada's face fell. Gobindo noticed this and added kindly, 'Very well, I won't charge you the full amount. Pay half. Five rupees per person.'

'Five rupees per person! Even the little ones?'

'Fifteen rupees in all. That's final. And remember, I do this as a favour. Because it's you.' He held out his hand for the money.

'I don't have it now,' Bibhupada said. 'I'll give it to you as soon as I can, I swear on Ma Kali.'

'Hmph!' Gobindo grunted. 'A loan today, a debt tomorrow. That's not how I do business.'

'It won't be a debt,' Bibhupada pleaded. 'I'll give it to you in a few days. Ma Kali's—'

'These are hard times, Bibhu,' Gobindo interrupted. 'Even gods and goddesses are not to be trusted.' Shaking his head sadly, as though moved by Bibhupada's plight, he added, 'Come along then.'

The children had been listening to this exchange, wide-eyed with apprehension. Now they ran pell-mell and clambered onto the van. Sushil, being bigger and stronger than the others and with the right of primogeniture on his side, pushed and shoved his siblings aside, intent on securing the best position. Now he jumped to the front of the van, now to one side. Finally, he settled for the back where he sat, feet dangling over the edge. The other two were made to sit cross-legged in the middle. Bibhu and Suro sat on either side, for balance was an important factor. Sushil had sat in a van-rickshaw once or twice before and knew how it felt. He had run behind them and hitched a ride till the irate owner pushed him out with shouts and curses. For Sudha and Chhotu it was a unique experience. To sit in comfort eating muri and going where you wanted to at the same time! They squirmed and giggled and made faces at the unfortunate folk walking on the road. Walking ... but still being left behind. What fun this was! Who knew life could be so delightful?

'Ma! Look!' Sudha pointed a finger. 'Two fan palms are stuck together like one. Are they twins, Ma?'

'Why is that dog chasing those birds? What birds are they, Ma?' Chhotu was always full of questions.

'Vultures.'

'Do vultures walk on the ground? Why is that man carrying a pole on his shoulder, Baba? Where is he going?'

'He's going home.'

'Look at that temple. It's broken. Why is it broken, Baba?'

'Why? Why? Why?' Bibhupada waved his hands impatiently. 'It's broken because it's broken. Now stop jabbering and dropping your muri all over the place.' The villages in this part of Bengal looked exactly alike. But in the eyes of the children, everything appeared unique and wonderful.

'Where are you off to with your wife and children, Bibhu?' Gobindo asked presently.

'To ... to Ronkalipur.'

'Why Ronkalipur?'

'It's ... um ... my wife's paternal village. She'll be staying there for some time.'

'O ho!' Gobindo grinned from ear to ear. 'Why don't you say straight out that you are going to your father-in-law's house? Good, good. A fine meal awaits you.' Turning to the children, he said heartily, 'You're going to your mama'r bari! What fun!' In a cracked, tuneless voice he sang the old jingle: *'Clap your hands, just so/ To mama's house we go go/ Rice and milk to eat/ No one to scold or beat.'*

'Are we really going to our uncle's house, Ma?' Sushil whispered in Suro's ear. 'How long will we stay there?'

Suro glanced at her husband. 'We'll see,' Bibhu replied, shifting uneasily. 'Hold on tight to the edge of the van and don't ask so many questions.'

'Do you want some muri, Baba?' Sudha held out the pile knotted at the end of her sari.

'No,' Bibhu answered absently.

Chhotu had recovered from his father's rebuke and now he let loose a new string of questions: 'Which bird flies higher, Baba? A kite or a vulture?' 'Why is that girl crying?' 'Is that a cow or a buffalo?' The older children giggled at his foolishness but his parents weren't amused. Surobala sat in stony silence and Bibhu snapped, 'Open your mouth once more and I'll wring your ear.'

Gobindo's vehicle continued on its way, stumbling and lurching over puddles and potholes. To make matters worse, a truck roared up from behind and occupied all the space, forcing the van off the road. Squashed between the truck and a paddy field, Gobindo jumped off and started waving and gesticulating. The children found this hugely entertaining. A huge truck and their tiny van-rickshaw were engaged in battle! Who would win? They watched wide-eyed as Gobindo lowered his vehicle into the field and then climbed back onto the road and began to pedal furiously, leaving the truck behind. 'We've won! We've won!' the children clapped their hands and cheered in glee. 'Our rickshaw is stronger than the truck!'

Surobala brought her face close to her husband's. 'Will you be able to cook for yourself and the children?' she whispered.

'Why not? There's nothing to boiling a few handfuls of rice.'

'Potatoes are cheap this season. Drop some into the pot. And … and Sudha has learned a bit of cooking. She can help you. Only, don't let her light the fire.'

'I won't. Don't worry about anything. By the way, I was thinking of sending the eldest one to school. What do you think?'

'What is in your bundle, Ma?' Sudha's voice broke into the dialogue.

'A few saris.'

'How many uncles do we have in our mama's bari, Ma?' Chhotu turned an eager face to his mother.

But it was Sushil who provided the answer. 'You'll know as soon as we get there,' he said with all the gravity of his position as the eldest. Sudha and Chhotu looked at each other nonplussed. They had never gone to their mama'r bari. They hadn't even known such a place existed.

After a couple of hours, Gobindo stopped his rickshaw and said, 'We've reached Sanatanpur. You must get off here. Take the road to the left for Ronkalipur. It's not too far. And don't forget the fifteen rupees, Bibhu.'

The party started on the walk to Ronkalipur. This was a better road, without too many potholes. The Keleghai river that ran alongside was choked with water cress and hyacinth. Reaching their destination, they walked to the far end of the village, where eight or ten tile-roofed shacks huddled together. There were a couple of shops nearby with bamboo benches on which some men sat chatting animatedly. Bibhu stopped and took his wife's hand. 'Do you *really* want to do this, Suro?' he asked.

'Yes. I've made up my mind.'

'We could go back if … if…'

'No. I won't go back.'

'It wasn't my idea, remember that. I didn't force you.'

'No, you didn't force me. I made my own decision.'

The children became restless. Their mama'r bari was right in front of them. Why were their parents standing on the road wasting time?

'Let's go, Baba.' Sushil tugged at his father's hand.

'Listen, children,' Bibhu cleared his throat, 'your mother is going by herself just now. The rest of us will return to Chhoto Saturhi.'

'Why?' the three cried out as one. 'Why only Ma? Why not us?'

'Because children are not allowed in there. Your mother will come home in a few days. Until then you will stay with me.'

A frown appeared on Sudha's brow. Girls mature faster than boys. While the other two didn't know what to make of this information, Sudha found it unacceptable. Why shouldn't children be allowed into their mama'r bari? she reasoned silently. Who were the ones the rhyme referred to if not the nephews and nieces of the house, the ones who were given rice and milk to eat and were never scolded or beaten?

Chhotu, too young to question his father's logic, clasped his mother's thigh and burst into tears. 'I want to stay with you, Ma,' he cried piteously. 'I won't be any trouble. Let me stay.'

Surobala looked at her husband and two older children. Gently disentangling the child's arms, she said, 'Be a good boy, Chhotu, and go with your father. I'll bring you here another time.' Turning to her daughter, she said, 'Take your little brother's hand. You must look after him while I am away.' She bent down and touched her husband's feet and then turned to the children. She held them to her breast and hugged them tightly. Then, releasing them with a jerk, she started walking towards the cluster of shacks.

Halfway there, she turned back. 'Don't leave just yet,' she told her husband. 'Wait a few minutes.'

The men sitting outside the shop looked her up and

down as she passed them. 'There,' one of them said, pointing a finger, 'go to the biggest shack. She's waiting for you.'

Walking down a lane slippery with mud and slush, Surobala glanced at the houses on either side. Some of the windows were open. Women of various ages and appearances stood at them, eyeing her curiously. At one point, the lane forked into three alleys. Surobala stopped, uncertain which one to take.

'The left one!' said a female voice behind her. 'Take the one to the left. Don't you see her, the demon goddess Kali of Ronkalipur?' There was a muffled giggle from somewhere but the voice continued, 'She's sitting right in front of you.'

Suro turned to the left and saw a woman sitting in a veranda. Monstrously obese, mouth bulging with paan, massive legs stretched out before her. A younger woman sat by her side, thin and bony as a mynah bird.

'O Mashi!' the mynah twittered gaily. 'Is this the new one?'

The older woman looked at Suro. 'Come, child.' The betel juice that filled her mouth rendered her words indistinct. 'Come and sit beside me.' Running her eyes expertly over Surobala's form, she asked, 'Widow?' But she corrected herself before Suro could answer, 'No, no, of course not. There's sindoor in your parting. I wonder I didn't see it. Going blind in my old age, I suppose. So? What happened? Your man ran off?'

'No,' Surobala answered meekly. 'He's at home.'

'Hmph!' the woman snorted rudely. 'Worthless guy won't work. He's looking to you to feed him. How many children?'

'Three.'

'Three!' Mashi's eyes nearly fell out of her head in shock. 'How old is the daughter?'

'Six or seven.'

'Aha re!' The booming voice softened and the probing eyes grew moist. 'Still a long way to go before she's wed. Children are nothing but a curse. We hold them in our womb and suckle them at our breast but the moment they learn to fend for themselves they spread their wings and fly away without a thought for the poor mother they've left behind. I had two strapping sons. Where are they now?'

'My son too,' the yellow-beaked mynah chirped feebly.

Stuffing a fresh paan into her mouth, Mashi held one out to Suro. 'It is our destiny, child,' she said, making soft clucking sounds. 'Our parents marry us off with big dowries in the hope that our husbands will look after us. But if the good-for-nothings can't give us a handful of rice at the end of the day ... Tch, tch! And three children on top of that! Beaks open twenty-four hours, waiting to be filled. So the lazy lout sent you here, I suppose.'

'No,' Suro answered quietly. 'I came on my own.'

'You were right to do so.' Mashi picked up the spittoon that lay by her side and sloshed a mouthful of blood-red betel juice into it. 'A woman must live and keep her children alive. Does anyone shed a tear if she dies of virtue and starvation? Forget your man. Kick him out like a dog if he ever comes sniffing in here.'

'He's sick. He coughs and coughs day and night. Sometimes there's blood...'

'Nonsense.' Mashi stopped her with an imperious wave of her hand. 'I've heard that story before. What's in your bundle? Let me see.' Grimacing, she picked up the saris Surobala had brought and then dropped them. 'These won't do,' she said, shaking her head. 'You'll need at least one with a gold border. Can you get it by the evening? There's a shop nearby.'

Surobala shook her head. She looked at the older woman nervously but it seemed as though the latter had prepared for such a contingency. 'Don't worry,' she said, 'I'll lend you one or two for the present but you must buy your own later. By the way, the rule here is that each one provides her own meals. Nothing is on the house. Whether you eat bellyfuls of rich food or starve yourself to death is no concern of mine. Shefali here,' she gestured at the mynah, 'will explain everything to you. Another thing, I can't give you a separate room just now. You'll have to stay with Mokshada. The wench is sick with the dropsy. Can't eat a morsel without throwing up. It has left her looking like a bunch of twigs. Not a drop of juice or sap, not even in her bones. It's made her really irritable and nasty. Squabbling and bickering all the time, even with the clients. I have received three or four complaints already. *A molo ja!* Clients are our gods. They put food in our mouths and clothes on our bodies. Can we afford to neglect their wishes or find fault with them? I'm going to turn the bitch out one of these days and give you her room. But you must put up with her until then. Don't answer back even if she hits or abuses you. I'll do what needs to be done. An empty cow shed is better than one with a rogue cow in it. Now go with Shefali. She'll show you everything.' But Suro didn't budge. 'What's wrong with you, girl?' Mashi gave her a little push. 'Didn't you hear me? The clients will start arriving soon...'

'Can you lend me some money?' Suro muttered, eyes on the ground.

Mashi's expression changed. Her cheeks turned fiery red. 'Money!' she exclaimed. 'What money?' Her voice was harsh and grating. 'You haven't even started work and you have the gall to ask for money! Did I beg you to come? Look

here, girl. If you want to stay you have to follow the rules.
Live in my house, work hard and make all the money you
can. Pay me my share and do what you please with the
rest.'

'I need the money desperately!' Surobala said in a rush.
'I need it today.'

'Who doesn't need money?' Mashi wagged her head
philosophically. 'Who in this wide world isn't dying for
money? But why should I give it to you? Just because you
ask for it? Have I opened an alms house? If this place
doesn't suit you, you're welcome to leave. I never keep
anyone against their will.'

'The children are waiting outside,' Suro murmured
helplessly. 'There isn't a grain of rice in the house. They
will starve if I don't...'

'The children are waiting outside!' Mashi exclaimed in
shock. 'You've brought them *here*? What sort of mother are
you? Don't you know this is a den of sin with lumpens and
criminals lurking in every lane and alley? They'll think
nothing of devouring your seven-year-old...'

Surobala burst into tears. 'Have pity on me,' she cried. 'I
can't bear to see my children starve.'

'Pity,' Mashi echoed. 'In our profession there's no room
for pity. Pity isn't going to put food into our mouths.'
Turning to the mynah, she said, 'Give me a hand, Shefali.'
Shefali rose and hauled the older woman to her feet. The
two looked on as she lumbered into the house, her huge
body creaking and swaying on tiny puffy feet.

Surobala sat shamefaced and silent, her eyes on the
floor. Her husband had pleaded with her but she had
insisted on coming. He was a very sick man, racked by a
cough morning, noon and night. Sometimes the phlegm

was speckled with blood. The medicines from the general hospital didn't seem to be working. The doctors said he needed nutritious food. But where was it to come from? He thatched huts for a living but it was hard work and he felt breathless and faint after a while. No one sent for him any more.

Surobala had tried to make ends meet by scouring vessels and wiping floors. But the houses of affluent people who employed servants were quite far from where she lived. Besides, most families preferred live-in maids who were prepared to do everything from cooking to washing babies' bottoms and soiled kaanthas. Even that hadn't deterred Suro. But the wages were pitifully low, not enough to buy them one square meal a day. She didn't mind starving herself but she couldn't bear to hear her children beg and whine for food. Was it their fault their parents couldn't feed them? Had they asked to be brought into the world?

Husband and wife had discussed the situation for nights on end but they saw no light at the end of the tunnel. Their few possessions—an aluminium pot, a couple of brass bowls and Suro's wedding sari—had been sold off already. They had nothing left. Nothing—except the flesh on Surobala's body. The strangest thing was that so many months of semi-starvation hadn't left her dried-up and wizened. She was thin but strong and supple. As full of sap as a bamboo shoot…

Mashi waddled back, holding a flimsy, garish sari in one hand and a bunch of assorted notes in the other. Shoving the money into Surobala's hand, she said, 'I never give an advance. Ask Shefali, she'll tell you. You're the first. Go and give it to your husband and send him packing. Then come back and get ready for work. Tell that bastard he and the children must never set foot here again.'

Suro came out of the warren of alleys to see Bibhu standing under a wild fig tree, holding Sudha by the hand. The boys were lurking outside a grocer's shop, staring at jars of boiled sweets and toffees with greedy eyes. They ran back when they saw their mother.

Suro thrust the fistful of soiled notes into Bibhu's hand. 'Buy the rice first,' she said. 'Buy quite a lot. And some salt.'

'Do you think rice will be cheaper here?'

'Don't strain the rice. The starch is nutritious and fills the stomach. Buy some potatoes. They're cheap this season. The children mustn't go hungry…'

'Can't we go inside our mama'r bari just once?' Sudha begged. 'Just to see what it's like?'

'Not now.' Suro stroked her daughter's head. 'Another time maybe.'

'Ma will be coming back soon,' Bibhu said in a voice he strove to keep level. 'She won't be staying long.'

'Yes,' Surobala echoed. 'I'll come back.'

The younger boy's face crumpled and he burst into tears.

'Buy them some toffees,' Suro said to her husband. 'Take your brother's hand, Sudha.'

The word 'toffees' had an electrifying effect on the children. Chhotu stopped crying at once and ran towards the shop, his short legs trying to keep up with his siblings. Bibhu and Suro stood looking into one another's eyes.

'Take care of yourself.' Suro's voice was as stiff and frozen as her face. 'Don't forget to take your medicine and gargle with salt water when the blood comes…'

Bibhu's lips trembled. His face started working and tears glittered in his eyes. He wanted to say something. But what could he say? What can a man say to his wife at a time like this? He lowered his eyes and wiped them on his sleeve. When he looked up, he saw Suro walking away from him with firm resolute steps.

The children ran ahead of Bibhu. It had been such a wonderful day for them—an outing with their parents, a ride in a van rickshaw. And now they had toffees in their mouths and in their hands. *The taste of nectar.* Leaping and dancing with joy, they ran...

THE BROKEN BRIDGE

THERE IS NO way of crossing the Keleghai river to Chitalmari these days except by boat. A bridge still stands on which buses and cars plied until last monsoon, when a part of it collapsed, leaving a gap of about ten feet right in the middle. Luckily, there was no traffic on it at the time, no pedestrians either. The only exception was Goni Mistri's youngest son, Monku, who was taking his goat out to graze. Suddenly, the concrete under his feet crumbled and he and his goat were flung headlong into the river amidst a shower of bricks and mortar. The people standing on the bank saw it with their own eyes.

Three men jumped in to rescue them but found no trace of Monku. The goat was retrieved and now stands tethered to a post in Goni Mistri's yard, alive and well. Goni has decided not to sell it.

The broken bridge presents a strange sight. It looks perfectly solid and sturdy from both ends but there is a yawning gap in the middle. No one uses it any more. Naturally. Is it possible to jump across a stretch of ten feet? How did such a thing happen? And when will the bridge be usable again? No one has any idea.

The village elders remember a time when a bamboo bridge spanned the stretch of water to Chitalmari. The paths on either side were nothing but mud tracks, so no automobiles plied on that route. After the tracks were firmed up with gravel, the need for a concrete structure arose. Appeals were made to the authorities and applications sent. It took a long time—nearly ten years—and several meetings before the bridge became a reality.

Building it took a decade. How long will it take to repair it? Another flood of appeals, processions and gheraos of the panchayat office. The job looks simple. The structure is intact except for the gap in the centre. All the authorities need to do is rebuild a length of about ten feet. That shouldn't take too long or cost too much. Or so the villagers think. The reality is different from what the lay eye perceives. A bridge cannot be mended like a broken shoe. When a man's spine cracks, he loses use of his arms and legs. It is the same with a bridge. The collapse in the centre has weakened the supports on either side. Engineers have examined it and given their opinion. The entire structure has to be demolished and rebuilt.

A new bridge? How long will that take?

Moniruddi's ferry service is back with a bang. The poor man had lost his vocation for the last few years and was hard put to make a living. The only business he got was from ferrying bags of paddy from this bank to that one. Now he can barely keep up with his passengers. Crowds of people—office goers, college students and school children— clamour morning and evening from one bank or another. Moniruddi plies two boats these days.

But this is not a story about broken bridges or ferry services. It is about people.

One evening a young man stepped off Moniruddi's boat at Chitalmari. It was obvious from his appearance and expression that he didn't belong to these parts. He had a sleek, plump body and a round face with luxuriant whiskers waving from it. He wore a tightly buttoned waistcoat over a dazzling white dhuti and kurta, and a pair of gold-rimmed spectacles were perched at the end of a nondescript nose. His hair was closely cropped. He lit cigarette after cigarette with a glittering metal lighter and exhaled smoke from his nostrils. A cloth bag was slung across one shoulder.

While crossing the river in the boat, he didn't speak a word to any of his co-passengers. They didn't speak to him either. Even rural folk these days have learned not to display curiosity or ask unnecessary questions. It was only after the boat had grazed the bank that Moniruddi spoke to him.

'Are you going to Chitalmari?' he asked.

The stranger nodded. 'There!' He pointed a finger. 'I can see the Shiv mandir...' His voice was oddly thin for such a macho man and he had a marked city accent. Taking out his wallet, he paid Moniruddi and climbed out of the boat. The other passengers stared as he strode confidently in the direction of the village. It seemed as though he had the topography of Chitalmari at his fingertips.

Reaching the Shiv mandir, he lit another cigarette. Then, looking this way and that, he approached a man in a lungi with a gamchha hanging from his bare torso.

'O he, korta!' he called out heartily. 'Tell me. That cottage with the tiled roof, the one next to the two palm trees ... doesn't that belong to Raghab Das?'

The man stared speechlessly at the stranger for a few seconds and then nodded twice. Whereupon, the latter started walking in the direction he himself had indicated. For no apparent reason, the other man followed. As they approached the house, two storks who had been sitting on one of the palms flew off with a flash of white wings. A mangy mongrel lying on the ground raised his head and whined dolefully.

The young man cleared his throat. 'Is anyone home?' he called out. A middle-aged woman in a striped sari hurried out of the open door and looked wonderingly at him. 'Nomoshkar.' The stranger brought his palms together. 'Is Raghab Das moshai in the house?'

'No.' The woman shook her head.

'My name is Bijoy Sarkar. I am Annapurna's colleague. We work in the same bank. Are you her mother?'

The woman nodded. Bijoy Sarkar smiled and, stepping forward, touched her fungus-ridden toes. She stood, undecided, for a few minutes. It was difficult to trust anyone these days. But when someone touched your feet you couldn't exactly drive them away.

Though she was a poor man's daughter, Annapurna had always been a good student, her lack of beauty compensated for by her brains. She had passed her class ten examinations from Madhabpur High School and found a job in the cooperative bank of a nearby district town. No other girl from Chitalmari had left home to work in a town before. Not only did Annapurna find a job, she also organized her own boarding and lodging. She lived with the family of a reputed lawyer of those parts. In return, she tutored his children.

Annapurna's mother was puzzled. Wasn't it strange that a man had come all the way from town to look up a female colleague? Had something happened in the office? Annapurna had been at home for about a fortnight or so. She said she was on leave. Could there be another reason? Her face grew dark with anxiety.

'Is... is something wrong?' she asked.

'No, no. Nothing's wrong.' The stranger smiled reassuringly. 'I'm on my way to Nirula's granary. I have some work there. I was passing through your village so I thought...'

'I'll call Annapurna.'

Annapurna came running out. She had been working in the kitchen and her shabby, soiled sari was stained with turmeric. A look of alarm sprang into her eyes at the sight of her guest. She stared at him, speechless. But the young man was unfazed.

'Ki re!' he cried out heartily. 'Why do you look at me like that? Don't you know me? I'm Bijoy—your Bijoy-da. I've come to see your village. Besides, the bank owes you some TA. I've brought it along.' He drew out a slim brown envelope from his satchel and handed it over. The envelope was unsealed and some fifty-rupee notes nestled within.

The man in the lungi and gamchha stood a few yards away, mouth agape. It was clear from his expression that it was only a matter of minutes before he would start spreading the news.

'Lekhon,' Annapurna's mother, Lakshmimoni, called out to him, 'on your way back, inform Anna's father of what has happened and tell him to come home as soon as he can.' Turning to her daughter, she said, 'Take the gentleman inside. Give him some water to wash his feet and make him comfortable. He is our guest...'

Though Lakshmimoni lived in a village where families tended to be large and sprawling, her own was relatively small. Of her three daughters, the middle one had died in childhood. Her eldest, a widow, preferred to live with her parents-in-law and take care of them. But her husband's aunt, a woman younger than herself, had been part of her household for many years now. She had a son named Sudhanya.

Annapurna, being a working girl, enjoyed the rare privilege of having a room to herself. And it was here that she brought her guest.

'You!' she gasped the moment they were alone. 'What have you done? Does anyone come like this?'

'Why?' Bijoy laughed. 'What's wrong? I wanted to see your village. And you too. It's been a long time.'

'But ... but ... like this? Like a dandy in a fine dhuti-kurta?'

'Just a whim.' Bijoy smiled sheepishly. 'I felt like dressing up a little. By the way, I hope you'll let me spend the night...'

'How is that possible?' Annapurna raised her eyebrows in astonishment. 'What will people think?'

'Why should people think anything? Don't village folk have house guests?'

'What if someone finds out? No, no. My father...'

'I'll manage your father.'

'You should have written first.'

'I missed you desperately, Anna. I haven't seen you in so long! Nearly three weeks. You're looking pale and thin. What's the matter? Have you been ill?'

'I'm worried about my job. Is there any chance of getting it back? I've told everyone at home that I'm on leave. But any day now they will find out I've been lying. Is there ... is there any chance?'

'No. Your job was temporary. Besides, the post of record supplier has been abolished. But you don't have to worry. I'm getting transferred to Asansol. I'll find something for you there.'

'Asansol! That's a long way off. I don't know anyone there. Where shall I live?'

'With me. We'll live together.'

Annapurna's father owned a small grocery shop in the village. It stood on the path that led to the bridge and its favourable location had ensured good custom all these years. After the bridge collapsed, he lost most of it. People didn't pass by his shop any more. The ferry ghat was some distance away. Raghab Das didn't own any land. The little he once possessed had been washed away in last year's flood. Now it was lodged in the womb of the river. The government had given some compensation but it was only a fraction of what he had lost. He wouldn't have survived if it weren't for the money his daughter sent him every month. Leaving his aunt's son to keep an eye on things, Raghab Das hurried out of his shop. Lekhon's description of his guest intrigued him. He wondered what the visit was all about.

Bijoy touched Raghab's feet and said, 'Your village is so quiet and peaceful. Where I live, the ears are constantly assailed by sounds of traffic. Noise and bustle from morning till night, not a moment's peace.'

Raghab was impressed. This nice young man was an officer in his daughter's workplace and he knew that subordinates had to be especially respectful of their superiors.

'Sir...' He folded his hands ingratiatingly. 'I have a humble suggestion. We are poor folk, but since it is getting dark, do me the honour of spending the night under my roof.'

'Please don't call me "sir".' Bijoy touched his ears and bit his tongue. 'I am your daughter's colleague. I can stay in your house as a family member. In fact, I'd like to. I hope to explore some of the villages in these parts.'

A rooster was killed that night and cooked into a curry for the special guest. Annapurna gave up her room and slept with her grandaunt. Four days passed but the young man showed no sign of leaving. He had said that he wanted to explore the surrounding villages but he seemed to have given up the idea. The only sightseeing he did was to stroll down to the river every now and then. But he always returned in half an hour. He spent all day in his room chatting with Annapurna. Raghab and Lakshmimoni began to get anxious. Why was the young man sticking to their daughter like a leech? Why wasn't he going home? One had to be cordial to one's daughter's senior officer and extend the warmest hospitality—but for how long?

Lakshmimoni and Raghab's aunt took turns to spy on the pair. They barged into the room, as though by mistake, to see if the door was locked or if the two were in a compromising position. Which they weren't. Ever. All they did was talk. So softly no one could hear a word. Sometimes it sounded as if they were quarrelling and the aunt heard Annapurna sobbing once or twice. What was going on? No one knew.

It was difficult to trust anybody these days. News came in all the time of girls being kidnapped from villages and shipped off to the Gulf. Why, only the other day a middle-aged woman had appeared in Nanda Sapui's house, claiming to be a distant cousin. She looked respectable enough and Nanda had taken her in. Nanda's daughter Gouri was seventeen and quite pretty. She had a wheatish complexion and big eyes, though one of them had a slight squint. She had some education too; she had studied till Class Five.

Marriage proposals came for her but not one matured. Her father was poor and couldn't afford a substantial dowry. 'Why do you keep the girl idle in the house?' the aunt said to Nanda Sapui. 'Send her to a nursing college. There's good money in nursing these days. I can make all the arrangements.'

The woman took the girl away. Months later a letter came in Gouri's handwriting, full of spelling mistakes and grammatical errors and splotched in places as though with tears. The aunt was a demon, Gouri had written. She had sold her and now she was in a brothel in Mumbai. It was a filthy place and she was very unhappy. She was beaten every day and forced to perform sinful acts. Nanda Sapui reported the matter and the police swung into action. But it was in vain. The Mumbai police raided the premises and found no one called Gouri. She had already been packed off to another destination.

This was four months ago. The fear and anxiety that the incident sparked off in the village hadn't quite died down. Now they were fanned into flames once more. Tongues started to wag. Men were the masterminds behind all cases of kidnapping and selling of women and they often took up aliases. Who knew if the young man was really an officer at Annapurna's bank? Officers were busy people with hectic schedules. Why should one of them sit cooling his heels in an obscure village for days on end?

People started coming to Raghab's shop and asking uncomfortable questions. Their voices had an edge that troubled Raghab. The seemingly innocent queries could turn into open threats any moment now. The ring leader, a man called Bhairab Mandal, had taken upon himself the responsibility of being the moral police of the village and his diktats were accepted by the villagers. Bhairab had warned Nanda Sapui that if his daughter came back and he took her in, he would be ostracized by the community.

Why wasn't Bijoy Sarkar going home? Raghab tried talking to his daughter but her eyes widened in panic and she had nothing to say. Raghab decided to take his wife's advice and tell the man to leave the house.

Bijoy hurried to the door on hearing his host's voice.

'Er, Sarkar babu,' Raghab cleared his throat, 'I have something to say to you.'

Bijoy Sarkar was an intelligent man. From the expression on Raghab's face he guessed what was coming. Without giving him a chance to speak, he bent and touched the older man's feet. 'Uncle,' he said, 'I have something to say to you too. Please allow me to speak first. I have been discussing the matter with Annapurna for the last few days and we have come to a decision. We wish to marry. Please give us your blessing.'

Raghab's eyes were ready to pop out in astonishment. This fine young man wanted to marry his daughter! But Anna was so plain! It wasn't as if her face and form were disfigured or deformed, but her skin was dark, exceedingly dark. Black as charcoal. Her nose was quite flat too. A girl like her could find a husband only if her father offered a big dowry. Raghab had given up hope of his daughter's marriage long ago. It was enough for him that she was educated and earning her own living. But in his heart he felt sorry for her. A married woman commanded a higher status in society than a working one. Besides, a single woman was unprotected, vulnerable. And if, god forbid, she fell in love and entered into a relationship, she would be condemned by the community and brutally punished. On the other hand, how she fared after marriage was no one's concern. Her husband could beat her up and starve her, even drive her out of the house. No one would interfere.

With Bijoy's proposal, things changed. The news spread all over the village and tongues stopped wagging. Raghab and Lakshmimoni had a long conversation with their future son-in-law and learned that Annapurna had lost her job—not through any fault of hers, the post itself had been abolished. But, Bijoy hastened to add, he would find her another one as quickly as possible and she would continue to help her family. In the meantime, he promised to send Raghab the exact amount his daughter used to send him every month. To establish his bona fides he handed a sheaf of documents to Raghab. They corresponded perfectly with his claims. He was indeed an officer in the cooperative bank where Anna worked and was presently under transfer orders to Asansol.

So far so good. But there was one hitch. Bijoy wanted a Hindu wedding and he wanted it soon—in a day or two. Raghab was flummoxed. How could he organize a traditional wedding so quickly? And where was the money to come from?

'We'll keep it simple,' Bijoy suggested. 'Just family. There's no need to invite outsiders. As for the expenses, don't worry, take what you need from me.'

The village was agog with excitement. The news of a Hindu wedding put all doubts and fears to rest. Everyone marvelled at Annapurna's luck. Who would have thought that a plain, dark girl like her could snare such a husband? Educated, good-looking and an officer in the bargain. Compared to her, he was a prince! He had excellent manners, too. Ignoring Bijoy's plea to keep it within the

family, the villagers rallied around Raghab to help. Bhairab
Mandal offered to provide the fish for the wedding feast.
Everyone was running around doing his bit. Even the
bridegroom was helping out. The story should have ended
here. Such things don't happen in life. But sometimes they
do...

Calamity struck at dusk, just before the rites began. The
bride and bridegroom were ready. Bijoy was wearing a
waistcoat over his brand-new dhuti-kurta like he always
did. The priest looked at him in surprise and requested him
politely to remove both his upper garments. For a Hindu
wedding, he explained, the bridegroom had to sit with a
bare torso while pronouncing the mantras. Bijoy agreed to
take off the waistcoat but not the kurta. In fact, though the
evening was hot and humid, he insisted on wearing a
shawl.

Bijoy sat on his plank, a stubborn expression on his
face. Under the shawl, his body streamed with sweat, and
drops as large as sandalwood markings were beading his
brow.

'Hee hee! Hee hee!' Suddenly a small boy giggled and
pointed. 'O ma!' he cried. 'Look at the bridegroom's whiskers!'

All eyes turned in Bijoy's direction. One of his whiskers
had slipped from under his nose and was dangling
precariously above his lips. The wedding guests stared at
one another. Why was the man wearing false whiskers?
Was he concealing his identity for some reason? Some of
them burst out laughing at his frantic efforts to readjust it.
Others gathered in knots, whispering feverishly.

Bhairab marched up to the bridegroom and yanked the
shawl off his shoulders. Two mounds were clearly visible,
pushing up through his fine kurta.

'Are these fake too?' he demanded sternly.

Bijoy was silent for a few minutes. His face was flushed, his eyes downcast. 'No,' he said at last. 'I'm a woman.' His voice trembled. 'My name is Bijoya. I love Annapurna.'

The last sentence went unheeded. A woman! The wedding guests set up a racket. What was a woman doing here in the guise of a man? Up to some mischief, no doubt. What about the documents he had shown Raghab? Those were probably fake too.

'No, no,' Bijoy hastened to reassure them. 'They are genuine. I *am* an officer in the cooperative bank. Bijoy and Bijoya have the same spelling in English—VIJAYA.' Annapurna, she said, had told her about the strange woman who had appeared in Nanda Sapui's house and lured his daughter away. That was why she had decided to assume a male identity. Her intentions weren't evil. She truly loved Annapurna and wished to marry her.

Marry! Could two girls get married? The Shastras didn't sanction anything like that. The woman was talking nonsense. She must be a decoy. She had deceived Raghab and was planning to take his daughter away.

'Treachery!'

'Deceit!'

'Impersonation!'

Angry voices broke out from the crowd.

'Forgive me.' Bijoya folded her hands. 'Have pity on me. I truly love Annapurna and we wish to be together. Why don't you ask her if you don't believe me?'

'It's the truth,' Annapurna cried out sharply. 'I know her. We love each other and we…'

Love! Lakshmimoni's blood boiled at these words. She stared at her daughter for a few seconds and then sprang forward, grabbed her by the hair and slapped her hard on the cheek. 'Bitch!' she shrieked. 'Dirty, filthy bitch! Do you know what you are saying?'

'Is this a woman or a eunuch?' someone asked.

'Could be anything.'

'Quite possible.'

A chorus of voices rose in the air.

'Let's strip the creature and find out.'

This was a new game the men of rural Bengal were playing these days. The moment they heard of some misdemeanour on the part of a woman, they stripped her naked and paraded her through the village.

'No! No!' Bijoya shrieked. 'Forgive me! Have mercy on me!' Bursting into tears, she pushed past the crowd and started running as fast as she could. Out of the house and down the path. Her dhuti had slipped from her middle and all she wore under her kurta was a panty. To prevent Annapurna from running after her, some of the men held her forcibly to the ground.

Bijoya ran like a hunted animal down the path towards the river, the mob behind her yelling and hooting like a pack of wolves till they reached the broken bridge. Here they stopped short. But Bijoya ran on and on, sobbing bitterly. Her pursuers stood on the bank and watched her figure grow smaller and smaller. Then, suddenly, it vanished.

Will Bijoya's terrible death go to waste? Maybe not. The news will spread. Reporters will come to the village and questions will be asked. A photograph of the broken bridge might appear in newspapers and get flashed on television screens. And who knows, the authorities might even hasten to repair the bridge.

ONLY HALF A CENTURY

1

Three old ladies were sitting on a mat, legs stretched out, a box of paan between them. One of the grizzled heads was tonsured. Widows had to give up all the good things in life, even hair. Her hair had hung like a cloud, black and rippling, down her back and over her hips. But even as her dead husband made his way to the burning ghat, an old midwife had snatched up a pair of scissors and chopped it off. Now a niece of hers had taken upon herself the onerous duty. Every month she snipped off what little appeared on the ancient head.

'There isn't a single mango tree here the size of our *Tia thunti*,' the woman shook her cropped head and muttered ruefully.

'You remember the pond at the back of our house?' One of the others looked up brightly. 'How it used to swarm with fish! I used to catch puntis by the dozen. It had two huge carps in it the size of husking pedals. They were a couple and always swam together.'

'The fish here is tasteless.' The third old lady frowned disapprovingly.

The first woman, a widow, hadn't eaten fish in years.

She had even forgotten to regret this fact. She preferred talking about fruit. 'Have they cut down the *Tia thunti*?' Her voice was wistful. 'Have you heard any news of it?'

'Aa lo, boro pishi!' The second woman gave a short laugh. 'They've cut the country in two, and you're crying over a tree.'

2

The young man was leaving home. He had a suitcase in his hand. It was made of tin and had a rose painted in one corner.

The name of the place was Badu. It wasn't too far from the city but mercifully the licking tongues of the latter hadn't reached it yet. Theirs was an extended family. Including men and women, young and old, they numbered nearly twenty-eight members. 'Nearly' is an odd word to use when counting human beings. The fact is, theirs was a shifting population. Two or three left every year, and two or three appeared in their place. The house was a semicircle of seven rooms, some built with brick and mortar, others with mud and thatch. The family owned two shops in the bazaar and was well off. Rice was cooked in a huge black pot twice a day and everyone got a dollop of ghee.

Yet Sadeq, their first graduate, was leaving for East Pakistan. What else could he do? He couldn't sit in a shop measuring out lentils and spices, nor could he crush mustard in the oil crusher. He needed a proper job. Why else had he taken the trouble of doing his graduation?

Sadeq's world had changed dramatically in the last few years. Retrenchment had begun soon after the war and gained momentum after independence. The streets were full of unemployed graduates. Independence and chopping off—were the two synonymous? Or was Sadeq being rejected again and again because he was Muslim? Tired of doing the rounds of government and other offices, he had decided to give tuitions. A number of his college friends were doing that while they waited for a real job. But even here he found himself up against a wall. Muslims in these parts were poor and uneducated. They didn't want tutors. Hindu households wouldn't employ him. Though he lived in Madhyamgram, he was prepared to go as far as Barasat. But everywhere he went it was the same story. The moment they heard his name they shook their heads and doled out excuses. Some said they were looking for a female tutor, some that they were getting an MA at the same rate.

It wasn't as though Sadeq was under any pressure. The neighbourhood was peaceful and Hindus and Muslims lived quite amicably. Even when Kolkata was burning, there had been no rioting here. His family didn't mind feeding and clothing him. Yet Sadeq was going away. Ignoring his mother's tears and entreaties and the advice of his father and uncles, he was leaving the country. Didn't people go out into the world to seek their fortune? he said to them. But his heart was heavy with resentment, his face dark with humiliation.

3

This is the land of Gobindo Ganguly's dreams. His sighs can still be heard wafting in the air. The pond, which had once been as clear as a crow's eye, is choked with sedge. The temple where bells had rung out morning and evening is on the verge of collapse. A huge peepul tree has caught its dome in a fierce, crushing embrace. The temple has no deity. Two snakes slither through the dust and dry leaves on the floor.

4

The basti in Beleghata has disappeared. Its narrow alleys were once lined with hovels of potsherd and tin. The occupants, mostly tailors and cotton-shredders, were Muslim, though the basti belonged to a Hindu. Now a double-storeyed market stands in its place. On one side is an apartment complex, on the other a children's playground.

Remember the year Maniktala and Bagbazaar entered into a competition? Not of sport, of murder. From one side the *nara-e-takdeer*, the slogan 'Allah hu Akbar'. From the other, 'Bande Mataram: Bharat Mata ki jai!' A river of blood in-between, the air filled with the stench of decaying corpses. The game found its way into Beleghata. Kerosene splashed on roofs and walls. The hiss of licking flames. Within hours the entire basti had burned to ashes.

Hedayat Hossain was in Kolkata. He had come from Narayanganj, not for a holiday but on work. Though advanced in years, he was tough in body and a shrewd businessman. The hosiery trade on the other side had been controlled by Hindus until the Partition forced many to abandon all they had and flee to India. Hedayat Hossain was quick to take advantage of the void thus created. He had prospered, the enhancement reflected in both his widened girth and his swelling bank account. The latest machines were available only in Kolkata and he had come to buy some. Crossing the border openly involved passports and visas and he couldn't be bothered with such formalities. Taking the ferry in the dead of night was a simpler option.

Hedayat Hossain's work in Kolkata was done and the arrangements for his return finalized. Now, dogged by nostalgia, he decided to visit Beleghata, where he had spent the golden years of his childhood and youth. Walking past the market, he found himself standing in front of a five-storeyed mansion. Two fair, chubby-cheeked children were playing at the gate, climbing up and down the rungs. As he watched them, Hedayat was transported to the past. His father's tailoring shop had stood on this very spot. Abbajaan had fled with his family to the other side. But he hadn't managed to take them all. His youngest son, Hedayat's brother, was left behind. The engulfing flames had swallowed him.

Tears dimmed Hedayat's eyes. The fire he had seen so many years ago burned in his breast. He felt like taking a gigantic hammer to the building that stood so proudly before him and reducing it to dust and rubble.

5

Karim saheb had a flat in Dhanmundi, where a group of senior officers congregated every evening. Karim saheb was a wealthy man. He owned a house in Savar too but preferred to live in the quarters allotted to him by the government. He hadn't rented out the flat. He had turned it into a little club for his friends.

The club had nine members, all men. Women were debarred entry, as were outsiders. Privacy was what the group sought most keenly. The doors were locked as soon as the members had assembled and cards and bottles were brought out. The gaming and drinking went on long into the night, spiced with small talk. They were educated, cultured men. They recited Shakespeare and sang snatches of ghazals composed by Mir Taqi Mir. The country was passing through a pro-Bangla phase. People, the younger generation in particular, were clamouring for a revival of the indigenous language and literature. But these men considered Urdu far superior to Bangla and lost no opportunity to show off their expertise in it. In fact, they often competed with each other to determine the quality of their Urdu.

Karim saheb didn't keep servants in the flat for the simple reason that he didn't want anyone to see what went on there. Who knew what garbled message would be leaked out to the media and what repercussions would follow? Yet someone had to be in attendance to serve soda and water, to pass around plates of chips, nuts and kebabs, to replenish stocks when they ran out. The only person the group trusted was Finance Secretary Haider Ali's driver. Haider Ali was bolder and less touchy than his colleagues. Besides, he knew his driver wouldn't dare open his mouth. He was so humble, his behaviour bordered on servility. No one had heard his voice. All he did was bow his head and obey orders.

'Thank you.' Haider Ali looked up as the man approached them with a tray. 'Please put the things down on the table and kindly uncork one of the bottles, if you don't mind.'

'You speak very politely to your driver,' Rafiqul saheb had said to him the first day. 'It is a good habit.'

'It certainly is a habit, good or bad, I can't say. The man is elderly and hails from our village. His name is Haren Bhattacharya.'

'Bhattacharya!' the others exclaimed. 'A Hindu and a Brahmin!'

'That's right.' Haider Ali nodded. 'I'm surprised you recognize Brahmin surnames. The man, and his father before him, performed all the pujas in the village. I've seen the kind of reverence they commanded. We too were taught to respect them. During the riots, the entire Hindu quarter was wiped off. Most unfortunate. They were good people. I used to call the man Haren-da.'

'He stayed behind?' Rafiqul asked curiously. 'Why didn't he run off to India like the rest?'

'Who knows, maybe his roots wouldn't let go of him. He lost his vocation—there were no Hindus left—and became a pauper.'

'So you've kept a Hindu Brahmin as your driver. Very good.'

'My uncle taught him how to drive. But he's handy in other ways too. He can even dish up a meal when the cook absconds. He's very grateful. He knows he wouldn't be alive if it weren't for us. We've kept him safe in our house.'

'Brahmins are good cooks...' Karim saheb murmured reflectively.

'True. It runs in their blood. Haren-da makes an excellent beef curry—better than what you'll find in any five-star hotel .'

Karim saheb burst out laughing.

6

'When did you come here last, dada? Which year?'

'In 1948. That makes it twenty-four years. Oof! What a lot of time has gone by.'

'Why didn't you come earlier? Didn't you want to?'

'Of course I wanted to. I used to dream of it time and

again. But there was a wall before me as invincible as the one in Berlin.'

'Why? You belong here...'

'Our ancestral home was in Rajshahi. But I don't belong here. This is not my country.'

'Do you have any family left in Rajshahi?'

'My maternal uncle was there till 1965. He migrated to India after the police looted his house in an armed dacoity...'

'The police! Dacoity! What are you saying, dada?'

'Yes. That's the tragic truth. An ordinary dacoity is easy to understand, even accept. But if the police arrive in the dead of night and take everything away at gunpoint, when they molest your women in front of your eyes—what do you call it?'

'Protector turned predator. Ha ha ha!'

'I'm glad you find it funny. Other funny things used to happen at that time. The two Bengals were separated only by a river. Dhaka and Kolkata were a few hundred miles apart. Yet telephone calls had to be routed through London. Did you know that?'

'Yes. You had to know someone in London and he would make the connection.'

'Circling the head to touch the nose. Politics! Nothing but politics. Even top officials played this game.'

'Dada, you must visit my house before you go back. You must leave the dust of your feet on my threshold.'

'Arre arre! My feet are still coated with the dust of Kolkata. Why should I leave that on your threshold? I'll go back with the dust of this land on my head. It may not be my country but it is still my birthplace.'

7

Samar Mitra, the famous singer, was on a visit to newly independent Bangladesh. He was no ordinary warbler. His patriotic songs had fired the hearts of Muslims and Hindus alike during the nine months of the country's freedom struggle. Debdulal Bandopadhayay and Samar Mitra had both become legends in their lifetimes. People waited eagerly to hear the news and music in their respective voices.

It was Samar Mitra's first visit to independent Bangladesh. Large receptions were organized in his honour and he was showered with felicitations. He gave musical performances which people attended in vast numbers. The wealthy elite of Dhaka vied with one another for his time. Invitations poured in thick and fast and he had to eat at three or four houses every day.

That evening, as he stood in front of the dining table at a newspaper editor's house, his eyes widened in dismay. It was a huge table, groaning with food. There were so many dishes on it that the very thought of tasting them all alarmed him. In a moment of carelessness he had mentioned to someone—he didn't remember who—that he enjoyed eating dried fish. The news had spread like wildfire, and now wherever he went he found an assortment of dried fish on the table, cooked in a dozen different ways: dried Bombay duck in lentils, dried minnows in greens, mashed potatoes and aubergines cooked with dried prawns. The list was endless. In addition there was an enormous range of fresh fish: fat rui from Sirajganj; ilish gleaming like moonlight, caught fresh from the Padma river; fierce, flat, silvery chital from the Meghna; huge lobsters. And with all this there were several preparations of mutton and chicken.

His hostess, Suraiyya bhabi, was a fine cook. She was very beautiful too and had a sweet, melodious voice.

'What's all this, Suraiyya bhabi?' Samar turned to her with a smile. 'Do you want to kill me with so much food?'

'I won't force you to try everything.' The gorgeous lady smiled back. 'Take what you like and as much as you like. And don't worry, there's no beef in any of the preparations.'

'Worry! About beef?' Samar laughed. 'Do you know, as a student I survived on ruti and beef kebabs. They were the cheapest food available...' Samar took a spoonful of rice, white and fragrant as jasmine petals, and small servings of a few other dishes. Plate in hand, he withdrew to a corner and seated himself.

'Sir.' A young lady darted towards him from the other end of the room. 'What do you think of our country? Do you like it here?'

'Of course!' Samar Mitra replied. 'The people are warm and generous and there's so much spirit and energy in the young. Even the air smells fresh and sweet—of independence. My own country seems jaded in comparison. But I have one problem with you. You are too lavish with your hospitality. In India a newspaper editor, even an owner, wouldn't dream of spending so much on one party. They aren't as wealthy either. Baap re baap! The houses of the rich here make my head spin.'

'But the newspaper market is booming in Kolkata,' a young man hovering nearby put in. 'Many more are sold...'

'True. I hear there's a dearth of buyers for the dailies here. But your editors are much more affluent.'

'People in Bangladesh like to show off their wealth. They know very well that no one can eat thirty dishes at a time and still they...'

Samar Mitra was alarmed. Suraiyya bhabi was standing
a few feet away. What if she heard them? 'You know what I
wish for at times?' He changed the subject quickly. 'I wish
I could stay here with you. If you allow me to, of course.
Bangla is bound to flourish here. Language, literature *and*
the arts. It isn't the same in Kolkata. Everything is turning
hybrid. And the love I receive from you…'

'Stay! Please stay!' a clamour of voices rose from all over
the room.

Sitting in a corner by an open window was Mijanur
Rehman—the editor of another newspaper. He held a glass
of whisky in his hand. Taking a long sip, he shook his head.
'Don't even dream of it, Samar babu,' he said. 'Wipe that
wish away from your heart. What you think of as love is
mere infatuation. And infatuation evaporates with time.
Do you know what will happen if you decide to stay here?
Other singers will feel threatened and go after you. And the
public that fawns upon you now will take a U-turn and
denounce you as a Malaun—an idolatrous Hindu. They'll
spare no effort in trying to drive you away from the country.
If you—'

'That's not true,' Suraiyya bhabi interrupted, her face
pink with embarrassment. 'Mijanur bhai speaks a lot of
nonsense.'

'Our Mijan bhai is a cynic of the first order.' Her husband
laughed.

But Mijanur saheb was unfazed. 'I only stated a fact.' He
took another sip from his glass. 'Just analyse the past and
you'll have to admit the truth. When the Indian Army came
forward to help our Mukti Bahini and eminent men from
West Bengal spoke out in our favour, we were ecstatic. We
raised slogans like "Indians are our friends", "All Bengalis

are brothers". How long did the euphoria last? And this isn't only true of us, such turnarounds are a fact of history. The same thing happened after America released France from the clutches of Nazi Germany. It didn't take long for the French to wrinkle their noses in disgust when they saw Americans on their streets. The Indian Army lost eighteen thousand soldiers in our war for liberation. They lie in unmarked graves on this very soil. But mark my words, we'll soon forget them. History books will carry no mention of their sacrifice. In fact, Bangladesh will deny that India had anything to do with their struggle for independence. This is the way of the world. History repeats itself.'

Voices rose in protest. Samar Mitra took their side. 'I think you are being a little too pessimistic, Mijan saheb,' he said with a smile. 'I don't know how India and Bangladesh will deal with one another politically, but I do believe that ordinary people from both countries will continue to love and cherish—'

'Forget politics,' the young woman who had asked him what he thought of her country interrupted forcefully. 'Bengal is divided but its language and culture are not. In fact, we've forged a bridge between us now. Pakistan had robbed us of this connection all these years.'

'We won't let go of you, Samar-da.' Suraiyya bhabi turned dark, melting eyes on her guest. 'You will stay here with us and give us music lessons. We will all sing together. And...' She glanced at her husband. 'We're thinking of buying a house in India. We would like to spend a few months each year in Kolkata.'

Mijanur Rehman poured more whisky in his glass. A small smile hovered around the corners of his mouth.

8

In one of the side streets that meander away from Elgin Road there stands a haunted house. All the other old houses in the area have been converted into brightly lit apartment complexes. Only this one remains. Dark and mossy, buried in trees and shrubs with gaping holes in place of doors and windows. The price of land here is worth its weight in gold.

The house must have had a fine garden once, where little children played and pretty women with red velvet slippers on fair feet sat under striped umbrellas, sipping rose-flavoured sharbat from tall crystal glasses or Darjeeling tea from cups of Belgian porcelain. The owner of the house, Monirujjaman saheb, had left the country after Partition, migrating not to East Pakistan but to West. He hadn't been able to sell the house before leaving. For one thing, there was an error in the title deed that needed to be rectified. For another, he hadn't found the time. He had meant to go back when things calmed down and do whatever needed to be done. Unfortunately, with increased travel restrictions between the two countries, that time had never come.

For the first few years Monirujjaman prospered in his new country. He managed to set up a good practice in Islamabad and was recognized as one of the city's leading barristers. He even dabbled in politics and was made a junior minister in the Cabinet. The trouble began after the 1971 war. People woke up to his Bengali identity and the tables turned. Bengalis and traitors were synonymous. Hadn't they started a civil war and split the country in two? Monirujjaman felt a net of hatred and suspicion closing around him. When his youngest son got killed by

Mujahideen bullets, it became clear to him that this country was not his. He had to get out. But where would he go? His two daughters were married to Pakistanis and had adopted the language and customs of their new families. And there was no place for him in Bangladesh. He had sided with the enemy. Old and enfeebled, Monirujjaman saheb had become a 'nowhere man'. He bought a ticket to London and, as he crossed the black water, lost his identity as a Bengali altogether.

Monirujjaman's wife's brother, Habibullah, lived with his family at his ancestral home in Chandannagar. Habibullah was a lawyer in the lower courts and his third son, Kamaal, worked in an advertising agency. Kamaal had recently married Tehmina, a schoolteacher, and all three found the commute from Chandannagar to Kolkata strenuous and time-consuming. They were looking for a flat in the city and since Tehmina's school was located on Southern Avenue, something close by would be ideal.

Kamaal knew that a huge house belonging to his uncle had been lying abandoned near Elgin Road for many years now. It was so old it was crumbling to the ground, yet nothing was being done about it. There was no chance of his uncle ever returning to this country and Kamaal, his sole relative here, didn't possess any documents. His heart surged with self-pity each time he thought of the possibilities. If he had the title deed he could have handed the property over to a builder. He could have kept two flats for himself and sold the rest. And with the money that came in he could have lived a life of leisure for all time to come, just like his zamindar ancestors. He was lucky the house was still standing—the government could have acquired it long ago. Or else the stream of refugees from

East Pakistan and now Bangladesh could have found their way in. But the thought brought little comfort to Kamaal. He sighed. He didn't have any documents and, as such, not a ghost of a chance of possession.

'Look for a place in the Muslim quarter of Park Circus,' his friend Shamsher advised. 'You won't find a house anywhere else.'

Kamaal didn't believe him. Kolkata was a cosmopolitan city where different religious and ethnic groups had lived side by side for centuries. Besides, weren't they surrounded by Hindus in Chandannagar? But even though Kamaal combed the streets of South Kolkata, he found no available house. Wherever he went—Southern Avenue, Ballygunge, Jodhpur Park—it was the same story. He was prepared to pay the market rent, even give a deposit, but he was rejected each time. He couldn't understand why.

At last a ray of hope was brought by Tehmina. Her student, Bishakha, had informed her that the ground floor of their house in Jodhpur Park had fallen vacant and her father was looking for a tenant. Bishakha promised to put in a word for her teacher and more or less told her that the place was hers if she liked it.

One Sunday morning, Kamaal and Tehmina went to see the flat. It was bright and airy and stood in a quiet and respectable neighbourhood. There was no question of not liking it. Bishakha's father, Ranganath babu, was not at home. He was in the fish market, his daughter said. He loved fish and took a long time in selecting the freshest and the best. While they waited, Bishakha served them tea and pastries and kept up a lively conversation.

'This is my miss, Baba,' Bishakha introduced the couple as soon as her father returned, 'and this is her mister.'

Ranganath sat with them, plied them with more tea and cake, and talked of this and that. But when Kamaal brought up the subject of the flat, he shook his head sadly.

'I would have loved to give it to you,' he said, his voice faltering, 'but ... unfortunately ... Bishakha must have told you ... I'm in the tea business. I've expanded it recently and the staff has increased by twenty per cent. My office in Khidirpur is chock-a-block ... there's no space to move. I've decided to shift the accounts section here. So I'm sure you'll understand ... I'm not renting the flat—for now anyway. I'm very sorry. Please forgive me.'

Bishakha accompanied Kamaal and Tehmina to the taxi stand. Returning home, she found her father standing on the balcony with Kamaal's card in his hand. 'Are you really converting the flat into an office, Baba?' she asked. 'Why didn't you tell me?'

'I haven't made up my mind about that yet. But one thing is certain, I don't want Muslim tenants. I don't trust them.'

'But my miss isn't a typical Muslim. She's a cultured lady, a good teacher and very kind and loving. And she sings Rabindra sangeet...'

'That may be so but it's best for them to live among their own kind. They should go back to Pakistan, they'll be better off there.'

'Dhaka isn't in Pakistan, it's in Bangladesh. Really, Baba!'

'It's the same thing.' Ranganath shrugged his shoulders contemptuously. 'Bangladesh is turning into a replica of Pakistan, I hear.'

9

The terrible news spread quickly and chaos descended upon the city. Shopkeepers pulled down their shutters, buses and trains stopped running. The department of health, in which Hena worked, advised its employees to hurry home before the traffic came to a complete halt. Hena managed to get onto a bus but it was stopped midway by a group of men shouting slogans. She got off and started running. In her hurry she dropped her umbrella. Not daring to turn around to pick it up, she left it on the road and ran faster, not stopping until she reached home. She locked the door and commanded her servant Saiful: 'Don't open it, no matter who knocks.' Breathless and panting, she rushed up the stairs.

Her husband Alam was in bed, reading a book. He had been feeling feverish for the last few days and hadn't gone to work. He looked up, astonished, at his wife's red, sweating face.

'Haven't you heard the news?' Hena burst out. 'Indira Gandhi is dead. She has been assassinated.'

'Hyaan!' Alam cried out in a shocked voice. 'What are you saying? Who killed her? A Muslim?'

Before Hena could answer, the telephone rang shrilly. 'Hena apa!' a woman's voice screeched from the other end. 'Have you reached home? Shukre Allah! Don't go out again. You heard what happened?'

'Yes, yes. But who do you think killed her?'

'Nothing has been announced on our channels yet. But the BBC has reported that it was one of her security guards.'

Putting the phone down, Hena turned to her husband. 'Are there Muslims among the prime minister's security guards?'

'I'm sure there are. She keeps Muslims and Sikhs around her as well as Hindus.'

'But why should a Muslim kill her?'

'Why not? He could be a Pakistani agent. Many Indian Muslims dislike her.'

'But she wasn't communal. She stood by Bangladesh when it needed her help.'

'That's the crux of the matter. Many Muslims blame her for splitting Pakistan, particularly the ones from north India. Even we Bengalis ... Haven't you heard Karim chacha call it an act of Hindu diplomacy?'

'What if the killer is a Muslim?'

'Then there'll be hell to pay. Hindus will go on a Muslim-killing spree. Sooner or later, the Muslims will retaliate and there will be full-scale riots.'

'I admire Indira Gandhi immensely. She was right to split Pakistan and give Bengalis a country of their own. West Pakistan has always suppressed the East and treated it as a colony—thrusting Urdu on Bengalis, denying Mujibur Rehman the prime-ministership. Besides, it was Bengali Muslims who started the war of liberation. Indira Gandhi only helped them achieve their goal.'

'Admire her all you will and sing her praises. That won't change anything. Why did she lose the last elections? Because the Muslim vote went against her. Who knows if some crazy religious fanatic took it into his head to pump a few bullets into her?'

Suddenly they heard the sound of running feet and the loud shouting of slogans from the street. A shiver rippled down Hena's spine. She glanced fearfully at her husband. He had switched on the radio and was listening to the news, his face grim.

It was late evening when they got the news: the killer was not a Muslim. The prime minister had sent the army into the Golden Temple to smoke out the terrorists hiding in there. This was their revenge. A Sikh from among her own bodyguards had splayed her body with bullets.

Across India, in the capital in particular, a terrible massacre was unleashed upon the Sikh community. Sikh houses burned, women were raped and children butchered. Fortunately, things couldn't go too far in Kolkata. The police stopped it with a firm hand. But in Siliguri, a petrol pump was set on fire and its owner, an elderly Sikh, was pushed into the flames.

Not a Muslim, a Sikh. Hena breathed a sigh of relief. But deep down, she felt a sense of unease. All this while she had been mourning Indira Gandhi's death, at least that was what she told herself. But was that the truth? Wasn't she thinking obsessively of what might have happened to them had the killer been Muslim? Wasn't her heart quaking with fear every time she heard voices in the street? Wasn't she living in fear of assault by a frenzied mob every moment? Why such helplessness? Why this insecurity? Didn't she have the right to live here just like everyone else?

10

Rabeya stretched her hand across the counter and handed her form to the clerk.

The old man adjusted his spectacles and looked it up and down. 'Why have you left the space marked "Religion" blank?' he asked.

'My religion is my personal affair,' Rabeya answered quietly. 'I don't wish to announce it to all and sundry.'

'There's no need to be impertinent. Fill the form properly and bring it back.'

Rabeya refused and, in consequence, was sent to the principal. 'If you have no religion,' the latter's lip curled in contempt, 'you may write "Atheist".'

'I'm not an atheist, I have a religion. But why should I be compelled to put it down on my admission form?'

'That's the rule. Another thing. You've stated that you are married. What is your husband's name?'

'Do I have to declare his name? Is that also the rule? Well, since you ask, it is Satyen Basu Choudhury.'

'That means your husband is a Hindu. Why haven't you taken his surname?'

'I don't know if he is a Hindu. Only he knows what he is. But does the law compel a woman to change her surname after marriage?'

'You're wasting my time. If you don't fill up your form properly there's no question of your getting admission.'

'I insist on getting admission.'

'Are you threatening me? Do you want me to call the darwan and have you thrown out?'

'You could do that but I won't give up. I'll get a court order and take admission in this very college. I'll take my case right up to the Supreme Court if necessary.'

Satyen Basu Choudhury had left his ancestral home after marrying Rabeya and moved to a small flat in Madhyamgram. It was a government flat so no questions had been raised about caste or religion. But changing the ration card had posed a difficulty. 'You've married a Muslim,' the inspector told him. 'That's all right. But husband and wife must have the same surname.'

'Suppose we don't want it that way?'

'It's the rule. There is no other way.'

'Whose rule? The British started this system but why should *we* follow it? And for your information, Muslims don't have surnames. They have one name—a long one, sometimes—but one. By the way, do you remember your grandmother's name?'

'My grandmother's name!' The inspector was startled. 'Why do you ask me that?'

'Because I'm sure your grandmother didn't have a surname. Do you know what the poet Rabindranath's wife was called? Mrinalini Debi—not Mrinalini Tagore. Hindu women traditionally have first names followed by the suffix Debi or Dasi, in accordance with their caste. Isn't it better for our women to be known by the name their parents gave them without advertising their caste?'

That evening, Satyen and his wife went out. They had meant to visit a friend but a sudden shower of rain forced them to stop and take shelter under a tree. One isn't completely protected even under a tree. Rabeya and Satyen were laughing and dodging the raindrops that splashed onto them from the leaves. Through the branches above their heads they could see the sky. It was always there, above them. But how often did they care to look at it? It was only at times like these that one looked up and thought, isn't it amazing that we all live under the same sky?

CROSSING

THEY TWISTED MY arms behind my back and tied my hands with a nylon cord. My eyes were bandaged with a thick black cloth. Wedging a large ball of cotton wool into my mouth, they sealed my lips with sticking plaster. Then two or three men—I'm guessing the number—carried me a hundred-odd paces and set me down on a plank. 'Start walking,' a voice as bright and sharp as a knife cut into my ears. 'Take one step at a time. There's no need to hurry.' I put out one foot tentatively. The plank was about nine inches broad. Around it was an empty expanse...

It was a dark, moonless night and the air was thick and humid. Not a leaf had stirred in the trees as my car lurched and rolled up and down the hills and came to a halt in the middle of a jungle.

Is this a bridge across some mountain river?

The men laughed and answered the question I had asked myself. 'Yes. This is a temporary bridge across the Teesta. The water flows five hundred feet below. One false step and you'll turn into pulp. No one will see you again.'

Why are you making me cross this bridge? I wanted to ask but the only sound that came out of my sealed mouth was an indistinct 'Bu-bu-bu-boom.' They understood what I was trying to say—how, I do not know.

'It's a game,' they shouted.

What if I don't wish to play this game? I asked exactly as I had before.

'Then we'll push you off the plank.' Their voices were gay with laughter. 'You'll go twirling through the air and fall into the river. We'll flash our torches and watch you.'

What if I manage to reach the other side?

Another burst of laughter. 'You'll see what happens then. Something pleasant, surely. Now start. We'll count to ten. If you don't start moving by then ... One, two, three...'

I put my right foot forward. It didn't seem too difficult. The wood felt firm. The trick was to move slowly, I told myself. Very slowly. To make sure one foot was secure on the plank before lifting the other. A moment's inattention and the river would swallow me up. But I had played dangerous games before. And this one...

I had taken three steps before they finished their counting. What did they think I was? A coward? Just because they had outnumbered and captured me in an unknown jungle after my car broke down? Were they expecting me to weep and plead? To beg for mercy? They didn't know me! How long was the plank? The Teesta was quite wide in places. I had crossed Jubilee Bridge a number of times but it might be narrower over the hills. What place was this?

Oh! Why were my legs shaking? My head was calm and clear but my feet were unsteady. As soon as I raised one foot, the other wobbled on the plank as though it didn't have the strength to hold up my body. I wondered why. People could stand on one foot for a fair amount of time. It used to be standard punishment in school. So? Ah! Standing on one foot was easy but setting down the other in front of it was damned difficult. That was the problem. People didn't learn to walk right from birth. Babies waddled the first few days.

'Why did you stop?' someone shouted. 'Do you want a shove on your backside?' My mouth was bound. They knew that, didn't they? Then why were they asking me questions?

'Either we push you into the river,' another voice entered my ears, 'or shoot you dead. Which would you prefer? We'll count to ten again, and then shoot. One, two, three...'

If only I had a lathi, I could find a better balance. A lathi! Hah! They hadn't even left my arms free. If they had I could have stretched them out ... I had used this technique as a child when walking along a boundary wall or a railway line. It worked. At times like these, arms turned into wings.

The visibility was nil tonight. Yet they had bound my eyes. I wondered why. I've heard that in times of dire necessity, it is possible to see in the dark. Even if that wasn't true, even if I couldn't see *in* the dark, I could *see* the dark, couldn't I? Darkness has its own beauty, its shades and variations. My legs were trembling violently now. So violently they were totally out of control. Once, I swayed to the left and almost fell. This was an unfair game! I would never make it to the other side. There was one thing, though, that brought a glow to my heart. I was beyond the reach of their lathis. They couldn't poke or push me. They could shoot me, of course, but ... Here I took a vow. I wouldn't die of bullet wounds. I would jump into the river before their counting was done.

'Neelu! Neelu!'

My father's voice. But Baba had been dead and gone for many years now. Was his soul calling out to me? But a soul, if such a thing exists, is not a bird that can wing across a river and speak in a human voice. I know I am imagining it, conjuring it up from all the stories and novels I've read. Had I, crying out from within the deepest layer of my unconscious self, asked for my father's help?

'Neelu! Neelu! Shall I hold your hand?'

'My hands are tied, Baba. Do *you* have hands?'

'No, I don't. But you must not, you cannot stop. Take the next step, and the next. Slowly. Carefully. Tell yourself your mother is waiting for you just ahead.'

Did mothers stand in front of their sons or behind them?

A tiny breath of wind rose from the river and passed over my hot, perspiring limbs. Oof, what a relief! But then the wind started blowing in gusts. That was bad. Already my body felt light and fragile, like a leaf or a flower, as though it could be blown away any moment.

No. I can't. I can't do this any more.

I could hear the counting behind me. One, two, three … seven, eight…

'Don't jump, Neelu!' My mother's voice. But why did it sound so different, both in tone and texture? 'Don't jump. Keep going. Come. Come to me. Don't you know who I am?'

'Rini! You're Rini! I didn't recognize your voice at first. And I thought I would remember you all my life. Isn't that strange?'

'You forgot me! Did you really forget me, Neelu?'

'No, Rini, I didn't forget you. Not entirely. It's true, of course, that I haven't thought of you in years … Where were you? You got lost and…'

'It wasn't I who got lost. It was you who drifted away.'

'My eyes are bound, Rini. I can't see you. Do you still look the same? You had the soft, wondering eyes of a young dove. A body as light as a floating feather.'

'Don't talk, Neelu. Concentrate on walking towards me. Here, take my hand.'

'I can't, Rini. I'm losing my nerve. See how long it is taking me to raise one foot.'

'Yet there was a time when you left everything and came rushing to me.'

'It was you who drew me like a magnet. Can't you do that again?'

'I doubt it. Too many years have passed since. Listen to me, Neelu. Turn sideways and shuffle slowly along the plank. Your legs will stop trembling because you won't need to raise your feet. Come. I'm here, right in front of you, holding out my hand.'

'You're right. Walking sideways is so much easier. How did you know, Rini? Have you crossed such a bridge yourself?'

No answer. Rini wasn't there, I knew that now. It wasn't she who had spoken to me from the darkness. It wasn't she who had advised me to walk sideways. I had thought up the trick myself. Rini! I had moved away from her. I had lost her. Yet at one time, I had darted towards her like the light of the sun that travels millions of miles in the direction of the earth. The spark that enters the pores of our animate and inanimate bodies and is carried through our veins and arteries sets us aflame. Flesh, blood, tissue, fibre, sinew, bone and muscle—all, all are illuminated! So had I … no no, it wasn't I who had turned on the light. It was Rini. On a hot, brooding afternoon, when the world slept and the only sound was the plaintive call of a kite,

Rini had lifted her hand and said, 'Look at the tip of my forefinger and tell me what you see.' I looked and saw … eternity. Yet we lost one another. But it couldn't happen again. I couldn't lose her again. I would pretend that she was waiting for me, ten steps away, holding up her finger. I could see its glowing tip. I had to take those steps. I had to reach her.

'Neelu!' Rini's voice came to my ears again. 'I'm standing exactly ten steps away from you. Come to me. Very slowly. You can do it.'

'Will you rip the covering from my eyes when I get there? I want to see you once. I yearn to…'

'It's a good thing they bandaged your eyes. Looking down at the river would make your head spin. There's a glimmering light in the water. Right at the bottom…'

'I don't want to look at the water. All I want to see is the tip of your forefinger glowing in the dark.'

I walked the ten steps. My feet didn't tremble. But Rini wasn't there. I could hear some sounds now. Where were they coming from? The river? Ah, yes, it must be the river cackling with mirth as it leapt and whirled hundreds of feet below me, carrying dangerous currents on its breast, rushing headlong to meet the sea.

O-he! I called out to my subconscious. *Why couldn't you summon up the power to turn my fantasy into a flesh-and-blood Rini?* I was a fool to imagine that she stood ten steps away. Why hadn't I thought of fifty? Guided by the glowing tip of her tender finger, I could have walked those fifty steps and reached the other bank. Like a miser I had thought only of ten and, spending them, I had lost her. I could rave and rant against my subconscious all I wanted, but Rini wouldn't come back.

'Why do you stop? Eyi, haramjada!' There was a harsh growl behind me. 'You want to keep us here all night? Shall we start shooting?'

Were those six (I had counted them) flashing their torches to see how far I had gone? Were they keeping an anxious vigil so as not to miss a moment of the sight of my body falling into the river? Perhaps they had indulged in a betting game and were waiting with bated breath for the result. I thought of a scene common in action films. The hero misses his footing ... the hearts of the viewers go *thump-thump-thump*. But he doesn't fall. At the last moment he clutches the branch of a tree with one hand. He hangs in space for half a minute. The open jaws of a crocodile wait below him but he is undaunted. He manages to swing himself back to safety. But I wouldn't be able to do that. My hands were bound. I wouldn't be able to grasp the plank with my teeth either. There was a gag in my mouth. I couldn't afford to make a mistake. No, not even a fraction of a mistake. I was no hero and this was not a film.

Was living so important? What was wrong with dying? Another scene rose before my eyes. A straw thatch on a mud hut with a gourd vine clinging to it. A grasshopper fluttering fragile, iridescent wings on a tender, downy leaf. Living joyously, rapturously. Oblivious of the fact that a shalik with needle-sharp eyes was watching it, ready to dart from the sky and snap it up in its yellow beak.

Why had this thought crossed my mind?

How much further did I have to go? Was I halfway there? It was a moment's decision. If I took that moment by the horns I could leap into the water and rid myself of this prolonged agony. Falling from such a great height, I would be dead before I even hit the water. The air pressure would

kill me—so scientists say. I thought of my lifeless body
floating on the silver waters of the Teesta. Was there a
better way to die?

The bridge had started swinging. Gently at first, then
harder and faster. Why was that? Were the lumpens shaking
it deliberately? So that was their game. They wouldn't let
me win. All the skill and intelligence I had employed would
come to naught. They would compel me to fall.

But … could there be another reason? This was a long,
narrow plank with no support other than the two banks. I
must have reached the middle. The plank, curving under
the pressure of my body, was swaying from side to side.
Either way I was as good as dead. I couldn't stop the plank
from moving.

'Neelu! Neelu!' Another voice. 'Swing your body this
way and that. Synchronize your movements with that of
the bridge, then you won't lose your balance.'

'Ke? Gagan-da? Where did you come from?'

'Don't talk, Neelu. Concentrate on swaying from side to
side and move forward bit by bit.'

'I can't, Gagan-da. I'm exhausted. The water is dragging
me down. I'm falling…'

'No, Neelu. You won't fall. Have courage. Tell yourself
you'll succeed and you will. Follow my instructions and
you'll reach the bank. You have to…'

What was all this? There was no Gagan-da. It was my
subconscious playing tricks with me again, telling me to
swing my body and walk at the same time. That too on a
narrow plank across a river in spate. Was I a gymnast or a
magician?

Gagan-da had always given me the wrong advice. As a
college student, he encouraged me to give up my studies

and join an armed movement. He insisted I abandon the genteel tongue I had spoken all my life in favour of a rustic dialect. He said I must banish love and tenderness from my heart and harden it to the extent that I wouldn't bat an eyelid before plunging a dagger in my best friend's chest. And I had obeyed him blindly, followed all his instructions. Eventually, when the scales fell from my eyes, I realized that he didn't practise an iota of what he preached. He was living a cushioned, comfortable life, bogged down by nothing. No ideals, no principles. When I asked him the reason, he looked me up and down and said, 'Who are you? I don't know you.'

Baba, Rini, Gagan-da. Why were they rising from my subconscious? In which deep, dormant layer had they hidden themselves all these years? Walking on a nine-inch strip of wood that was swinging high across a turbulent river, was I playing out an allegory of life? Was this nightmarish journey merely a powerful metaphor? Teetering on a razor-thin edge, swaying between existence and non-existence— was that what life was all about? The Upanishads said … Bah! All that philosophy was rot. Utter rot. Six armed assailants had pounced on me from god knows where and put me through this ordeal. What they had against me and why, I hadn't the foggiest notion. Why, instead of lodging a bullet in my head, they were making me play this grotesque game was the moot question. And I was playing it. Knowing full well that if I made the slightest slip, I would be hurled headlong to my death. That was the hard truth. As was this endless night…

One, two, three, four, five…

I'm moving, guys. I'm moving. Who doesn't cling to life? Who doesn't strain every nerve, teeth clenched, just to

remain alive? The swinging seemed to have stopped. Perhaps
I had crossed the middle of the river. The wind had died
down and it was beastly hot. If only I could take my shirt
off. And if I could shed my pants, even better. I would be
able to walk more freely. Thank god they had removed my
shoes before setting me on the plank. They must have done
so by mistake, for it had given me an advantage. Like my
primeval ancestors, I was curling my toes at the edge of the
plank to get a better grip.

'Don't be afraid, Neelu. I am with you.'

'You've come again, Baba. Do you remember how often
I used to lose my way home? But I always found it again.'

'Neelu! A father's or mother's love is strongest when a
child is in trouble. It gushes out of their hearts and wraps
him in a protective halo. Wise men say love is like a
mountain stream—it flows downward. That is why we
humans receive love from our parents, but when it is our
turn to give we pass it on to our children.'

Why did you bring my father back? A tight knot of pain
formed in my throat as I questioned my subconscious. *His
presence is weakening me. I have hurt his feelings—not once, not
twice, but innumerable times. I know that now. I wasn't present at
his deathbed. I ignored his advice. It was good advice but I preferred
that of my friends. Their company was stimulating, enjoyable. But
is this the time or place for regret and self-flagellation? Dear brother
Subconscious, if you must bring someone to me, bring Rini. If nothing
else, the sound of her voice will strengthen me.*

It was my own subconscious yet I was pleading with it.
I was unable to control it. I wanted Rini but it had brought
Gagan-da instead. What was the point of bringing Gagan-
da? Men like him only mouthed platitudes and preached
sermons. A few might benefit from them and reach their

goal. But what of the hundreds and thousands who fell by the wayside? I was one of those who fell. But I want to live. Really and truly, I swear by Ma Kali. I yearn and yearn for life. Even if it is of the poorest quality imaginable! Even if it means hanging outside the dining rooms of the rich and eating their leftovers. I don't want to fall into the river and have my limbs torn from my torso by deadly currents. I don't want to die. Oh god, I don't want to die!

Right foot. Left foot. Right foot. Left foot. My subconscious had abandoned me. Now all I was left with were my feet. Eyes bound, hands bound, lips sealed—only my feet could see me through. Were those six still flashing their torches and keeping their guns in readiness? How much further did I have to go? I had walked far … so very far!

I could hear voices close by. Were they really voices or was it my subconscious again? No, these were voices, pure and simple human voices. Had I reached the bank? Was I saved? Thank god, they hadn't plugged my ears! I could hear every word quite clearly. 'Buck up!' someone cried. 'Buck up! You've reached. Only a few more steps and your ordeal is over.'

'My god!' An angry exclamation. 'The haramjada's made it! He has the nine lives of a cat.'

'One is to four.' Another voice. 'Didn't I tell you the pull of life is so strong the guy will win? You've lost your bet. You have to pay up…'

I stopped in my tracks. The voices were familiar. They were the ones I had heard when I was being gagged and blindfolded. But how did they reach the other side? There must be another bridge close at hand, wide and safe, across which they had run on flying feet.

'Why do you stop?' a voice, kinder and more encouraging

than any I had heard that night, called out to me. 'Just a few
more steps. You've made it, man! You have nothing more
to fear.'

'He's really something. We should give him a prize.'

'Of course. We must show a sportsman's spirit. We'll
declare him winner the moment he steps on the bank. O re
… What would you like? A house on half an acre of land? A
foreign trip? An agency for a chemist's shop? A road-
building contract? Name it and it's yours.'

My legs were trembling violently. I remembered the old
adage: *Three elbow-lengths of a date palm*. Date palms had
rough jagged surfaces that were very hard to climb. The last
three elbow-lengths were the toughest. Many who managed
to make their way up fell in this last lap. Like a boat that
sways and totters over unruly waves for hours but sinks
minutes before it touches the shore. These last few steps …
I couldn't take them. My strength of mind and body had
gone…

What are you doing, you fool? My subconscious appeared at
my elbow. It began pushing and prodding me. *You've reached
the end of the plank*, it hissed in my ears. *You're standing on
solid ground now. The water's behind you, just two or three more
steps. Even if you fall now it won't matter.*

I laughed and turned my head. The men had promised
me a prize if I reached the end. It was a game to them. Like
everyone else, I too wanted to live. But was simply being
alive enough? Even worms and insects lived. Human beings
were different. Their lives had to have a certain quality.
Self-worth and self-respect were part of it. A carrot dangled
on the other side and I was straining every nerve to reach it
… *Death if you lose, a carrot if you win*. These were the rules of
the game they were playing. Was this what I wanted? Why
should I play by their rules?

I turned and started walking in the opposite direction. 'Arre! Arre!' Shocked, bewildered voices rushed into my ears. 'What is the man doing? Is he mad? O re! This way. This way. You're saved.'

My mouth was bound but I spoke to them in a resolute voice: 'Your game is over. Now watch me begin mine.'

A Peacock Feather

THE DOORBELL RANG four times in succession. That was his signal. Tinni glanced around the room quickly. Was everything in place? Hari babu hated a room in disorder. Bits of paper on the floor, an empty teacup on the table—these things enraged him. And far worse were open windows. Tinni hastened to close them. As she reached the last of the three windows, the one in the corner, she stood for a few moments, her eyes filled with longing. Then she snapped it shut and ran to open the door.

A man aged between forty and fifty stood outside. Spring, summer, autumn or winter—Hari babu looked the same. He wore a dark brown suit and a cream tie. He held a leather briefcase in his hand. His thinning hair was combed carefully over the bald patch above his brow.

'Were you asleep?' Hari babu asked pleasantly.

'No no,' Tinni answered, a little flustered.

'Then why did you take so long to open the door?'

'I didn't take long...'

'Yes, you did.'

'Oh! I remember now. I was in the bathroom.'

Hari babu entered the room, took off his shoes and shoved them under the bed. He didn't take off his socks. He wore them all the time; he even slept in them. Walking up to the bathroom, he peered inside. What he saw or thought only he knew. He sat down on the bed and beckoned to her.

'Come. Come to me.' Seating her in his lap, he pressed his thighs tightly against her hips. 'You're pretty,' he told her, 'but you look even prettier with lipstick. Why aren't you wearing any?' Even before completing his sentence he slapped her hard on the cheek. His voice changed, becoming a hiss. 'Why did you lie? You were standing by the window, weren't you?'

Tinni was silent. She knew that if she opened her mouth, be it in acceptance or denial of the charge, more beatings would follow.

Hari babu started stroking the soft cheek he had marked with his hand. 'A-ha re,' he commiserated. 'It's turned quite red. Guess how I found out?' His teeth glittered as he smiled. Without waiting for a reply, he continued, 'I make it a point to look up at the windows the moment I step into the street. I saw all three open and you standing at the corner window like a seductive Radha. Who were you looking out for? Me?'

Tinni was silent.

'Answer me.' Hari babu's lips curled in a grimace. Still Tinni remained silent. 'Haramjadi!' He gripped her long hair and twisted it, dragging her head back. 'Why don't you answer me?'

'Who do I have but you?' Tinni whispered in a broken voice. Tears filled her eyes and rolled down her cheeks.

Hari babu stared at the upturned face for a few seconds and his expression changed. The ferocious lines relaxed. He stuck his tongue out and began to lick away the tears with as much relish as if he were licking an ice cream. He didn't loosen his grip on Tinni's hair, though. He continued twisting it as he said, 'Of course you have me. Don't I give you everything you need? What more do you want? Ask and you shall have it. You're a good girl. Everything about you is good except your habit of standing in front of open windows. Next time I catch you, I'll flay the skin off your back, remember that.' Hari babu let go of Tinni's hair and opened his briefcase. 'Look what I've brought for you.' He drew out a bottle of whisky and two cartons of Chinese food. 'Fetch some plates and glasses,' he commanded.

It had been three years but Tinni was still sickened by the smell of whisky. Yet she had to take a glass and sip from it now and then. The more Hari babu drank the more garrulous he became. But for all his jabbering, he watched her with a hawk's eye. If he thought she wasn't drinking, only holding her glass, he would punch her in the face or grab her ear with fiery fingers. And when he was completely drunk, he would kick her forcefully on her behind. He got a lot of pleasure out of kicking her. 'Hee hee hee!' he would cackle gleefully. She would fall to the ground with every kick and then stand up and get ready for the next one. The game would go on until, tiring of it, he would tumble into bed and start snoring.

It was Basana who had taught him the kicking game.

Hari babu finished his first peg and lit a cigarette. 'Do you feel like a caged bird, Tinni?' he asked conversationally.

'N—no.'

'Why not? This room is like a cage.'

'Yes—no, no. I mean, the bathroom is nice.'

'You're quite right. The bathroom is *really* nice. It has a telephone shower, even a bathtub. Cages don't have bathrooms, do they? But the question is, are birds happier in cages or out in the open?'

'I ... I don't know.'

'Right again. How do we know what birds think? After all, they don't have the gift of speech. They can't express their thoughts. Well, no, I don't mean exactly that. I'm sure they can communicate amongst themselves. The trouble is we humans don't understand their language. But one thing is certain. In the open they have to fend for themselves. They have to find their own food, don't they? Inside the cage they don't have to take the trouble. Their food is brought to them. Tell me, Tinni, do you think birds weep?'

'I don't know.'

'True. How would you know? Long ago, I read in a book that birds and animals cannot weep. Only humans can. From that, doesn't it logically follow that creatures who don't have emotions cannot distinguish between liberty and bondage? The freedom of unhampered movement— what pleasure can it bring to them? Birds fly about because they have to find food.'

'Are they looking for food all the time?'

'Of course they are. The moment they've eaten their fill they fall asleep. What else can they do? Go and see a film? Take a dip in the Ganga? Hee hee hee! Tell me, Tinni, do you feel like a prisoner?'

'No.'

'Why not? Isn't this room like a prison cell?'

'No ... I mean ... the bathroom is nice.'

'You have a thing for bathrooms. But you're right. Prison cells don't have attached bathrooms. And prisoners aren't fed Chinese food. As for jewellery...' He reached out and swung Tinni's earring gently. 'Who will bring jhumkas for a prisoner? Eh, Tinni? Who will bring jhumkas? Yet you keep your windows open. Why?'

'I won't do it again.'

Hari babu's hand closed over her ear and gave it a fierce tweak. 'Remember that.' He grimaced. 'If I catch you again, I'll...'

Hari babu needed four pegs of whisky to reach a high. Another hour, during which he did whatever else he needed to do, and then it was time to switch off the lights and go to sleep. He started snoring the moment his head touched the pillow. Tinni lay beside him, wide awake, staring at the ceiling. It was a pattern she was familiar with. It lasted three or four days. Then suddenly one morning he was gone. He might return the next day or a week later.

When he was with her he didn't step out of the room even for a minute. He kept all the windows closed and opened the door only twice a day to let in a man who brought them food. Tinni knew nothing about Hari babu other than his name. It was quite possible that Hari wasn't his real name. It was also possible that he had another home, a wife and children. He never spoke about himself. He had told her about some maternal uncles who lived in a remote village. He never mentioned his parents, not even when he was completely drunk. He kept a lot of money in his briefcase. Tinni had seen him counting it once or twice.

Hari babu slept soundly all night. He woke up once, at dawn, to urinate, and then fell asleep again. He was very quiet during the day. He didn't beat or abuse Tinni. He seemed lost in thought...

Tinni rose from the bed, very quietly, and placed her feet on the floor. There was an air-conditioner in the room and it was cool. But the smell of whisky and of the man lying beside her sickened her. She longed for a breath of fresh air. Why was Hari babu so hell-bent on keeping out fresh air? She couldn't figure it out.

Tiptoeing to the bathroom, she clicked the door shut and stood by the window. She opened it and leaned out, breathing in great draughts of clean, cool air. The room in which Hari babu kept her was on the second floor of a five-storeyed apartment building that stood on a wide street. There were some smaller houses opposite it. From the bathroom window she could look straight into one of them. It was well past midnight but a light still burned in a room that stood by itself on the terrace. The windows were open—they were open at all hours of day and night—and through them she could see a bed spread with sparkling white linen. At a table sat a young man in pyjamas and a sleeveless vest, poring over some books. Tinni gazed into the room, her eyes wide with curiosity. It was something like looking at a still-life painting. Morning, noon and night, it looked exactly the same. Except for a couple of hours in the evening, when he went out, the man was always at the table, sitting in exactly the same position. The scene drew Tinni like a magnet. How far into the night did he study? From where did he get his intense concentration?

On rare occasions he walked about the room, book in hand, pausing briefly to look out of the window. One morning, a few days ago, he had seen her. At first he seemed somewhat preoccupied and then suddenly his eyes looked full into her face. The next moment he had moved away. Was it in embarrassment? Yes, Tinni realized that he was embarrassed. Because from that day onward he stopped standing at the left window, from where he could see her

clearly, and moved to the right one. Tinni was amused.
Were young men in this day and age ashamed of looking at
women? She had never seen anything like this in her life.
Yes, in all her life she hadn't encountered a shamed male
gaze. She had seen anger, lust, envy, cruelty and cunning in
men's eyes. Even pity. But not shame. Never shame.

Tinni was shy and retiring by nature and had been so
from childhood. She had never asked for food even when
she was hungry, never opened her mouth to protest an
injustice. People called her a good girl, a gentle, submissive
girl. Afraid of unknown people, she had always hidden
herself in the presence of strangers. This trait had enraged
her father and he had often beaten her for it.

In all her twenty-three years the only kind man Tinni
had known was Shibkumar, the gatekeeper of the house in
which she had lived prior to this one. He was a big, muscular
man in his prime. He wore khaki shorts over a sleeveless
vest and sat all day on a stool at the gate, stroking his
enormous moustache. A man called Jhandu had brought
her to that house. He had wheedled her into coming away
with him from her village in Coochbehar with promises of
marriage. But the moment she entered the house she knew
something was wrong. It was full of women. Tinni
understood at once, and why wouldn't she? Hadn't she
seen dozens of films with brothel scenes in them? She was
twenty at the time and Jhandu forty. He didn't even belong
to Coochbehar. It was Suro mashi who had arranged it all.

Suro mashi had said wonderful things about him. Not
that Tinni believed everything she said. But desperate to
leave home, she had wanted to believe. This was her only
chance. Her mother had died in her childhood. Her father
came home drunk every evening and beat his children

mercilessly. A few months ago, her elder brother, unable to bear it any longer, had struck back. Picking up a heavy knife from the kitchen, he had stabbed his father on the shoulder and run away. He hadn't returned. They had an aunt living with them who had hated Tinni from the very beginning— Tinni had no idea why. She made her do all the difficult household work, cursed and beat her and even starved her at times. Tinni had put up with her aunt's cruelty but her son Bhaba's repeated attempts to rape her was the final straw. She decided to run away from home like her brother.

Men had troubled Tinni from the time she turned sixteen. Though she didn't understand the exact implications then, the way they touched her made her blush with shame. Freeing herself from their clutches, she would run into the house and hide. But that was possible with outsiders. What did one do when a ferocious beast was a member of the household? Bhaba lived in Siliguri, where he was a bus conductor. He came to see his mother every now and then and whenever he did, he had a go at Tinni. He looked like a demon and obviously thought of her as food over which he had a legitimate right. He could eat her whenever he felt like it. And his appetite was insatiable. He raged with hunger all the time. If he had bitten off chunks of flesh from her body and eaten them, Tinni wouldn't have felt so revolted. But what he wanted to do with her was a sin—a terrible sin. Her own cousin! If she allowed it, her soul would rot in hell. No, even hell was too good a place for one as depraved as she.

She had complained to her aunt once and been sharply rebuked. She was told that it was her own fault. It was around that time that Suro mashi arrived on the scene— from where, Tinni didn't know. She had never seen the woman before. 'A-ha re,' Suro mashi had consoled her in a soothing voice. 'You'll have to suffer this torment all your life. Do you think that selfish drunkard, your father, will ever arrange a marriage for you? As for that aunt of yours, she is inhuman. She'll put you up for sale! If you want to be saved from such a fate, place your trust in me. I'll find you a husband.'

Tinni believed her. To escape Bhaba, she ran off with Jhandu.

Later, she discovered that Jhandu's profession was trafficking and Suro mashi was his partner. Together they sought out helpless, unhappy girls, won them over with promises of marriage, brought them to Kolkata and sold them into brothels. Tinni cursed herself. Why hadn't she seen through them? But even if she had, what difference would it have made? Could she have gone on living the way she was? With her meagre education, could she have found a job? She had attended Maharani Harsha Mukhi Vidyalaya till Class Six before her studies ended on an abrupt note.

One rainy afternoon she was coming back from school with two other girls. By the time they reached the bazaar all three were dripping wet. Tinni was tall and voluptuous for her age, unlike the other two who were small and scrawny. As they went past the tea shop, the tailor's son, Lotka, jumped up from the bench and rushed at them. He was big and hefty and his eyes were inflamed with ganja.

'Come!' He grabbed Tinni's hand and yanked her towards him. 'I want to measure your chest.'

Tinni screamed and struggled but Lotka wouldn't let go until a crowd gathered and pulled them apart. When her father and aunt heard about the incident, they decided to end her education. She had had enough schooling, they told her, and of what use was it, anyway? Her father had studied up to Class Four and her aunt didn't even know her letters. Thus Tinni took the punishment for Lotka's action while he swaggered around, his chest puffed up like a lord's.

Tinni had escaped her aunt and Bhaba but, in doing so, had fallen from the frying pan into the fire. She wouldn't let the men who came to the brothel do what they wanted and that enraged them. They complained to the madam and demanded their money back. Tinni was beaten black and blue but she wouldn't submit. She wept and pleaded but her tears and entreaties didn't strike the slightest chord of sympathy in any heart. Then one of the girls, Basana, gave her a piece of advice. There was nothing to be gained from resisting, she told her. The more one wept and begged, the worse the beatings became. 'Learn to smile,' Basana said. 'It won't come naturally but keep one fixed on your lips. This is an artificial world and you'll learn to adapt to it. The sooner you do so, the better it will be for you.' But how could Tinni smile when her heart was breaking? When terror and revulsion were filling her soul?

The other girls of the house heard of Tinni's disobedience and obstinacy and were shocked. The madam was spending good money on her upkeep and getting nothing in return. Clients were complaining. They were saying she behaved like a wild beast. The brothel was getting a bad name. What could one do with a girl like her but beat her into submission? The harsher the beatings, the sooner she would come to her senses.

Only Shibkumar, the darwan, tried to help. Coming into her room one afternoon, he whispered, 'Do you wish to escape, daughter?' As she looked up eagerly, he continued,

'Do you know anyone in this city? Tell me where you want to go and I'll take you there myself.'

Tinni shook her head. She didn't know anyone.

'Where will you go then?' Shibkumar looked at her with pity in his eyes. 'This is a bad house but the streets are far worse. A young woman like you will be torn to pieces the moment you cross the gate. You'll be gang-raped and then smuggled out to the Arab countries where the men are worse than devils. Your voice will be silenced forever.' Frowning, he added, 'Can you take up a job? Do you have any skills? What is your education? Can you speak English?'

'No.' Tinni shook her head.

'That son of a bitch Jhandu brought you from Coochbehar with the promise of marriage, didn't he? He's done that with many girls. Tell me, would you like to go back? I could buy you a ticket and put you on a train.'

Back to Coochbehar! Tinni looked at Shibkumar with bewildered eyes and shook her head. She knew, without being told, that she had lost her place in her father's house. Girls who crossed the threshold were never taken back. And even if she was, Bhaba would be waiting for her. What he wanted to do with her was incest—the vilest sin in the world. She would never submit to it. Shibkumar looked at the weeping girl and tapped his forehead in resignation. He could not help her. But he had been kind. His words had fallen like balm on her wounded spirit. She had to succumb in the end but felt eternally grateful to him.

Hari babu was a frequent visitor to the house and often asked for Tinni. Whenever he came to her, he took perverse pleasure in kicking her plump buttocks. Once, Tinni had cried out in shock and pain and Shibkumar had come running in. He had pulled Hari babu back by the nape of his scrawny neck and told him to behave like a gentleman. Could Hari babu swallow such an insult? Of course not. He bought her from the madam the next day and installed her in this flat. Now he could kick her as often and as hard as he liked.

Hari babu had employed an elderly woman who shopped, cooked and kept an eye on Tinni. She lived in the adjoining basti and slept in the flat on the nights that Hari babu was away. Tinni wondered how long this phase of her life would last. She often thought of running away but where would she go? She knew nothing about the city, she knew no one here. Shibkumar had warned her that the streets were worse than a brothel. If only someone held her by the hand and took her out of this hell! But who? And why? She was an ordinary girl with little education and no skills. She wasn't even brave; she couldn't conquer her fears. For a girl like her, there was no hope. She was trapped in this flat for who knew how long.

Somewhere, in one of her Class Five textbooks, Tinni had read that God watches over those who have no one in the world. And so she kept calling out to him. Again and again. But God didn't seem to hear her. She couldn't blame him. There were so many people with so many problems begging him to help them. What could he do? How many grievances could he redress? And who was Tinni anyway? Why should he bother his head over her? Tinni understood God's difficulties. Yet she went on calling out to him.

What did God look like? A picture of a brilliant blue Krishna she had once seen in a calendar rose before her eyes. Another, an image of Shiva with serpents twining around his neck, followed. Did God look like one of them? But Durga and Kali were gods too. Well, not gods exactly,

they were goddesses. So were Lakshmi and Saraswati. A
strange thing was happening to Tinni these days. Whenever
she closed her eyes and tried to think of God, she saw
neither Shiva nor Krishna. Nor even Durga, Kali or Lakshmi.
She saw a young man of about thirty. He had a wheatish
complexion, thick black hair and was clean shaven. He
wore sparkling white pyjamas and a sleeveless vest and
held a book in his hand. He looked much older than a
school or college student but he studied all the time. She
realized she was calling out to him to save her. But how
could *he* save her? He didn't even know her. Their eyes had
met briefly, just once, after which he had moved away. A
gentleman never stared at a woman. It was a boorish,
uncivilized thing to do. He had even stopped standing at
the window from which he could see her. But Tinni stared
at him all the time. His form filled her eyes. It filled her
heart. She could never get enough. Her eyes burned and
hot tears coursed down her cheeks. But these tears were
different...

One afternoon, Tinni saw a girl in his room. At first she
thought she was a boy for she was wearing pants and a vest
and her hair was cropped. But she was a girl, Tinni realized
soon enough. Who was she? His wife? His girlfriend?
Tinni's heart skipped a beat. But why? Everyone had
relatives and loved ones. Why couldn't he? What right did
Tinni have to feel envious?

Tinni saw the girl in the young man's room several
times after that. They would sit together for an hour,
sometimes two, conversing in low voices. Tinni couldn't
hear what they said but she watched them with as much
concentration as she would a film. She noticed that they
showed no sign of intimacy. They neither kissed nor held

hands. Was she his sister then? Yes, she must be his sister. Waves of relief washed over Tinni at the thought.

When the young man went out and Tinni looked into the empty room, her unhappiness and desolation became sharper and more poignant. She stood by the window, her eyes glued to the street, waiting for him to return. She noticed that, here in the city, quite a few people walked with dogs beside them held firmly on a leash. In the village, cows were led by a rope to the meadows to graze. Domestic animals both. She too was a domestic animal. She belonged to Hari babu. Only, Hari babu never took her anywhere. But she didn't mind. She didn't want to go out with him.

The woman who worked for her was called Thako. She was kind and had offered to take her out once or twice. 'Would you like to go to the bazaar with me?' she had asked. 'You stay cooped up in this room day and night.' But Tinni had shaken her head. Had she wanted to, she could have crossed the street and waited for the man who had become her God. She could have seen him from closer quarters. But she didn't. She was a depraved creature, worm-eaten. What if her God turned away from her in disgust?

What was his name? In her mind, in her prayers she called him 'Debota'. But she wanted to know his real name. What a beautiful face he had, so clean and bright. Such a smooth forehead and high, aristocratic nose.

On the afternoons that the man was out, Tinni spread out a mat and lay down on the floor. Her room had a fine bed on which she slept with Hari babu. But she hated it. She avoided touching it in his absence. Hidden under the bed was a bundle that she had brought with her from Coochbehar. Hari babu had found it once and kicked it across the room and out of the door. Thako had found it and brought it back. It didn't contain much: two saris, two sets of salwar-kameez, a hand mirror, two bead necklaces, a plastic watch that had stopped long ago, some Class Six textbooks and a peacock feather. She didn't use any of these things now. Hari babu had bought her expensive saris and jewellery and ordered her to wear them all the time. She had to look beautiful even in his absence, for who knew when he would land up? Yet Tinni couldn't find it in her heart to throw her old things away. They were reminders of her past.

Sometimes, when Hari babu was away, Tinni locked the door and draped one of her old saris. She stood before her dressing table and tried to gauge how much she had changed. She turned the tattered pages of her textbooks and read them. She told herself the story of the crane and the jackal and recited some of the poems. Taking the peacock feather, she brushed it gently across her cheek. How soft and soothing it felt. No one had touched her body with such tenderness. Of all her possessions, this was her favourite. Peacocks were rare in Coochbehar but they appeared once in a while and dropped their gorgeous feathers here and there. She had found this one lying in the street and picked it up before anyone else had the chance. She had an uncanny feeling about the feather. It was long and lustrous and seemed to have been waiting for her. As though someone had blown it across the skies for her. A gift from an unseen world.

What if her Debota appeared before her one day and said, 'I've come to save you, Tinni. I'm going to take you away.' What would she do then? A scene rose before her eyes. She was touching her head to the ground and placing flowers at his feet. The more she thought of it, the more real the scene became. He was standing before her in his spotless white pyjamas and sleeveless vest and holding out his hands. 'Come, Tinni,' he was saying, 'don't be afraid. I'm taking you to a place where no one can hurt you. Where you will be safe forever.' But Tinni had no flowers. Where would she get flowers? Her eyes were burning but she pushed back her tears and placed the peacock feather at his feet...

The scene vanished. Tinni was back in her everyday world. She looked around her. Daylight had faded and the flat was dark and empty. She rose and went to the window. Across the street stood the house that drew her to it like a magnet. A light was burning in the room and at his study table the diligent scholar pored over his books with unflagging attention.

Hari babu came a few days later, a changed man. He didn't beat or abuse Tinni. He didn't even kiss or caress her or force her to sleep with him. He drank an entire bottle of whisky, laughed and wept for a while and then fell asleep.

'We'll have to leave this flat,' he told her gravely when he woke up the next morning. 'The police are after me.'

He walked out of the door without even brushing his teeth and returned only at dusk. There was a man with him, a huge, hefty man with a black beard. Hari babu had brought strangers to the house before but whenever he did so he pushed Tinni into the kitchen and bolted the door from outside. She had to stay in the hot, steamy darkness for hours before he let her out. But today, just as she turned away on seeing another man, Hari babu gestured for her to stop.

'Wait,' he said. 'Stand still.'

The stranger's eyes raked her face and body for a good five minutes. 'Hmm. Not bad,' he said, 'but I'll have to examine her spine.'

Hari babu placed his hands on Tinni's shoulders and turned her around. The man's hand travelled down her back, his fingers pressing every bone from the base of her skull to the cleft of her hips. 'She'll do,' he told Hari babu, 'but I can only give you five minutes. I'll leave after that.'

'Pack your things,' Hari babu barked at her. 'You're going to Delhi.'

Delhi! Where was Delhi? Tinni looked at her protector with dumb dog eyes. What was happening? Was he selling her? She ran to a corner of the room and folded her hands in supplication. 'I don't want to leave you,' she begged. 'Please don't make me.'

Hari babu made a long, sad face. 'Do we always get what we want?' he said philosophically. 'Life changes for all of us from time to time and we have to submit to it. There is no other way.'

Still Tinni wept and pleaded. There was something in the bearded man's eyes that sent shivers down her spine. She had been with Hari babu for some months now and knew his ways. She was convinced that he was a better deal.

'Will you come quietly?' the man said to her in a low, hard voice. 'Or shall I be obliged to carry your corpse?'

'No no,' Hari babu put in quickly. 'You won't need to use force. She is a good, obedient girl and will go of her own accord. The first one or two days might be a little difficult but a few cigarette burns will do the trick. She will become your slave. Thako!' he called out to the serving woman. 'Get her things together.'

Thako was waiting outside the door.

'There's no need to pack too much,' the stranger said to her as she came in, 'just her saris and jewellery.'

Thako stuffed Tinni's belongings into a bag and pulled out the bundle from under the bed. 'Would you like to take this with you?' she asked softly. There was a strange expression in her eyes.

'What!' the two men exclaimed in horrified voices. 'That filthy, smelly stuff! Throw it away.'

But Tinni had taken it from Thako's hand and was clutching it to her breast. Hari babu pounced on her and snatched the bundle away so forcefully, the knot came undone and its contents lay scattered on the floor. The two men cackled with laughter at the sight of the cheap saris, books, bead necklaces and plastic watch. Noses wrinkled in disgust, they stamped their feet on Tinni's girlhood, grinding it to dust. Tinni gazed on the scene with vacant eyes and felt the heels of their boots on her heart.

Did such men have no childhood memories? No past? Had they come all the way kicking and breaking everything that lay in their path? Tinni picked up the peacock feather before their feet could touch it and thrust it into her bosom. It had been sent to her as a gift from another world. She wouldn't let these men destroy it. Darting to the window, she flung it open. She drew out the feather, soft and warm, from her breast and set it afloat in the cool night air.

In the house opposite, the light burned as it always did in the young man's room. He was Tinni's god but, like real gods, he had no time for suffering women like her.

Just then a strong wind rose from the south and lifted the feather on its wings. Tinni saw it swaying this way and that. Where would it go? Whom would it reach? She did not know.

P.S.

Insights
Interviews
& More . . .

On Tagore, Gitanjali and Translating Poetry

Sunil Gangopadhyay

Rabindranath Tagore received the Nobel Prize in 1913 for the English version of his *Gitanjali*, originally published in Bengali in 1910. Though the translation was undertaken by the poet himself and the two books were given the same title, there are some differences in them. Several additions and deletions are found in the English version.

The Nobel for *Gitanjali* surprised and continues to surprise critics and scholars. Some of Rabindranath's best poetry collections such as *Manasi, Sonar Tari* and *Chitra* had appeared prior to *Gitanjali*. If one were to conduct a comparative evaluation of the poems of the earlier anthologies with those of *Gitanjali*, there is no doubt that the latter would appear somewhat feeble. One wonders why Rabindranath chose to translate, for his foreign readers, the poems of *Gitanjali*, actually a collection of songs, in preference to the ones which, in terms of poetic excellence, were far superior. Could it be because Europe, at that time, stood on the brink of a devastating world war and its people were staggering under a load of anxiety and depression? Did Rabindranath feel that, at such a juncture, readers were

'Preface', *Songs of Tagore*, Neogy Publishers

not in a mood for intellectually stimulating poetry? That they would prefer the refreshing, spiritually optimistic verses of *Gitanjali* which soothed the mind and brought peace to the soul? In all probability that was the reasoning behind the choice of *Gitanjali*.

Rabindranath chose an archaic form of English for his translation. Something like the language of the Bible. That, perhaps, was an added attraction. Even Yeats and Ezra Pound, who used a robust, modern English for their own poetry, declared themselves spellbound by the oriental poet's quaint, old-fashioned expressions. The euphoria, however, was short-lived. A few years later, Yeats started taking an active dislike to both Rabindranath's language and his spiritualism – so much so that he instructed the publisher to refrain from publishing the Indian poet's other work.

We, who have read the original *Gitanjali*, do not appreciate the translated version. When Rabindranath wrote in his mother tongue, he used the living language; a Bengali that, in his hands, became more vigorous and expressive with each new effort. Why did he choose a dead, archaic medium for his English translation?

There have been several other attempts at rendering the poems of *Gitanjali* into English since Rabindranath's own but none have proved worthwhile. The reason for this, obviously, is that translating poetry is a far more demanding task than translating prose. Translating songs is even more difficult – well nigh impossible. Rabindranath often composed the music first and incorporated the words later. The translator should, properly speaking, be able to infuse the translation with the rhythm and cadence of the original composition. But that is easier said than done. Translators, in general, learn the source language and carry the poem over into English in ordinary prose, missing out the finer, more delicate nuances of the original Bengali. I'll give an example. An eminent Western translator used the word 'prisoner' as an English equivalent for 'bandi' in one of his translations. But though one English equivalent is, indeed, 'prisoner' the word in the original poem stood for *bandana kari* or 'the one who sings a song of praise or salutation'. That this was Rabindranath's intention is obvious in the context in which the word is found – *bandi ra dhare sandhyar taan* – which means that the bandis are singing an evening raga. The use of the word 'prisoner' is totally out of context here.

Aruna Chakravarti's mother tongue is Bengali and the language of her education, English. She has a fine grasp of both languages and understands their subtleties and cultural nuances. She has received a number of awards for her translations but mostly for her prose work. These days one doesn't see her translating poetry. Yet, in her first publication, she displayed the rare courage of translating some of Rabindranath's songs into English.

In this connection I would like to narrate a personal experience. About twenty-five years ago the editors of a popular journal *The Illustrated Weekly of India* wished to interview me for one of their issues. They sent a photographer who took me around to several places in Kolkata and clicked a number of pictures. One of them was to show me reclining in a boat on the Ganga, reading a book. My table was littered with books sent by various publishers which I hadn't even opened. I picked up one at random and got ready for the photo shoot. It was a translation of some lyrics of Rabindranath by one Aruna Chakravarti. I didn't know her at that time. In fact I hadn't even heard of her. I opened the book and carelessly, half-heartedly, I read the first poem. I sat up startled. The translation was so natural and spontaneous that the shift from Bengali to English was hardly noticeable. And I felt as though I could hear the primary tune and rhythm of the original composition. I read a few more and my amazement grew. I came back home and, over the next two days, read the book again and again.

Aruna writes in English but knows her Bengali well. She also sings Rabindrasangeet – an advantage other translators may not have. I'm sure she hums the lines to herself while translating. That is how she gives her renderings an added dimension. I do not know if any other translations of Rabindranath's songs have matched hers in authenticity.

The book has been out of print for many years now. I'm very happy that another, revised edition titled *Songs of Tagore* with some more inclusions is to be published by Neogy Publishers in this one hundred and fiftieth year of Rabindranath's birth. I have no doubt that, among the innumerable books that are seeing the light of the day, this one will find an eminent place.

A Conversation with Sunil Gangopadhyay

Aruna Chakravarti (AC): Sunil da, you have maintained in a number of your public statements that, as a young writer, you had no great admiration for Rabindranath. Neither did your contemporaries of the *Krittibas* group. You considered his work sentimental and archaic and wanted to get out of his shadow. Which you did by writing in a very original and dynamic way. Yet, now that you are in your seventies, we see in you a great admirer of Tagore. You have read his works conscientiously. And I'm told you can sing at least two lines of each of the two thousand songs composed by him. Not only that. You have made him the central character of your novel *First Light* and used the awakening of his poetic inspiration as a metaphor for the awakening of an entire nation. When and how did this change take place?

Sunil Gangopadhyay (SG): Yes, we were rebels who wanted to write in a stronger, more down-to-earth and powerful language. We rejected Rabindranath as a model and had mixed feelings about his work. Some of his poems we thought were dated and some others were too long. But that does not mean we did not admire him. We *did* admire him, particularly his lyrics which we knew, even then, would be immortal. In one of my prose pieces I have said that even if everything else Rabindranath has written dies out with time, his songs will live. My friends and I used to compete with each other as to who knew the greatest number of his songs. We would spend our evenings singing Rabindrasangeet and reciting his poems. Some of us could recite reams of pages. But it is true that we admired him in private and rejected him in public. We made our dislike of the Rabindra scholars, who lionized him shamelessly, quite apparent. They declared that he was the last word. That the pulse of poetry had stopped with him. They turned him into a god. We couldn't accept that. We were young and hot-headed and reacted strongly. And sometimes we used abusive language. One of my friends declared publicly that he had kicked out a collection of Rabindranath's poetry. But, in reality, nothing like that happened. And we hated the term Gurudev. Why Gurudev? Why such blind adulation?

AC: Has any of your work been influenced by Rabindranath's?

SG: No. We tried, very cautiously, not to imitate Rabindranath and if we found the faintest trace of imitation in the work of any of our friends, we ridiculed him.

AC: I don't mean consciously. And I'm not referring to your early writing. Later, when you realized the value of his work, did it not rub off in any way? Subconsciously perhaps?

SG: Can any Bengali writer escape Rabindranath? I've learned the basics from him. Poetic structures, the use of rhymes and metres … from where else did I learn all this?

AC: Though you started writing while still in your teens, it was exclusively in Bangla till 1987 when your novel *Arjun* was translated into English. Which makes it a little over a couple of decades that you started reaching out to a Western readership. Something similar happened to Rabindranath. He wrote from childhood in Bangla then, suddenly, chose to turn bilingual at the age of fifty when he translated the lyrics of *Gitanjali*. Why do you think this happened? As I see it, neither of you had any particular compulsions to make your work a part of the literature of the West. Please share your thoughts on this in the light of your own experience.

SG: Rabindranath had travelled widely by that time. He, as we all know, was the most widely travelled man of his times – a kind of roving ambassador for India. He had met many eminent men and women from other countries who were impressed with his personality and curious to know what and how he wrote. They urged him to translate his work. And he did so. That was the primary reason. His family didn't think much of this endeavour. Dwijendranath Tagore, his eldest brother, writes in his memoirs that one day he saw Rabindranath lying on his bed with books and papers spread out before him. On asking him what he was writing, Rabindranath told him that he was translating some of his work because the sahebs wanted to read it. Dwijendranath was quite annoyed and told his younger brother, 'If the sahebs want to read your work they should learn Bengali.' People did not care for translations then. Bankim translated his own work but did not like them at all.

AC: And what about you? You have said, often enough, that you are perfectly content with your Bengali readership and with using Bangla as the sole language of your literary expression. Yet you *did* commission translations of your work. Why was this?

SG: Aruna, I must tell you that I've never, in my whole life, requested anyone to translate my work. People have done it. I have not stopped them. There is a reason for it. I consider myself a poor writer and believe that my books do not merit translation. I do my best but genuinely believe that I am yet to write a really good and perfect book. Besides, my English is not so good. I can't tell if the translation is worthwhile or not. You have done an excellent job with *Those Days* and *First Light*. People who know English tell me that your translations are better than the originals.

AC: Really, Sunil da! Please don't embarrass me. But let's move on from this to another point. From the advent of English education in India, writers have sensed a tension within themselves regarding choice of language. Michael Madhusudan and Bankimchandra began their literary careers in English, then switched over to Bangla. With Rabindranath the opposite happened. But not quite. He continued to write prolifically in both languages. But it seems as though he chose English for certain genres and Bangla for others. English to express his ideas on politics, religion, education and philosophy. In short, he chose to use it as a language of communication with a wider world. But Bangla was the language of his heart. It was his language of communion, the language of his music and poetry. Here I'm reminded of the song '*Gaaner bhitor diye jakhan dekhi bhuvan khani*' in which he concedes that it is only through his music that he can commune with God and all created things. And, though he doesn't say so, the fact that he can do this only in Bangla is implicit. It is interesting to note that he did not write a single song in English. He could have done so. He was sufficiently knowledgeable about Western music and his English, too, was impeccable. We see traces of Western influence in some Bangla songs. But he never, ever, wrote an English song.

SG: Quite true. He loved Bengal and the Bengali language. He travelled to so many countries and wrote so much during those times. But the places he visited are conspicuous by their absence in his poetry. Even during his travels the focus of his songs and lyrics was fixed, unwaveringly, on his own land. Wherever he went – be it Iran, Italy, England or Argentina – he never recorded his experiences there in song. Rather, whatever he composed during those times, reflected the melancholy of parting and a bittersweet nostalgia for what he had left behind.

Another thing: Rabindranath always maintained that the

English renderings were not good. And I agree. Leave alone the works of others, even his own translations are a feeble shadow of the original. Sometimes I wonder why Yeats and Rothenstein liked his English *Gitanjali* so much. It is nothing compared to the Bangla. And I don't think his best work has been translated. There are no good translations of the poems of *Balaka* and *Purabi*. His work in English is remarkably slender. It runs into fifty-six volumes in Bangla and in English we have only four.

Rabindranath may have been a world writer in his views but he had the heart and soul of a Bengali. He loved Bengal and loved her language. During the Partition of Bengal in 1905, when the language was threatened, Rabindranath came out on the streets, for the first time in his life. He was not that type at all. He hated publicity. But he led his people in protesting against what he considered was an infringement on the lives of Bengalis and a move to crush them by diluting the power of their language. Fortunately, the partition of Bengal did not happen in his lifetime. It happened six years after his death as part of the partition of India.

AC: Coming back to your comment that, during his travels, he never composed a song on the land in which he was staying, I am put in mind of the song he wrote in Germany once just before Durga Puja. He wrote '*Chhutir banshi bajlo... ami keno ekla boshe ei bijane.*' To move on to another aspect of Rabindranath's engagement with the West: we know that Rabindranath fell back on the notion of the gurukul when he started his school in Santiniketan. He conceived it as a brahmacharyashram with himself as gurudev or preceptor. This was an expression of his lifelong discomfort level with the Western system of education. He had fared badly in all the English schools to which he was sent, including the ones in England. Yet, Rabindranath responded enthusiastically to European literature, art and music and even studied the new scientific theories with interest from his early youth. The poetry he wrote in his teens was largely inspired by that of Dante and Petrarch. Another interesting fact is that he had not only read the major poets, he was also aware of the obscurer ones. For instance, he had read the boy poet Chatterton and saw a close resemblance between himself and Chatterton ...

SG: *Bhanu Singh er padavali?*

AC: Yes. This was particularly apparent when Rabindranath was writing the lyrics which were published as *Bhanu Singh er padavali.* Both young men were incurable romantics and obsessive dreamers who lived in a visionary world they half believed in. Like Chatterton, who concealed his identity behind that of the non-existent medieval poet Rowley, Rabindranath used the pseudonym Bhanu Singh, a non-existent Vaishnav poet. Do you see a contradiction between his absorbing interest in everything European and his rejection of it in terms of an educational process?

SG: Rabindranath couldn't stand the rigid discipline of the British public school system. He hated confinement of any sort and the notion of being dosed with quantities of knowledge within the four walls of a schoolroom was obnoxious to him. That is why he fared badly in all the English schools to which he was sent, both in India and in England.

AC: His brother Somendranath who wasn't quite normal as a boy and became distinctly unhinged in later life fared better. But Rabindranath's inability to benefit from a structured system of education wasn't restricted to English schools. His brother Hemendranath, who had taken charge of the primary education of the children of Jorasanko, told his father often '*Robi mon dei na*' (Robi doesn't pay attention) His music tutors complained that he didn't attend his classes regularly and, even when he did, was inattentive and careless. Yet, Rabindranath rose to be one of the world's greatest composers and could be numbered among a dozen of its most learned men. What, in your opinion, lay behind the strange amalgam of qualities that made up Rabindranath?

The meticulous self-education he put himself through with no aids other than simple lexicons and dictionaries indicate rigorous self discipline. A wondrous ability to imbibe knowledge and an instinctive rejection of a formal, structured process of education! How does one explain it?

SG: Well, he was a genius, Aruna. And who can gauge the psyche of a genius? Or even try to analyse it? And what is more he developed his art slowly and carefully. He did not rest on his extraordinary abilities. He worked hard at them. He was one of the most disciplined and hard-working men born in this world. He made some mistakes in his life but doesn't everyone make mistakes? When he established the brahmacharyashram, he did it on the advice of his friend Brahma Vidya Upadhyay. The idea appealed to him but he did not realize that it was a highly impractical one. Impossible to implement. He began by enrolling students without charging fees. But he could not keep it up. He had to sell his wife's jewellery, even his own favourite watch, to pay his teachers. But how long could these funds last? He couldn't make ends meet. Finally he had to start charging fees. Another defective system he introduced was the observance of caste. Brahmin boys would not touch the feet of Kayastha teachers. But Kayastha teachers would touch the feet of their Brahmin colleagues. Even that had to be given up. But the great thing about him was that he never failed to admit his mistakes and rectify them. He realized that even a guru has to grow and evolve. And he learned steadily and continuously from the journey of his life. He was truly successful with his experiment of Viswa Bharati, the meeting of Bharat with Visva, India with the world. He realized that India's greatness lay not in her ancient system of education but in her ability to assimilate and bring together all the nations and cultures of the world. *Ei bharater mahamanaber sagar teere.*

AC: Very true. But some of the systems he introduced in Santiniketan have remained to this day. For example, his belief that a child can learn only if he's in the midst of nature, which must have been behind the concept of the 'open-air school' he started, is still respected. No classrooms. Learning only on bedis under the trees.

SG: That was a foolish idea! And it didn't work. It rains three months in the year in Birbhum and the rest is either burning hot or bitterly cold. There are only short spells of pleasant weather in spring and autumn. The open-air school was impractical. It was at best a gesture. And it has remained a gesture. And to tell you the truth: I've never understood why Rabindranath had to open a school. He was a poet and should have remained content with writing poetry. Why did he have to pose as an educationist? Where was the need?

AC: Time is running out, Sunil da. I had many more questions and was looking forward to hearing your views on the conflicting Western responses to *Gitanjali* prior to the Nobel Prize and after. But it looks as though I'll have to keep it aside for a private discussion. I'd like to end with one observation. Though it is not a question I would be happy to have your response. Many of your admirers, among whom I count myself, are of the opinion that no other Indian writer has come closer to Rabindranath's prolificity, his vast range of genres and the depth and expanse of his vision than yourself. Many of us see you as Rabindranath's legitimate successor and feel sure that you will be recognized as such and invested with his literary mantle in the not-so-distant future. Would you like to respond to this prophesy?

SG: Thank you, Aruna. But no, I have nothing to say.

AC: Thank you, Sunil da, for your inputs. They have been most interesting and have certainly pushed the borders of our understanding of Rabindranath substantially. Thank you once again.